The Gods of Nazus Trilogy
Book Three

When The Gods Wage War

The Gods of Nazus Trilogy
Book Three

When The Gods Wage War

Kefira Zink

Contact Info: kefirazinkauthor@gmail.com

ISBN: 979-8-9928400-8-7

Table of Contents

Dedication

For the people who will fight
Even when there is no hope
To make their home better
For the next generation

Grab your magic, bitches, let's ride!

Author Note and Trigger Warning

If you are related to me, either stop here, set the book down, and walk away, or get really cool about some stuff really quickly. This is book three, you know what's up by now. If you read book one and two, this is more of the same. If you didn't read it, or read them and now aren't sure if you should have, put this book down. Again, I love you, fam, but not every book is for every reader.

Okay, for everyone else and the family brave enough to continue, here's my warnings. There is still a lot of **swearing** in the book. Fuck and shit are still these guys favorite words. There's **sex** too. Multiple guys, one girl and they all love each other a bunch and show it. There are also references to **past child abuse** and **SA** (all remembrances, nothing any of the main people did, they were the victims).

There is **war** as well, if you didn't figure that out from the title. War comes with a lot of stuff, including:
- Blood
- Violence and death
- Torture
- Prisoners of war
- Manipulation of emotions through magical means
- Abject poverty
- Governmental overreach and abuse with talk of a superior race

Basically, this book runs the gamut. As I said for book one and two, if you have any specific triggers you would like spoilers on, please feel free to reach out to me on social media/email and I will willingly tell you as much or as little as you want to determine if you will feel comfortable reading this book.

All the AI stuff still applies. This is not AI made. Nothing you believe you know about what signals something is AI applies here because it is 100% human made. My work always is and always will be. And for the love of all the gods, stop it with the so-called AI checkers!

Final warning, this book also contains a very hated trope (not saying which one, because spoilers) but it's there and I will not apologize for the real-life stuff these guys go through. It's their journey, I just recorded it like the good little Gods Games dictation worker I am. So, enjoy it and remember that Jinx's jinx always works for her in the best ways in the end. If you made it this far and are still reading, buckle up because this shit is about to get wild.

Love, Kefira Zink

Note from the Council of the Gods Games Realms-wide

The following is a recording of the true events of the aftermath of the Three Hundred and Seventy-Fifth Gods Games, in the city of the gods, Veirveil, on the continent of Nazus. The records have been obtained from transcripts of the council of the gods of Veirveil meetings about this, and interviews with the surviving gods and humans involved. Since the events recorded are a direct result of the conclusion of the Three Hundred and Seventy-Fifth Gods Games, it has been determined that this record is covered under the official rules of the Gods Games, and must be recorded as part of the Manuals of the Gods Games. As always, the record has been written from the perspective of the leading human witch. This is the third manual for the Three Hundred and Seventy-Fifth Gods Games. If you do not have the first two, return to your distributor and obtain a copy of both before reading this.

In following of the regulations of the creation of Manuals of the Gods Games, this record will be translated into all known languages for available access by all gods and humans after passing their twenty-fourth birthday and, in the case of the humans, a blue blood test. In an effort to allow the greatest understanding by the largest number of readers, all scientific information, including names of animals, foods, plants, magical workings, etc. will be translated to something of a similar nature known by the land to which the translation will be sent. Original transcripts in their original language are available by request with proof of the linguistical understanding of requesting persons. Any requests may be sent to the Council of the Gods Games Realms-wide in lieu of the officiating council of the gods, as such a council is not stable enough at the time of printing to fulfill such requests.

Chapter One

ANARUS IS DEAD. HE'S dead. His body is limp in my arms and I press my hands to his chest, desperately trying to force my magic to let me back in his heart, back in the vision, back to the bridge so I can pull, push, fight to get him back in the land of the living. I know, I KNOW, if I could just get back there, I could do it. Fuck the wilde hunt, fuck Death, fuck Winter, fuck every single one of the original gods.

I want him back. I need him back. My heart is tearing itself apart and I cannot, cannot let him go. I scream until my throat tears and bleeds. The salve on my hands has long since worn off but I refuse to stop and apply more, so my hands are a mess of burns and blisters as I force every single drop of magic I have through them into him. My arms are shaking, my head is pounding, the gods around me are talking, yelling, fighting, but I. Do. Not. Care. Anarus is dead and I will get him back.

"Jinx." A hand runs gently down my back. "Beautiful, you need to stop." Ydum's voice is quiet, but still breaks through all the noise.

Another hand cups my cheek. "You can't keep this up, baby girl. I know it hurts, but you have to come back to us now." Byder's words are tense and emotional. I know he's in pain too, but I can't focus on him right now. I need to get him back. I need to get Anarus back. I can't do this without him.

"No. I can save him." I cry. Tears are hot on my cheeks, my real cheeks. I know I am only dreaming. The memory is only a dream now, but I don't want to let it go. It's already fading, though. Ydum is pulling me into his arms, squeezing me close to his chest, his tears falling on my face as he rocks me softly.

The moment I actually open my eyes, the nausea hits, like it always has after this dream. Which is the only dream I have anymore. I push out of Ydum's arms and race out of the room into the washroom next door just in time to vomit hard. Byder is behind me, holding my hair and rubbing my back. I know that, like every time before, Ydum will have a cool washcloth and water to rinse my mouth out.

They take care of me, even though the pain of the broken bond hurts them too. I think it hurts them just as much as it hurts me even though we were told it wouldn't. Our bond isn't a normal one so they don't know what the fuck they're talking about. It isn't the same as it was when Anarus held them in his heart, weaker, only large emotions showing through them, but it's all three of us instead of just me and Byder and me and Ydum like they said it should be. We feel each other all the time, even though it's only the big feelings now. Because that's all we have left, the big feelings. The big, gaping, bleeding, raw feelings of pain, grief, and love.

As my roiling stomach relaxes, I lean back against the washroom wall. "It's been a month. A whole fucking month. Thirty-two fucking days. When are they going to decide?"

"I don't know." Ydum sighs and slumps down the wall to sit next to me. He takes one of my hands in his. With his other hand, he reaches out to Byder.

Byder sits on the floor in front of us, facing us, taking Ydum's proffered hand. "I wish they would just get on with it. The whole fucking world feels like it's on pause waiting."

I look at the two of them and see the tear tracks on their cheeks that probably mimic mine. I think we could fill a lake with the amount of tears the three of us have shed in the last month.

Eiran, Ydum's father, pokes his head in the open washroom door, a soft look of compassion fliting across his face. "More ginger tea?"

I nod and Ydum tells his father, "Thanks, Dad," weakly.

We have been staying at Ydum's parents house while the original gods decide what they're going to do about us. While they decide what they are going to do about Anarus. I know it hasn't been easy for his parents to have us here, with all three of us hurting so much, grieving but not really because I refuse to accept that we won't get Anarus back, and Byder and Ydum wanting to believe that too even if they doubt more than me. Our nightmares don't help the issue because they are stuck hearing me scream every night then get sick from it every morning. Byder's screams when he dreams of the same moment as me. Ydum's screams. The three of us tense and wanting to hold each other but sometimes feeling so raw that the touches hurt more than they help.

But Eiran and Otuna have both been so kind about it all, not once commenting when Byder, Ydum, or I end up sleeping on the couch in the sitting room because we cannot stand to touch the other two with the bonds so exposed and painful. Not once commenting when we are distracted or angry and snapping a little too much, our anger coming out at the wrong people. They are all angry too. Ydum's parents, and sister and brother-in-law, and Byder's parents are all angry too. Zimuna and Greg have been over often, and they are both struggling to find reasons not to just kill the entire council and be done with it.

They saw it all as well, that day the three of us see in our nightmares every time we try to sleep, so of course they are angry. They saw the council attempt to refuse to let Anarus even try for his mantle, but change to making him try for it without my help when we argued with them about it, because I couldn't hold all three of their hands at the same time.

Because gods forbid he just touch another part of me to channel the power of the crowning of his mantle through me as it settled on him. That he just held the back of my neck like he did when we were practicing before the tenth game. And Winter didn't take the wilde hunt off him first when, according to Death, she wasn't even supposed to give it to Anarus until after he had settled with his mantles as the god of the bridge between life and death and the ender of bonds.

When Death felt his child enter his lands, actually enter it at only twenty-two years old, he immediately had come back to Nazus, violating his banishment, to see why. He could only do it, use his power to travel to Veirveil, because the parents of all gods in the Gods Games are supposed to be invited to watch their child attempt to take their mantle in the Veirveil Colosseum. The fact that no one invited Death has been glossed over, since no one but Winter and Inspiration knew who Anarus's dad was until that day. And Inspiration only found out when he used his power to know Anarus's true name as a god, right when we entered the Colosseum.

Since Death is Anarus's father, he had every right to come to Veirveil for that moment. Unfortunately, he didn't know it until it was too late. Had he known, had Winter told him they put Anarus in the games early, Death could have been there to stop everything, force Winter to take the wilde hunt... No. I can't keep going this way. Down the path of what if and what could have been.

What actually happened was, when Death realized where we were, the tenth game in the Gods Games, Death lost his cool. Anarus should not have even been in the games for another three years, so what the fuck was he doing there at all, dying taking his mantles after winning the games? While I had been fighting to try to get back into Anarus's power, just like I did in my nightmare, Ydum's dad told me later that the whole thing dissolved into chaos.

I had blamed Death for Anarus carrying the extra power, the full mantle of the god of the wilde hunt, which at least contributed to his failure to take his actual mantles properly and his death. When Death heard that, losing his cool was an understatement. He literally shot white and blue flames of cold fire from his eyes. It took six gods to restrain him from killing Winter on the spot because that power wasn't Death's but Anarus's mother's, Winter. Since it was created from both their powers, and needed the bridge that would be Anarus's power when he took his mantle, she and Death had agreed it would be transferred to Anarus after he was crowned with his mantle, according to Death. After, not before.

Eiran had told me that most of the gods claimed they didn't even know Anarus was Winter's child and were angry and horrified at how his life growing up had been because she denied him. Then, when they figured out that the thing that caused him so much loneliness and pain, his shadows and all the outward manifestations of his power that came from him when he was far too young, were actually because she gave a newborn child a fully crowned mantle of power to try to control, they were livid. Add on that she played dumb about why his power was doing that every time the council tried to figure it out to help him, letting her own son continue to suffer so much, a few of the original gods were ready to let Death kill her. Instead, they settled on imprisoning her until a decision could be reached about how to punish her for her crimes, and maybe clarify exactly what those crimes were because, wow, did she do a lot of fucking damage.

The problem is, while they decide that, Death had to agree to wait before resurrecting Anarus. He feels he should be allowed to, and Anarus allowed to try again to take his mantle. Without the extra power this time. Apparently, according to Eiran, bringing a god back to life if they actually die is a thing Death can do if he catches that death in time. Or maybe, Eiran thinks, that is only something Death can do for Anarus. We're not exactly sure yet, and Death isn't really clarifying the issue right now.

As I thought when I looked at Anarus's power, the god of the bridge can send people who are technically dead back to the land of the living as long as they haven't actually crossed the bridge yet. Since Anarus had yet to take his full mantle, that power is still technically Death's, but we're not sure how that works because Death never controlled the bridge before but only met people at it after they crossed, so the specifics here are murky. And I think either Death is too confused or too angry to really explain what he can or can't do, except to insist he can bring Anarus back, if the council will let him.

But the council is telling us doing so should be agreed necessary and for a valid reason by the council. Which mostly means he would have never been allowed do it before, if he could do it, because he was banished and could never come to Veirveil to ask for the right to. I mean, technically, he could have done it anyway, but then the council might just re-kill that god over and over until he stopped trying without their permission. Or something like that.

Eiran said that Death never tried to violate the law we didn't know was a law until Anarus's death, so he doesn't know what actually would have happened had he tried. But right now, Death is respecting the brand new but supposedly old law around Anarus and is only allowed to preserve his physical body in a stasis until the decision is made. We're not even sure if he has crossed the bridge between life and death yet, and Death really isn't telling us, so who knows anything at all.

This obviously creates problems for me, Byder, and Ydum. Actually, it creates a whole host of problems for a whole bunch of people. Without knowing if Anarus actually failed to take his mantle or not, we don't know if we completed the tenth game or not. If we did, the full mantles Byder and Ydum successfully claimed, and have so far been allowed to keep, should be theirs and I should be made immortal, which hasn't been done yet. We are the winners of the Three Hundred and Seventy-Fifth Gods Games. If not, and Anarus should stay dead, Byder and Ydum should be stripped of those mantles, made mortal and we lost the Gods Games, and someone else won.

This means that the council of the gods isn't even sure who is on the council to make the decisions in the first place. If Anarus is considered treated unlawfully, and should be brought back to try for the mantle again, and he does take the crowning successfully, I should be in the human seat on the council right now, Byder in Hunt's seat, and Ydum in the Nature's. Death's seat is in question, because he is technically here right now, so whether it would be Anarus or Death in that seat is another question entirely.

—

4

If the decision is made that Anarus was treated lawfully, just not nicely, then Nature and Hunt keep their seats and one of the other humans in the games with us, probably Damek if Ydum's guess about who ended up in second place overall is right, should be in the human seat. Based on how long each team took, Ydum says Damek should have taken first in the tenth game, us second, Isis third, Raven fourth, and Wren fifth. If they all survived it, that is. And fuck all knows who should be in Death's seat right now, if neither of them should be since Death is technically banished and Anarus is technically dead. And no one can agree on the solution to any of the problems.

So, all we are getting is more fights on top of more fights, and the fucking council hasn't figured out a damn thing in a month now and soon Death will have to leave for a bit to move the wilde hunt back into the land of the dead since Anarus isn't here to and Winter can't from her prison cell. Or wherever they are keeping her.

He already had to go back once to fix the bridge between life and death that fell apart when Anarus died. A temporary fix until he knows whether the bridge is still uncontrolled, since it was never his to take care of after he first added death to the land of Nazus, or passed on to his son to care for as is his power. Luckily, we have a while until winter is supposed to end and we have to figure who can make it relent to Spring.

"Tea's ready." I hear Eiran call out from the kitchen.

I close my eyes and take a deep breath. I have to get up off the floor now. I have to start another day without him. Just today. I only have to make it through today. Just worry about making it through today. I tell myself this every morning, and try to find peace, but I have none to call on with my magic, and Byder and Ydum don't either so I can't make more out of nothing.

Just stand. That's step one. Just stand. I stand up and Byder and Ydum stand too. The washroom in Ydum's parents' house is much smaller than the one we had in the games and is not really designed for three people to be in at once. Byder steps out of the washroom so I can grip the sink and wash off my face and mouth. Ydum stays behind me, taking over rubbing small circles on my back as I stare into the tiny mirror above the sink.

Both of our faces reflected back to me are far too pale, mine devoid of all color, except the dark smudges under my eyes, and his showing far too much green tint and the same smudges from lack of good sleep. We both look haggard and drawn from worry. I know that Byder's face carries the same stress, exhaustion, and worry as ours do.

I step out of the washroom into the tiny, one-person wide square of hallway that connects the door to the washroom in the middle behind me, the doors to two of the bedrooms in the right and left walls, and the doorway into the dining room in front of me. The left bedroom door from the washroom leads to Ydum's room, his when he was a child and where the three of us have been staying. The one to the right is Zimuna's childhood bedroom. She and Greg still stay there sometimes.

Through the doorway into the dining room, to the left is the front sitting room, front door beyond that, and on the left side of the sitting room, a door to the third bedroom, Eiran and Ydum's mom's, Otuna, room. But I go right into the kitchen.

5

The kitchen is a nice size for the house, especially considering the kitchen in the home I grew up in. My childhood home had basically just a wall of rickety cabinets along one wall, a tub sink we had to fill with water from a well to clean dishes in, and a hob in the fireplace for cooking. A large, scarred wooden table in front of that wall was the workspace for the kitchen as well as our dining table and the rest of the room was the front sitting room. Ydum's family has a whole room just for the kitchen, with beautiful cabinets, a deep sink with running water, both hot and cold, and a cast iron stove and oven rather than a hob over a fireplace. They even have an indoor ice box.

When I enter the kitchen, Byder is leaning against a counter, chatting with Eiran, who is pouring mugs of tea for all of us. At Byder's feet, an old bloodhound is curled up on the floor asleep. The dog is named Xudbug, and is Byder's dad's old hunting dog who has been having some problems with arthritis. Since Byder and Ydum were at least temporarily allowed to keep their full mantles, Eiran and Otuna agreed to let the dog come here so that Byder could help her with her pain.

I know that, even though Byder doesn't seem to be paying any attention to the dog, his bare foot under the Xudbug's head is actually transmitting some healing power to her to soothe her cold morning aches. He'll stay there, leaning against that counter, until she wakes up and is able to stand on her own. I think Eiran and Otuna hoped the dog might help us, give us some comfort or at least a task to focus on. She has, a little.

Eiran hands me a cup of ginger tea, and I take it before leaning against Byder. I think about peace as much as I can for Xudbug, to help him make her feel better. I can find peace for the dog, but not for me or my gods. Apparently, a dog's type of peace is different than a human's, or god's.

Otuna comes into the kitchen, giving Eiran a quick kiss on the cheek before nabbing one of the teas. "I still think we may want to consult a human healer, Jinx. I know you have been through a lot of pain but I'm worried about you having such horrible nightmares that you end up getting sick every morning."

Ydum takes his mug and stands next to his mother. The two of them are so similar looking it's almost uncanny. Both are tall, Ydum almost six and a half feet, his mother just an inch or so shorter. Both have blonde hair with soft wavy curls, Ydum's falling to just around his ears and over the neck of his shirt, and hers to just below her shoulders. Both are slender with narrow waists and long, graceful fingers, and the slight tinge of green to their skin I have discovered is common among even partial nature gods. They have the same expressive, vibrant green eyes, although Ydum's are dulled right now, and same nose and mouth. I have seen Otuna smile the same smiles I used to see on Ydum in the games. The only thing Ydum inherited from his father was the pensive look when he's thinking and the mannerisms he does when he's thinking or talking academically.

Zimuna looks more like Ydum's dad, except she lacks the academic looks and mannerism and does have her mother's green tint. Both Zimuna and Eiran are shorter than Ydum and Otuna but taller than me. Their hair is darker, more of a light golden brown, Zimuna's to her waist, and Eiran's cropped closer to his ears, and straight. They both have golden brown eyes and Eiran is stocky while Zimuna is curvy. Neither of them has the long, graceful fingers either. I know

Zimuna may come over with her husband, Greg, soon.

I call Greg her husband but I have learned that the gods don't do anything so formal as a hand fasting ceremony. When a god comes home from the games with their mated bond mate who has been made into basically an immortal demi-god, the idea of something like a wedding seems superfluous to having survived the games together. Instead, it's just assumed that the bond is all that matters and terms like spouse, mate, bonded, partner, whatever are all used interchangeably. Technically, by all rights, Byder and Ydum are considered my husbands now, or mates, or whatever, but I still just call them my gods like all of us humans in the games spoke about our gods.

I suddenly realize that Otuna had been speaking to me and, lost in thought, I ignored her. "I appreciate the concern, Otuna, but I don't think any healer could help me with this. What would help is a decision from the council."

I don't want to see a healer. I don't even want to think about seeing a healer. I don't want to know the things a healer would say to me. I want to feel all of this and a healer would probably put me on something to make me sleep without dreams but dreams are the only time I see Anarus anymore. It's not fair to them, everyone else in the house, I know that, but until Ydum and Byder push for it, I will keep my nightmares and my anger. And I will let them keep theirs.

Otuna just shrugs and doesn't fight me on it. We all drink our tea in relative silence, the only noise coming from the Xudbug as she wuffles and gives a half bark then wakes up. Byder kneels down and scratches her head for a moment before Xudbug stands fully and Byder takes her outside to do her business.

When he comes back in, Ydum looks into my mug and, seeing I have drunk all the tea, says, "You know what you have to do now, beautiful?"

I give him a half-smile. "Run?"

Ydum nods. "Run." He smiles back at me but neither of our smiles are real.

We started running after our first week back from the games. Not a real run like we did during the games, but more of a gentle jog around Ydum's neighborhood. My hip still gives me some issues since the gods have not made me immortal yet. I must have hurt it more in game ten. Or maybe, like Xudbug, it's just the cold mornings. But doing it, going running, gives us a task to do. It gives us a schedule. It's familiar even though it's no longer in a hallway and foyer but actually outside.

Byder, Ydum, and I get dressed and put on our boots. I have ones that fit me now. And my own clothes. Mostly, it is all simple shirts and pants like Ydum wore throughout the games. Like most of the nature gods and their bonded witches wear in Veirveil. Plant based fabric and long-sleeved shirts. But I still have my dress from home and I wear it whenever we go in front of the council so they remember who and what I am, what they have done.

I comb out and braid my hair, then put Byder's hair in a bun for him. He can do it himself now, I just like to. I add the warmer clothes, gloves and a thick sweater to keep away the winter chill that doesn't affect my nature or hunt gods as much as it does me.

We go outside on the wide front porch that stretches across the whole front of the house and go down the steps to the wide paved sidewalk in front of the house. All the houses in this neighborhood have wide front porches, nice but small front grassy lawns and paved sidewalks that edge the cobblestone paved roads. After we stretch, and watch the small puffs of white from our breath fill the chilly December air, the three of us jog to the north together, Ydum next to me and Byder behind us. I focus on the houses we pass, seeing their immaculate gardens and good construction, real windows, and smoke curling out of chimneys to become puffy white clouds against the backdrop of the gray, winter sky.

We turn left at the second street crossing and go three more streets down. This corner is where Damek and Iella always join us. Iella grew up only ten blocks away from Ydum. It was only on accident we found them so close by. We were out on our run the first day and literally ran into them doing the same thing.

Byder grew up in a completely different neighborhood, close to Esnir. But Byder knew where Esnir lived and, as soon as we met back up with Iella and Damek, we took a trip to Esnir's parents' house to see if he and Isis were there.

Now, Esnir and Isis sometimes travel here to join us on our run, meeting us at the same spot as Iella and Damek. But they aren't here today. I haven't seen or heard from Wren and Kutar or Raven and Uesis. Neither has anyone else. We aren't sure if they survived Kutar and Uesis taking on their mantles or not and no one has told us. And none of the four gods know where their parents live to go ask.

"No word from the council?" Damek asks as he and Iella fall in line with us, behind Byder.

He asks us this every morning. Their lives are on pause to some extent just like ours are while waiting on the council's decisions. Damek and Iella are the most likely winners of the Gods Games if we aren't, and don't know what they are supposed to do while they wait for the decision either. I mean, they are less concerned with it than we are, but they also miss Anarus too, just not like we do.

"Nope." I pop the p to show my frustration. We used to get daily updates, and went almost every day to the council hall, but it didn't help, leaving us more frustrated and rawer rather than less, and the updates have become less frequent. Now we only go once a week to make sure they are still actively debating the issue. Although their debates are just talking in circles. We are going again today, after we run.

We run north through the east side of neighborhood and into the middle of Veirveil. Veirveil is set up like wedges of a pie. Ydum's neighborhood is the most southern wedge, where there are mostly smaller houses with three- or four-bedroom homes with a small front lawn and larger back garden on tree lined streets.

To the east around the circle of the pie, the wedge is full of larger houses, mostly four- or five-bedrooms with two washrooms instead of just one and two stories tall. They have larger front lawns, larger back gardens, enough land for a horse and carriage to be kept, and wider streets with more trees around.

To the west is the apartment buildings where Byder and Esnir grew up that I saw in the painting in the third game. Squat, two-story buildings with one- and two-bedroom apartment with one washroom, four to a building, on narrow streets with a small bit of lawn around and between each building.

West of the apartments, the wedge is mostly businesses. Shops and markets for just about everything. A lot of used to be witches work in them. Byder's mom, Daisy, runs a meat market there using meat Byder's dad, Xolios, and other hunt gods hunt for and prepare for sale. The hotel we were in was probably in this district.

To the east of the large houses is the area with the schools, lots of parks and public buildings. The Colosseum that the tenth game was held in is there.

The final wedge, the most northern wedge of the city, is the government. The council building is there, and a lot of other government buildings too. It's also the wedge with the grandiose homes the original gods live in.

The closer you go to the center of the circle in any of the wedges, the less there is of pretty much anything. Lots of trees and open land, but less roads to cut through the center to another wedge.

In the very center of the city, where all the roads converge at one point, is the clock tower Iella told us all to meet at on December twenty-second at noon. It's December tenth, so we have twelve more days until that. I occasionally hope that, on the twenty-second, we will meet with Raven and Wren at the tower so we can know they are okay.

On the outer edge of the circle, past where the city of Veirveil technically ends, is a large wooded area. The whole city is set up on a plateau that rises above the rest of the land. A forest that extends for quite some ways in a circle around the circular city, big enough for Xolios and other hunt gods to hunt there often, gently dips and rises in meandering hills in every direction out from the city of the gods until it finally flattens out and extends into the rest of Nazus. Apparently, the cave from the beginning trial is in the forest there somewhere.

Past the forests, small crops of human villages spread outward in every direction. No regular humans actually live within the city, but some do travel there for things or work there on special occasions, like to assist with the games.

Close to the forest surrounding Veirveil, after the land goes totally flat, there are lots of small villages that do rather well for themselves. The further out into continent of Nazus you travel, the further apart the villages get and the poorer they get. My village of Greenbriar is one of the farthest away, and therefore one of the poorest.

I have no clue how the social systems work in Veirveil. Byder's mom, as an immortal witch who survived the games bonded to a god, works an actual day job, but Ydum's dad doesn't and he is the same, a witch who survived the games bonded to a goddess. I have no idea why Byder grew up in an apartment and Ydum didn't. I know that Xolios spends his days mostly hunting or raising and training hunting dogs to sell to other hunt gods and sometimes even humans in the off season. Occasionally he provides services of healing to others with hunting animal with injuries or illnesses. I know that Otuna mostly spends her days growing flowers in their gardens out back, and the greenhouse they have built back there, and those get sold in a market stall. I have no idea what Zimuna as a stone goddess, or Greg as a crystal witch, does every day they aren't with us plotting to take out the council.

I know all three of the gods are called on occasionally to go to the council and meet with gods from the nature pantheon, for Zimuna and Otuna, and from the hunt pantheon, for Xolios. It has happened twice in the last month that Otuna was called by a nature god and we saw Xolios there once after he met with another hunt god. I have no idea if it's rare they are ever called on or if they have been called on less than normal lately. But beyond the council meetings we go to so we can fight for Anarus, neither Byder nor Ydum have ever been called there to meet with anyone or do any type of pantheon work.

I should be learning these things. I know I should, but I just don't fucking care right now. Since part of me wants to burn the whole thing to the ground, it's hard to find the desire to give a flying fuck.

I think I'm afraid if I learn about how everything works here, I'll get angrier. Angrier that the humans in villages like mine are doing without while the gods here have so much. Angrier at the potential injustices between what different gods in different pantheons get for being who they are, how they were born, things they had no control over. Angrier that Xolios got an apartment while Otuna got a small house and the original gods get mansions.

We round the clock tower and move to turn back. This makes us head away from the unpopulated top of the small homes wedge close to the clock tower and back towards Ydum's house. As we run along the western edge of the city wedge, Ydum catches my attention.

"Feeling vicious, Jinx?" He glances at me as we run.

I try to smile. "Aren't I always?"

Byder actually laughs. It's still kind of hollow, but it's a laugh. "Yeah, well, you're feeling a little extra stabby stabby today. Maybe we should actually get some coffee."

"Jinx didn't have coffee this morning?" Damek's gasp is far too loud to be real. "How are you two still breathing?"

I turn my head to glare at him and Damek blanches and looks away.

When I turn back forward to watch where I am running, I hear Iella admonish him. "So not an appropriate joke, Dame."

And I feel bad about it. I feel bad about getting angry at him over just a normal joke we made so many times during the games. But coffee. Grumpiness without it. Anarus. I can't help it. Everything brings me back to the hole in my heart that's jagged and painful.

I hate this. I hate my life being on standstill. I hate everyone feeling like they have to walk on eggshells around me because I am so frustrated and on edge all the time. I want my life back. I don't want to be this way, but I can't make it stop. I don't know how. I want to move on with life. But I am afraid to.

If Anarus comes back—

No.

When Anarus comes back, how do we explain that we just went on living life while he was dead and frozen in time? But life is moving on and if something doesn't change soon, I am going to have to figure out how to move with it. All three of us will. Life has a way of forcing you to move on when you're alive, and our lives will do the same. Somethings even pain can't make stop, and life is one of them. Even when all you want is for everything to stop, wait, let him come back and be a part of it with us.

We get back to the corner where Damek and Iella turn the opposite way than us and wave them off. Then, we get to the house and, once inside, all three of us shower, dress in clean clothes, me in my dress, and head back out to go to the council building. We walk, taking the direct path straight through the hub and past the clock tower instead of the circuitous path we did while running.

The council building looks a lot like the testing center from Greenbriar, only a lot bigger. Stone and brick with a real roof, like all the buildings in Veirveil. No huts made with mud and daub and no real windows and thatched roofs here. Ydum's house even has wood floors. Wood floors instead of packed dirt. The council building has polished stone floors. And looks large, tall enough for three stories but actually is only one for most of it.

Inside the large, polished wood double front doors, there's an entryway and several offices on either side of a short hallway. The hallway has a runner carpet in red. There's a set of stone stairs off to one side that go up somewhere but I've never gone up them to see where. The whole thing is lit up brightly with gold magicked light sconces every few feet. Fancy artwork similar to the first paintings in the games decorates the blank spaces of the walls.

At the end of the hallway is a small sitting area, with nice chairs and a square of red carpet, for people to sit and wait to speak to members of the council or to be let into the council chambers. Beyond that sitting area is a small podium where a guard monitors who comes and goes and another set of impressive large polished wood double doors lead into the council hall.

When Byder, Ydum, and I walk into the sitting area before the council hall doors, the god there that works as a gate-keeper for who can go into the hall barely looks up at us. He's a god of felicitous meetings, his name is Drew or something, I think. We have been here so much in the past month that he doesn't bother asking if we are on the scheduled itinerary anymore because there is no itinerary for the council anymore. We are the only topic at all.

The council hall is disgustingly opulent. There are twenty-one large, plush leather chairs and ten smaller chairs that are wood with a small bit of padding on the seats. The backs of all but one of the chairs face the doors. The doors of the council hall open to a walkway lined with the red carpet that goes between the wood chairs, five on each side, and then the leather ones, ten on each side.

Beyond that, is a podium that face toward the thirty chairs where whoever is speaking stands. Usually Inspiration. On a raised dais, two steps higher than the rest of the room, accessed by stairs on either side of the dais, is one more plush leather chair, facing the same way as the podium. A door on the side of the dais leads to a back hallway and, I assume, the back entrance to the building.

The ten wooden chairs are for guests, which right now, Byder, Ydum, and I are. The twenty chairs on the floor are for the gods who currently have a council seat, which right now is all the original gods, minus Winter. While Winter is in prison, her daughter, Phylidria, the goddess of season's change, is in that chair. Spring, Summer, and Fall are all supposed to be in their rests right now but have come out early because of, well, us. The last chair is for the human that won the right to be on the council by winning the last Gods Games.

Currently, the human from the Three Hundred and Seventy-Fourth Gods Games is still sitting there, but whether she should be is one of the questions up for debate and why the council can't reach a consensus.

I've never even bothered learning her name. Not that I blame her for any of this. One of the reasons things are such a mess is because her position is more just for show than actually holding any weight in the council. She's blameless, a victim of the original gods, just like all the other Gods Games participants over the last three hundred and seventy-five years.

The ceiling above the council hall is three stories high, stone with arching wood beams and four decorative pillars that appear to hold up the ceiling but really just make the room look grander and more overdone. Four large magically lit chandeliers light the whole room.

All the buildings in Veirveil are magically lit. No gas burning lanterns, candles or just the fireplace for light here, but freaking magic.

When we finally get to visit my village, I think my gods will be shocked by how stark the difference really is. We talked a lot about our homes during the games, and I know they believed me about the conditions I grew up in, but, seeing Veirveil now, I don't know if there's any way they actually wrapped their minds around it. My village was poor even for human standards so I had less than even Damek or Isis did growing up.

We walk through the doors and take the first three seats in the wood chairs. We have sat in these seats for so many days, listening to Drila give an account of the games and every moment of it scrutinized. That was a diversion for the longest time as the gods argued over whether my works to unite the teams counted as sedition and nullified everything we did in the games.

Eventually, it was decided that it did not, even if we did use the words rebellion and revolution often, since our goal was not to actually undermine the games or trick them in any way, but look to change something we thought was unfair about them after the games were completed in accordance to the current rules.

The fact that they knew the things we had said, even in the privacy of our rooms, caused me to be quite upset for a long while. They never told us they would be listening to that. Apparently, somehow, they could watch too, a recording made of everything that happened, but they didn't show that in the council meetings.

They heard and saw everything. Every single thing. Every private moment. They knew the exact moment every team consummated their bonds because they heard us and saw us. There's an ick at that I cannot get out of my mind and hope to never forget.

The gods also spent three whole days debating whether I should have been in the games at all with my blood test results, an issue that was basically set to the side as unimportant because no one could tell why my results were what they were and I obviously had every ability to do the magic for the games, even if it was weird. They did insist on retesting my blood for any god ancestors through a different type of blood test, but that came back clean too. There has been some discussion of the Fates examining my destiny a little closer to see why I am whatever I am, but so far nothing has come from that either. At least, not that they have told me.

There was another two days of debating the legality of the cave putting three gods on one team. But Knowledge, who apparently made the cave magic originally, said the cave does what the cave does and everything the cave does must be legal because he made that shit for the games specifically based on the rules.

If there's a clash between something the cave thinks it can do and what people think the rules say, then the fault must lay within the interpretation of the rules, as decided after the fiasco after the Three Hundredth Gods Games, when the two gay candidates were paired in a straight bond together and couldn't opt out without dying. That ended that argument completely.

Now, they're stuck in the endless cycle argument. Death wants a ruling on if he can bring Anarus back and have him retry for his mantle. Every time he asks for a vote on this, some gods insist that Winter needs to be dealt with first so that she can have her vote, if she should be given one.

Others argue Death can't call for or participate in the vote because he's still technically banished and only here as a nicety. Still others argue that no decision can be made about either of those problems without a council vote and the council vote requires that the proper members of the council be determined first. Meaning should me, Byder and Ydum be on the council or not.

Then, gods will argue they can't answer that until Anarus is either considered failed and should not be brought back or was not given a legal attempt and needs to be brought back to try again, starting the whole thing over again.

As we sit in our chairs, the council of the gods take their seats in the hall as well, entering from the door at the front of the room near the human's dais. I look down when Death comes through the door. I'm no longer mad at him, since I've realized none of this is his fault and he's just as angry about it all as we are, but it just hurts too much to look at him.

Anarus was, is the spitting image of his father. The dark umber skin, coarse black hair braided to his waist, dark amber eyes with streaks of black, muscular frame that isn't the sculpted muscles from working out all the time but real strength, solid and broad, all the same for both of them. They even wear their facial hair the same way, a trim moustache with a neatly trimmed goatee.

The only thing that's different about the two of them is their height, with Anarus being shorter than his father by almost two feet. Not that Anarus is short at six feet tall, but Death is just huge. That, and the shadows that swirled around Anarus and don't around Death. They never met in life, but looking at Death hurts because all I see is his son.

Byder grabs my hand and grips it tightly, and one look at his face tells me he feels the same. Ydum too. I take Ydum's hand in mine and try to give both of them the same comfort he and Byder are always trying to give me.

Like always, I look down at Ydum's hand in mine for one small moment. The pinky finger on his left hand is still gray from when I accidentally harnessed Anarus's power of death and used it on Ydum. He still has complete range of motion in the finger, but no sensation in it at all. Since the gray skin has stayed to just that finger, never spreading past the second knuckle, and it doesn't bother him at all, we haven't worried about it.

Well, he doesn't worry about it. I always do. But it still looks fine, so I can stop worrying about it right now.

Once the gods are all settled in their seats, Inspiration goes to the podium and calls the meeting to order, reminding everyone that when they adjourned yesterday, Sadness, one of the four Fates, was speaking about calling for a temporary extension of the Gods Games winner from the previous year's term of service to solve the issue of who should be on the council, at least as it concerns the human vote.

I do not like Inspiration. He was the one who announced the decisions in the tenth game concerning Anarus and, while I know that was more of a group decision, he was the one to say it and not give us time to rebuttal before effectively killing my god. In the Colosseum, the gods were sitting mostly in shadows since the majority of light was aimed at the Colosseum floor. I could only see that he was short like me, or well a normal human height like me since I am not exactly short for a human but am so for a god. He has long, straight, silver hair and gold eyes.

Now, having seen him often in the bright light of the council hall, I know that he tends to always have an expression that looks like he's scheming. Which in all honesty might have more to do with his power than that he's in any way conniving or bad.

"Sadness, do you have more to say on the topic now?" Inspiration asks.

The goddess of Sadness, one of the four living Fates along with Anger, Happiness, and Peace, stands. She's a tall god but doesn't look like it. She seems so much smaller than she actually is. Her hair is a limp dull gold, and her eyes a cloudy blue. She always speaks softly. Not softly, not actually, but again it feels like it. Her words are muted, not powerful like many of the gods, even though she's quite a powerful goddess.

"I do not believe so." Sadness tells Inspiration. "I would just like the vote called, using who is present among the gods. Once this determination is made, if we vote for it, we can move forward with at least something to work with."

Inspiration looks around at the other gods on the council. "Do any of you have any objection with the nineteen council gods that occupied the seats on November seventh, the day before the conclusion of the last games, minus Winter who will be represented by her daughter Phylidria, voting on this?"

No one says anything.

Inspiration looks to us. "Does the human and two gods whose status on the council is in question, have an objection to this vote?" Had we not been here today, they wouldn't have waited to ask us, I know. He's just being polite since we are here.

Ydum looks at me and Byder. I keep my eyes on Ydum because I'm trying not to hate Inspiration and Death is too painful to look at, and shake my head slightly.

"No." Ydum says out loud. Byder must have agreed as well.

"A vote has been called." Inspiration says. "The nineteen gods and the human on the council on November seventh will each cast a vote. Yea or nay. Should we extend the terms of service for the winners of the Three Hundredth and Seventy-Fourth Gods Games until the council is able to declare a clear winner of the Three Hundredth and Seventy-Fifth Gods Games? I say nay."

The goddess of the Sky stands next. Her hair is white and she seems average height for a god. I can't see them with her back to me, but I know her eyes are sky blue, of course, and her face is soft rather than the normal sharp lines of most goddesses. Her voice sounds strong and powerful but soft and lilting at the same time.

I'm realizing that a lot of the original gods look like what they are the god of, and Sky is no exception. Her skin ranges from a milky white to a kind of odd gray color that looks like clouds before a thunder storm, depending on the day.

Sky answers quickly then sits back down. "Yea."

The god of Nature stands next and Ydum shifts in his seat a little, showing his nerves. Nature is his direct ancestor, but more than that, if we actually are considered the winners of the games, Ydum unseats him for a year. The blood relationship between Ydum and Nature is evident in some ways. The green tinge to their skin, the curly almost strawberry blonde hair, and the green eyes. But Nature is not quite as tall as Ydum nor so slender but powerfully built.

"Yea." Nature sits down quickly. He just voted in the first step to potentially being unseated and his vote could make that happen.

The god of Water has the smallest tinge of blue to his skin. Without seeing them, I know his eyes are the color of seaweed. He seems to sway even when standing perfectly still.

"Nay." His voice sounds like waves crashing.

These similarities to their powers are strange, especially since, beyond Ydum's green tinge and both his and Byder's tattoos, none of the other gods in the games seemed to have such striking affectations. Water sits again so that Hunt can take her turn.

The goddess of the Hunt is Byder's direct ancestor, the same way the god of Nature is Ydum's. But the similarities between Ydum and Nature are not repeated with Byder and Hunt. Hunt is very thin and very tall. She's an almost sickly looking thin, like if she turned sideways behind a pole, no one would see her. She's not as tall as Death, but is taller than Ydum. Byder is the shorter than Ydum but only slightly taller than Anarus and packed with broad muscles, especially in his shoulders and thighs. He's power incarnate and she's a wisp that looks like she might blow away. Her hair is a mottled brown and her eyes are mud colored, interestingly, the same mud brown as mine.

When she votes, she also votes against her own self-interest. "Yea."

The four seasons gods, Spring, Summer, Fall, and Phylidria filling in for Winter, all stand together. Spring, Summer, and Fall all bear similarities to the season they control. Spring's eyes are purple and pink, like the blooms of a flower and has pink tinged cheeks, like he's always almost blushing. Summer always radiates a warmth and always seems just a little sunburned. And Fall's hair is various shades of red, orange and brown like the leaves that change color during his season. Phylidria has the pale complexion of her mother, but that is as far as the similarities between her and Winter, or winter, seem to go.

They speak as one group, even though their votes will count individually. "Yea."

The god and goddess of Fertility also both stand together. They stand together so closely, I would think they are one person. Their black hair seems to flow together behind their backs. I've asked about them and the odd way their bodies seem to almost blur together if you look at them too long and Otuna told me that no one has ever seen them apart. She's not even sure they can be apart. Like, not more than inches apart.

They speak as one. Not the way the seasons did, but more like their combined speech makes one voice, giving their two votes. "Nay."

The four Fates all stand as one. They each represent their emotions by their facial expressions as well as demeanor. Happiness is exactly that, happy looking. His face is open and inviting, always seeming to be just on the edge of laughing even when he's serious. Peace is calm, her face always serene, and looking at her feels calming. Anger has a permanent scowl and his black eyes always seem to be snapping.

Sadness speaks for the group. "Three yea, one nay."

It's surprising for the Fates to disagree. I wonder which one was the nay.

Inspiration interrupts before the god of Knowledge can vote. "At this time, the yeas have ten votes, the minimum required for a majority. No more votes are needed. The decision has been made. The terms of service for the winners of the Three Hundredth and Seventy-Fourth Gods Games will be extended until the council is able to declare a clear winner of the Three Hundredth and Seventy-Fifth Gods Games. All further votes will assume those in the chairs of the council have the legitimate right to vote on any further issues, minus Death whose position has yet to be determined."

I hear Death growl softly, a noise I heard Anarus do often. I think he's as frustrated by the bureaucracy of it all as we are.

Inspiration calls for a vote over whether Death's banishment should be temporarily lifted since it's his power that they are discussing. Several gods stand and there are tense moments as Inspiration tries to determine who should be allowed to speak first. I see Death's head hang down and after a lot of talking, some yelling, and a whole lot of accomplishing nothing but going in circles again, Death casually stands and walks to the back of the council hall and out the doors.

I tap on Ydum and Byder's arms and thrust my chin to the door when they look at me. The council accomplished something, but it's two steps forward, three back for them. Same as it has been for the last month. The last thirty-two days. If we wait, they will argue this new point of order for another week.

Instead, I want to follow Death. He never leaves the hall, especially when they are talking about him and his powers. Or his son. But he left. And not out the back door, but out the front, main doors. Ydum and Byder get my meaning and we quietly follow Death.

I haven't talked to him since the moment at the Colosseum when I was ineffectively trying to punch him to make him bring Anarus back. Sometimes when we have been in the same room, Death has glanced our way, but he always looks down and away quickly. I wonder if he realizes how hard it is for us to look at him. Maybe it hurts him to see us, the three people who love his son so much we are willing to fight for him when he didn't. Or maybe he feels guilty for never coming back and checking up on his son before he died. Maybe if he had...

No. I stop my train of thought there. I will not blame Death for what he couldn't know. He trusted Winter. It's all Winter's fault.

Either way, I haven't interacted with the male at all in the last month. So, when we step out into the sitting area and see Death, his back to us, shoulders slumped, groaning to himself, I think he's surprised when I call his name. He snaps up, standing straight, but doesn't turn around.

"Jinx." Gods, his voice is even the same. "I'm sorry. I just couldn't stand another moment of," Death waves his hand around as if gesturing to the whole building, "that. I know I should be in there fighting for you three but I just can't anymore. I just can't..." He lets out another groan that sounds almost more like a sob.

Death hasn't turned around. I can see in the lines of his back that he's hurting. In my pain, I've ignored that Death lost his son, a son he never even got to know but had to watch from afar, only seeing him through the parts of their powers that crossed over, and even then, only in hazy snatches because Anarus wasn't really there and didn't have his mantle. He has never talked to Anarus. He knew nothing about Anarus's life, and by the time he learned how the council, how Winter was treating his son, it was too late for him to do anything.

I take a few tentative steps forward and place a hand on Death's arm. "Nothing in there is going to help us. They are immortal gods. They can argue for a hundred years and have lost nothing. We're the ones who are hurting. We should be the ones making decisions since they can't."

Death turns his head slowly and looks at me. His brow is furrowed and his mouth turned down. If this was Anarus, I would think he was having thoughts about doing something crazy and totally unprecedented. Like having all the gods in the Gods Games work together to teach all the humans to fight so that less of us die in the combat game.

A small piece of me lights up at this, a small fire burning to remember how to be rebellious too. Why are we giving the council a damned choice, again? When have they ever done anything to earn that right? Oh yeah, never.

Death's eyebrows shoot up like my face surprises him. Then, he shakes his head. "Not here. We cannot talk here."

Ydum is behind me, his hands in his pockets. I think he felt my stabby stabby viciousness grow and is trying to give off an air of casualness because Drew or whoever he is may be watching and listening. "Death, you've never been formally introduced to the families of your son's bonded mates. Would you like to come to lunch at my family's home today? We could get Byder's parents and maybe even introduce you to some of our friends from the games."

Oh, slick cover, Ydum. I love my genius god. I shoot Ydum a small smile.

Death takes a moment to decipher this statement, then also smiles. "That would be good, I think."

Ydum gives him the address and direction and they agree to meet there in an hour or so.

Chapter Two

WE LEAVE THE COUNCIL building casually, slowly, leaving Death in the sitting area. As soon as we're out of the building, Byder deviates from our path. "I'll run and get my parents and meet you back at your place, Ydum."

"Get Esnir and Isis too." I tell him.

Ydum nods as we start to trot back to his house. "Maybe see if their parents want to come as well? I have a feeling this might turn into more than we expect."

With some sort of action we can focus on, all three of us become more animated. Byder leaves us with a terse nod and Ydum and I make our way quickly back to his place to help Otuna and Eiran prep for an impromptu small lunch party.

As soon as we are in the house, Ydum is loudly calling for his parents to come to the front sitting room. Zimuna and Greg were already here, so they come too, after Greg fetches Otuna from the greenhouse in the back. Ydum gives everyone a quick rundown of what happened at the council building and everyone now headed their way.

They spring into action, Ydum, Greg, and Eiran quickly counting off how many people may actually be coming and deciding if they need to get extra chairs or move the furniture to make space. Otuna leads me and Zimuna into the kitchen to start on making refreshments.

One of the good things about being a nature god is that it's very easy to throw together some fruit and vegetable party trays. Otuna watches me thoughtfully as she works This is the most animated she has seen me in, well, ever in the month she's known me.

Hopefully, I'm calming some of her fears that make her want me to see a healer. I really, really do not want her to bring that up again and make my gods actually consider it.

It doesn't take long for Byder to show up with his parents. Byder isn't the spitting image of one of his parents, like Ydum is, but a mixture of the two. His mother, Daisy, has the same brown eyes as Byder and is wearing a blue dress that looks similar to what I always wore in my village. She's the only witch turned immortal that I've seen who still wears the styles from the human villages. Her hair is a lighter brown than Byder's and she is a few inches shorter than me, slight and willowy. Xolios, his father, looks close in body to Byder, broad and muscular, with the same chin and determined, demanding expression. He is wearing the same clothes Byder always does, a black and white mottled pelt shirt without sleeves and black soft leather pants.

On his right forearm, I see several thin tattoo lines going from his wrist up his arm. As they stand next to each other, I realize just how many more Byder hunt lines has than his father. He told us this during the games, and even said it was expected since Byder is a full hunt god and Xolios isn't, but the father's lines stop about halfway up the forearm while the son's almost go to his elbow.

"We brought some shaved meats and sliced cheese trays." Xolios says quietly and Greg directs him to put them on the dining room table with the fruits and vegetables. Eiran makes gallons of cold tea and juice and we officially have a nice lunch buffet.

Which is good because Iella and Damek show up with Iella's parents, Yorr, also a chance god, and Leona. It doesn't seem like the chance gods have a special type of clothes they wear because Yorr, Iella, Damek, and Leona are all wearing a mix of leather clothes, homespun fabrics like the humans in the villages wear, and plant-based fibers like the nature gods wear. Neither Iella nor Leona are wearing a dress, but all of them are wearing long sleeves, sweaters, and pants, dressed for the cold.

Iella is also a mix of her parents. Her father's golden blonde hair and her mother's pale alabaster skin. She shorter, like her mother, but not as short. Leona is probably not even five feet tall, making her look as tiny next to the average height of Yorr the same way the average height of Iella looks tiny next to Damek's taller than Byder frame.

Right after them, before they have even fully moved away from the front doorway, Esnir and Isis show up with Esnir's mom, Ayja, goddess of the battle, and his dad, Troy. Troy and Esnir are the spitting image of each other. If it wasn't for those tiny, tell-tale signs of age, I wouldn't be able to tell which stocky male with dark hair cut into a crew cut and gray eyes was Troy and which one was Esnir. Both Ayja and Esnir are wearing pants and shirts with utility pockets in a camouflaged print. That quickly, our small lunch party grew quickly to seventeen people, and Death isn't even here yet.

Eiran just shakes his head. "We need to move some stuff around. Not everyone will fit."

He immediately directs the young guys to start removing the food from the dining table set in the center of the square dining room back into the kitchen. Then, he has them move the table into the center of the square kitchen, reload it with the buffet, set in the center of the room so people can navigate around it to get food.

Otuna quickly moves to make more fruit and vegetables while Zimuna and

Leona help. Eiran enlists Yorr, Troy, Ayja, and Xolios to help him grab some extra chairs and dishes from the shed in the back yard.

With the table being moved out of the way, Iella, Isis, and I move the dining chairs around to the walls and set up small, folding tray tables between them to have seating for everyone.

Iella gives me a shy grin. "Looks like the revolution planning is happening a little earlier than scheduled."

I shake my head at her. "I just wish we knew something about Wren, Kutar, Raven, and Uesis. No one has seen or heard anything and I worry what that means."

"We could ask Death." Damek offers, lugging heavy pitchers of drinks to the kitchen. "He would know if any of them went into his lands. At least we would know something then."

I nod at this. It might be an idea for later. Maybe when there aren't so many people around.

We finally get everything as set as we can, and the games people hang back, finding spots to sit while the parents, Zimuna, and Greg get plates of food and drinks for themselves from the buffet. Once they are done, the rest of us do the same.

We don't talk much, an eerie silence falling, as if we all know how dangerous this meeting might end up. I'm not exactly sure what we are really planning, or what the others think we are planning, but if the original gods thought us talking in the games about changing them was sedition and rebellion, there's no way whatever this becomes wouldn't be worse. My nerves play up and I find it hard to actually eat any of the food on my plate.

Soon enough, though, Eiran is opening the door and letting Death inside. Around so many people, I realize how absolutely massive he is. He has to duck to fit through the door. I thought Ydum was very tall, but he barely comes to Death's shoulders.

Damek lets out a low whistle. "Fuck, he's tall. Anarus got all his looks from Dad, that's for sure. Death couldn't deny him if he tried."

Eiran, ever the socially adept, introduces Death around, since most gods haven't seen him before. There are a few tense moments as Death says hello. He seems about as socially on par as Anarus was. One more way they are so alike it hurts.

Eventually, we all settle into seats with food or drinks. There aren't enough seats for everyone in the small dining room, even with the table removed, so some people find a place to perch in the sitting room where they can see the rest of the main house through the wide double-sized doorway between the two rooms.

Ydum, Byder, and I end up standing along one wall that's visible from the whole dining room and most of the sitting room. Death is a few paces away from us, also standing but more uncomfortably. Everyone else is looking at the four of us, waiting.

Shit, they want me, or Death, to say something. But Death is just looking at the floor and I have no clue what to do now. This was all spur of the moment and is now so much more than we planned.

Ydum puts his hands in his pockets and makes himself the academic so he can talk for us. "Okay, so just to check, everyone here knows the real story of what happened at the tenth game? You all know the real truth about Anarus?"

"His parents are Winter and Death, right?" Yorr says. "Winter made him carry an extra, full mantle as a child and that was why he had all the shadows."

Ydum nods. "Yes, that's true. Winter gave the power of the mantle of god of the wilde hunt to Anarus when he was born instead of after he obtained his own mantle, as agreed to by Winter and Death at his, was it conception? I dunno. He carried that shit for twenty-two years without it killing him or anyone else, which is a miracle in and of itself.

"Winter lied about it to the council and hid that she was his mother. Those shadows are actually the souls of the people in the wilde hunt. Anarus couldn't always control them because they are not a controllable thing, but actually people in their own right. They would choose to listen to him sometimes, but other times they would act of their own accord, responding to his emotions or what they thought were his needs, since they seem to like him, but were not his.

"They have no allegiance except to the god of the wilde hunt, which, even though they were with Anarus, was still technically Winter. Every time he was faulted for not controlling the shadows, is wasn't his fault because he couldn't. Winter could have fixed that at any time by commanding them herself to obey him, but she didn't. She also didn't take the wilde hunt off him when we went into the tenth game, and, since it was after October thirty-first, the wilde hunt was free. The souls swarmed Anarus before he could even attempt to handle his actual mantles."

Ydum pauses, making sure everyone is still following before continuing. "Anarus had two mantles of his own, god of the bridge between life and death and the god of the ender of bonds, something we didn't know could happen but did. Combine all of that, two mantles of his own plus the wilde hunt, and add in that the council refused to allow him to touch his witch, Jinx, the power was overwhelming and he died. If they had allowed him to touch another part of her, or took the wilde hunt off him when it clearly wasn't his, the outcome could have been different. Would have been different."

"Bullshit." Troy spits, interrupting Ydum, vitriol dripping from his voice. "I don't see how any of that was legal, or even just right. That wasn't his lack of ability to handle his mantle. Or mantles. They purposely denied him his witch while making him carry too much power. Power that wasn't his and had no ability to control. I don't see how that's anything less than murder."

I try to hide the stab of pain over my heart at that word. Murder. I have been refusing to think it because it hurts too much. But Troy's right. Anarus was murdered.

Byder takes my hand in his, squeezing it tightly, and when I look at him, his eyes are dark and angry. I can't tell his thoughts as well as I could when Anarus was holding our bonds, but I don't need Anarus to help with this. Byder is as incensed at that word, murder, as I am. Anarus was murdered by the council.

Ydum ignores our feelings I know he must sense through the bond, and talks more. "That's our thoughts too. But the council just goes around in circles and won't decide if Death is allowed to resurrect him and give him another, proper, try or anything really. They are stuck in the politics. Honestly, I'm of the opinion that they are trying to hide their clear and total culpability and illegal actions."

Huh, Ydum has never voiced that out loud to us. I wonder if it's a new thought from Troy's use of the word murder.

"If the council's actions are illegal, like my father and I agree they are, then they have no right to make rulings about any of this." Ydum answers my question without meaning to. He and Eiran must have been talking about this for a while, maybe even researching Veirveil law for a while already. "The question now is, what can we do? Do we declare them part of the problem and act without the council's approval? Is it even physically possible to and if so, what does that acting mean? Do we risk it? What happens if we do?"

Eiran shifts in his seat. "The first step should be to stop waiting for the council's permission. They can't be the criminals breaking the laws then also be the jury to decide if their actions were illegal. If we are deciding they broke the law, then it's up to us, or really you three as the aggrieved party, to decide what reparations need to be made for their actions. I vote we just bring Anarus back. But doing that poses questions of logistics. Where exactly is Anarus's body and what would Death need to bring him back?"

Everyone murmurs their assent at this and looks at Death. "He's being kept in the council building. I can get him. It would eventually be noticed that his body is missing, though. Even with that, getting him is the easy part. Bringing him back might be difficult at this point. His essence is in the land of the dead. Last I saw, he was staying near the bridge, but that was a while ago. It could be anywhere by now. The land of the dead is a mirror image of the land of the living. When something goes there, they live in rest, moving backwards from how we move in the land of the living."

"What does that mean, moving backwards?" I interrupt Death.

Death shifts slightly. "In the land of the living, things are born or created. People, gods and humans, but also plants, animals, anything alive. They are born and grow, then die. When they die, their essence moves over to the land of the dead. When a tree is cut down here, that tree's essence appears there, as a tree again. You've seen glimpses of the land of the dead, Jinx. Each of those trees you saw across the bridge were ones that had at one time been alive in the land of the living. Over time, as the physical parts of that tree are used, rot away, destroyed, burned, whatever, that essence there fades into pure energy. Once there's nothing left of the physical thing here in the land of the living, the essence in the land of the dead is freed to be recycled into a new life, a new tree seed in the land of the living. It's a continuous cycle of birth, life, death, decay, rebirth. It's not reincarnation, since the new tree will be a wholly new creation, maybe even a different tree type, but will just reuse the energy from the old one. The tree's essence, its energy, now completely free of the old life will become a new life, a new tree."

Death stops for a moment, considering his words. "There are a few exceptions to this pattern. The wilde hunt is one. Lost and angry souls that choose not to decay. Or ignore their own decay because I'm not sure how much they realize they're dead. Another is when the essence is purposefully taken and given to someone else."

Death looks at Byder, Ydum, and me. "You three already have experience with that. In one of your games, you transferred the essence of a rabbit to a dead witch. Because the rabbit did not die naturally, didn't know it was dead, and its essence didn't cross the bridge, the rabbit was able to steal Ydum's essence when he stepped into the light of the cycle. You caught the rabbit and put it back and, by then the witch had expelled the rabbit's essence, the rabbit actually came to the land of the dead properly. Had you not given Ydum back his essence, he would have been dead but not able to move through the rebirth cycle properly until the rabbit died. Even then, if his body had already decayed, he might have been stuck, his essence confused what to do. Anarus's essence would not be able to decay towards rebirth right now because his body's decay has been unnaturally halted. His essence might be confused by this. It might hurt. I honestly don't know because I've never tried that, holding the dead in stasis this long, before. I don't control the land of the dead, only death."

Esnir stands from his spot in the sitting room and walks to the large doorway to the dining room, leaning against it. "Wait, if you don't control the land of the dead, who does?"

Death shrugs. "I don't know. I don't know that anyone does. Like I said, it is a mirror of the land of the living. There may be a god of rebirth there, or something else. The land of the dead was not something purposefully created by us, the original gods. When the twenty of us made the land of the living, there were other realms that already existed. We knew that and we knew they were governed by other beings like us. When we created this land of the living, it was only one of many lands of the living, one of many realms. When the other gods asked me to add death, when I spoke the word death over the land, the bridge to the land of the dead was formed. I knew it would do that, but the land of the dead already existed. Our bridge is not the only bridge into it. Our beings are not the only beings that go to it. My only power is to allow the beings from here to be allowed to go there, and to decide how the cycle works. I made the cycle birth, death, rebirth, and made the exceptions. Other realms have other cycles."

"Anarus was supposed to be the god of the bridge." I say. "If he had succeeded at taking that mantle, what would your powers control then?"

"Death." Death answers. "Anarus would just maintain the bridge. Physically maintain it, fix anything that breaks on it, but also maintain who can use it. Let those who have died pass over it and end their bonds with the living so I can help them find where in the land they should go, our realm's part of the land so to speak. He would have refused crossing for those who should not be dead, or aren't actually dead. He would open the bridge at the required times for the exceptions I make, like the wilde hunt or letting someone be brought back to life when I ask for it. The bridge is a one-way valve. When I allow it to work the wrong way, he would have to hold it open for me. I cannot hold it open and move the essence the wrong way at the same time."

"So, you allow dead things here to go to the land of the dead, take the dead to our place within it. Without Anarus, anyone could cross the bridge but then they would be stuck being dead, except the wilde hunt that Winter gave the power to move back and forth, and the bridge would just exist as it was when you first made it. With him, Anarus could have made sure no one went into the land of the dead accidentally or at the wrong time, kept that bridge in good working order, and made it easier for exceptions to come back to the land of the living. Once settled in the land of the dead, though, they are someone else's problem, except that the other person would follow your plan of eventual rebirth of that essence." Byder shakes his head, confused and in wonder. "That is quite the crazy system."

"It sound confusing and messy." Isis mutters from her spot on a couch.

Death takes in a deep breath. "It is confusing and messy. Especially with me banished. Having my son to help me was supposed to make it easier. That's why I chose his mother to be Winter, so that he would be able to handle the wilde hunt for us."

"Why was the wilde hunt created?" I ask. "It's both you and Winter's powers combined. Why did you two decide to make that?"

Death chuckles darkly. "It was Winter's idea. Before I actually added real death to the creations, Winter believed her season was going to be the one people feared the most because food would be scarce and water is frozen. But then, people didn't fear it like she hoped. They thought the cold and snow was beautiful. They loved the nights around a fire. They used the frozen water for recreation, to skate on and the snow to sled and ski. She wanted something. Something that would make her season feared. She thinks fear equals power. We are a bonded pair, so I agreed to help her and we made the wilde hunt, a group of humans and gods that would have their essence trapped and forced to ride through the winter hunting other souls.

"It was never supposed to be like it is now. Winter unleashed the power in frightful ways. I never should have agreed to make them. I should have never bound us like that. When I saw what she did with the wilde hunt after I made death, the only thing I could do is limit their power by making them subjects of the land of the dead who can only access the bridge on October thirty-first to get out and must return on the winter's solstice.

"When the bridge started to decay, I realized I couldn't do everything I needed to. I knew I needed a child with my power. I was already bound to Winter, and we both knew that the wilde hunt had been ignored for too long, allowed free reign for too long. She wanted rid of it because no one feared it anymore so it was useless to her. We agreed that the child, as the manager of the bridge, would also handle the wilde hunt. She would give the wilde hunt to the child after they got their mantle at twenty-four. His second power, the ender of bonds, was not our choice, but a second power he was given by destiny itself.

"As soon as we found out Winter was pregnant with Anarus, we knew he would have the power we purposely gave him, the bridge, the power Winter would give him after he finished the games, the hunt, and the third one that was what he naturally had, the bonds. It was already more than any other god ever had with just the two when we discovered there would be the third, but I had already broken my banishment to talk with Winter and create the child. Winter said she would make sure he would be taken care of and I left before I was found out. I'm not exactly easily hidden."

Several people chuckle at this and Death gives a rueful smile. But it fades quickly. "I trusted her to do right by the child. I thought she would love her own child at least, even if she had never loved anyone else. I was wrong. I was so wrong and my son suffered for it. If I had known." Death balls up a fist and slams it on the small folding tray table near him, making several people jump. He looks at me, Ydum, and Byder, his face twisted in pain. "If I had only known! I swear I would have never left him like that had I known."

I reach out and take his hand in mine. There is so much anger and sadness in both of us, I don't know if my touch is actually comforting at all, but I try. "I believe you."

Everyone is silent for a while, giving Death and the three of us a chance to reign in our feelings.

Byder's mom, Daisy, eventually brings us back to our task. "So, retrieving his body isn't a problem, but retrieving his essence to put it back may be. What would you need to do to that?"

"We would need to convince him to cross back over the bridge and reattach his bonds to himself." Death keeps his eyes on me as he talks. "And I do mean we. I would need your help, Jinx. For him to cross back, he has to take back the bridge again. He has to rebuild it. I temporarily fixed it so that essences can cross over to the land of the dead, but Anarus would have to open that one-way valve the wrong way himself, as is his power. He would need to take on his mantle as he comes back to life. At the same time. And he would need his witch's help just like he would have originally."

I would have to help. I should have guessed. I close my eyes, and take a deep breath. "Would we have to physically go somewhere or would it be magical, like when I looked at his power?"

"Neither and yes." Death says, confusing me. "We would not be going to a physical place, nor a magical one. The bridge is accessed through your essence. When you accessed his power before, you were not using magic but your essence."

I rub my face, trying to understand. "It's not magically that I accessed their powers?"

"For Byder and Ydum?" Death tells me. "Yes, it was magical. You saw their powers, but you went to Anarus's. Anarus's power over the bonds is magical, the same as Byder and Ydum, but the power over the bridge is through his essence rather than magic, and tied to a place which is where you went to him. Didn't you notice there was a difference between seeing their power and going to his?"

I had but I never really thought about it. Byder and Ydum's powers were always a silver or green light shining in them. Once I pushed past the well that was the wilde hunt in Anarus, it wasn't power within him but a vision. There were the gold bond lines and gold in his eyes and hands, but I always went into a vision of the bridge.

Death whispers to me, quietly, so that only the three of us can hear him. "You might have to let your essence actually step into the land of the dead. You might have to die to help me bring him back. If we fail to bring him back, you may be stuck dead. You did it before though, when you tried to drag him into the land of the living right when he died. You were technically dead too for about two minutes in the tenth game. The only reason you weren't stuck there was the wilde hunt was moving through the broken bridge. That held it open and you came back quickly, before your body realized you were dead."

"If we do this, without the council's permission, it will cause a war." Ayja says firmly, not realizing the quiet conversation Death and I were having.

She looks at her son, Esnir, who also nods. "The council will come after us. All of us. Not just Jinx, Byder, Ydum, Anarus, and Death. Their families too. And their friends."

She looks at her son again, Isis, Iella, and Damek. "And their friends' families. They will claim sedition. That we should have waited for their decision."

"Do we care anymore?" Esnir isn't really asking a question. His body seems to be almost vibrating with frustration and anger. "The games are wrong. They were wrong before we ever stepped foot in them. They want to call us wrong for saying fuck their politics bullshit? I say we tell them how they are wrong. All the ways, not just what they did to Anarus, but to all the gods and humans in the cave. The fifteen thousand or so people who have died in all the games."

"Sixteen thousand, nine hundred, and thirty-three." I say. I did the math from the number Anarus gave us. I refuse to include him in that math. "And that's only if Wren, Raven, Uesis, and Kutar are alive."

"They are not dead." Death tells me. "They did not come to the land of the dead. And this would not be the first war against them, but the third. Why do you think there's a pantheon of war that isn't part of any of the twenty of us original gods' pantheons? The second war was when the non-magical humans warred with them for the right to leave Nazus. The original gods managed to barricade themselves against the humans and it became a stalemate. The original gods worked to make a power to help them fight the humans, to make a new pantheon of gods, the pantheon of war. The humans turned to me, asking for help. I was already gone by then, but I heard the humans' pleas through their offerings, and made another land for them. They left and it was too late for the council to stop it by the time they finished making the gods of war. That's why I was banished. Not because I made death in their creation, but because I acted against their will and took away their humans who hated the magical dominion of the gods."

"Did the gods actually make us humans?" I ask. It doesn't matter right now and is off topic, but I'm curious of how much Anarus got right about the story of creation.

"Yes." Death tells me. "They did. But not like they say they did. They made humans from themselves. There were other gods beyond those twenty including me. Others who did not agree to the plan of making these lands. That was the first war, the war of creation, one the twenty of us won. We stripped the gods who lost of their immortality, made them more susceptible to illness and injury and tried to get rid of their powers, but that only half worked. The witches are just the descendants of those stripped-down gods that managed to keep some of the magical abilities from their god ancestors, The non-magical humans are just humans that didn't. Without the same level of power, the magic feels different, but really isn't. Just weaker. Except Jinx. Except your magic that seems to be very god-like even though you are very much human. Still limited by comparison, but more god-like than anything the gods have seen in a long, long time."

"That's when you added the death that upset the other nineteen original gods?" Leona asks. "Making the gods that lost the war human and mortal? Was that when you ran?"

Death tilts his head to the side, thinking. "Sort of. It wasn't that simple. The death I added to the land was a three-part process. The first creation of death was for the animals and nature, which the original gods were happy with. The second part was death for the gods who lost the war, making them what we know now as humans. Unfortunately, allowing human death also brought a form of death to the gods who never had such a thing before. That's what angered them. They didn't understand that humans and gods are the same. Bringing death to one brought death to them all. The original gods were horrified by that. But they didn't listen when I tried to tell them that would happen. They insisted I do it anyway. So, I did, then ran before they could get angry with me."

Death sighs and shakes his head, as if the memory of that time weighs heavily on him. "Once the gods could die, their essence had nowhere to go until I made the bridge. The bridge into the land of the dead was the third part, adding the word of death to make the bridge and the plan of how the cycle worked. I did that in an attempt to pacify the nineteen original gods that now hated me."

Death pauses, looking around the room. I do as well and take in the sea of faces that look as confused as I feel. I can see Esnir and Damek both with furrowed brows, counting on their fingers. Isis and Iella are both shrugging at each other.

Zimuna tilts in her seat to whisper to Greg. "Did that make sense to you?"

Greg shakes his head, frowning.

Eiran steps up to the center of the dining room where everyone can see him. "Let's take a five-minute break. Everyone, feel free to get more to eat. Death? I think I'm going to grab a white board from my office. Maybe if you draw it out, it will make more sense to everyone."

Everyone starts wandering, stretching, and a line forms at the washroom. The noise level in the room ticks up as everyone talks. I know that this information really shouldn't matter right now, but for us to really make any changes around here, we have to know the truth. This may be the only time we have an original god who was there to explain it honestly.

The three of us don't move as everyone else does. We don't talk either but just wait as Eiran rolls a large white board into the dining room and hands Death a black marker. The people who had been sitting in the dining room all shift their chairs to face the board and the people who had been in the sitting room all stand in the opening between the two rooms. The whole thing ends up feeling like a class in school, where we are the students and Death is our teacher.

"Making death for nature, making death for the gods and humans, and making the bridge were three different things." Death starts once everyone is settled. He draws one box and labels it 'death of nature.' Even with the first box, he makes and labels a second box, that says, 'death of gods and humans.'

He points at the two boxes. "I made both of these at different times. Nature first, everyone is happy. Gods and humans second. They only wanted humans, but gods and humans are the same thing as far as our essence goes, so the ability to die for one is the ability to die for both. Gods are now mad."

He makes a third box that says, 'bridge and cycle' under the first two boxes with an arrow pointing from them to the new box. "I tried to calm them down by making the bridge to the land of the dead and the cycle of life and death, giving death a purpose. It did not help."

"I was in control of all three of these." He taps the three boxes with the marker, then draws a fourth box off to the side, labelling it 'the wilde hunt.' "This was Winter's. It only interacted with mine because the souls had to cross my bridge the wrong way."

"Once I was banished after the war with the non-magical humans, it was too much for me to manage my three tasks." He taps the nature, gods and humans, and bridge and cycle boxes again. "Which is why I wanted to give one of them over to my child." Death taps the bridge and cycle box. "I planned to give over control of the bridge and the cycle to my child."

Several people mutter or grunt. Zimuna calls out. "That makes sense."

Death chuckles. "Well, that was my plan. It didn't actually work like that. Apparently, we're not supposed to plan a child's pantheon power, try to control it, and the uncontrollable power of the inevitability of destiny, that is something outside of everyone's control, even the gods, got mad at Winter and I for trying something we shouldn't have. It messed up our plans."

He erases the word 'bridge' from the bridge and cycle box. "The cycle split off from the bridge power. I still control both deaths and the cycle."

He keeps talking while drawing on the board again. He draws yet another box by the wilde hunt and writes 'bridge' on it, then draws another box under that one and labels it 'fate.' "This left Anarus supposed to control the bridge itself. He also was to control the destiny of death, the other end of the destiny lines from the Fates. I didn't know that existed because I'm not a Fate. Maybe it never did before and destiny added it because it was pissed at us."

The board is now a mess. On one side is a line of boxes, nature deaths and gods and human deaths with line connecting them to the cycle of death. All Death's powers. On the other side is another line of boxes, all in a neat line. Bridge, fate, and the wilde hunt. What should have been Anarus's powers.

Death taps the marker on the side of the board with Anarus's powers. "With him gone, I don't know who controls these two. The bridge and fate. The wilde hunt is still Winter's, I know. And they are out, hunting, so don't need much for now. I know I don't control the Fate part, like I never did, but the bridge?"

He just shrugs. "I have no idea. It's not me again because my attempts to fix it failed and I could just do basic things to make it usable. Just enough that human and god essence, which is all really just god essence since humans are just mortal gods, can cross it."

"Fuck, Ani was basically completely right." Ydum whispers.

Byder laughs softly. "Jealous he was smarter than you about something, Ydum?"

"No." Ydum says defensively, but both Byder and I smile, knowing his feelings say otherwise. "Fine, maybe. But don't you dare ever tell him."

Isis brings us back to task again, walking over to the board to examine it. "So, all the control the gods have exerted over us, over the humans, they never deserved to? Not really? We are only like this because they wanted to control us and won a war against our god ancestors?"

"Yes." Death admits honestly.

"Maybe it's time humans took a little of that control back." Esnir says, his voice turning angry again. "Why do the original gods get to be in control of everything just because they made the world by force? Why do they get to be the ones still in control of it? Why isn't the system more democratic than one basically worthless human chosen because they just survived a cruel game? Ydum is a full nature god, with as much power as Nature. Why doesn't anyone else get a say on which one of them gets to make up the rules we are forced to live by? Why is war not included on the council as well, since we are our own pantheon? Why don't we have a seat at the table at all? Why has no one fought any this before?"

"Because the gods lie." I tell him. I stand up taller. This is what we were saying in the games all along.

I step further out in the room, surer about myself, surer about this. "Because the original gods make it seem like Ydum can't possibly be the same as Nature. Nature knows more and is better somehow. They don't even tell us that the gods of war are their own pantheon, but just let you wonder who you really belong to and who is in charge. They don't want you to have power that isn't what the nineteen of them give you. They teach everyone the world was made by them. The humans were made by them and are little more than animals, with aa far less caliber of magic than gods. The humans are weak, frail, nothing powerful, except the few ones that manage to survive a game the gods let us play because we meet some standard they won't even tell us what is."

Byder stands up taller too, moving to stand next to me. "What would happen if we told the humans the truth? What do you think they would do? All the ones in Greenbriar that Jinx said are so poor they don't even own shoes while we have magical lights. If they realize the only reason they have so little and the gods have so much is a lie. What would they do?"

"They'd fight back." Eiran says quietly, almost angrily. He seems so similar to Ydum in that anger. An anger rarely displayed, but when it is, it feels all-encompassing and righteous. "My village would want to fight back."

"Mine too." Daisy adds. I look around and all the humans are nodding. Every human village has suffered. Every human village has sent children to the games.

"So, we tell them. Then, we fight back." I look at Death. "Will the wilde hunt listen to you?"

He shakes his head. "I don't know. I'm not even sure I can force the them back across the bridge in ten days. They are all each a shadow of a soul, a remnant left behind. They aren't even just one thing, but the same as any group of people, with each member having their own memories, feelings, and desires. The remnants were trapped for so long, and became angry because Winter ignored them. Then, she moved the remnants to Anarus, and were in him for twenty-two years. As far as I can tell, they believe he freed them. You gave them their first offering in generations. They may listen to him. Or maybe even you, Jinx, if he isn't here. Me, I don't know."

Esnir catches what I'm getting at. "The wilde hunt would be a damn good start to an army. There are," he stops, counting, "eight human villages represented here. Ten if we find Wren and Raven. How quickly could they organize? Get the information to other villages?"

Isis answers. "Depends on the village. My village? It's only a few hours from here, with several other villages within a few hours of that. I've visited Veirveil on vacation before with my parents. Other villages are further away, further apart."

"It took me from just after sun up until sunset to get to the cave from my village." I tell them. "I went to the testing center at six-forty in the morning and arrived at the cave just before the trial of the cave started. We never had any gods visit or High Priests or Priestesses from other villages. I don't even know where any other villages are because I never went there or saw people come to us. No one comes to Greenbriar on purpose."

Eiran nods at me. "Greenbriar is one of the most remote villages in Nazus. I think that, if we plotted out the villages represented in this room on a map, Ydum and I could devise a system of each of us going to our known villages, talking to the humans there, then having others go to the next, prechosen, village until we hit most of them and know how long it would take to amass and come here. If we want to use the wilde hunt, we would have to have a plan that has everyone back by the nineteenth."

"But what do the humans fight with?" Ayja asks. "We can get bodies here, but battles take much more than bodies."

"That part would be up to you, Esnir, any other war gods you can wrangle up, and maybe Death and Anarus to plan." Eiran tells her. "Although, I'm pretty sure Anarus would want to stay with Jinx when she goes to Greenbriar. I don't see those four letting any of them out of each other's sight for a long time." Eiran chuckles at this and so do the people that were in the games with us.

I take a deep breath. "We have a plan then, or at least the start to one? Death and I bring back Anarus. Everyone else will stay here, working with Eiran and Ydum to plot out who goes where. Esnir and Ayja will draw up battle plans, and everyone else will go to their assigned villages, leaving the message to meet in the forests to the south of Veirveil by the morning of the nineteenth. From there, Esnir and Ayja can gear everyone up, or whatever, and be ready to fight by sunset when the hunt can join us, if the council doesn't just relent before that."

"Only one part of the plan I disagree with." Ydum turns to me. "I am coming with you and Death."

Byder looks at me as well. "Me too. The three of us are going together with Death."

Eiran chuckles again. "Told you."

"How much time do you need to get ready, to get Anarus's… get Anarus?" I ask Death.

"Less time than it will take you three to pack to go to Greenbriar and meet me at my home in the government sector." He tells me. "I have a feeling, if we do this, if we bring Anarus back without the council's permission, your four will need to disappear quickly. I would suggest you be ready to go to Greenbriar immediately without returning here first."

I nod and activity starts up around us. Eiran goes into Zimuna's room, which has become almost his study now that she doesn't live at home anymore, and grabs maps.

The dining table is brought back into the dining room. The chairs are moved out of the way so the table can be used as a war strategy table with one map. The gods huddle around it, Esnir, and Ayja taking control of discussion. Another map is hung over the white board and the humans, led by Eiran, start plotting there.

Death starts to walk to the door to leave, but gestures for me to speak with him privately, shooting a look at Ydum and Byder, indicating he means even privately from them. When I'm next to him at the door, he asks me. "Are you sure you can do this? With Anarus? Are you sure you should try with how you are right now? It will be painful and will definitely take a lot of energy. You could die. There could be other complications."

I grit my teeth. "You need me to bring him back?"

Death nods. "I'm almost certain of it, but I know you will be needed to help him take his mantles either way."

"Then, I can do this. Nothing else matters but getting him back." I tell him, my face hard and determined, daring him to argue with me. "Anarus once told me he would light his own funeral pyre to save the three of us. Right now, I am willing to sacrifice anything for him."

Death stares at me for only a moment before he just nods once and opens the door and leaves. I go back to Ydum and Byder. We sneak away into our room to pack and prepare. Inside the room, Ydum starts pulling bags from the closet, but I stop him.

"First things first." I say as I grab my witch's kit from the top of the dresser. It's the same one from the game, still in Byder's knife box. I pull out the red string. "I lost my bracelet from Anarus when the vision kicked me out when he… when the bridge fell. I need to check our bracelets and make new ones."

"Smart witch." Ydum tries for a smile, but again fails and just sits on the bed with his wrist out. Byder does the same. I run my fingers over both of their bracelets and find no defects. Then, I run my fingers over them again, thinking protection and strength. Then, they both check mine, and add power to them. Both of them are fully mantled gods now. Their powers are much stronger than when we made them almost three months ago.

To replace the bracelet I lost form Anarus, Byder and Ydum take two new red strings and braid them together, then braid those two braids together to make me a third bracelet. Finally, I help them make each other a bracelet plus another one to represent Anarus for each other. Our bond is no longer just me with each of them, but each of us with each other, so our protective bracelets should match that.

"Okay, now we can pack." I say and Ydum chuckles.

"Do you want to stay in your dress for this, Jinx?" Byder asks. "Or do you want to change? If we leave straight away from Death's house, we may have to travel through the night to Greenbriar. Or we may need to give Ani time to rest and have to wait a few days to leave."

I contemplate this. I want comfortable clothes. Pants might be nice for a large magical working. But at the same time, I want comfortable clothing. I want home and the strength of witches I've known my whole life with me. My dress was made by my mother. There's a power in that.

"Stay in the dress for now. I may change before we travel." I finally decide.

Byder only nods. They trust me with so much magically.

Once we're packed, assuming several days gone, we head out into the main parts of the house to leave. I see Eiran talking to the other humans and making dots on the map in different colors. I don't know his system, so I check in with him before we leave.

"Is there are any other villages we should be sending people to?"

Eiran looks up and shakes his head. "No. You don't know when you will be able to actually leave for Greenbriar and, with it so remote, you may not have time to get to any other villages. We'll plan that Greenbriar is the only village you go to and cover the rest."

The three of us head out into the city of Veirveil to walk to the government sector once again. Byder, Ydum, and I soon find ourselves outside a rather large looking home near the clock tower in the government sector. Since Death was banished, his home he was technically assigned was the farthest from the actual heart of the government buildings. This works to our advantage, since it's too far away for anyone to see and question why we're at Death's house with our bags packed.

The house looks more like a small castle, made completely out of rectangular smooth stones with small mortar lines, two stories tall and a large, half circle front porch with a second story balcony over it and so, so many windows and chimneys. It would feel grand and imposing if it didn't look so neglected.

There are overgrown vines clinging to the walls and the front lawn is overgrown. There is a wide front drive past the wrought iron gates at the road ending in a circle with a small, cracked fountain in the center of it that's dry and covered in moss. The front drive is also cracked, weeds sprouting between the cracks and once beautiful bushes are spilling out from the edged flower beds in front of the house, wild and untamed.

The numerous windows have heavy curtains drawn tight over them. If I didn't know better, I would say the house was abandoned. Which it was until a month ago. Death has obviously not worried too much about putting his house to rights with his son's life hanging in the balance.

I knock on the heavy, gilded, double doors and the sound echoes inside the house in a way that makes me think the house is empty. Death opens the door quickly and ushers us into an ornate foyer with curved staircases against both side walls.

The floor is smooth and shiny, like polished black stones that have white veining through them. There's a set of double wood doors to the right and the left of the foyer, at the base of each wooden staircase and black carpet runners up the middle of the stairs. Beyond the stairs, through the middle of the foyer, I can see hallways go off to the right and left. The foyer itself is just empty all the way to the back wall that has large windows and glass doors onto a patio that looks as wild and overrun with plant life as the front of the house did.

I look up and see that the foyer is two stories tall, except past the stairs. There's an ornate gold and black chandelier, hanging from the second story ceiling, surrounded by a faded fresco of dark, stormy clouds with lightning bolts and black horses that seem to be running in mid-panicked states.

Death leads us up the left staircase and down a hallway on the second floor. There are four black wood polished doors with gold handles along the hallway.

Death walks by these, taking us to the black wood polished double doors at the dead end of the hall. No paintings hanging on the walls and, while there are no cobwebs or really any dust, the gold light fixtures that are the only accents in the hall are a muted gold. I would guess they are tarnished, or developed a patina, but I doubt they actually are. They just look like it because the magic lights don't seem to be operating at their full strength. The hallway carries the same abandoned air as the rest of the house.

Death opens the doors and shows us into a large room. It is the only one I have seen that actually feels somewhat lived in. In the center of the room, situated with the head against the back wall, is the largest bed I've ever seen. There's a decorative wood headboard and footboard, but I don't pay any attention to that, or the rest of the furniture in the room, because on the bed is Anarus. Or his body is. He would look like he's just sleeping if it wasn't for how pale he looks and how limp his body is. I have watched Anarus sleep. He radiates strength and power even in the softness of sleep. There's no sense of power or strength coming from him now.

I rush to his side anyway, tears threatening, as I trace his facial hair with a gentle finger. My heart feels like it's caving in, and I realize Ydum is sitting at his feet on one side of the bed and Byder is sitting next to Anarus on the other side. They both are touching his legs, as if they couldn't help themselves either, and their eyes are glassy with unshed tears. I'm feeling all three of our pain, and so are they, through the bond.

Death is speaking softly. "No wonder you could hardly ever look at me. He looks so much like me."

I only nod. Death takes the bags Byder and Ydum were carrying and sets them to the side. Then, he comes over to the bed and sits across from me at Anarus's head.

"You understand this may not work?" He asks me. "You understand that if it does work, he may not have a mated bond with you anymore? He may not be the same person anymore? He may be changed from his time in the land of the dead?"

"Yes." I whisper. "I don't care."

Death looks at Byder and Ydum who both also say, "Yes."

"Then, let's do this." Death begins. "Jinx, I need you to touch me and Anarus."

"Wait!" Byder stands, digging in his pants pocket. He produces a small glass jar and hands it to me. "Don't forget this."

The burn protection salve. I had forgotten all about it. I used it in the games to protect myself from getting magically burned touching their powers. But Byder remembered.

"Thank you, Byder." I rub my hands, covering them in the salve, then touch my eyelids gently. "Okay, now we are ready."

Death starts again. "I need you to touch me and Anarus. I will guide you to the bridge, but I think you will have to do the work once we are there. Find Anarus, get him to take his mantle and fix the bridge, then cross back over through it to the land of the living so his essence returns to his body. Byder, Ydum, I'm not sure what you can do. Lend your strength to Jinx, maybe. Be another anchor point to his body for her."

Byder comes around the bed and he and Ydum situate themselves so that they can both touch me and Anarus. As soon as they are sorted, I reach out a hand to touch Death's arm. My other hand is already holding Anarus's hand. Death takes Anarus's other hand in his.

I close my eyes. "Peace. I need peace." I take a deep breath and blow it out slowly. I can have peace. We're getting Anarus back. "Peace, strength, and power. I need to get Anarus back. I need peace, strength, and power." I feel a warm sensation settle over me and the vision shimmers into my mind.

The land is still covered with snow on both sides of the tiny creek. The trees nearby have shed their last leaves and the bare branches are swaying slightly in the gentle breeze. The river is frozen still and over it, a small rope bridge dangles down into the cracked icy water. The rope railings are still frayed, but the wood slats that had broken when Anarus fell on it have been replaced. I can tell the difference between the old rotting wood and the new uncured wood.

There are gold lines, braided together, stretching over the bridge from somewhere deep into the woods on the land of the living side to deep into the woods on the land of the dead side. They look almost the same as they did the day Anarus died, except there are three black lines running through the gold braid now.

The black lines go slack just over the bridge. I follow their lines, and find Anarus sitting in the snow, staring at the bridge, holding the frayed ends of the three black mate bonds in his hands. I stand at the bridge just on the land of the living side.

"Anarus, you need to stand up." I say softly, my heart in my throat.

Anarus doesn't seem to notice me or hear me, so I speak louder. "Anarus, you need to stand up."

He still doesn't respond. Can he not hear me because he is dead? I move a foot closer, my toes now on the frozen river. "Anarus. Stand up."

"No." Anarus growls, not looking up. "I won't leave here without them. I'll wait for them."

"Who are you waiting for, Anarus?" I ask.

"Jinx, Byder, and Ydum. I won't leave without them." Anarus still isn't looking at me. "I don't care if the bonds broke. I'll wait for them."

"Look at me, Anarus." I try to bite back my sob. He's waiting for us. He thinks we are all mortal and that he can wait for us. "Anarus, who am I? Look at me."

"Why?" He asks harshly. "There is only three people I want to see and you aren't them. You aren't anyone. You are just in my mind."

"Why do you think that, Anarus? Why do you think I'm only in your mind?"

"Because you sound like her." He sighs heavily. "Because you sound like Jinx and even if they were made mortal, they wouldn't end their lives and leave each other to come here to me."

"Anarus, look at me please." I say softly.

Anarus finally actually looks up at me and gets angry. "No. You are not her!" He rakes his free hand through his hair. "Fuck, first I'm hearing things. Now, I'm seeing things. Jinx wouldn't come here. She wouldn't dare leave Ydum and Byder behind."

He laughs, the sound ragged and sharp. "I'm losing my mind. Maybe it is degrading with my body. Maybe I should let go and go where I should be in the land of the dead."

"No!" I slam a hand out, reaching across the bridge to Anarus even though I know it's too far for me to touch him. "Don't give up. It is me. Anarus, I'm here for you. It really is me."

He looks down at the three black lines in his hand. "I've held on too long. The bonds are dead. I should let them go. Let Byder, Ydum, and Jinx go." His voice softens. "I don't want to. They loved me. Someone finally loved me. It hurts holding on like this. But I don't want to let it go."

"Then don't, Anarus." I carefully take another step forward. "I'm still on the side of the living, but just barely. "Don't let go. Come back. Stand up and come back with me."

"I can't. I'm dead and you're not real." Anarus loosens his grip on the three black lines and they tug out of his hand just a small bit.

My mind races for anything to convince Anarus I'm real and really here. "You split Ydum's lip only twice in the games but always threatened to do it again if he pissed you off."

Anarus scoffs. "Everyone knows that."

I try again, becoming desperate. He really looks like he is going to let go and leave. "After we bonded, I told you that you are beautiful and you thought I was talking about the stars on your back I was touching, but I told you, no, you are beautiful. You are my beautiful, beautiful man. Anarus, please, just look at me for one moment. Please."

He looks back up. I stretch my hand out as far as I can across the bridge. "Touch me, Anarus. Feel me. I'm warm. I'm real."

Anarus takes my hand with his free one and his eyes go wide. "You're... you're warm. You're real."

His hand holding the lines snaps tightly closed on them again and he stands up, yanking his other hand out of mine violently. "No! It's too soon. Go back, Jinx. Go back. It's too soon. Don't cross the bridge. Go back to Byder and Ydum. I can wait for you. Fuck, why are you here already? Go back!"

"I'm here for you, Anarus. I'm here to bring you back with me." I try to explain.

Anarus shakes his head, his hand holding the ends of the mate bonds clenched tight. "I can't go back. The bridge is broken and I'm dead. Go back, Jinx. I love you. Please go back."

I squeeze my eyes tight for just a moment, trying not to cry. "Death brought me here, Anarus. Not because I've died, but because you haven't. Not really. He's holding your body in stasis so you can come back. You have to fix the bridge so you can come back."

He snarls. "You're trusting Death? The god that made me carry a second power and abandoned me! And you're trusting him? Now I know you aren't real. Jinx would never trust him after what he did to me."

He's pulling away again and I speak in a rush to stop him. "It wasn't him, Anarus. It wasn't him but Winter. Winter was supposed to hold the wilde hunt until after you took your mantle. It was your mother's power, not your father's."

"It was Winter's?" He scowls at me, not believing. "Why would it be

Winter's power rather than Death's?"

In broken, rushed clips, I tell Anarus everything Death told us. "You were right all along. The only thing we got wrong was that it was Winter who gave you the extra mantle when you were born, not Death. Anarus, think about it. If Death was banished, how would he have been able to be here, in Nazus for that long, without ever being spotted? Long enough to make a child with Winter and still here when you were born? It doesn't make sense, right? He couldn't have. It was Winter."

He looks down at the three black lines, his mouth moving with no sound coming out. Finally, he looks at me again. "You're right. It doesn't make sense for it to have been Death. It was Winter."

Anarus shifts, confused and, I can tell, scared. "Jinx, I can't fix the bridge. I didn't take my mantle so I can't fix the bridge. And I can't open it to come back if it isn't fixed. You need to leave. You need to go back before you can't. Please, I'm fine here. I promise I'm fine. I can wait for you. I'm fine."

"But I'm not, Anarus!" I yell at him. "I'm not fine. Byder's not fine. Ydum's not fine. We need you back. I can't do this without you, Anarus. You have to come back. You have to take your mantle and fix the bridge and come back."

"How?" Anarus yells back. "How do I take my mantle when I'm already dead?"

I groan under my breath. "Fuck it."

The moment I step on the bridge, Anarus starts screaming. "No, Jinx! No! Stop! You won't be able to get back. Stop!"

But I don't stop. I cross the bridge, the freezing water chilling my bare feet and wetting the bottom edge of my dress. I walk right across and take Anarus's face in my hands. I kiss him, tears running down my face making our lips taste salty.

"Now, you have to fix the bridge." I whisper. "You have to take your mantle and open the bridge so I don't get stuck here and die. So that we don't die."

Anarus pulls me tight against him, kissing me roughly. "Fuck, Jinx. Why did you do that? Why?"

"Fix the bridge, Anarus." I take his empty hand in mine and lead him to the bridge. When we are close enough to touch the rope of the bridge, I guide his hand to the frayed bits. "Fix it, Anarus, and we can both leave the land of the dead together."

"I don't have my power."

"Use mine. You can have mine until you find yours." I put my free hand on his chest, right over his still heart. I need Anarus to use my magic. Let him use my magic. Give him all of it. Anarus needs my magic.

Anarus takes a quick, sharp breath. "Fuck!" I feel the draw against my magic. It hurts but when I look down, gold is shining out of his hands into the frayed rope that is rebuilding itself. His hand wavers over the rebuilding rope.

"Keep going." I tell him through gritted teeth.

He shakes his head. "It's hurting you."

"I don't care. Keep going. Don't let us die, Anarus. Keep going."

Anarus looks into my eyes, his feelings on display so clearly, I know them even without the bonds. He is terrified of hurting me.

I speak softer this time, masking the pain. "Keep going, Anarus. You can do this. I trust you."

He sighs heavily and looks back at our conjoined hands. The gold light starts shining out of them again and I feel the draw against my magic again. The frayed rope keeps rebuilding itself. It is slow and painful, the rope not responding well to my magic filtered through Anarus. I bite my lip until it bleeds, masking the pain of my magic being siphoned from me.

Moving together, we touch every part of the bridge. Every piece of rope is bathed in my magic through Anarus's hand until it's clean, tightly coiled rope, taut across the creek again. Sweat drenches my back as the pain becomes almost too much. I can feel my magic waning.

We move to the slats of wood that make up the steps of the bridge. Every board becomes perfectly weathered as we touch them. Not so new, like Death made the temporary fixes, that they could easily become waterlogged and rot. But not so old that they are crumbling either.

I stop sweating and bite the other side of my lip. I have never felt so exhausted before, but I hide it from Anarus. He would want to stop if he knew how bad this is for me, but we need to do this. He needs to do this. So, I hide it.

The wood fixed, we move to the posts on either side of the river, attaching the bridge to the land. These parts of the bridge fight against my magic fixing them more than the rope and wood did. Or maybe I'm running out of magic and that's what's making it harder. But we struggle through, Anarus and I. Soon, every fastener and knot is tightened down, rust falling away under his hand.

When we reach the other end of the bridge, the one connected to the land of the living, Anarus stops. Again, he seems confused on what to do.

"I can't leave the bridge, but I can't not go into the land of the living and become alive again." He says.

I think about this. "Before you tried to take your mantle, you were always standing with one foot on each side. Not on the bridge itself, but one foot in the land of the living and one foot in the land of the dead. Could you do that again?"

"You go first, little human." He tells me. "Go into the land of the living and I will try."

I shake my head. "No. I'm afraid if I go back there, it will take me back to my body and I don't want that until we know we're right and this works."

Anarus grumbles. "Fine. We'll try it your way." Anarus positions himself in the middle of the now fixed rope and wood bridge. He extends one leg until he can set his foot down in the land of the dead. He shifts the foot in the snow, moving it until he's sure the foot is on steady land, not ice and slick snow. He pauses, considering something. Then, he holds out his hand gripping the three mate bonds.

"Take these. Do not let them go. They keep trying to pull away from me. Do not let them."

I nod and grab the three black bond lines in my hand before he lets go. They burn my hand to touch and are trying so hard to yank out of my grasp. Once he's sure I have them, Anarus places one hand on each rope railing. Then I hold my breath as he lifts his other foot, setting it down in the land of the living, shifting it until it's solidly holding his stance.

Immediately, Anarus fills overflowing with gold light. He screams and almost lets go of the rope.

"Don't let go! Anarus, don't you dare let go." I say as I place my free hand back to cup his cheek and the hand with the bonds in it over his heart. "It's your mantle. I think it's the mantles of your power. Let it settle on you."

Eyes, heart, hands. That's where the gold always was for him. I need to help him. I look at his heart. The well is gone and I can see his heart shining gold. The braided cord of mate bonds and destiny that was running from the land of the living straight to the land of the dead is trying to anchor on his heart again.

Let it anchor there, I tell his heart. That's where it is supposed to be. Let it anchor there.

Nothing happens. I look down at the mate bonds in my hand. They are still black. His power can't hear me. I'm not his bonded witch anymore, so it can't hear me.

"Anarus, you have to reconnect our bonds so I can help you." I'm not sure if he's hearing me, though. His power trying to settle the full crown of his mantles is causing him so much pain, I don't think he can hear me. He's writhing and twisting, howling in pain. A full mantle is a hard enough thing to settle, and Death said he has two of them naturally, even without the wilde hunt. He can't concentrate on anything but that.

Fuck it. I'll do it myself. I push the bonds to his heart. My hand burns like all the skin is being stripped off, but I don't stop. I keep pushing. Take the damn bonds back! I could be pushing through a brick wall for all the progress I'm making. But I keep pushing.

"Anarus, you have to help me. You have to let our bonds back so I'm your witch again."

His eyes are wild with pain, but he tries to focus on me. "You're my witch. You'll always be my witch, Jinx. You're the only witch I ever want."

That admission from him must have loosened something because my hand starts to make actual progress. I can feel my hand tugging the black bond lines through his skin, both the power of moving them and they themselves burning my skin. The drain we already made on my magic means I have even less power to do this with and fatigue makes me sloppy. The bond lines want to pull away, but I keep pushing through the syrup that is the way to Anarus's heart, glad that it isn't a brick wall anymore.

By the time I touch the bonds to his heart, my hand has gone from burning hot to ice cold to completely numb. I'm sweating again and shaking from a pain that's so great, my mind is rejecting even feeling it anymore. Take the fucking bonds back! I scream through my magic.

As I hold the bonds against his heart, I watch as slowly, far too slowly, the black frayed ends tendril their way around Anarus's heart, the slightest shimmer of gold crawling down the black lines.

I know the exact moment the bonds take root in his heart because I hear Anarus screaming in my head. I feel his pain alongside mine. I feel Byder screaming in pain. Ydum screaming. Kinshra, who I haven't felt or talked to in a month, howls long and loud. Her pack howls with her, sharing the load of her pain at the rebuilt familiar bond and her joy at it being restored. The bonds between all five of us restored completely, the lines are now solid gold.

Now, take the rest of them. Let them anchor within you, I tell his heart. This time it listens. I am Anarus's mated bond mate and it will listen to me now. The heart allows the rope of coiled bonds to find its ending anchor in his heart. I breathe a sigh of relief and pull my hand from his heart.

As I watch them attach, I see the difference in the two golds. The gold of his heart and the gold of his eyes and hands are two different golds. Anarus's power was always two-fold, even before Winter put the wilde hunt in him. His heart is the opposite side of the mated bonds and destinies from the living Fates that created them. He is a Fate just as much as they are, that power different than being a god. For the Fates, their godly power is only that of a Fate, I think, creating the start of people's destinies and their mated bonds. But for Anarus, he is both, a Fate and a god. His power as a Fate is to end those destinies and those mated bonds when they die.

The eyes and hands are the bridge mantle. This is his power as a god, the separate power from his power as a Fate. With his hands and eyes, he cares for the bridge and shepherds the dead across. They are related powers, but distinct, with their own mantles. The ender of bonds mantle settles on Anarus peacefully and I can turn my attention to the bridge mantle.

I move my thoughts to the eyes. You know your duty? I ask them.

They answer quickly. Yes, we see the dead and show them the bridge. We see the living and turn them away. We examine the threads of their bonds to know the difference. We follow Death's instructions about whether a person stays in the land of the dead, recycles their essence, or is allowed to move between the living and dead. You are not supposed to be here yet. Your destiny is not done. Your Fate is not yet complete. You need to turn back so you can complete them both.

I will soon, I tell his eyes, ignoring that spoke of me as if I have a different fate than destiny. Aren't they the same? Soon, I still have work to do.

His hands next. Do you know your duty?

His hands only scream. It's too much! The bridge is too feeble. We cannot hold it. It is too hard. We need to let go.

No, I tell them. Hold the bridge together. That is your job. Keep the bridge between the living and the dead open, allowing only the dead to pass through into the land of the dead, and not allowing any dead to pass through into the land of the living. Not unless Death says they may.

But the bridge is too weak! They argue with me.

Then, build a new one, I tell them. One hand can hold the bridge open for those who need to cross it, and the other build a new one. A stone bridge that will be stronger. When the new bridge is built, you can move there and hold that one easier.

We can do that, Anarus's hands tell me. Build a stone bridge on top of the wood and rope one. A stone bridge will be strong and last.

Anarus lifts his left hand from the rope railing and I see the edges of the bridge along the land of the dead start changing into stone. It is slow and seems like he's working hard to do it. Anarus's face is shining with sweat, but his eyes are open and he's not screaming anymore.

"I'll have to work quickly." He tells me. "The bridge will not hold when the wilde hunt comes back. I need it to be stone in time."

"What about the wilde hunt? Are they yours?" I ask.

He shakes his head. "I don't know. They won't come back yet so I can't ask."

I twist my lips in thought. "We will need them on the nineteenth. Can you keep trying to call to them, see if they will listen to you once they are close?"

"What's on the nineteenth?"

I bite my lip. I feel weak and so very tired. The other side of the bridge that I can see over Anarus's shoulder looks tempting. That side is the land of the dead. I could rest there, I know. I close my eyes and sigh. Rest would be good. I'm so tired. The pain of my life has been so great, for so long. The games, mourning Anarus, and now, the work of bringing him back. I could rest without all that pain. If only I went to that side, I could rest, free from pain.

"Jinx." Anarus growls at me. "Get off my bridge. Go back to the land of the living. I'll meet you there, but you need to go back now."

"But…" I start to say. It looks so peaceful there. I could rest. I would love to rest. Everything has been far too hard for far too long.

"Go. Now!" Anarus yells at me, bringing my attention back to him. "You can't stay here anymore!" His hand that was building the stone bridge comes up to my chest and shoves me backward.

"Go, little human. You need to go." He shoves me again and I stumble backwards, falling down in the land of the living.

I open my eyes and see Anarus on the bed, Byder and Ydum next to me and Death on the other side of the bed. My red bracelet, the one Ydum and Byder made me to replace Anarus's, falls on the floor, burned and black. I notice that both of them have lost a bracelet too, theirs still red on the floor of the room. All of Anarus's are gone. Not just on the floor like ours but completely gone. There is ash on the mattress, under his wrist.

Pain flares all over me and I scream. I fall off the bed into a heap on the floor. My right hand is on fire and everything else hurts like it did after the sixth game. Every muscle and bone in me feels like it has been pounded. The world swims and I think I will throw up. I do.

Hands are pulling on me. "You foolish, little hex! You foolish, foolish little human. Why did you do that?" I am being gathered into arms in a lap.

I can only cry and pant from the pain. "I had to save him. He wouldn't come back so I had to go get him."

"You got me. You got me." Anarus says, cradling me in his arms. "Fuck, your hand is a mess. All of you is a mess. This is worse than when you kicked Damek in the balls."

I give a watery chuckle, then what he said makes its way to my brain. I force my eyes to focus through the pain on Anarus's face. I'm in Death's bedroom and Anarus is holding me. Talking to me. He's alive. I don't care about pain anymore. I throw my arms around him, crying harder as I claim his lips.

Anarus pulls back from me. "As much as I enjoy this, little human, you and I are both very hurt and the Fates felt the bonds reconnect. I'm not sure if they'll tell the rest of the council, but they seemed pretty pissed. I hope you guys have a plan because I have the distinct feeling that we should probably run or something."

"Or something, man." Ydum says, chuckling. "That phrase tends to get you in trouble. Can either of you walk? Or move at all?"

Anarus cocks his head to the side, thinking. "Me? Not well to be honest. Her? Not a chance."

"You're alive, Anarus. I'll run if you want." I tell him. But I know he's probably right. I wiggle my toes slightly and groan at the pain that shoots through my foot. "Tomorrow, I can run tomorrow. Why do I hurt this much?"

Death answers. "Well, let's see. You stepped into the land of the dead while still alive. Fed your magic to Anarus, all of it. Your entire magical being was controlled and used by him. Most people would die from that alone. Then, you, a human that isn't even immortal yet, held onto three mate bonds with your bare hands and shoved them into a full mantle of power by a sheer force of will. And if that isn't enough, you assisted in rebuilding the bridge between life and death. Something you should not be able to do at all. Even Byder and Ydum can't do that. Even I can't. Only Anarus should be able to do that."

I lay my head on Anarus's shoulder. "Oh. Is that all? Sounds like an average day at the games."

All four males laugh at me. All four. Although Anarus's laugh sounds tired.

"Alright, beautiful. You get to come with me now." Ydum takes me out of Anarus's arms and I groan in protest. "I'll give you back. Be patient. But we have to leave and Ani can barely carry himself, much less you."

"My carriage and driver are right out front. I had some food and water put in it, as well as your bags." Death tells us. "Go to Greenbriar. Don't stop until you get there."

I feel Ydum nod. My eyes are so heavy it's hard to keep them open, but I look over his shoulder as he carries me down the stairs. I see Byder with his arm around Anarus, who is walking but leaning heavily on Byder. Outside, Byder helps Anarus into the carriage first, then Ydum lifts me in on the same bench, my head on Anarus's lap as I lay across the carriage bench. I reach out and take Anarus's hand in mine, holding it tightly.

"Your hand." He says softly.

I shake my head. "Is not letting yours go ever again."

I feel more than see Ydum and Byder climb into the carriage and barely feel us lurch forward to start moving before I fall asleep. I don't dream.

Chapter Three

WHEN I WAKE UP Byder has my burned hand in his. The carriage is dark except for a small silver light coming from his hand on mine.

"What are you doing?" I ask him quietly. I can see that Ydum next to him is sleeping sitting up, his head tilted back to rest on the back wall of the carriage and Anarus curled around me is breathing regularly like he's probably asleep too.

Byder looks up at me. "Sorry, baby girl. I didn't mean to wake you. I was just trying to see if my healing could help."

"You heal animals." I pull myself to sitting up, but don't take my hand away from Byder.

In response, Byder just shows me my hand. The blisters have subsided some, not much but some. "Better than nothing."

"You shouldn't waste your energy." I say, but at the same time Anarus says, "Keep going."

I look at Anarus as he sits up and he's watching me. "Let him heal you, Jinx. He can sleep and recover quickly. That hand will take weeks to heal on its own and, according to what they told me about why the nineteenth, we don't have weeks."

I pretend to be affronted and whip my hair like Iella does. "I'll have you know I fight best broken and battered." I drop the act, slumping back in my seat. "Or well, that's the only way I've ever fought so it's what I know."

Byder laughs at this but keeps working on my hand. When I see his silver light start to sputter, I pull my hand away. "That's all you can do for now, Byder." I tell him and examine my hand. It feels significantly better but only looks a little better. Less blisters that aren't as big.

"How are you feeling, little human?" Anarus asks me.

"Better." I tell him. "The all over pain and exhaustion are gone. You?"

Anarus groans. "Good." Then, he grabs me by my waist and lifts me onto his lap, facing him. "You good?"

"With you? Always." I say as I kiss him with everything I am. My hands curl into the hair at the nape of his neck as I press as close to him as I can. I want to touch him with everything, everywhere. When he moans, I use the opening to slip my tongue in his mouth.

"Fuck, I missed you." Anarus moves his lips from mine to my jaw and ear. His hand is questing for a way under my skirt. I lift my left knee off the bench seat, pull up the fabric of my skirt that was caught under it, and give him the access he wants.

"I missed you, Anarus." I breathe out as I sit straight up in his arms, forcing his head lower, down my neck to my chest. He wastes no time untying the ties on the bodice of my dress with his other hand and freeing one of my breasts to wrap his mouth around the nipple, sucking hard.

His other hand finds what it was looking for and Anarus lets out a frustrated growl. "Who the fuck gave you underwear?"

Ydum, who I already knew was awake because the bond is back in full force with Anarus back to being the hub of it, laughs. "That would be my mother. When she saw Jinx wearing my clothes, she went on a little shopping spree for her. I think she thought it would help Jinx settle."

"Well, I hate it." Anarus grumbles, which only makes all of us laugh. He lets his hands quest around my underwear, pushing it to the side so his fingers can graze my core. His mouth resumes its ministrations to my breast while his other hand toys with my other nipple.

I moan and press myself against Anarus's questing hand. I want more. I want all of him. I don't care that we are in a carriage, his father's carriage. I pull on his face, bringing his lips back to mine to kiss him fervently.

I pull back and look into Anarus's eyes. They are hooded and his hand is still moving against my skin under my dress but refuse to actually go where I want them to, but I see lines of exhaustion still lingering on his face and pull away from him.

"You're still recovering, Anarus." I push on his chest, and attempt to move off of him, forcing him to grumble a resentful acknowledgement of that truth.

Anarus disentangles himself from me, annoyed, and pulls the curtain back to looks out the window. Light shines through the window blinding me for a second. I realize it was only dark in the carriage because the thick black curtains pulled over the windows in the doors. I straighten my tangled and undone clothes, then pull back the other curtain to look out.

I recognize the area we are in. I think. It looks like the woods around Greenbriar. But then again, all woods look like woods. As I watch, I start to see things that are familiar. Actually familiar. Old Man Gantry's hut on the outskirts of the village is visible between the trees. Unless some other old codger living outside some other village proper in the woods made his hut out of metal sheets too, that has to be Gantry's place.

"It doesn't matter now, because we are almost there." I tell my gods.

As if to reinforce my statement, the carriage stops and I feel the driver get down. He opens the door and leans partially inside. "We're just outside Greenbriar. Where in the village am I heading?"

I give the driver the directions to my parents' hut the best I can and after we start moving again, I try to quell my nerves.

"What's got you tied up, baby girl?" Byder asks me.

I look at my three gods. All three of them. Gods, I love them. But fuck if I'm not nervous about this. My parents' home is so different than theirs. Even Anarus, who never had his own home, only ever stayed with other families in Veirveil, where Byder's apartment is worlds away from my hut. Worlds better. Not for the first time, I think about how almost impossible it is for the three of them to understand the level of poverty they are about to see. The level of lack and want I lived in for all but the last three months of my life.

I think about my parents. What do they know? Anything? Nothing? Do they know the real point of the Gods Games? Will they understand? If it comes down to a choice, I know without a doubt I would turn my back on my parents and leave again in this carriage with my gods, but I don't want to have to make that choice. Will they accept that my bond is with three gods, a type of relationship that may be unusual in Veirveil, but was never, ever acceptable in Greenbriar?

On top of all of this, there's a point to this visit. It's not the leisurely we survived the games visit we had planned but a call to arms. Which probably means talking to the High Priest.

No, which definitely means talking to the High Priest because, oh fuck, where are we supposed to stay while we are here? My parents don't have the room. Not with only two bedrooms and Orphelia and Catarina still living at home too. Most visiting gods would stay at the High Priest's home but the fuck if I am doing that. Not even with all three of my gods.

"Jinx." Ydum says softly. "Everything will be okay. We'll all be okay."

I don't have time to respond because the carriage is stopping again. I peek out the window and see the dirt road, nothing more than frozen mud at this point, giving way to what would be a front garden if it was able to grow much in the way of grass, a small well that is actually shared by several houses on this street situated in the middle of the not a garden dirt area.

The mud and daub hut, with its straw thatched roof that is showing some black spots of rot, meaning it probably needs to be replaced again soon, a dull gray in the watery gray sunlight of a winter day. There are planters in front of the hut, on either side of the front door. A door that is little more than thin sheets of wood screwed together, no door handle except a piece rope strung through a hole with a knot on the outside of the door and another on the inside.

The planters are empty now, showing how they are ringed with odd stones and scraps of wood, an attempt to make the house better, more welcoming. It doesn't look like much from the outside, and I know it looks like even less on the inside, but it's home to me.

My mother is standing in the open front door, her dark blue eyes and light brown, almost blonde hair to her waist, and lithe form so familiar. As is the homespun gray dress she's wearing that looks exactly like mine. And the used to be white but is almost gray from a million washes apron tied around her waist that she's wiping her hands on as she peers out the door curiously at the large, expensive carriage with an actual horse and driver that stopped outside her house.

I know she's curious why such an expensive carriage would be stopping here. We never see actual carriages, except every September fifth, when one comes and waits in case someone needs to be transported to the games. Except for this year, that carriage would sit behind the testing center, then leave Greenbriar as empty as it arrived every year. But this one stopped in front of her home, or close to it at least.

As soon as the carriage stops, my worries melt away. Mostly. It's Mom, and I can see Catarina peering out behind her. I open the carriage door and step out. It takes only one second for my mother to recognize that it's me coming out of the carriage.

Mom instantly yells, running towards me, to grab me in a tight hug. "Jinx! Oh gods, Jinx. You're home! You're alive!" Mom pulls back from me, looking my up and down, while also glancing back over her shoulder, yelling out for Dad. "Maddox! Maddox! Jinx is home!"

My father, with his mud brown eyes like mine wide in shock and his graying hair, a little too long, getting tousled as he runs, comes barreling around the side of the hut at a full run. He doesn't even stop but grabs me around the waist and lifts me off the ground in a tight hug, even though he's almost the same size as me and has that small gut most older males develop.

He cries into my shoulder as he hugs me. "My baby girl."

It's Catarina who notices my gods first. "Who are they?" She asks almost breathlessly.

I know from the first time I saw them, or any gods, that the three males behind me will be instantly recognizable as not human, their too perfect skin and features, and Ydum's green tone, announcing their godhood for them. My father sets me down and stands a little taller while Mom smooths down her hair. Catarina just gapes at them. Orphelia must not be home because her nosy butt definitely would already be out here with this much noise.

"Um, Mom, Dad, this is Ydum, Byder, and Anarus. They…" My words fail. I don't know how to explain this here in the middle of the street with the neighbors poking their heads out their doors and pretending to not listen. Just as much as Mom was looking curiously at the carriage because such a thing on her street was completely out of the ordinary for her life, so is everyone else who lives on this street, and probably the few streets around this one too.

Ydum feels my distress and comes to my rescue. He steps forward towards Dad, holding out his hand. "We were Jinx's team in the games. I'm the one that's Ydum." Along with being a genius, good fighter, and god of nature, apparently Ydum is also great in social situations. I had seen enough evidence that Eiran was very socially adept. He must have passed that on to Ydum along with his love of knowledge and learning. Good to know. Is there anything that male can't do? Sometimes, I think the answer is no, because every time I've ever seen him in a situation that called for a new skill, he just. Does it.

My father takes his hand and shakes it. "Maddox Bloodmorrow."

"I figured by the way you came running when Jinx's mom screamed Maddox." Ydum says teasingly. He moves over to shake my mom's hand who, blushing and whispering, tells him her name is Avalon. Ydum turns to Catarina next. "You must be either Catarina or Orphelia, right?"

"You're green," is the only response Catarina gives.

I groan and mutter, hanging my head down, a hand going to my forehead. "Oh, for fuck's sake, Catarina."

But Ydum takes it in stride. Smiling and putting his hands in his pockets, after he jerks his thumb at Anarus. "Could be worse. Ani used to have shadows everywhere all over him."

"Still could, maybe, after the equinox when the wilde hunt returns." Anarus grumbles out.

"Oh, my gods!" my mom exclaims. "I'm so impolite. We haven't even invited you in out of the cold. Please! Jinx, baby, bring your... teammates, I guess? Inside."

Byder walks up to stand next to me. "Should we mention the fact that your mom just said oh my gods and we are actually gods? Now I know where you picked up that phrase." He gives me a wicked grin and I playfully slap his stomach.

"Be nice, Byder!" I hiss quietly.

We all move inside and my sitting room has never felt so small. Mom and Catarina turn around two chairs from the dining table to sit on, leaving the two threadbare blue and gray couches for me, Dad, and my gods. Dad gestures for them to have a seat, and Byder and Anarus do but Ydum turns to me.

Whispering close to my ear, he asks. "Hey, beautiful. Washroom?"

My cheeks flame. "Outhouse in the back." I point to the door in the kitchen wall, and look down at the floor.

Ydum puts a finger under my chin, lifting my face back to look at him. "Why are you embarrassed? Your parents seem nice. Your home looks like there's a lot of love shared here. You have nothing to be ashamed of, beautiful." He kisses my cheek gently. Then, he casually strolls to the back door, saying louder, "Don't mind me, long carriage ride. Be right back."

"Who's carriage is that anyway?" Catarina asks while eyeballing me hard. She saw Ydum kiss me. I ignore her stare, knowing far too well that she is memorizing every single second of this to tell all of my other sisters about it. Jinx, home from the games, with three gods, one that kissed her cheek and called her beautiful. Oh, the gossip will not end from them.

"Um, Death's." I answer her and go to sit between Anarus and Byder on one of the couches, leaving the spot next to my dad for Ydum when he gets back.

"Like the god of Death, Death?" Catarina's mouth is hanging open. Yeah, she's soaking all this in.

"My father, the god of Death. Yes." Anarus tells her.

When Catarina looks like she is going to say something else, Dad interrupts her. "Caty, dear, why don't you go tell your sisters Jinx is here. They'll want to know."

"All of them?" Catarina asks, seeming upset to be kicked out.

Mom fixes a look at her. "Yes Catarina, all of them."

Catarina groans but slides on the boots next to the back door, the shared ones that everyone but Dad would use for going to the outhouse during winter, and wraps a blanket from the blanket ladder next to the kitchen door around her shoulders. She mutters as she leaves out the back door to head to, I assume, Shearah, Myrna, and Ganna's first since it's the closest if you cut through the back way.

As soon as she's gone, Mom speaks again. "We weren't told a lot after you left, Jinx. Just got these notes delivered." Mom stands and goes over to the mantle above the fireplace and opens a small wooden box I never saw before, taking out several small papers. Her hand shakes a little as she touches the box. "We got one a week for nine weeks, after the first two, then nothing for almost a month now. We didn't know what that meant and I feared the worst."

It suddenly dawns on me that the small box holding those small notes is an urn. My urn. The urn my parents bought to remember me with. Because my parents thought I was most likely dead and they didn't even have a body to bury, a grave to mourn at. They were mourning my supposed death while I mourned Anarus's actual death.

Mom hands me the papers and I look through them. They are all the most basic missives the gods could possibly send to update my parents, handwritten on creamy paper. The first one says, "Jinx Bloodmorrow has found a team in the Gods Games. She will do weekly challenges for ten weeks. As her next of kin, you will be updated on her progress after each game." The next one only says, "Jinx Bloodmorrow and team have passed game one." That's it. And the rest are the same, except to change, saying game two, three, and so on until game nine. Nothing more than my team passed. And nothing at all about game ten, of course. Anarus takes the slips of paper from me when I am done reading them to look at himself.

"I didn't think the teams were ever more than one human, one god." Dad says thoughtfully, with an edge of some emotion I can't place. "How did you end up with three, princess?"

"Good question." Byder jokes, but I blush.

"It's not all as simple as we were taught." I tell Dad. "The games, there's, well, the teams aren't just teams, but..."

Thank fuck Ydum comes back in. His entrance distracts us from the question for a moment. He seems to have a knack for smoothing this stuff over and talking in uncomfortable situations. But then again, Ydum has never had a problem talking at all, that I know of. As soon as he figures out what we're talking about, he takes over the explanation. The way his voice changes when he starts talking about things academically will help smooth over all the embarrassing stuff. I hope.

"The initial trial for the Gods Games determines if a witch and any of the gods of that year are destined to be bonded mates. Most of the time, that does only mean one human, one god, but can mean one human, two gods. Three gods, like us, is a unique situation, but the magics for discovering these bonds is nigh on failproof and ancient. If it said the three of us, then the three of us it is."

"Bonded mates?" Dad caught that. "Mates as in, married?"

"Yes." Byder says calmly.

"With all three of you?" I can tell by Dad's tone he's not happy.

"Yes." Anarus answers this time.

"Jinx, did you agree to this?" Dad is definitely not happy. "Were you given a choice? I know you didn't have a choice to go, but with this, were you...?"

"Jinx had…" Anarus starts to interrupt Dad, but Dad interrupts him right back, his voice growly, not happy at all.

"I was not asking you. I was asking my daughter." Dad is very angry now. Standing, and almost vibrating with barely controlled rage. "The gods stole my child, then wouldn't even tell me if she was alive or dead, and now here you are saying she's yours. Three gods are now bonded to her? Did you have any choices at all? Did the gods give you any choice at all?"

"Yes, Dad." Oh fuck, peace. Give my dad peace to understand this. His anger makes sense. He thought I was dead. He bought an urn for the only piece of me the gods would give him to mourn and now, three gods are saying I'm not his baby girl anymore but their bonded witch. Dad doesn't know. Dad doesn't see the difference between the gods that stole me from him and the three sitting here now, who are just as much victims of all this as me, as him.

"The pairing for the teams was not my choice, but everything after that was. I had the choice for everything that happened with the three of them after that. They never forced me into anything, or even asked for anything." I take a breath, maintaining that magic of peace. "The gods in the games with me were given as little choice in the makeup of our team as I was. And they were given less choice about being in the games at all. There's no blood test for them. All the gods go to the games or they die. The only thing forced was the deadly games the original gods made us compete in for our lives. My relationships with Byder, Ydum, and Anarus were our choices. My choices."

"And you chose Ydum?" Mom asks. She looks at him. Ydum had chosen to sit in the seat Catarina vacated, so is sitting right next to Mom. "You kissed her cheek and called her beautiful."

I inhale deeply. Fuck it, peace for everyone. Pretty please, peace for everyone. "No, Mom. I chose all three."

Dad looks like he is going to speak again, and definitely does not look like what he's going to say will be nice and peaceful, so I speak again before he can. "One more time, for the last time, mated bonds, my choice, Anarus's choice, Byder's choice, Ydum's choice. No one else's." I look closely at Dad. "No one else's. We have gone through far too much shit together in even the last twenty-four hours, much less the last three months, to argue about this with anyone. Not even you, Dad. All three of them are mine. My bonded mates that I chose and still choose. And they chose me back."

"Well, then," Mom stands, rubbing her hands with the apron again, her nervous habit, "how long do you think you'll be able to stay for? I should get clean sheets for your bedroom, Jinx. I'll see if Catarina and Orphelia can go stay with any of your sisters once they get here. I assume the one room is fine for all four of you? It's not much, but… Unless you were planning to stay at the High Priest's home?"

"No, thank you." All four of us say at the same time.

"Here's good, Mom." I tell her. "It'll only be a few days this time. We will have to talk to the High Priest at some point, that's why we're here now actually, but we have a few days." Mom only nods and goes off to the bedroom, I know to change the sheets and pillows to the best ones, the guest ones we always called them.

"That's it? That's all you got?" Ydum is looking at the notes my mother showed us, but now he's frustrated. Anarus had given them to Byder and Byder to him. "Shit, my parents got full updates, point tallies, the works. Of course, they were there for week ten, so wouldn't have gotten anything even if it hadn't gone sideways, but damn. They left you so in the dark."

Dad nods. His arms are crossed over his chest and he's eyeing up all three of them, as if he's trying to decide if he likes them or not, but at least he's speaking with a polite tone now, not so angry. "Especially because of Jinx's birthday. She went to the testing center in the morning and I never saw her again until now. We didn't get that first note until she was gone a week. Then, the next one came two days later, then just weekly until the game nine one. When we didn't get the tenth one, the one for the last game, we assumed that..."

Dad sighs in a way that makes me glance back at the box. At the urn. I know what he thought. "We aren't really taught much about the Gods Games here, unless you get a blue test, so Avalon and I didn't really know anything except passing probably meant Jinx was okay and had no idea what finding a team meant. We definitely didn't know it meant, well, what it does, apparently."

"I went straight from the testing center to the cave." I explain to him. "The team pairing trial. I was the last one to arrive so it started as soon as I got there. The first actual game was the next day, then one every week thereafter."

"You were the youngest there, then, too, right?" Dad asks.

I shake my head. "I should have been."

"I was sent into the games three years early." Anarus says. "As an orphan, the gods didn't really know what to do with me."

Dad cocks his head to the side. "I thought you said your father is the god of Death."

"We know that now." Byder says snidely. "Not so much three months ago. It's a whole thing, long story."

"So, Anarus. Anarus, right?" He nods at Dad that he's saying it right. "You're only twenty-one instead of twenty-four?"

"Twenty-two." I correct. "His birthday is October first."

At that moment, the front door bursts open, and in pours all seven of my sisters, and Dahlia's husband Finnegan. Catarina must have run to get all of them here that fast. Either that, or someone said something about the carriage and they were all already headed here.

Of course, as is the norm with my sisters, they're all talking over each other, but clearly above the rabble, I hear Orphelia say, "Catarina said that Jinx is alive and back home and she brought three hot gods with her and one of them is green. Tell me what a liar... she... is." Orphelia sputters out the last two words as she looks around and sees the four of us.

"Why the fuck do I have to have so many embarrassing and loud sisters?" I whisper under my breath, dropping my head into my hand, and Byder has the gall to laugh at me.

My dad stands, as if he is going to introduce them all. But Ydum is still on smooth things over with the, I guess, in-laws duty and tells him to wait. "Let me see if I can figure this out." He starts pointing to one sister after another, guessing which one is which from freaking memory of me talking about them during the games.

"Well, you're easy, Catarina. We already met you. And you must be Finnegan, because of course, and the beauty on your arm would have to be Dahlia then." Dahlia only nods. "Hm, next to Dahlia is Shearah?" Samantha shakes her head no. "Aw, Samantha then." Samantha blushes. "If she's not Shearah, then you must be." Shearah nods emphatically. "Orphelia is next to Shearah?" Orphelia smiles and fakes a curtsey. "And that leaves Myrna and Ganna, right?" Both of them nod that he got it right.

"How did you manage that?" Finnegan smiles and shakes his head. "It took me two months and you got them all without ever having met them before?"

Ydum smiles broadly. "Jinx told a lot of stories during the down times of the games. A lot of stories."

"When he wasn't making me run." I complain. "Still hate you for it."

"You love me and you know it." He winks and sits on the arm of the couch next to Byder, his long arm draped behind both of us. And I know exactly what he's doing. It's the same thing Byder's doing by holding my hand. Claiming me. Letting my sisters know without words who they are here for. It's the same reason my hand is on Anarus's knee.

All of which I know my seven sisters are all taking in with greedy, gossipy eyes. I love them all, don't get me wrong, but in a village like this? Choices are slim for eight sisters. That's probably why only Dahlia is married now even though several of my sisters are already past thirty. I'm betting that at least a few of them have had talks with the High Priest about working on arranging marriages with someone from another village.

Finally, Orphelia finds her voice again. "Okay, so, when are you going to tell us their names? And, girl, you literally went to the Gods Games, stories! You must have good stories. What was it really like?"

All of my sisters fan out, getting comfortable in the too small, over full room like only we can after growing up here. Once they are situated, I introduce my gods. "Anarus, god of the bridge between life and death and ender of bonds. Byder, god of the hunt. And the green one," I glare at Orphelia, "is Ydum, god of nature."

Ydum, still being a good sport, but at the same time sending a small worry over Anarus down the bond, pushes his shirt sleeves up slightly and gets the exact reaction to his moving vine tattoo that he expected. My sisters and dad immediately are fascinated, Dad doing a better job of being discreet about it. I use the distraction to pull Anarus away with me into the bedroom. The whole hut only has the three rooms, so there's not much private space. Mom is still in there but sees us come in and, because she's smart, ducks immediately out.

"Hey, you okay?" I ask as soon as we are alone.

Anarus sighs. "That's a lot of family."

"And you were dead yesterday." Immediately, I grab him, pulling him in my arms and kissing him.

Anarus groans into my mouth and turns us, pushing me so my back hits the wall next to the door to the room, his hands in my hair gripping me tightly. He molds his body against mine so that there isn't one part of us that isn't touching. I wrap my arms around his waist and slide my hands up the back of his shirt to touch his skin.

"How the fuck do I get to be inside you with so much fucking family in such a tiny hut?" Anarus grumbles. He's trailing kisses down the arch of my neck. His hands have moved down to my sides, moving everywhere as if he is reminding himself of the shape of my body.

"Quietly." I tell him. "You do it quietly."

He turns us again, and I can tell he's angling us towards one of the two beds in the room. The two low beds, the whole things coming no higher than my calf, with thin mattresses on metal frames, are the only furniture in the whole room. My sisters and I often complained that it would be better to just have the mattresses on the floor than on the metal slats that act as a box spring. Most of the metal springs running from one edge to another on them have sunk, warped or straight out broken and had to be fixed with whatever we had on hand. But under the bed was the only storage space we had for our clothes, more blankets for the cold months, anything at all. So, the frames that probably made the beds more uncomfortable rather than less had to stay.

When the back of my legs hit the edge of the bed, I push Anarus back. "Beds squeak at the slightest shift."

"Shit." Anarus groans again. He takes one step away from me and runs his hand over his hair, looking around the room. The dirt floor layered with rag rugs over it for warmth. The rough walls of mortar and stone. The two windows with wooden shutters pulled tight against the cold that creeps in because there's no glass in them.

He sighs heavily and slumps down to sit on the bed, which lets out a loud squeal in protest, proving my point about them. "All eight of you slept in here your whole life?"

I smile as I feel him assimilating the stories I told at the games with the reality of the room he's in. "For the first ten years of it or so. Then Dahlia took her test on her twenty-fourth birthday, it came back red and she and Finnegan basically got married as fast as possible. Then, a year and change later, Samantha took her test and found work, moving in with a few friends from school who all shared a small hut together to be out of their parents' houses. From there, it was a slow trickle down as each of them turned twenty-four, got a red test, and found lives to make of their own elsewhere. Only Catarina, who is twenty-seven, and Orphelia, who is twenty-eight, still live here too. And, well, me until three months ago."

A loud burst of laughter filters into the room. Anarus looks at the door. He's feeling a lot of confusing things. "You should, I'm keeping you from your family."

I step between his legs, forcing his knees wider apart so I can stand directly in front of him, and trail my fingers down his cheek. "You are my family, Anarus. I'm worried about you. Are you doing okay? Really? Besides the there is no place in this whole hut private enough frustration?"

Anarus places his hands on my hips gently and looks up at me. "Honestly? It's overwhelming a little. Not just the family thing, but everything. I feel awkward. No shadows, none of that cold weight I've known my whole life. In its place is this simmering power I'm not sure what to do with."

It has been a bit different to not see Anarus trailing tendrils of black smoky looking shadows everywhere. "What's happening at the bridge? I mean, you're here. Right here. I know your power's different than Ydum and Byder's. Death explained you work through essence not magic, but how's that working right now?"

Anarus doesn't speak for a moment. I give him time to examine himself. "There's this little corner of my mind where I know part of me is on the bridge, still rebuilding it with stone. People have died while we talked to your Dad and a sliver of me knew that and let them cross the bridge, ending any bonds they had. It was like an awareness that I could just ignore if I wanted to. Another part of me has an eye out for the wilde hunt. Not that I know exactly where they are and what they are doing, but just know they are not in the land of the dead and have exactly so much time before they need to return. I'm in all three places at once. I remember this feeling from before. I didn't know what it was then and it grated, like an itch I couldn't scratch. Now, I know it, I understand it, and I know how to let it settle in me without irritating me so much."

I nod. "You have your full mantles now, so you aren't trying to do something your power isn't ready to do."

"Yeah," he sighs, "I'm not sure how to be. How to be me. I was so angry all the time, except when a certain witch helped me." He gives me a small smile. "When I woke up in that bedroom, I knew everything. I knew exactly how long I had been sitting at that bridge. I knew what you did, coming to get me. And I was exhausted in a way I never have felt exhausted before. But I slept in the carriage and when I woke up, you were there. You, Byder, and Ydum and it was like there was nothing for me to be angry about anymore. I mean, there is, the original gods, Winter, all of that. But all that is normal angry. Not that oppressive angry that made me want to fight the whole world. I've been angry for so long. That angry, the itch I couldn't scratch, the cold fire and shadows, the pain in my chest, I've known that my whole life. It was just who I was. And now it's gone. And I'm not sure how to be without it."

"When Byder, Ydum, and I first came to Ydum's house, we were so heartbroken and worried, there wasn't a lot of energy for anything else." I tell him, turning to sit on the bed next to him, taking one of his hands in mine. "But then Byder started rubbing this spot on his hand over and over. It became like a nervous habit he didn't even know he was doing. Finally, I asked him why he was doing that and he was startled by the question. He finally realized that it was his power. He described it exactly the same way you just did. Like an itch he couldn't scratch his whole life that was suddenly gone. Ydum thought about that too, and found the same thing, like there was an ache that he hadn't realized had just always been there had suddenly vanished and his body didn't know what to do without it now. They took longer to notice it, but that probably has more to do with you carrying the wilde hunt on top of your own power and us being distracted with the whole Anarus died and we are fighting to get him back while hurting because the bonds broke thing."

Anarus looks at me, concern marring his face. "Did it hurt, when the bonds broke? I just felt empty."

I let out a long, stuttering sigh. I don't know if this is something we should be talking about yet. If I try to cover now, make it not what it was, it will eventually come out and Anarus would feel worse that I tried to protect him from the realities.

I choose to be honest and we'll deal with the fallout. "When they first broke, I felt like I had been stabbed in the chest. I could feel the frayed end like it was in my hands. After a while, it was an exposed nerve that any tiny touch made jolt and pain would shoot through me again. Byder and Ydum were the same. For a while, we couldn't even touch each other because our frayed bond ends would rub together and it was like lightning hit all three of us. They, the original gods, their parents, kept saying it would heal and settle down, but it didn't. That the bond between the three of us would go back to how it should be, just me and Byder and me and Ydum, but it never did. And the pain never really went away, we just learned to live with it."

I look down at the floor, hiding my expression even though I know he will feel my emotions through the bond. "I thought it was my fault for a while because I didn't want to let you go. I thought I was hurting them because I wouldn't let go of the bond. I dreamed of that moment in the Colosseum every night and got sick every morning from the pain all over again. Otuna kept saying we needed to take me to a human healer but I refused because I knew they would give me something to stop dreaming and, as much as it hurt, I couldn't let it go because it was the only way to still see you. But Byder and Ydum said they felt it too, dreamed of it too, and couldn't let go either. It wasn't my fault, I wasn't giving them the pain, I just had it worse than they did."

"It was me." Anarus groans. "It was me still holding onto the bonds, wasn't it? That's what made it hurt so much for you three?"

"I think so." I whisper.

As soon as I feel the guilt in him, I snap my head up and speak louder. "You do not feel guilty about that. You held onto them, and that was a good thing. If you didn't, they would be gone now and, even though we brought you back, we wouldn't still be bonded. Fuck, I don't think we could have brought you back without the bonds. When I tried to help your mantle settle, it wouldn't listen to me until I forced our bonds back into your heart. You would have died all over again from your mantle before you even lived again. So, don't you dare feel guilty because that pain saved your life. I would feel it for another thousand years if it meant having you back."

Anarus takes my injured hand in his. "That's how you did this. Forcing the bonds back into my heart."

Before we can talk any further, the bond trembles with a feeling of being needed. Not anything too anxious or overwhelming, but it definitely isn't a calm feeling either, so Anarus and I both worry. We open the bedroom door and a man I used to think looked tall and imposingly powerful is standing just inside the door to the hut. Behind him is his younger copy.

My heart skips a beat in fear at the sight of them, but then I remember who is here with me in my parents' hut. I remember who I am and that I don't need to be afraid of them anymore.

"High Priest Breedlove." I say, my voice faltering only a little. "And Jacob."

That's as much of a hello I can give them. Anarus immediately is tight behind me and that anger he said he didn't have any more is roaring back. I can feel Byder gripping his emotions tightly and Ydum tense. I know without even looking at them that Ydum's hands are clenched tightly in his pockets as he stands looking casual enough, leaning against the wall between the two bedroom doors. Byder is still sitting where he was on the couch, not hiding his clenched fists.

High Priest Reuben Breedlove is probably about an inch or so shorter than Anarus and, before I went to the games, was the tallest male I had ever met. His black hair always slick looking with the creams he uses to keep it perfectly tame and neat, and his brown-gold eyes in a sharp face with angular cheekbones and a strong chin, snaps with what I used to think was intelligence. His slender, whip-like body always felt like it was bridled with power. As the High Priest, he would be the most powerful witch in our village.

Jacob is his spitting image, almost. Jacob has always let his hair grow longer, keeping it in a perfectly tousled mess that looks as if he doesn't care but probably actually takes a lot of styling to get precisely right. He doesn't carry as much power in his body as his father, but will eventually when he becomes High Priest when his father dies.

A small tremor runs through me, seeing them. Fear tries to make a home in me again. Anarus sets a hand gently on the small of my back in a very discrete move of protection and safety, and I fight off that fear, looking at all three of my gods.

Next to Byder, the High Priest and Jacob don't look strong but just average. Compared to Ydum, neither of them is smart or tall. Against Anarus, their magic looks like something a child would do. The prettiest boy in our village can't hold a candle to my three gods. I finally see Jacob for the small, backwater High Priest's son who can only feel powerful by hurting others that he is. He isn't anything special, just a speck of dirt on the dirt floor of my family's hut.

"You have more power in one word than they have in both their bodies combined." Anarus reminds me in a hushed tone in my ear.

I only nod and take in a deep breath, squaring my shoulders to stand tall. "To what do we owe this visit?" I try to emulate Drila's overly sweet fake tone and Ydum coughs over a laugh.

"The driver of your carriage came to my home to rest the horse and seek lodgings during your visit and I thought it strange that three gods came to visit my village and did not come to my home first." High Priest Breedlove says, his voice silk. "I thought it only proper that I come and introduce myself and offer my dwellings to them, a place to stay more befitting of their station."

Wrong answer. I have to hide the smile when all three of my gods feel like punching him at the same time. I step further into the sitting room. It's very crowded with my seven sisters, Finnegan, my parents, my three gods, me and now Jacob and the High Priest. But I move forward just enough that it becomes clear that Anarus has purposefully stationed himself behind my left shoulder rather than that he's stuck there because of the fullness of the room.

Ydum stops leaning against the wall and moves to stand directly behind my right shoulder. Byder slowly stands up. He can't move next to me without having to actually step over people, but slowly turns to look at me, putting his back to the High Priest and his son.

The action could be mistaken as the three of them just looking at me to see what I'm going to say, but the way the High Priest's body registers confusion and frustration, I know he knows the move for exactly what it is. All three of the gods just deferred to me, as the leader in this situation, rather than to him, or at least even one another, and that confuses the fuck out of the High Priest.

Ydum is the one who answers the High Priest. Dad's expression says he registers the change in the way my fun-loving, academic god was speaking with them and the way he's now speaking to the High Priest. That his voice went from casual and joyful to radiating power in an instant.

The power of a god resonating in it, showing him as an undeniable force to be respected. Not just another being but a god, a full god in his own right with the crown of his mantle declaring his magical superiority. I find it interesting to hear him speak this way, with power like this. I never heard it before. But then again, he would never use such a voice with me because he respects me, and most other people, as equals.

But not them. So, for them, he uses the voice of unbridled power and dominance. "I believe the home of our mate's parents is perfectly befitting our station. We will require a conversation with you at some point in the next day or so, but I believe that our mate should be able to have some time to reconnect with her family who has been worried about her for the last three months before we get to the business of our visit. It is only proper that Byder, Anarus, and I get to know our mate's family first, don't you agree, High Priest?"

Damn that was smooth. He said mate three times. And both the High Priest's and Jacob's faces show they caught it all three times, their same right eye twitching each time Ydum said it.

The High Priest is rattled, the silk of his voice faltering. "Of course. Of course. I did not realize the, um, nature of your relationship with the young Miss Bloodmorrow. I thought that potentially you were just escorting her back from the games. I apologize for the mistake, and of course, would gladly meet with you at your leisure. The offer of accommodations stands, if you change your mind."

"The young Miss Bloodmorrow, as you called her," Byder says, exuding the same power-filled voice Ydum did, but not moving to look at the High Priest, keeping his eyes on me, "is no longer Miss Bloodmorrow. She is now Jinx, emotional control word witch, the winner of the Three Hundred and Seventy-Fifth Gods Games and thrice mated bond of myself, a full god of the hunt, Ydum, a full god of nature, and Anarus, the twice-mantled god of the bridge between life and death and ender of bonds. We do not escort her, but she leads us, as our witch, the binder of our powers."

Well, fuck, Byder. The winner part is a little bit of a stretch since that actually hasn't been decided, but I let it slide because the look on Jacob's face is priceless. If he gets any paler, I think he may pass out.

The High Priest tilts his head ever so slowly. "Emotional control word witch? I don't think I've ever heard of such a thing." Of course, that's the only part he pays attention to.

When Anarus allows the power to ring through his voice, I expect it to be weaker than Ydum's and Byder's, with everything that's happened and because, while Ydum and Byder are both full pantheon gods, Anarus only got a specific power from the death pantheon. Well, two specific powers and potentially one borrowed one, but still. Instead, his is deeper, almost more terrifying. Maybe that's because death is terrifying to most mortals.

"We wouldn't expect someone of your low magical station to have ever heard of it. It's quite a rare, and extremely powerful, magic." What he doesn't say is that it's so rare, I'm the only one ever known to have it, and we still don't exactly understand what it means or how I came to have such magic. But they don't need to know that, either.

I feel a small question of wanting down the bond from Anarus. He's asking if I would be up to making them shit themselves by doing a demonstration. Oh, fuck yes.

Ydum speaks again, his power still ringing in his voice. "The power of an emotional control word witch is not a delicate thing, nor weak. Jinx? Shall you introduce them to what such a power can do?" I note he says power, not magic, trying to draw a distinction between the two of us, the high priest and me, again.

I tilt my head to Ydum, giving the same affirmative answer that I already had through the bond.

Without a word out loud, I reach for an emotion. Happy silliness, I need silliness. The High Priest and Jacob need to understand what I can do, so give them happiness so deep they cannot contain the giggles. There are enough of my sisters in the room that the silly giggles are quite present for me to draw from. Make them giggle. Not laugh but giggle with a silly tickled fancy.

The High Priest's mouth twitches. Jacob is rubbing his lips, as if he's trying to hide them. More, more silliness. More foolishness. Make them unable to contain their giggles. The High Priest burst out with a sudden giggle that he cuts off quickly. Jacob's shoulders are shaking as his hand is clamped hard over his mouth.

To prove it was not just a coincidence, I pick another emotion. Fear. I can tell that Jacob is already afraid of these gods. He's never seen gods before, but that's not the only reason he's afraid of these gods in particular. They are my gods and he's not sure what that means for him. He used to think he was the most powerful person in my world, besides his own father, and that meant he could abuse that power around me. Now, he's nothing and he knows it.

I pull on that fear, make it expand. Give fear to the High Priest. Make it bigger for Jacob and move to High Priest Breedlove too. When the High Priest goes from clenching hands to hide his laughter to clenching trembling fists, and Jacob's hand over his lips trembles as well, both of their eyes going wide, I know they have felt what I wanted.

That's good enough. I end the magic and see the look of shock and awe on the High Priest's face and Jacob does actually manage to pale more without fainting.

"What was that?" Orphelia asks, looking from the High Priest to me and back again. I only needed the two of them to feel the emotions that strongly, but I know from our experiments with Damek and Iella in the games that others around me will notice the emotions but wouldn't know why.

"That was," the High Priest shakes his head slightly, messing up his perfect hair, "an interesting demonstration. For a witch that has such a small amount of skill…"

Anarus cuts him off, growling, that ring of power in his voice going even deeper still. "Her skill was never small. Her training was inadequate."

If I'm not mistaken, I think Jacob might have just shit himself. He looks at the floor, hiding his face from Anarus's power.

"We will be in contact shortly to arrange that meeting, High Priest Breedlove." Ydum says smoothly before the High Priest can balk at that statement. "I suggest, though, you find alternate entertainment for your son during our meeting. He will not be welcome to join us. Thank you for stopping by." Ydum has dismissed him, the High Priest knows.

Jacob's eyes widen yet again as he looks up at me. There's a level of shock and horror around his eyes as his mouth trembles with words he's biting back. He knows they know something. He's scared what they know, how much I told them. He knows that, whatever I told them, however much I told them, they'll hold it against him. He knows that three powerful gods now see him as their enemy. Three powerful gods and a strong witch. He swallows hard as I give him a slow, knowing smile. The fear in him now is not one I'm creating, but all his own doing. Jacob flees out of the hut, his father leaving slower, still trying to hold onto the idea he has any control.

After the High Priest and Jacob left, my gods deflate that power immediately. Byder sits back down and Ydum leans back against the wall to go back to chatting with my sisters. I see Mom puttering around in the kitchen area. She seems concerned but trying to hide it. I wander through the bodies littering the floor to talk to her.

"I know this is a lot." I say, leaning back against the cabinets as she looks into one then another.

Mom stands up, trying to smooth away the concerned look as she anxiously rubs her hands down her apron. "Oh, Jinx. No. I'm so happy that you, that you're okay. We didn't think, most people who go to the games never come home. I thought I would never see you again. We thought you were..." Dead, she doesn't say. They thought I was dead. "And your, your gods, I guess, seem lovely. That Ydum is a very nice man. I mean, he's not a man, not really, I know, but," Mom lets out a frustrated sigh.

I chuckle lightly and wrap an arm around my mom's shoulders. "Don't worry. I was just as flustered when I met them too. Well," I consider it for a moment, "not really. But then again, I had just fallen on my butt getting out of a hiding spot in a cave after watching Anarus and Ydum get into a fist fight, so, there was that. What I mean is, you're fine, Mom. Everything is fine."

She smooths her hands over her apron again, not looking at me. "Will they, will you, really be okay staying here? We don't have much. I mean, you know how it is, Jinx. It's not even the solstice yet." Mom's gaze wanders over the cabinets she had been rummaging through and suddenly I feel horrible.

Mom's worried about the food. Winter is the hardest time. It always was growing up. Game is harder to come by. The canned vegetables and fruit that were set by all fall are never quite enough to make it through the whole winter. No matter how much you plan and scrape together, it never seems to be quite enough.

I suddenly see my mom and dad with new eyes. Three and a half months and I forgot the struggle, the toll it always takes on them. Two and a half months of three large, if simple, meals a day just appearing in our room, then another month at Ydum's house, where Eiran can just pop out to the shops and buy more meat or Otuna can whisk out vegetables from thin air, and I forgot.

My parents aren't young anymore, in their sixties. How much hunting has Dad really been able to do this winter while he was worrying because his youngest daughter was gone, maybe dead? How much has Finnegan been doing for them, trying to support both his own home and theirs?

Fuck, just looking at my feet, I suddenly feel awful. I have on nice, new boots. Catarina had slipped on the shared boots that have sat by the back door of this hut my entire life to go collect my sisters. Boots we have mended so many times they are more patches than original material anymore. Most of my other sisters are wearing homemade shoes that barely protect against the cold and don't protect against the wet at all. But the four of us all have on brand new, waterproof boots of our very own. Boots nicer than anything I had ever seen before September fifth.

If we are here for a few days, even if most of the time it's just them, Orphelia, Catarina, and us four, it would be a huge drain on their resources. Resources they need to survive after we go back to the comfort of Veirveil. Even Veirveil at war would be easier. Maybe we were wrong to turn down the High Priest's offer. I furrow my brow and realize that Mom and Dad would never say a word but if we stay here, they might starve after we leave.

Byder is next to me, leaning on the tub sink. "What's going on, baby girl?" He felt my guilt through the bond.

I glance at my mom, who went back to her cabinets. I turn into his arms to whisper in his ear. "They can't feed us. They don't have enough to feed us, Byder. If we stay here, they'll use up all their winter store and have nothing left to eat when we leave. They'll starve after we leave if we stay."

Byder laughs and pushes a nonexistent hair behind my ear. "Oh, is that all? Jinx, do you think that Ydum and I haven't already thought about that? We knew way back in the games that when we came here, with how you talked about home, that we wouldn't be leaving until we were sure your parents were well provided for. Shit, I've been excited since we got into the carriage. You realize I've never even gotten to hunt yet since I took my mantle?"

I hadn't realized that. "With everything, I never even thought about it."

He nods at me. "We weren't going to say anything yet, with all your sisters around, because we wanted to let you introduce us. But if your mom is worrying about it, if you are, we'll take care of the food situation now so she knows she doesn't have to."

I lean my head down on his shoulder. "I love you."

"And we love you, baby girl. Which means we automatically love your family too. It's a rule or something, I think." Byder stands up straight and I move out of his way.

I see him look at Ydum and jerk his head. Ydum only nods back and Byder walks back around the table. "Well, looking at the time, if I don't get out to the woods soon, there's no way I can have my famous rabbit stew ready for us to eat tonight. Finnegan, Maddox, would you like to join me? I'll need someone to show me around the woods here."

No, he wouldn't. I know he wouldn't. I know the lie even though I've never seen him hunt, before his mantle or after. He's including them even though they will probably actually slow him down.

"Oh, you don't have to do that." My mother, the ever gracious host, balks. "You're the guest…"

"The guest that's a god of the hunt." Ydum says, coming over to her, with a smile. "Let the male hunt before he gets too itchy at being stuck inside. Byder, potatoes, carrots? Anything else?"

Byder turns his head to the side to think, as if this whole thing between them isn't scripted. "Hm, onion and mushrooms too if you can?"

Ydum puts a hand over his heart. "You wound me! As if fungus is hard for me, or something."

"Fine." Byder grumbles. "You want a challenge? How about sage, bay leaves, and parsley?"

Anarus moves to sit in the seat Byder vacated. "Byder, you're in a witch's hut. You think Avalon doesn't have that shit in abundance already?"

"No parsley, sorry." Mom says tentatively.

"Hah!" Byder says to Anarus, crossing his arms over his chest.

Anarus only scowls back, as Byder asks Maddox and Finnegan if they are ready. My dad and brother-in-law had been shrugging on their coats while my gods had talked. Byder turns back to me and kisses my forehead.

"I'll be back soon, baby girl." I smile back at him, my heart bursting with pride in them. Who would have thought this is how they would be, when three months ago Byder was confused by my lack of shoes and Ydum and Anarus ended most conversations close to, or actually with, a fist fight?

Chapter Four

AFTER BYDER LEAVES, YDUM nudges me with his hip. "You're in the way, beautiful. Go sit with Ani." He smiles at me, though, before turning back to the tub sink.

He puts his hands into the sink and pulls out four carrots that were not in there before. He just grew them in his hands. With everything else, we haven't really experimented with their powers with their full mantles. But Ydum just pulled four fully grown carrots from nothing without even breaking a sweat. My mom's mouth forms a perfect O as he asks her if she thinks we'll need more than four.

I do as Ydum told me and go sit with Anarus. My sisters, in true Bloodmorrow fashion, move around to fill in the now vacated spots left by Dad and Finnegan. With seating always in short supply, the rule has always been move your feet, lose your seat.

"So, Byder is going to hunt using his magic?" Shearah asks. "I mean, finding enough rabbits for stew for all of us, now, this late in winter? There's no snow right now, but it's still cold."

"Yeah. Well, not magic the same as we know it, but basically, it's the same. Just a lot more of it, and stronger." I tell her. "Just like Ydum is growing vegetables in the sink in seconds using his nature power." Half of my sisters twist in their seat to stare at him, their mouths forming perfect O's like mom's did after he whisks a handful of potatoes from nothing.

"What about you?" Samantha asks Anarus. "What do you do?"

Anarus shifts uncomfortably. He got his power yesterday, and it's death. How would he explain being a god of death to mortals without freaking them out? "Um, my power isn't quite as outwardly demonstratable as all that."

Orphelia pushes the issue, oblivious as always. "Yeah, but what is it? Ydum said life and death. What does that mean?"

I put a hand on his arm and give him a look. You don't have to talk about it if you don't want to, I want to tell him.

But he does anyway. "Well, right now, an old man just died after being ill for a long time. Part of my essence helped him cross over the bridge between the land of the living and the land of the dead so his essence can rest until it's time for his energy to be reused in the cycle of birth, death, rebirth. He was very bonded with his wife, so I cut that bond so she can grieve and heal from the loss and he can rest properly."

"But you're sitting here. How'd you do that from sitting right here?" Ganna asks.

Anarus looks at me, unsure how to explain it. I try, unsure myself. I use Damek's explanation of how magic works for most witches. "It's like how you can access your magic, see it, but it isn't really something tangible. You can do things with the magic, and maybe the result is something you can see but maybe not. What does it look like, what do other people see you doing, when you add strength to a yarrow plant? Nothing, right? You did a lot with your magic but other people only saw you sitting there, staring at a plant. His magic was doing something and you couldn't see it, just like he wouldn't see you do anything to the yarrow."

"When did Jinx become the smart sister?" Myrna laughs. "She's gunning for your spot in that, Ganna."

Ganna only shakes her head. "She isn't gunning for it, Myr. She took it by a mile. She won the Gods Games. I guarantee you did some crazy things, didn't you?"

I blush and just shake my head.

"Nope." I hear Ydum say from the table, where he is cutting up potatoes. "Don't downplay it, beautiful. She did. She made it rain in our washroom. She moved the life essence from a rabbit to a dead witch so we could hear a message she had for us. She channeled a wolf. Actually, she could be talking to that wolf in her head right now."

"I'm not. Kinshra would be sleeping right now. I wouldn't disturb her sleep unless it was an emergency." I say.

My sisters all stare at me. "You have a wolf? In your head?" Orphelia asks incredulously.

"Not in my head." I roll my eyes at Ydum. Thanks, I think sarcastically. He only smirks at me, the brat. "She's my familiar. We are bonded through Anarus, so we can talk through meditation sometimes."

My sisters all continue to stare at me like I grew a second head. Catarina breaks out of the trance first. She sits up from her spot lounging on the floor, excited. "What else? What else did you do?"

We continue talking, each telling stories about the games. Well, Ydum and I tell stories. He keeps telling ones that highlight things I did and I rebut them with ones about the three of them. He tells them about me thinking of making spears out of ice to defend against the yetis, and I tell them that he made those ice spears out of thin air. I tell them how Byder and Anarus made it cold on the island so that Damek's weather would be snow. He tells them that I made it rain on two islands across the ocean from us. He tells them about my protection circle with Byder, and I tell them about the carnivorous plant we all created together.

As we talk, Anarus sits quietly, his hand tangled in mine at our sides. Occasionally, he adds a detail here or there, not letting either of us downplay our own contributions. But for the most part, he just listens and lets Ydum and I be the storytellers. When Ydum goes to carry the large pot used to cook soups out to the well out front to fill it, Anarus offers to take it for him and Ydum tells him no, you rest, prompting questions about why Anarus needs rest.

"Not something we really want to get into a whole lot of details about right now," I say, "but he was sort of dead yesterday."

"Dead?!" All seven of my sisters exclaim at the same time.

Anarus chuckles slightly. "Yes, dead. Long story, but yeah. Jinx burned her hand going into the land of the dead to bring me back." He looks at my right hand like he just remembered it, checks it, then says. "Make sure Byder looks at this again, little human."

This pronouncement from Anarus does nothing to quell my sisters' questions. Everyone talks at the same time.

"Jinx went into the land of the dead?" Mom's concern is evident.

"Why Byder?" Samantha asks.

"Little human?" Orphelia giggles. "You call Jinx little human?"

Shearah asks. "How did Jinx go into the land of the dead if you only go there through your magic?"

They are all, thankfully, distracted as Ydum comes back in carrying the pot full of water. My sisters' eyes follow his progress as he, without seemingly any effort, carries the pot it usually takes two of us to carry when only half full of water to the fireplace and sets it on the pot hook. They gape at him, and he completely does not notice. I don't even think he was trying to show off his strength this time, but truly did not realize how heavy that pot is, nor the fact that all of us know it. My sisters are not the only ones watching him with fascination at his effortless strength. I'll admit, I like it a little too. Okay, maybe I like it a lot.

With so many bodies in the house, the fire has been neglected for lack of needed warmth. Ydum needs the fire stoked to start the icy water from the almost frozen well boiling. "Beautiful? A little help?"

He could have just fueled it the normal way after adding some wood. He could also have just used his own power to encourage it, since fire is a part of nature. But I think he wants to show me off. Beyond just hearing the stories, he wants my family to see I'm powerful in my own right.

I glare at him for a moment but relent. He's still feeling a little peeved from the encounter with the High Priest. Anarus is too. They want my sisters to have stories of Jinx, the girl everyone underestimated because their high priest said she wasn't good at magic. The girl who was taught wrong but still managed to become a seriously strong witch. And they want me to remember that too.

"Sure." I close my eyes and find my peace. I speak the first part out loud for their benefit. "We need the fire stoked." But then, I only think because, well, it would make more questions and I really don't want to explain Ydum carrying a volcano's fire in his eyes. Use Ydum's fire to make the fireplace have exactly what we need to cook with. I open my eyes as my sisters gasp. There is a tidy little fire burning cheerily in the fireplace and Ydum swings the pot hook over the blaze.

"You didn't," Orphelia stammers, "you didn't even go over there or anything."

Anarus chuckles. "Like we said to the high priest, Jinx is a word witch. She doesn't need anything beyond the words to do her magic." Again, not a strictly true explanation, but Anarus remembers how hard it was to explain how magic really works. It's easier just to say I use words than to try to teach my sisters what High Priest Breedlove failed to teach us all in school.

Catarina squeals. "That's amazing! Do something else, Jinx!" While everyone at the games with me would have been able to do the same, or even better than me, my sisters have never seen magic that clearly evident before. Something as outward and tangible as making a smoldering ember a fire without any effort. Well, except Ydum just now with the vegetables. But they'd expect that from a god, of course. Or maybe from Granny Helen or the High Priest.

But from an average witch? Their sister they've known their whole life? They never saw anything like that from someone like me, just living a normal life in our village. They don't even realize they could probably do that too, if only High Priest Breedlove had let them be taught properly.

Ydum chuckles. "Rosebud?"

"Fine." I say, huffing. How did I not realize that he would be such a show-off? Of course, Ydum's showing off me, but still, show-off.

Ydum sits on the arm of the couch next to me. He holds up a closed fist, then opens it, dirt and a single rosebud nestled in his palm. That alone gets aww's from my sisters.

I speak out loud even though I don't need to, again for my sisters' benefit. "I need you to bloom." Since Ydum isn't fighting me like he did when we did this in the games for practice, the rosebud opens easily into a tiny rose. He plucks it from his fingers and hands it to Orphelia with a wink. Then, closes his hand so the dirt vanishes.

When Orphelia looks like she is about to ask me to do more, I'm saved by Byder, Dad, and Finnegan returning. Dad and Finnegan both have excited gleams in their eyes and their cheeks bright from the cold. Byder has three braces of rabbits in his hands.

"That was," Dad shakes his head, "something else. He found those rabbits and caught them by hand. By hand. And he let two go because he said they had kits too young to lose their mother."

Byder passes me on the way to the table, and stops for a quick kiss. "That was fun. I like your dad. Finnegan too."

"I'm glad." I smile at him.

He takes the rabbits to the table and, after Ydum confirms he doesn't need to use the table for vegetables again so there's no risk of cross-contamination, he puts the rabbits down and pulls a small knife from, well, nowhere. "Would you want the skins for anything in particular?" He asks Mom.

"Trading, more than likely." She responds curiously, watching him work.

Byder only nods at this before setting to the task of skinning and carving the rabbits. I watch him as well with an appreciative eye.

I've never really seen him using his power this way and it's actually kind of hot. His brows furrowed together in concentration, the muscles in his arms flexing, his fingers moving delicately around the small animal as he strips the fur pelts in one quick movement, then dissects the carcasses to gain the most usable meat from the bones. He has a small smile playing on his lips and cheeks, food and the ability to feed people one of his favorite parts of his power. Byder looks up for only a moment, his eyes glittering at me darkly before he bends his head back to his work, and I know he knows what I'm thinking.

"You like that, little human?" Anarus says quietly in my ear, his voice deep and smoky. The feel of his warm breath in my ear lights me on fire, making me skip a breath.

Ydum chuckles, running a discrete finger down the back of my neck, which I feel all the way in my core. "Oh yeah, she does."

Fuck. My sisters are watching. My parents. I try to hide the shiver and not moan right here on the sitting room couch in front of everyone. Horrible. They are all horrible, devious males I will make suffer for this.

What does not help me at all is when my mother accidently splashes Byder as she's pouring a bucket of water over one of the rabbit carcasses to rinse it out for him. His shirt is hit with water and gore from the carcass and my poor mother is stammering and fumbling to apologize.

Byder only smiles at her. "Don't worry. Happens all the time."

Byder doesn't even think about it but strips the shirt off and she immediately snatches it from him, promising to get the stains out. Now Byder is standing in my parents' kitchen, shirtless, and all seven of my sisters, even Dahlia sitting next to her husband, are staring unabashedly at his powerful and, I'll admit, sexy chest.

"Fuck me running." I say under my breath as I stand, intending to go into the room to grab him a new shirt out of the bags we stashed there.

Completely unaware of the scene they are making, Anarus stands as well, looking at Byder's chest, right above his heart. "You get that from your mantle?"

Oh right, Anarus has never seen the tattoo Byder got yet. Byder nods and Anarus goes over to look at it closer, letting fingers trail over the four symbols directly over Byder's heart. "Nice. The four disciplines. Does it do anything?"

I stop and listen. Even I don't know that yet.

Byder nods. "I felt it warm over the air symbol when I needed the wind to shift so I was downwind of the rabbits. It worked too."

"So, that was you. Thought so. The wind at my back was just suddenly gone then a slight wind started blowing on my face and I knew it had to be a god's doing." Finnegan says, shaking his head from his seat cuddled against Dahlia on the couch.

I continue to the room and grab the shirt out of Byder's bags. When I hand it to him, he doesn't put it on but does let his fingers brush against mine.

"Don't want to just mess up another one." He says with a twinkle in his eye. His eyes follow mine that I can't help but let sink down to stare at the top of that tiny trail of hair starting at his stomach and running down past the waist of his pants. He chuckles as I force my eyes back to his face and blush. Damn, I forgot how sexy these gods are. "I'll put it on when I'm done skinning them."

When I sit back down, no one having moved to take my seat between Anarus and Ydum, who's still sitting on the arm of the couch, Catarina stares at me, mouthing the words "damn, girl!"

I smile and blush. Yes, I know, Catarina. But they are mine. Don't go getting ideas.

"Jinx feeling jealous?" Ydum whispers in my ear again.

"No." I hiss at him, but I know I can't lie. "Possessive, there's a difference." Ydum laughs.

The rest of the afternoon, we spend telling stories. My parents embarrass me as only parents can with stories of my childhood, much to Ydum's delight especially. In return, they tell stories about their childhoods in Veirveil.

I realize as we talk that we never did anything like this with Eiran and Otuna. Or Xolios and Daisy. We were too busy mourning and fighting the council. This is the first time we have really relaxed since the games. Or, well, since ever because even the relaxing times in the games were always tinged by the fear of death or failure.

Byder shuffles back and forth between sitting in a chair by the table and the pot over the fire, tending the soup that fills the hut with the most delicious smells. Ydum stays by my side, perched on the edge of the couch arm and Anarus sits on my other side, holding my hand. It actually becomes almost comfortable. So similar to so many winter days growing up, just with the addition of my three gods who are fitting right in. Mostly fitting right in. As much as three gods can fit in with a room full to bursting with humans.

After we eat Byder's amazing rabbit stew, and my mother shoos my sisters out of the hut, sending Catarina and Orphelia to Dahlia's for the duration of our stay, my mother putters about, her nerves showing. She's nervous about the accommodations being good enough for three gods and I hate it.

I hate that she's embarrassed by the home I always loved. But I understand because I was too. But that's what happens when one group of people draw a line through the land and say these people on their side of the line are worthwhile and those people on the other side aren't. That's the whole reason we are here, to get people to help us fight that system that made my mother feel like she should be embarrassed by her home.

My parents eventually go off to bed, leaving us alone. We go into the bedroom that Ydum and Byder haven't seen yet.

"All eight of you in here? Really?" Byder asks and all I can do is laugh.

"That's the same thing Anarus said."

Ydum shakes his head. "How did none of your sisters ever complain about your snoring?" When I glare at him, he only laughs again. "No foyer here, beautiful."

"There is a couch." I mutter darkly. "Or an outhouse."

Ydum pulls me close, his hands running up and down my sides. "You really mad, beautiful, or can I finally fucking kiss you?" Apparently, I'm not the only one who suddenly remembered all of those feelings and desires we used to have before Anarus died.

"Oh, please do."

He wastes no time, claiming my lips fervently. He doesn't even break the kiss when he scoops me up in his arms. I think, as he steps around the room, that he's going to lay me down on one of the beds, but he doesn't. Instead, I find myself being lowered onto a blanket on the floor between the two beds.

As soon as I am safely down, Ydum's fingers get to work on the ties on my bodice. He pulls the top of my dress down and leans back on his knees to examine his work. "Fucking perfect. Shit, I've missed you, beautiful." Even though we've been together, and sometimes sleeping in the same bed, neither Byder, Ydum, or I had any romantic interests in the last month, the pain of the broken bond too much to even touch each other most of the time.

Ydum moves to my side, lying down stretched out next to me on his side, head propped up on his hand with his elbow on the floor. Languorously, as if he has all the time in the world, he palms my breast and starts rolling and pinching my nipple. He watches my face as he does it, smiling as he watches me enjoy the warmth from his touch that starts spreading through me. I trail my fingers through the curls hanging over his forehead, sighing in contentment.

Anarus steals the spot in between my knees from Ydum. He removes my boots and pushes my dress up to my waist, then grumbles softly when he remembers the underwear. "I want these gone, little human."

When I nod my assent, he hooks a finger on either side of the waistband and pulls them off quickly, inhaling sharply when he looks back at my now mostly exposed body.

"Fuck." He runs a finger between my legs, up to my clit. A shiver runs down my spine and I bite my lip at the sudden and overpowering need that lights up my skin. Anarus pulls away to take off his shirt. "You don't like being the only one naked."

When he brings his hand back, running a finger up and down me, I try to tell them the walls in the house are thinner than they think. But I get lost halfway through as his finger slides inside me and I bite back a moan.

"Oh, fuck." I breathe out. He moves the finger, curling it, and it's all I can do not to cry out. With every move of his finger, I fight a moan as my body tightens. He knows exactly where to touch to make me squirm and push my hips against his hand.

"Don't hide those sounds we like, baby girl." I don't know how but Byder is leaning over my head with his face. There's not enough space in between the beds for how we are, but somehow, they're making it work. I shoot a glance at the wall that, on the other side, contains my parents' bedroom. Byder chuckles darkly. "They have eight daughters. I think they know how this works. But, if makes you happy, I guess we'll just have to taste your moans instead of hearing them."

He lowers his head, kissing me as I moan again when Anarus adds a second finger and keeps moving them inside me. I arch against Anarus's fingers as I use the hand I don't have tangled in Ydum's hair to pull Byder closer to me, meeting his soft kisses with a forcefulness I don't think he was quite expecting. I missed them as much as they missed me.

Byder leans back for only a moment. "They taste as good as they sound. Make her do it again, Anarus." He leans back down, capturing my lips with his as Anarus curls his fingers again, stroking the spot that makes me moan again and squirm with pleasure.

—

Anarus's fingers pick up their pace, moving inside me to drive my need and desire for all three of my gods higher. Byder uses the opening to mimic the pattern Anarus is creating with his fingers with his tongue in my mouth. I battle him back, enjoying the power play between the two of us.

"Mm. Let me try." Ydum says, and he shifts, removing his hand from my breast so that he can switch with Byder to kiss me and let Byder fondle my breast. He moves to my head, kissing me with a slow passion, enjoying tasting me, as Anarus pressed his thumb against my clit, making me arch as the sensations stutter through me, making my heart race as I want so much more.

"Anarus, please." I breathe out. "Oh, fuck, please."

"You want me, little human?" Anarus pulls his fingers out of me and strips off his boots and pants. "You want me inside you?"

"Yes." I whisper as Byder and Ydum both melt away. I can hear them and see them, kissing each other right next to Anarus and me in the small space. But my mind only focuses on Anarus as he kisses my lips, lifting me to sit on his lap and driving his cock inside me. My gasp that becomes a moan is mostly caught by his mouth. I tilt my hips, meeting his thrusts as the tight heat in my core spreads quickly. My hands grip his shoulders and I know there is no way I am going to stay quiet enough.

"Anarus, please." I gasp out, needing something. I shift on him, feeling like that perfect pleasure is just out of reach.

Anarus groans and increases his pace. "How's your hip?"

"My hip?" I ask, confused.

"I'll take that as it being fine." He grinds out, then grabs my right leg under the knee and pushes my leg as wide as he can, my foot almost behind Ydum next to me and cupping my ass as he shifts me. This changes his angle and he reaches the spot I was looking for and my back bows as I cry out. Oh yeah, my parents definitely heard that. But I have stopped caring because I feel my pleasure, Anarus's, Byder's, and Ydum's and it fractures me.

"Shit, don't stop, baby girl. Don't. Stop." Byder says as he reaches between me and Anarus to palm my breast. I turn to face him and he kisses me. Ydum is now turned around, his back pressed to Byder's chest. Byder is stroking Ydum's cock with his other hand while his cock is buried in Ydum's ass, thrusting into him with a dominating force. Ydum has his hands planted on the ground in front of him, bracing himself to arch back into Byder.

"Fuck, handsome." Ydum moans.

Byder releases me, his hand moving from my breast to Ydum's shoulder, pulling on him to make him sit up more. "Kiss Jinx, baby. I want to see you kiss her while I fuck you." Byder's voice has taken on a deep throatiness he only uses when he takes control like this. That voice is like a fire running over me and I moan at the heightening sensations.

Ydum lifts his head, his eyes shining with desire. He tilts my chin toward him and kisses me as instructed. He grips Byder's hand around his cock tightly as he bites my lip until a wracking shudder passes through him. He leans his head back and lets out a low moan as he spills his seed over his and Byder's hands, his absolute pleasure spiraling into me, Byder, and Anarus, driving us higher.

Anarus growls and I turn back to face him. "Mine." He claims my lips for himself and his pace becomes frantic. His hands tense around me, splaying over my back as he holds me up. I have an awareness that Anarus comes, but he doesn't stop as the pleasure in me doesn't crest but just keeps rising. My entire body is just one tight coil of sparking nerves and every touch, every look from the three of them, burns the fire in me hotter and higher.

Byder grips Ydum's body tightly against him as he yells and tenses, coming as well. And I feel it all, Byder, Ydum, Anarus, and finally me. With their pleasure spent, my body finally explodes in waves of ecstasy that leave me breathless, panting and stars dancing behind my eyelids. The four of us don't move for a long time, enjoying the afterglow as fingers entwine with each other, none of us concerned about who is touching who, but satisfied by the four of us here, together.

I hear a sound and the bed on my right is shifted towards the wall. After spreading out another blanket, Ydum drops on the ground to stretch out next to me. Byder hands Ydum and Anarus cloths he got from our bags to clean up with, keeping one for himself. When everyone is as clean as we can get without going out to the well for water, Byder joins Ydum on the blankets. They both give me a quick kiss, after Anarus and I both also lie down, with him on my right, turning me towards him to kiss me as well. Both Byder and Anarus pull the pillows down off the beds and the blankets and we snuggle up right there on the floor.

"So," Ydum says, playing with a strand of my hair once we are all relatively comfortable, "I'd say the entangled bonds are back in full force."

I snort, my heart rate still not totally back to normal. "Yeah, I'd say."

Byder, on the other side of Ydum, sits slightly up, propping himself up on his elbow. "Did that bother you, Anarus? Me and Ydum like that, right here next to you? Touching you and Jinx while we were together and you two were together?"

Anarus takes a moment to consider before answering. "No. You followed what I said when we had that nice, embarrassing conversation about boundaries. Things between the four of us have always been a little bit of blurred lines, so, no. It didn't."

"Okay good, just checking." Byder lies back down. "We worry about Jinx's boundaries a lot, just don't want to forget yours either."

"Appreciate it, but other than the one, I think my boundaries aren't anything like I thought they were going to be." Anarus says quietly. He's never talked about why he made the boundaries he did, to never touch his ass, not like I have, but we don't push him to either. He'll talk about it if he wants to talk about it, when he's ready to talk about it, I think to myself. I know enough about his childhood to know it was shit.

"Anyone else not going to be able to look Maddox and Avalon in the face tomorrow?" Ydum raises his hand as he asks this. Byder, Anarus, and I all raise a hand too.

"Our attempt at quiet missed the mark by, I dunno, the whole fucking village." I joke.

"Sleep, little human." Anarus says, pulling me tight against him.

When I wake in the morning, I'm the first one up. I struggle out of the three males' arms holding me and quietly get dressed. After a quick trip to the outhouse, I find myself slipping into the normal morning routines I had at home before the games. Go to the well for a bucket of water. Stoke up the fire, which I do with magic for the first time really. Slice the bread leftover from last night's dinner for breakfast and set the slices and the coffee pot on the flat sheet over the fire. Then, while watching the toast, I comb out my braid and rebraid it.

Once the toast is done and the coffee ready, and I pour myself a cup, I look in the cabinets and find a jar of preserved eggs. I add a cast iron pan to the fire and cook them. The smell must have woken Anarus up because he comes out to the sitting room, mumbling about coffee. I smile and pour him a cup, which he sits at the table to drink.

"You realize you only put pants on, right?" I say.

Anarus only grumbles wordlessly, so I leave him be.

My father follows behind by only a few minutes, making the same grumbles Anarus was, and I give him his morning dose of coffee as well. He is where I learned my morning addiction. The two males grunt and salute each other with their mugs and I have a sudden realization that makes me stop and stare.

Anarus and my father are so similar. Oh, shit, not just similar but Anarus is just like my father. I bite back the laughter at this thought because, while I have had a full cup already, they just started drinking their coffee and wouldn't appreciate my mirth yet.

When Ydum strolls out of the bedroom, he looks in my mug on the table before kissing my temple, saying, "Morning, beautiful. Need help with anything?"

I shake my head, but he takes over the eggs anyway.

Byder and my mother come out of the bedrooms at the same time, just in time for the eggs to be done. I grab plates and load them up without thinking. Anarus and Dad both cock an eyebrow at me when I slide plates of food in front of them and, this time, Ydum and Byder are also swallowing their laughter too.

I point at Dad. "Mom always yells at you to eat real food in the morning." I turn to Anarus. "And you don't give me that full mantled gods don't actually need to eat shit. Otuna told me that was bull. Eat."

Anarus groans. "What about half dead gods?"

I just stare at him, my arms crossed over my chest. "Even Death eats."

Ydum stops hiding his laughter. "After all that fuss she made when we insisted she eat breakfast during the games." He shakes his head. "Like father, like daughter." He glances over to take in Anarus's and Dad's matching scowls. "Like father, like son-in-law too, I think."

After we eat and my gods put on shirts, we decide to head to the High Priest's home. We are supposed to meet Death and everyone else back in the woods south of Veirveil in seven days. The people who choose to come with us will need time to prepare. So, better to get it over with quickly, so they have as much time as they can.

It snowed a little overnight and there's still a light dusting over the roads. I call them roads but they are little more than large swaths of dirt that have had so many feet and carts over them for so many years, they no longer grow grass. In the spring and fall, they are a muddy soup that cakes your feet and the hem of your pants and dresses. In the summer, they are hard-packed earth that scorches bare feet and throw up dust at the slightest wind. Right now, in winter, they are soup frozen over with ice.

Compared to Death's house, or even Ydum's, the High Priest's house I thought was so luxurious is rather plain. It's brick and stone, like the testing center, with a basement that's used as the village school and two stories besides that. But the inside, I remember, is only thin wood panel walls and unfinished wood plank floors. Ydum's house has wood floors as well, but they shine.

The High Priest has indoor plumbing, but not a fresh hot water supply. He has gas-lit lighting rather than magic-lit, and fireplaces for heat but not the inventive ducting system that Ydum's house has that allows heat from the fireplace in the sitting room and the cast iron stove in the kitchen to spread throughout the house.

The High Priest has glass in his windows, a step above most homes in my village, but it's not the same as the high quality glass windows that keep out the elements for Ydum and Byder. While the cold comes right through the wood shutters closed over the holes in our walls we call windows, but have no real glass in them, in my house all winter long, the High Priest's glass blocks the worst of it, but not all of the worst drafts, adding a sharp chill to the inside of his house.

As I knock on the front door and wait for him to answer, knowing he might be in the basement with the school children at this hour, I remind myself that the fact that the High Priest doesn't have even the basic accommodations that the homes Ydum or Byder grew up in have is part of why we are here. Why do they get magic lights and my parents can't even get glass windows?

"Remember he is not our enemy right now." I whisper to my gods just before the door opens. "We need him on our side and believing us."

Anarus snorts derisively. "Yeah, him. Not his son though."

"Anarus." I say his name as a warning right as the High Priest opens the door.

Yesterday apparently forgotten, the High Priest is all smooth silk again, inviting us in and showing us to the formal sitting room. The room is well-appointed, but not at all comfortable. I know from my time in school here that this room was completely off-limits to Jacob, his friends, and any other children from the school because it's only used when the High Priest entertains "gods and people of higher social standings," as we were told often. Otherwise known as never since I think this is the first time any god has ever entered Greenbriar after they built the testing center.

There are three matching blue couches, formal with wood embellishments on the arms that run down to the legs, wood side tables next to each of them, and an oil lamp, currently unlit, on each side table. There's a patterned area rug in the middle of the U created by the couches that stops just short of the hearth of a stone fireplace with a large carved wooden mantle. On either side of the fireplace are bookshelves with books and knickknacks.

All of it is in good condition, and fancy, but all carries an air of being slightly older. Not in an antique way, but more as if has only been kept in such good condition over the years by being hardly used.

I let my gods talk to explain the situation, what happened with Anarus, what the council has done, and why this matters to him and the other humans of this village. Mostly, Ydum talks. I know if I was the one talking, High Priest Breedlove would disregard everything I say. I'm a woman who dared to wear pants to his house, and of, in his opinion, low magical power.

Plus, why would he care what the extra daughter of one of the poorest families in a poor village has to say when he can talk to three gods? They may be young and newly crowned, but they are gods nonetheless. Beings with power over him. Even if now, by all rights, I should be considered a demi-god, and therefore above him in station, he will never really see me as anything other than a small witch from a small village. Beneath him.

The High Priest listens respectfully and, when Ydum finishes, he tilts his head thoughtfully. "So, you are asking me to ask the men of my village to abandon their families in the middle of winter to go to Veirveil to fight with you because you didn't get the right prize for winning the games?"

Is that really his takeaway? I grit my teeth, but can't stay silent. "No. We are asking you to let us tell the people of our village, who have been badly mistreated by the current system that we, and many other humans and gods, want to change that system. That we invite any of them that want to, male or female, to join us in fighting for what they deserve, including a proper education, the right not to live in fear that their children will be killed needlessly in the games, and access to resources currently denied them with a real voice in how Nazus is run."

"The asking you part," Byder says, not using his full power voice yet, but still adding enough of a touch of it to his voice to remind the high priest who he is, "is honestly a courtesy. Just so you understand, even if you say no, we will be talking to the villagers. We just won't be doing it with your support. Frankly, if the villagers get upset with the gods about this, how do you think they will take your lack of support? They are not blind to the luxuries, albeit few, you enjoy that they don't because the gods decided you were better than them for some reason. They will also see that Jinx, a witch under your tutelage, has been shown to be incredibly more powerful than you allowed her to become. Do you think they will still see you as a leader they wish to follow, no matter what happens in Veirveil?"

The High Priest's face turns red around the edges. "Are you threatening me?"

"Interesting you would take Byder's comment that way." Ydum stands, his hands in his pockets as he wanders around the sitting room, looking at the paintings on the walls and fingering some of the High Priest's knickknacks. "No, if he was threatening you, he would have said something along the lines of we'll tell the council of the gods about the actions of your son at his seventeenth birthday party and that they happened under your watch and let them decide whether you are still fit to be High Priest here. But that's not what he said, was it?"

When the High Priest only looks confused, I beg Ydum down the bond to let it go. Ydum wanders back across the room and only I know that he's apologizing to me with his eyes. He sits on the arm of the couch next to me, and gently places a hand behind my back.

"Now," Ydum begins again, "High Priest Breedlove, what is the best way to gather the most adult citizens of Greenbriar as quickly as possible in winter?"

"Tell the school children." I answer when he doesn't. "They will tell their parents, who will tell the neighbors without school children."

"And how long will that take?" Byder asks me. "How long would we need for the message to be passed along?"

I snort. "In Greenbriar? An hour, two at the most, after school gets out. But to be safe, we should schedule it for tomorrow right after school gets out. Once the children get home, most people are rushing to get chores done before it gets dark, then making dinner. They won't want to venture out too much after sunset. The wilde hunt may not have actually ridden in many years, but the superstitions behind them still survive this far out." We were always told not to venture out after dark alone in the winter, that it was tempting the gods.

"And where could we hold the meeting where people would be out of the cold to listen?" Anarus asks.

I wait a beat to see if the High Priest will offer his basement school, where most town meetings are held in the colder months. But he doesn't, so I do. "Usually, we would use the school downstairs, but if the High Priest isn't willing to allow his house to be used, as is only proper, then the testing center, maybe? Normally, that would never be allowed, but with you three asking? They may allow it."

Ydum slaps his knee with one hand. "Wonderful. Sounds like we have a plan. The question is, High Priest, will you be telling the school children to have their parents meet us here tomorrow, or will we be telling them to have their parents meet us at the testing center tomorrow?"

"You don't have the authority to..." The High Priest is trying to hide that he's sweating.

Ydum stands again, this time there is a little power moving in his voice, all attempts at being friendly gone. "We don't have the authority to, what? Inspect a human school? Speak to the students in one? Byder, remind me, are we fully mantled gods of Veirveil or are we not?"

"We are." Byder says tersely. There was definitely a lot of power in those two words.

"Thought so." Ydum nods. "So, as such, under the Articles of God-Human Relations, section Five, subsection B, we do have every authority to enter a human school without warning, conduct an inspection of their accommodations and teachings, and the failure of the High Priest or Priestess to allow such access when requested by any fully mantled god of Veirveil can result in penalties up to and including stripping of Priestly status."

I really should have asked those questions about how all this stuff between the gods and humans works. I have no idea what Ydum is talking about, but the High Priest is blanching at it. He knows even if I don't.

"I will tell the children, and you can hold the meeting here." The High Priest mutters, looking away from my gods.

Ydum nods at Byder, Anarus, and me. I know we are leaving. "That's all we asked, sir. We'll show ourselves out. Have a good day."

We exit as a group, and the moment we're outside, Byder laughs. "Man, you memorized the Articles of God-Human Relations? When the fuck did you do that?"

"Before the games." Ydum gives a sheepish smile, scratching the back of his head. "I was getting paired up with a human when I'd never even seen one who wasn't already immortal before. What did you expect me to do? Ani memorized all three hundred and seventy-four Manuals and you never gave him grief about it."

"Oh, he gave me grief. He just never let you hear it." Anarus answers drily.

When we get back to my parents' hut, Finnegan is dropping off a load of wood to them, so we decide to test our speech on him, Mom, and Dad, and see what they think the villagers will say about it all.

The four of us stand along the wall in front of the fireplace, while Mom, Dad, and Finnegan sit on the couches, hearing us out. We take turns explaining the reality of what happened to Anarus, the truth of how he is both Death's son and was raised as an unwanted orphan. The reality of the story of creation rather than the ones the original gods tell our schools to teach humans. And how we've been screwed over by them our whole lives.

When I tell them about Veirveil, what it's like there, I see their faces reflecting our feelings. The feelings of anger and betrayal at gods who were supposed to be taking care of them. Gods they made offerings to their whole lives, only to be ignored and allowed to starve.

I don't expect quiet Finnegan to be the one who responds first, or so emphatically. "Jinx, you ever wonder why Dahlia and I have been married for fourteen years and don't have any children? We talked before we ever got married and decided we could never bring a child into a world that made us sacrifice them up like that. We didn't think our children specifically would ever have to go, the way things are now. But what happens if more witches think like us and the gods couldn't get enough children anymore? Would they change the rules we don't understand, making our children now potential victims? Even if not, why raise children in a world where they have to live with that fear? It was the only way we knew to fight back, but now, you are giving us a better way. One that might actually change things, rather than just passively hoping they get better somehow. Dahlia and I will both come."

"Same reason most of your sisters have chosen not to marry at all." Mom says, surprising me. I hadn't realized that their lack of marriages had been on purpose. "Half the children in the village the same ages as you and your sisters have made the same choice. Some are marrying but refusing to have children, like Dahlia and Finnegan. Others are just not getting married at all. You will have more support than you think. Especially since you went to the games and still say it's wrong. They try to tell us that getting a blue test is an honor, and our children will be happy and given opportunities never available here in Greenbriar, but we know the same stories everyone else does. The children go to the games and never come back. They're never heard from again."

"But you came back, Jinx." Dad's hands are trembling. I think from rage. "You came back, and are saying that if their children survived, they could have too. It's easy to lie to yourself and say they just didn't want to when no one ever has. It's a lot harder to hear your stories of the games, and still tell yourself they're alive. You sat here yesterday telling us stories. You laughed while I was shocked at how close you must have been to death so often. You told us only the good ones, didn't you, all four of you? You only told the good ones and still I knew it must have been horrible. What would I feel if you told me the bad ones, sweetie? Tell me the bad ones. Tell them the bad ones."

I shake my head, trying not to cry. "You don't want to hear the bad ones,

Daddy."

Dad only nods. "That one statement is more telling than anything else I've heard. The last time you called me Daddy was when that bastard of a High Priest's son hurt you and you were begging us not to make you talk to Sam the next day."

My eyes go wide and I whisper. "You knew?"

"Baby, you have seven sisters, all older than you." My mother says softly. "We learned to listen at doors when our daughters are alone with a man years before you had your first kiss. We heard what you said to Sam and were just waiting for you to trust us with it."

I can't. They knew. They knew the whole time. I turn and bury my face in Anarus's chest. I can't breathe.

"Breathe, little human." Anarus whispers. "Where are you?"

I speak into his shirt. "In my parents' hut with you, Byder, and Ydum."

"Are you safe, baby girl?" Byder says softly, as he moves to stand beside me and Anarus. Ydum is behind me, bracketing me between him and Anarus. I have an out if I wanted it, but I don't.

I don't respond at first, trying to tell myself the answer is yes. They are here. They are here and Jacob isn't.

Ydum runs a soft hand down my back, the lightest of touches. "Are you safe, beautiful?"

I take in a deep breath. "Yes." I stand up straight and breathe out. "Well, as safe as a woman planning a war against the original gods can be."

Anarus chuckles. "You're okay."

74

Chapter Five

THE NEXT AFTERNOON, BYDER, Ydum, Anarus and I go back to the High Priest's house just as school is letting out. Instead of going to the front door, I lead my gods around the back to the basement door. We walk down a set of narrow stairs to a hallway lit with oil lamps attached to the stone walls every few feet, in between wood sheet doors.

There are twelve doors, six on either side of the dirt floor hallway. Each door, I know, leads to a small classroom. Seven of the doors are for the younger children, separated by age from six to thirteen. After the seventh class, the thirteen-year-old students join with the fourteen- to eighteen-year-old students in four of the classrooms. Those four classes have all the fourteen- to eighteen-year-old students mixed together for high school, for the classes that teach us everything.

The last classroom door is one I never went in, never knew what was for while I was in school, but now know is where anyone who got a blue test would have been taught about the Gods Games and given access to the manuals.

After eighteen, young adult children in this village have six blissful years free of school or real work before they test and get on with regular life. Most young adults work at home for their families during that time, helping with the washing, hunting, chopping wood, and taking care of gardens and any livestock they might have, minding their younger siblings, and preparing for their real adult life, pretending they aren't afraid of their twenty-fourth birthday. But while in school, these small eleven rooms make up your whole world between the harvest in early fall and the planting in the late spring.

At the end of the hallway, is a thirteenth doorway. There's no door on this room. Inside is a large gathering space. It's where the young children play on breaks between classes when the weather is too bad outside. It's where the older children eat their lunches, talk to their friends, and hide from their younger siblings. It's also where every town meeting has been held during winter that I know of. All four of them that have happened in my lifetime.

It's also where the four of us will hold this town meeting. We are all nervous. We know what we're asking of them, the people who have been my neighbors, people who I went to school with, the people who all knew probably within minutes that Jinx Bloodmorrow's test came back blue and were whispering to each other about it as the games carriage rolled out of town with me in it three and a half months ago. The people who probably either offered my parents condolences or said that they tempted the Fates having an eighth daughter and naming her Jinx.

At one end of the room is a raised platform the boys in school always practiced doing backflips off of. The High Priest, scowling slightly, is already there, standing off to the side as if he thinks all of this is a waste of time.

We go up onto the platform and stand together, watching as people start filtering in the room. The first to arrive are the parents of the younger children or their adult older siblings. Of course, they would be, since they were coming here to pick up the children anyway.

I tell Ydum we should do something, they're bringing the children with them, and this probably isn't something the young ones should be part of, should hear. Ydum agrees and heads off the platform, talking kindly with the parents. He returns and I see the parents splitting duties, some taking the children home while the others stay and will fill them in later on what we said.

In fits and spurts, the room fills and my nerves grow. I see my father and mother, Finnigan and all my sisters, friends from school. Sam, Devon, Randy, Jacob, the man from the testing center, Granny Helen, people I've seen every day at the well in front of my house, all milling around, eyeing us four on the stage, waiting and wondering what we're going to say.

"You got this, Jinx." Byder stands next to me and encourages me. We know that with the High Priest, they were the ones that should talk, but here, with the people, it needs to be me. Someone they know, a human they can trust.

Eventually, the trickle of people stops and everyone is just milling around talking to each other. I'm not sure how to get their attention.

Ydum, ever helpful, lets out a loud whistle. Everyone turns and looks at me.

I start, hoping my voice isn't shaking as much as my hands are. "Okay, um, everyone. I'm sure you know me, Maddox and Avalon Bloodmorrow's youngest daughter, Jinx."

"We thought you went to the games." Someone calls out.

"I did." I tell them. "That's part of what this meeting is about."

The same person calls out again. "People who go to the games don't come back."

"Let the poor girl speak, Absalom." Someone else calls out. "Where do think a Bloodmorrow girl would find three gods, if not at the games?"

People chuckle about this, and I try to smile. "Yes, they are my teammates from the Gods Games. Ydum, god of nature. Byder, god of the hunt. And

Anarus, god of the bridge between life and death and ender of bonds. We survived the Gods Games together. And we learned a lot. A lot that says what you know is actually wrong. What you think you know about the games is wrong. What you think you know about the gods is wrong. And that wrong information is how a specific group of the gods are using you, controlling you, and leaving you to only one awful destiny after another."

I take a deep breath, steadying myself as I see people listening and continue. "The people who you say go to the games and don't come back, they are dead. All of them. None of them are choosing to stay in Veirveil because is so nice and there's so much opportunity there. The gods are encouraged to go back to their human's village to visit with them before settling in Veirveil together. Every person you ever knew or heard of that went to the games and didn't come back is dead.

"When I arrived at the cave, the first trial for the Gods Games, there were fifty-nine people entering the games. Thirty-six humans and twenty-three gods. By the end of that night, just that first night, thirty-seven of them, twenty-six humans and eleven gods, were already dead and the games had not even officially started yet. By the last of the ten games, ten more people, five humans and five gods, were either dead or close enough to it to be out of the games. Two of them died in my own arms. One by my own hand."

I wait while people chatter amongst themselves. I hear the noises about me having killed someone, and try to talk over them again.

A voice tries to shut me down. "You killed another person in the games? Doesn't that make you a murderer?"

I cringe at that word, murderer. It's not like I hadn't thought that about myself after I killed Aretha. I'm still working on remembering that it isn't my fault but the original gods who put me in that position. So, I tell them the truth.

"They doped everyone with petunias." I say this loudly and clearly, knowing the reaction it will get. Petunias are illegal for a reason in our village. "I'm allergic. I knew right away and was spared the indiscriminate anger that forced others to participate in the sixth game that was nothing more than a killing field. Others were not so lucky. It became about nothing more than sheer survival, and, yes, I killed Aretha. They made me make that choice. The original gods forced my hand. They forced Aretha to attack me and me to defend myself to her death. And that was just one of the ten games."

As my dad told me to, I start telling the bad stories. "I was magically blinded and forced to go through a maze. We were magically whisked into a winter forest and forced to defend ourselves against three yetis without proper protection against the weather and armed with only what my god of nature could make with his power. We were forced to defend ourselves against a succubus. Other teams were dropped into the sea and forced to fight octopi or sharks, fight wolves, and a hate wraith. Byder was attacked by a mother bear when the game left him without the ability to communicate with us.

"I broke my wrist and three toes, dislocated my shoulder, and tore a muscle in my hip. Another witch was mauled by a bear and left to bleed out right in front of us, in the place that was supposed to be safety, while the goddess in charge just stood by and watched us fight to save her. Fifty-nine people went into the games this year and only twelve came out. And this was the three hundred and seventy-fifth time they have done them. If you know of humans that went to the games and didn't come back, they're dead. And they died a brutal, painful death for no other reason than the original nineteen gods that made the land of Nazus decided the games would be no fun if there wasn't that risk."

"Why?" Someone calls out. "Why do they have the games anyway? If so many people die in them, what's the point?"

Another person yells. "It doesn't make any sense. The gods wouldn't go to all this trouble just to let everyone die."

"Ydum?" We already decided this is where he would take over.

The people in the room turn their attention to him easily, but some of them seem doubtful. Ydum had considered how to answer this question carefully. We want to make sure that the people of my village draw a distinct line between the original gods who are the cause of all this and the rest of them, the ones like my three, who are forced and hurt, killed, just as much as the humans are.

"Breeding." He says and gives that word a moment to sink in. "The gods, as a species, are all descended from the same twenty gods, what we call the original gods. After a while, the gods powers, and the gods themselves, became unstable and uncontrollable, dangerous. To fix the issue, the original gods devised a way to determine if a witch has the ability to bond with and mate with a god to make another god child. To control the pairing, and the humans that were rapidly discovering much of their magic, they set up the games and made the testing of all humans mandatory. Red is not fit, blue is and you go to the games.

"The gods, on the other hand, have no choice at all. At twenty-four, you go to the games, find your mate and survive, or die. Our powers are bound at birth until we pass the Gods Games. We are left as half a person, hurting in ways we can't understand, until we complete the games. Then, and only then if we have a witch that has also survived the games and chosen to accept a fated mate bond with us, can we have access to our full power, our full selves. With a distinct lack of powerful enough male witches, most parents of female gods just assume their child will die because they were unable to find a proper male witch mate in the cave at the beginning. They live their whole daughter's life knowing that when she turns twenty-four, statistically, she will die."

Telling Iella's, and I learned from Ydum's parent's, his sister's, story seems to have the desired effect. We were prepared for the inevitable questions about this, and are pleased when they included the ones we hoped for. I can't determine who says what, but know that several villagers speak all at once.

"What do you mean mates?"

"If this is true, why does Jinx have three teammates instead of just one?"

"Why don't the gods do something to stop this if they're just as hurt by the games?"

I talk again. "Mates means exactly what you think it does. Like Ydum said, breeding, making children. But all humans also believe in the idea of mated bonds, that two people can be mated to love each other. It's in every story we tell children here. I mean, you all know my parents, Maddox and Avalon. How many people over the years have joked about their love being destiny?" I wait while most of the people in the room chuckle and nod. Most everyone believes my gushy in love even now parents are mated lovers if anyone is.

"The test we take checks not only for ancestors who are already gods, and strong magic, but also the existence of a mate bond. If you don't have the first one and do have the other two, you get blue. Then in the cave, that initial trial, a complex magic system is used to lead the gods to their intended human. A human that the Fates have already declared to be destined for them. Most of the time, yes, that's only one god and one human. But sometimes that means two gods. We don't know why. My bond with three gods is still unique, but I know with everything in me that it is a true mated bond with all three of them."

I her some people start whispering, the ideas of human propriety making them lose the point. I step forward, allowing my footfalls to resound loudly, drawing their attention back to me. "But, don't forget the real problem. The only people in the cave are supposed to be twenty-four-year-old humans with a blue test and all the twenty-four-year-old gods. And the only bonds allowed in that cave are between one human and other gods. Not human and human, or god and god. My father is two years older than my mother, and they are both human. What if either of them had gotten a blue test? They both have strong magic and obviously have no god ancestors. What if they are a mated love bond? Could that confuse the test and given them blue instead of red? We don't know. They're lucky it didn't. You're lucky it didn't for you, either. How do you find your bonded mate in a cave when they aren't in that cave with you?"

I feel the energy in the room change as people really consider this and understand the implications. They are getting angry. Good. Get angry. I want them to be angry.

Byder takes over. We want them to see the four of us as a united front. Byder's voice holds the edge of anger in it, mirroring their feelings back to them. "Even if someone does manage to find their destined mate in the cave, that's not enough. They have to be one of the first ten teams to do so. A few seconds too slow, and you die anyway. You will hold the hand of your destined mate, a god you just met, and know that you will now die because you were just a little too slow. Be someone like Jinx, with her shitty birthday meaning she had no idea what she was doing, or someone from a village like this where the magical education is less than it should be, would they know how to do the magic the cave requires for that trial to be fast enough to survive? Jinx almost didn't. She had no idea what to do and just lucked into it."

Anarus speaks now, as much as he didn't originally want to. He speaks softly, and somehow, that makes what he says more potent as the people have to really pay attention to hear him. "And what do you think happens the first time a human sees a god, or a god sees a human? Then, they are immediately fighting for their lives? How would you feel if it was you?"

Anarus gestures to himself, Byder, and Ydum. "The three of us were considered children until we went to the games. We had never seen humans before. Jinx had never seen a god before. And we were just expected to accept that this stranger, this person from a species we knew next to nothing about, is our destined mate and that we can work our magic together, make stronger magic together, strong enough to fight and not die together. That first real game was only the next day. Jinx knew us for less than an hour when she was thrust into an intimate living situation with three gods and then given one night before she had to trust us with her life. How would you plan your survival like that? How do you trust them enough to even think about it?"

He shakes his head. "You don't. You can't. If it was you, how much time would you waste trying to just figure each other out? Time needed to plan how to survive. It wasn't you. But it could have been. Very easily, it could have."

The murmurs from the crowd grow, some are still doubtful but more seem to be swaying to our side. Anarus keeps talking. "And all this we are telling you is only just the games. The Gods Games are just one way the nineteen original gods, that control Veirveil and all of Nazus, have made your lives inconsequential and worthless in their eyes. When we came here two days ago, Maddox and Avalon were kind and wonderful, perfect hosts, but feeding the three of us? How hard is that in the dead of winter? What could we do to her if she refused to host us? What could you do if we demanded that of you? She didn't know us, or what we could do. And neither would you. I'm sure all of you would have had similar fears."

Anarus pauses here to let people think about how they would react if the three huge gods standing on the stage, that they had never seen before, showed up at their doorstep at the worst time of winter, when you know exactly how much your supplies won't last as long as you need them to. When he sees the faces of the villagers tighten, he nods.

"Exactly. Byder walked through your woods for one hour and caught six rabbits, and he's one of scores of hunt gods in Veirveil. Why are any of you ever going hungry at all? Why have human children crossed the bridge into the land of the dead, dying from hunger, when meat lasts long enough in Veirveil to go bad and be thrown out?"

Understanding and rage starts moving through the crowd. Everyone here knowing someone who died from a lack of food, or proper protection against the elements. I hear yells of, "Why doesn't someone do something?"

Other get angry back. "What are we supposed to do? It's not like we can fight back against gods." And I know the moment has come.

I step forward again. "Fighting back is exactly what we want to do. There is a better way and the four of us, and many more gods and humans back in Veirveil, know it. Initially, we had planned to fight within the system. As the winners of the games, one of the prizes is the human gets a seat on the council of the gods, the reigning government body that decides everything about Nazus, for one year. The winning gods also get to unseat the highest-ranking god with a matching power as them for one year. For most gods, this means being so low down the pole that they have almost no power, and with the god of Death banished, the twenty original gods that hold the controlling seats are actually only nineteen, effectively making the human's tiebreaker position worthless.

"But, when we were successful, as a full nature god, Ydum would unseat the original Nature, taking a seat with the nineteen. Byder as a full hunt god would do the same to the original Hunt. Anarus, as the child of the god of Death with a death power, would fill the twentieth seat, making my seat, the human seat, actually powerful. We would carry a lot of weight within the council then.

"But the original gods knew we were angry and sensed that their power and control would be threatened by us so, by several means, they tried to stop us.

Including making Anarus enter the games three years too early, then attempting to murder him to make us fail. Unfortunately, they found out it's actually kind of hard to kill the child of Death who controls the bridge between life and death and have him stay dead."

Several people chuckle at this, and I let them. "Working from within to change a system this flawed with the balance of power too tightly controlled doesn't work. We need to tear the system down and rebuild it from the ground up. That's why we and many other gods and humans, including the banished Death, have made a plan to meet in the woods south of Veirveil and challenge the original gods' right to rule. We want to make something new, something where everyone, human or god, with magic and without, have a voice and a choice about their lives.

"Other gods and humans are visiting other villages all across Nazus right now, gathering as many humans as we can to meet there in six days. We know this is a lot, and fast, for you in a time when just sheer survival is a fight. But we're asking any of you who feel you can to join us. Join us and maybe next winter you won't wonder if it will be your child that Anarus helps into the land of the dead, your child that sees blue and is sent to die for those nineteen gods' whim and entertainment."

Ydum takes on his academic stance, giving the people the real statistics of the situation, the real chances. We debated saying this next part, but he felt that the people deserved to know everything, laid out straight, to make their choice. "We won't lie. The original gods won't go down without a fight. The last time someone fought them, the magicless humans, they had to be saved by the god of Death who removed them from Nazus completely and gave them their own land to live in. But we have, at present, two gods of war, three nature gods, two hunt gods, two gods of chance, six powerful god-bonded witches, one of whom has a familiar bond with a wolf, and two gods of death, including one with full control of the wilde hunt. We may also have a god of storms and a god of music and their two mate-bonded witches. We don't know how many other human witches from villages just like this one, gods of Veirveil and potentially original gods may have already been turned to our side. The Fate goddess, Sadness, lost her son this year to these games, and where one Fate goes, the rest follow.

"We don't want to be them, the original gods, tricking you and forcing you. We want you to make your own choices, with the realities of the situation spelled out plainly. This will not be easy. We have no idea how this will go down. But we are prepared to fight and want you to choose if you would like to come with us and fight for your ability to make your own choices too. We leave for Veirveil in four days. Take your time, think about it, talk about it with your loved ones, and we will either meet you in four days, on December seventeenth or not. If not, no shame. Your lives are hard, harder than I could have ever imagined, and you are making the choice between two bad decisions. We respect your right to make those choices yourself, and we will fight for your right to do that whether choose to join us or not. That's all. We will be at the Bloodmorrows' for the next few days if you have any questions."

Before we could step away, like we planned to at this point, someone calls out. "Why hasn't High Priest Breedlove said anything? Are they wrong or something? Are they not telling us the truth?"

I turn to look at the High Priest, waiting, wondering what he will say.

He slowly moves across the platform from his corner to the side to stand in front of us. I can tell he is trying to envelop himself with some sense of being just as powerful as my gods and just as trustworthy.

The silk in his voice I used to think meant power now disgusts me as he uses it to twist our words in an attempt to hold onto his power. "I do not agree with this plan. I believe this is only four disgruntled games players who feel they did not get their just rewards. I taught Jinx Bloodmorrow for twelve years and never saw much promise in her magic, and now they want us to believe that she won the Gods Games?"

He shakes his head, giving the crowd a small, sad smile. "No. I cannot believe that. Her test wasn't even actually blue, but both blue and red. She is nothing special. This plan is foolish and foolhardy. I urge you all to ignore their ramblings and not to go with them to what will most certainly be your own deaths over nothing more than their disappointment they did not win."

"Says the man who always has shoes on his kid's feet and food in his belly." Someone calls out. I think it's my father. "You've never had to pray the wood in the fire lasts the night so you don't freeze to death. You've never watched your children shiver from hunger and the cold. But I know just about everyone else in this room has at least once or twice. Who gives you the power to not do that? Oh right, those original gods Jinx talked about. Why would you want to bite the hand that feeds you? What would you know of our suffering and if we should risk death? We risk death every day, just trying to live."

Another person, also a male, yells out. "If that girl's test was not blue, but blue and red, meaning she wasn't a powerful witch, how is she standing here, then? With three gods backing her up? If nothing else, we know she survived the games, and that says enough of her magic that anything you say is irrelevant."

"If she was too weak a witch with a messed up test, and the gods still made her do it," a third male calls out, "then aren't they everything bad she says they are?"

Someone else, a female this time, picks up where that male left off. "If that girl says the gods are wrong for this, I believe her and the gods with her, over you. You must have been too weak yourself to realize the strength of her magic. You're not someone I want teaching my children if you failed her that badly. I don't need four days to decide. I'm going to put my trust in the survivor of the games that came back and her gods, not a man who thinks he's posh because he sits in a big house while the people he should take care of starve."

The High Priest seems to shrink and starts sweating as the voices of the crowd grow angrier and start turning their back on him, talking to each other and not even listening as he tries to speak again. Ydum claps the man on the back, making the High Priest jump.

"Looks like you lost your power here, man. Might want to stop while you're behind." Ydum chuckles and the four of us move off the platform to leave. I know that the people will probably mill around for quite a while, talking and arguing with each other. We'll leave it to the High Priest to shepherd them out of his house.

Over the next three days, some of the people from the village do come by the hut. Most of them seem more curious about Byder, Ydum, and Anarus than to have any actual questions.

They all deal with that curiosity in different ways. Ydum is smooth and calm, smiling and giving academic answers to their questions, avoiding more personal information deftly. Byder tends to answer their curiosities with brisque, simple answers as he shifts in his seat, looking obviously uncomfortable. Anarus avoids the interactions as much as he can.

No one is ever bold enough to ask us outright about the nature of our relationship, the three of them and me, but many people allude to it, skirting a line where the questions asked are definitely not the ones they want to ask.

On the morning of the seventeenth, we wake very early, long before sunrise. The four of us are already packed and ready to leave when Death's carriage and driver arrives back at my parents' hut. The driver had stayed at the High Priest's house, in the loft above his carriage house where the horse was stabled.

My mother is not coming with us, and I am thankful for that. She decided that there are many people with too young children who are staying behind and that someone should be here to guide these young parents. My father, on the other hand, would not hear my arguments that he should stay too.

"They did this to my daughter." He finally tells me, slapping his chest. "My daughter! I know that you met your gods that way, and you are happy about that. All three of them are wonderful and I see how well they take care of you, Jinx. I love them for how they love you. But if your own father won't fight over what they did to you, how could I ask anyone else to? And who is fighting for Anarus? My son-in-law was murdered by them all because they were afraid of losing the power they never should have had in the first place. If you don't want me to fight for you, Jinx, then I'll fight for him."

Anarus blushes and looks away at this. Dad's opinion about my gods has definitely shifted over the last few days, that much is clear, and he loves all of them, especially hunting with Byder. But Dad and Anarus somehow bonded on a deeper level. I found them talking quietly to each other often over the last few days, and was always pleased with how often those conversations had them both smiling. So, my dad won't let it go, he's coming. For Anarus if not for me.

As are all of my sisters and Finnegan. As are a lot of other people, apparently. As we move down the road to the edge of the village, the driver has to move slowly because of the number of loaded down mule-drawn carts and people walking in the road. People wrapped in blankets to stay warm with their crude hunting weapons held in their hands. People walking in homemade shoes that will do nothing for them if it snows again. A hundred people, and maybe a hundred more walking. Walking all the way from Greenbriar to Veirveil for the hope of something better for their lives.

The four of us quickly feel wrong riding in the warm carriage with our good boots and warm clothes. Byder knocks on the wall of the carriage and the driver stops.

He gets out, muttering, "Fuck this."

I follow him out and see him go over to an older man, walking with a distinct limp and shoes that he made from tanned leathers that were old and worn ten years ago.

"I can cook." I hear the man tell Byder. "I may not be able to fight, but most armies need to eat. I can cook."

Byder groans. "Fine, but you're not walking all the way to Veirveil. Get in the carriage. I'll walk."

After that, the four of us end up walking the rest of the way. The carriage carries older or less abled people who insist they can help in their own ways. People take turns riding in it.

I spend a few minutes sorting through our bags, finding Ydum's warm woolen sweaters, Byder's hide shirts, and the lovely clothes Otuna bought me. I distribute them to the people I see who have the worst clothes.

Mr. Natry, who clean the streets of the worst of the trash and whose shirt has more holes than cloth, gets Byder's deer hide sweater that actually has sleeves, even though he swims in it. A kid I swear can't be more than nineteen gets my pants when he is only wearing shorts. Others are doing the same, but their quality of clothes is so much less than ours, it ends up just with people laying their hole-filled clothes.

Ydum uses the warmth in his eyes to heat up canteens of coffee and tea as we walk. He eventually gets one of the wagons to become the food station, so he can just stay even with it and warm cups up as they are handed out.

Walking this far with this many people actually takes a lot longer than we thought it would. We are moving at a good pace, all things considered, but it'll still take longer than one day to get everyone to the outskirts of Veirveil.

Most of the roads are muddy and the swinging temperatures have left them icy but not solid, meaning cart wheels get stuck. Sucking mud potholes are only covered with thin sheets of ice. With so many feet and wheels passing over them, the ice cracks and cartwheels sink into the mud. Anarus pitches in often to help get them free, working with the others to tilt the carts until the wheel is free and the cart can be pushed forward.

Twice, he uses his brute strength to crouch under a cart, the wheel popping free when he stands with corner of the whole vehicle perched on his shoulder. Once, he holds it there, one corner of the cart hovering in the air and several others bracing their backs under it to assist him as the cart owner works quickly to change out the wheel that had broken on a stone.

Even with the sharing of clothes, some people find their feet and hands getting cold and stops are made so that people with warmer clothes can trade off with others, sharing whatever they can to keep each other going. Byder does some spot hunting, grabbing what animals he sees with his hunting power and doing a quick and dirty field dressing for the meat to eat and the hides for warmth. The hides won't last, we know, with them only semi-preserved with his powers, but parts of the hides are passed around to be tucked into clothes for added insulation.

Stopping for lunch was a long affair, taking hours with this many people. By the time those of us at the head of the group have finished eating our meager rations, many of the people at the back of the group have just gotten their food and we wait for them. It may take more time we didn't account for, but no one is getting left behind or losing the opportunity to get something warm to eat. My three gods use every skill and power they have to make sure as many people get as much as they can, warmed as much as possible, quickly.

Just after sunset, we come to a crossroad and find Damek and Iella coming from Damek's village, Readrock, with their own caravan of people. They had actually been setting up camp for the night for the fifty or so humans that joined them. They took one look at the mass of ragged and tired people following us and are surprised.

"I didn't think that in such a poor village, many people would be able to come." Damek says as six of us sit around a fire with Damek's father, Beck, his older brother, Douglas, my father, and Finnegan, cooking game Byder caught to help supplement everyone's meals. My sisters are all around somewhere, I think helping others set up makeshift shelters and camp fires.

Dad chuckles. "It's easier to leave everything behind when you really don't have anything to leave."

The Readrock people, who obviously had a lot more to begin with, end up sharing with the Greenbriar people. It's inspiring to walk around the impromptu campsite and see extra boots, warm blankets and clothes, and food being passed between strangers that now share a common goal, and enemy.

The weather holds overnight. I'm not putting it past Ydum that he had a hand in it even though weather isn't exactly his highest power control. Maybe it's actually Iella and her messing with the chances of snow three days before the winter solstice. Maybe both of them together.

Either way, the morning dawns cool but not as cold as it could be and overcast. Anyone who has ever suffered through the worst of winter storms knows that cloud cover is better in winter. A clear day is a cold day.

My father and Damek's father hit it off from the start, but I guess that shouldn't be surprising. Beck got just about as much of an update on Damek as my dad did about me. When Damek arrived at his father's hut in Readrock with Iella, he's not ashamed to admit they both cried as they hugged for a long time.

Damek's mother passed away when he was fifteen and Beck's worst fear was one of his boys going to the games. When Damek's test turned blue, Damek said his father nearly lost it and wanted to hide him, make him run away rather than get into that carriage. It wouldn't have worked, and the prison sentence doled out to humans who refuse to test or refuse to play if their test turns blue is extreme, so Beck didn't actually make him. But talked about it often, thought about it often, and even considered if he could somehow get Damek to the non-magical continent between his test on September thirtieth and the start of the games on September fifth almost a year later.

The mood changes as we start walking in the morning, but not how I expected it to. With the mingling of the Readrock and Greenbriar people, the atmosphere becomes much more hopeful. Stories are being told as we walk.

Readrock doesn't tell those children's fairytales about gods and humans falling in love like Greenbriar does, but they do tell stories about the early days of the gods and the trouble the first children of the gods got into in the newly created Nazus. Apparently, trickster was a popular power for a child of two original gods and, since their powers weren't locked up until they were older like they do now, there was some funny messes the original gods had to clean up when their kids had a tantrum. There's a particularly funny one about a nature god child accidentally rerouting which way water flows and a bunch of very confused fish.

Some people start singing. I know the Greenbriar songs, mostly shanties meant to keep motivation and pacing when doing repetitive work, but they are adapted well to walking speeds. The Readrock people seem to have a lot of love songs, joke songs, and dancing songs.

Some people have brought out instruments, ones blown into and others with strings that are plucked. There is some fascination as the Greenbriar people are given a chance to tinker with them. I know about instruments, creative people will make an instrument out of anything, spoons, a dish, but the first time I ever saw any real ones were when Uesis played for us in the games. The air fills with laughter, music, and the cold recedes some, chased away by smiles and good moods. And improved road conditions as we move closer to Veirveil.

Even the six of us from the games seem to change.

We fall in to old habits easily, as if all we are doing is walking together to the next game. Iella tells us about taking her mantle with Damek and how her parents refused to open the missives from the games at all.

"My mom decided to just keep them all in a box on the mantle in the sitting room." Iella says, convincing me yet again how little difference there is between a god parent and a human one. "My sister said they made a tradition out of holding it, kissing it, as a way of kissing me goodbye, then putting it in the box every week. Then, when the next one came, they would cry in joy I had been still alive to have them get one until the tears turned to sorrow and the mourning started all over again. Nayla, my sister, was tempted to just open them after my parents went to bed, end the misery of the unknown, but didn't. Not until they got the invitation to the Colosseum."

Iella laughs. "Nayla said the moment Mom had the invitation in her hand, and they knew each missive would say I had survived, she grabbed the box off the mantle, dropping and breaking it in her haste to rip them all open and read how well we had actually done."

"Girl damn near toppled me first time I met her, jumping in my face to read me the riot act about how stupid I was in game two for failing to make sleet of all things easily." Damek chuckles, shaking his head. "Nayla is shorter than Iella but almost scares me more."

When Iella mock glares at him for that, he only shrugs. "What? It's true. Look in the dictionary for mighty midget, it'll have a picture of Nayla instead of a definition."

Both Iella and Damek are excited to see Anarus alive and well. They knew from the meeting at Ydum's house that it was the plan for us to bring him back, but had never heard if we'd been successful. We tell them all about me going to the bridge, him taking his mantles, and using my magic to fix the bridge.

I notice, as we walk and talk, exactly what my dad had been saying. We laugh about how badly I burned my hand shoving three bonds back into Anarus's heart when, in reality, there is nothing funny about what we had to do to bring him back. Like so many soldiers, we find humor in the morbid because we have no choice but to either laugh about it or cry. And laughing feels better and stronger. If we stop to cry, we would never move again from the weight of the horrors we have suffered.

We reach the southern outskirts of Veirveil close to dinner and I'm again in shock. The woods are already filled with people milling around. Campsites have already been haphazardly set up, as well as stations for food, medical help, and what I assume is something akin to a strategy center. My dad and Beck say they will take charge of the humans and getting them settled.

The six of us head to the strategy tent and find Ayja and Esnir hard at work, leaning over maps and diagrams, apparently disagreeing over something. Ydum clears his throat when they seem not to notice us.

Ayja looks up and swears. "Fuck, you're here already. I'm already struggling to figure out where to put everyone. How many did you bring with you and do you expect more?"

Damek answers first. "About fifty or so, we had runners to the four other villages Ydum's dad said to send them to. They left two days before we did to come here, not sure who they'll bring."

I answer for us. "We were only doing Greenbriar. I think somewhere between a hundred and two hundred. Maybe more? It was really hard to get an accurate count and I didn't know we needed one."

"A hun… You're shitting me, right?" Ayja's mouth is hanging open. "Fuck." She scurries out of the tent, mumbling about not being prepared for something this big and how the fuck are we doing this tomorrow already?

"Mom's losing her shit." Esnir says with a rueful smile. "Which, I guess, in the grand scheme of things, is actually good. People just keep coming."

"Any word from Death, Raven, or Wren?" I ask.

Esnir raises his eyebrows and nods his head. "Oh, there's been word from Death, all right. There's been a slow trickle of gods from all sorts of pantheons wandering their way into our camp. No clue how these people know what's happening, but they just keep coming. They're all saying a friend of their brother's neighbor, or some such thing, said Death is here and the Gods Games winners and him are challenging the council of the gods and, whatever we're up to here, they want in. Then, there's the original gods, each came by themselves, one by one. Sadness, Hunt, Nature, Fire, and Fertility, the female one only. Only one of the Fates, and only half Fertility."

He shakes his head. "I couldn't believe what I was seeing. I mean, I didn't know the Fertilities could go anywhere without each other. Just showing up, with the same story as the other, non-original gods, saying they knew we were up to something out here, pushing for some type of change and when they sought out Death, he said come here and join us. Since Death finally showed up, we've had him keeping a close eye on them, keeping them on lockdown in case they're spies."

He sighs and taps the table with one of his knuckles. "Wren and Kutar came yesterday. They heard about it from someone who came to Wren's village. Kutar failed to take his mantle. They're alive, but both mortal. They ran to her village to hide when they heard what happened with Anarus."

"Shit." Ydum closes his eyes and pinches the bridge of his nose. He and Kutar had similar powers, storms being a part of nature. "Where is he now?"

"Fourth tent behind this one. We're keeping all of us from the games and our families close together." Esnir tells him.

Ydum looks at me, Byder and Anarus, with a pained expression and I smile at him, nodding. He takes off to go to Kutar.

Esnir keeps talking. "Still nothing from Raven and Uesis. Death swears they aren't dead and we sent someone to check Raven's village but no one there has seen them either. We just can't find any word of them."

"Nothing?" Anarus pushes.

Esnir shakes his head. "Nothing. It's like they vanished." He sighs. "But it's not like we are very organized for search and rescue, Eiran's planning skills notwithstanding. It is completely possible they passed our runners somewhere on some road and got missed in a crowd of others coming here and will just randomly show up. I want to conduct a full, detailed search for them, but not now. There're too many humans who need us. Too many other people and they would both tan our hides for worrying about them when there are so many other people who need us more."

We all nod. He's right. Raven might have only cared about gossip most of the time, but she cared. She would want us to focus on this now. We will find her. We will find them. I shove down the ominous feeling that tries to worm its way through me and remind myself they are not dead so we will find them. Then probably laugh about it all later. Another story that isn't funny being funny to us.

"Where do you want us?" I bring us back to the task at hand. "What do you need?"

Esnir looks down at a drawing on a piece of paper on the table in front of him. It doesn't look like an actual map, but a hastily redrawn version of one, with colored marks and writing all over it. I move closer to the table to look at it and it appears to be a blown-up copy of a portion of the map underneath it that shows Veirveil and the surrounding woods. This section is just the woods directly south of Veirveil, where we are now, and the colored marks and writing are labels of where different people have been set up. Esnir sees me looking and explains it to me, pointing to different spots on the map.

"This is us right now, this tent that is the center of the whole encampment. Behind it, to the north, where I sent Ydum to Kutar, is where we have tents set up for the Gods Games people. When the gods from the council started showing up, we gave Death a bigger tent, the one we meant for you four, so that he could have them all in the one spot to watch over. The rest of the gods and their witches that are our families, my parents, and yours, Byder and Iella, Ydum's too, those people are to the west of us. To the east, we are putting the gods that aren't from the council but aren't any of our own people either. And south, we have started setting up the humans trickling in."

"We are trying to make every village able to stay together, with their own resources tent for food, fresh drinking water, what have you. Mom has tried to work with each group to have them set up their own people doing the things like cooking, fetching the water from the river here, at the most southern edge of the camp. But there are just so many humans pouring in from everywhere that our system is getting messy. Eventually, people are going to have to start staying on the other side of the river."

Esnir sighs, rubbing his face. "If this goes on for too long, we are going to run into issues. There's not enough food, even with the number of hunt gods and humans who know how to hunt we have. The woods around here couldn't handle what we would need for this many people in this level of winter for long.

There's also the issue of weapons. Many humans brought some level of weaponry with them, but they are used to hunting not fighting. And the gods brought almost nothing, not even pocket knives, minus hunt and war gods. And none of this takes into account the wilde hunt, Anarus, because Mom and I didn't have the foggiest clue what they may need."

Byder turns the map to look at it. "Seems like what you are saying is we have a great start to a show of force. But that show of force is just that, a show. In reality, it's a toothless dog."

"That's exactly what I'm saying." Esnir turns to lean against the table, crossing his arms over his chest. "We have no way to know what is even happening with the council. We are amassing a fucking lot of desperate and riled up humans, and for all we know, the council doesn't even know we are here."

"They know they are missing five council members." Anarus snorts. "Pretty sure they'd notice that."

"And your body." I point out. "You said the Fates felt your bonds reconnect, Anarus. Only one of the Fates came here. Pretty sure the other ones would say something to the council about thinking you might be alive again. Add that with Death just going missing, then five more council members, they would put it together that something is happening."

Esnir sighs and turns back to the table. "Which brings us to the next problem. Even if they do know something is going on, how easy would it be for them to just ignore us? You told us Winter was being held in prison, but Veirveil doesn't have a prison. There's only one prison in all of Nazus, and that's far to the east, in nowhere's land far from any other villages and only for and run by humans. Court things like that, trying of crimes, that's all human village stuff, run by their Priests and Priestesses."

"Problems like that with gods get decided by the council and the only punishment, real punishment, doled out is mortality." Esnir shuffles some papers around on the table, pulling out the map of Veirveil and looking it over. "So, where is Winter really being held, how is she being held, and if the dissenting opinions on the council are all here now, what's to stop them from bringing her back out of whatever lockdown they have her in and just letting her throw the worst of the season at us until all the humans die and the gods are left near enough to death we can't fight anymore?"

I groan. "This is why Death said the magic-less humans had to appeal to him for help in their attempt to fight the council. Without magic, they had no hope against the original gods."

"But we do have magic." Byder furrows his brows, looking at the hand drawn map again. "We have a fuck ton of it. Gods, a bunch of immortal witches that are bonded to those gods, and all the humans are some levels of witch. Even the most unarmed person here is somewhat armed. None of these people are children. These are all adult witches and fully mantled gods. And potentially the wilde hunt. And if we're really lucky," Byder looks at me, raising one eyebrow, "some wolves on top of that?"

"I could ask. Don't know that they'd go for it, especially in winter when the hunting is slim already."

Esnir rubs his chin. "Actually, that may make it more to their benefit, Jinx. We don't have a lot of food, but we do have food. And hunters. Leftovers from our food without having to hunt at all in such a hard hunting time? Could be a nice benefit."

Anarus laughs. "You trying to domesticate Jinx's wolf familiar and her pack?"

"Why not?" Esnir asks, shrugging. "At least temporarily. What's it hurt to ask?"

"Kinshra is pretty possessive over you, Anarus." I smile.

"No offense, I don't want to step on your toes here, man." Byder says slowly, tracing a finger around the colored sections of the map. "But I think you and your mom set up the camp wrong. We don't want the villages all segregated from each other, but intermingled. We saw that on the road here. How much the attitude of the humans with us changed when we met up with your people, Damek."

Damek nods in agreement. "Yeah, the people in my village were in pretty good moods before you guys showed up, but yours looked ragged and scared. By the next morning, only the next morning, everyone was much more hopeful. Like, as if knowing they weren't the only dogs in this fight bolstered them."

"Exactly. Don't keep them segregated but let them give each other hope." Byder says. "Shift the way they are organized. Magic type with magic type. If we put witches who are good with hunting all together and pair them with the hunt and war gods, as kind of the leaders of their division, the gods can help the witches know how to use their skills if it comes to a real battle. Same for other types of magic. Are you the village healer? Good, go with the other healers and set up a camp hospital. Are you good with plants? Everyone together, here's a nature god to teach you how to make vines and thorns that work as weapons. I mean, we pretty much only have tonight to organize and tomorrow to prepare, but it's something to prepare with."

Anarus shakes his head. "Keep us together. The Gods Games people, I mean. And your mom, Esnir. We lead the charge with this, I think. With maybe Jinx's wolves and maybe my wilde hunt. The council gods too, under Death's watch. We stay together, even Kutar and Wren."

I nod. "I agree, with all three of them."

Esnir moves away from the table, giving Byder full access to the maps on it. "Listen, I take no offense. My mantle ended up being war strategy and survival and Mom's a battle god, but those are only very specific parts of war. I don't even know if there is such a thing as a full mantle war god, since the pantheon was created rather than born. Mom will rip your head off if you try to disagree with her on the strategy in a specific battle. Basically, I'm logistics, training and the bigger picture. I understand how to train good soldiers and keep them a good soldier, able to heal them enough to keep them alive to either get back out to the fight or make it to the actual medics, how to ration food to feed an army and the other supplies you need, and how battle movements shift and flow over the course of a full war. But this? How to organize a war camp? That's not in either of our mantles. We have no clue about it. So, if you think this is a better idea, Byder, not sure how you know, but it sounds better than the just stick 'em somewhere plan we've been working with."

"It's how you'd organize a mass hunt. You don't want the tracking dogs and the cooks mixed in with everyone else because the smells from mess tent would drive the dogs crazy and they'd be worthless when it came time to hunt. For shame, don't put the medics near anything that tracks using blood, and keep the falcons away from the dogs." Byder explains.

Esnir bounces his head from side to side. "Makes sense when you put it like that."

"Someone should talk with the council gods, too." All four males look at me when I say this, as if confused by the idea. "It doesn't matter if they are spies or not, not really. If they are, and we talk to them, ask what the council knows and about their plans, they'll lie and maybe say different things. If they're not spies, they'll tell us everything quickly and the stories will be the same. We can't totally trust what they say, but it gives us an idea of what's happening in Veirveil. And maybe ideas to draw the council here, since there is no way that we want to take the fight to them. There are children in Veirveil, innocents."

Esnir rubs his hands together. "Sounds like plans coming together. As soon as Mom gets back, we can get on reorganizing the camp. It'll be a logistical nightmare, but better done now. We need to get someone on interrogating the council gods. And Jinx needs to talk to her wolf. If they agree to come, let me know what to look out for and when. We don't want people panicking because a whole pack of wolves come trotting right through the camp. Unless, you have some major objection, I'll put you four in the tent that was Death's before we stuck him babysitting the council gods. It's small, but it's what we got without shifting all of us around too."

Byder claps Esnir on the back. "Man, we just spent six days in a room half the size of one of the bedrooms in the games sleeping on the floor between two beds because the floor was better than those squeaky, lumpy things. No offence, Jinx, but a war camp tent of any size will probably be an upgrade."

"As for talking to the council gods, can it be me?" I ask. "Or really us four? If they really are here because they're over the council's shit, it's probably us that were the tipping point. I have emotional magic I can manipulate them with if need be. They may also be more open to talk when they see the used to be dead but now very much alive and fully mantled Anarus stalking around. They don't know he doesn't still have his shadows with the wilde hunt loose and would be terrified about what a child of Death and Winter's power would be. They'll apt to be more honest. And we'd want to do it one at a time and not let them talk to each other after."

Esnir smiles. "Alright, correction. Jinx is calling her wolves then becomes our lead interrogator. Damn, you sound like if it comes down to torturing our prisoners of war, you might have a handle on that too."

"No actual torture." I chuckle. "I won't go that far, but I'm pretty sure if I can make people feel peace, I can make them feel very worried about what might happen if they don't tell the truth. And how my magic works is a complete unknown to them. They can't fight what they don't understand. Not that I have that great of a handle on it either."

Esnir leans back, stretching. "Well, this is progress. A plan. But the other issue is having a purpose. When we confront the council, what do we want? I know the ideas we talked about during the games, no more death in the games, but with the humans showing up in the numbers they have, I don't think that's enough. They're angry, they're tired and they're sick of being second class citizens, pawns for the gods to control and use or ignore at their whims."

The four gods look to me and Damek. I tell them what I think, as one of the only humans in the room. "We need the council gone. As it is, gone. The original gods stripped of their power, answering for the horrors they have inflicted not only on the humans, and gods, who have gone to the games, but to all of them. The ones who starved and died under their leadership."

Damek nods, agreeing "The games need to be gone too. If the gods still want a way to test for mate bonds with humans, it needs to be done a different way. We should have a say in both our local leadership and the leadership of Nazus. The whole power of a village resting with a High Priest or Priestess whose power is passed from parent to eldest child, unless the gods determine someone else in the village is more powerful and therefore more deserving, is ridiculous. It breeds contempt and leaders that don't train the children in magic right for fear one of those children will grow up to take that power. And a human who is only ever the tiebreaker vote on a council they have to fight to the death to become is equally laughable. There needs to be real human councils in each village, ones chosen by the humans of the village, and humans really represented on the council of Veirveil, with a real voice."

Iella nods at this. "I think the gods feel similar things. Taking our mantle of power at an age where we can be responsible with it? Sure, that's a good idea. But who decided Kutar wasn't worthy to be who he was born to be? And why were they given that power? Keeping some level of the cave to find bond mates is good, but it shouldn't be finding your mate or die trying. Why did I, as a woman, have to fear my birthday so much just because there were not enough male witches to go around? Why should female gods be basically doomed from birth that way? Test humans and the gods for a potential bond mate, then if they test yes, let them find that mate when they find that mate. If they had waited to put Anarus through the games at the right age, he would have died in the cave because Jinx came through three years before."

Anarus adds to that. "We should have the freedom to live where we want, do what we want with our lives. Humans and gods. In Veirveil or in one of the villages. Gods shouldn't be stuck in someone else's shadows just because we only have a finite power. And humans should have the right to live here in Veirveil as much as the gods do. We should be equal with the humans, living side by side, not something held up as better, separate."

"So, dissolution of the games altogether." Esnir says, writing as he talks, making sure he has it straight. "Dissolution of the current council, at the very least, minus probably Death. And reconstruction of the council to be fair and balanced between humans and gods, with a local council in each village as well as the national one for Nazus. Maybe even add term limits on serving on the councils and voting by the people who the council represents. Sounds like a solid list of demands."

I shake my head. "One change. Not just dissolution of the current council and its remaking. But the original gods put on trial, stripped of their powers and made mortal, if not worse. They should never be able to hurt or control anyone ever again. We need to make sure of it. I'm not say no to executions if it's found warranted either. At least not right now, but that may be me just being a little pissy."

Anarus and Byder both look at each other, saying at the same time, "Vicious Jinx is back."

Chapter Six

WITH THAT SETTLED, WE leave Esnir to his planning and the three of us find our way to the tent Esnir showed us was ours on the map to drop off our things, then head to the one that Ydum took off to. He and Kutar are deep in talks, and Byder and Anarus join him while I talk to Wren.

"When Kutar failed to take his mantle, it was awful." She and I are sitting at a table, watching the guys talking. "He nearly died and they just brushed us off, sending us to some squat hut on the outskirts of Veirveil where we didn't know anyone. We were there for days, Kutar writhing in pain. I didn't know how to help him and the villagers wouldn't even look at us much less help us. We had no food, no anything, and I was too afraid to leave him alone. As soon as I had a clue where we were, I sent a letter to my parents. My father came and got us. It was awful. I can't imagine what it would have been like if he died though. I know you must have suffered so much, with Anarus dying and your bonds so deep."

I only nod. "It was excruciating for all three of us. But he's back now."

"When we heard about what was happening here, Kutar didn't want to come. He was afraid that no one would talk to him. Not a witch, not a god, he doesn't know who he is anymore. But Esnir took one look at him and settled him in here, with the rest of you, as if we were no different, saying just because he doesn't have the god's powers anymore, that doesn't mean he doesn't still have the knowledge." Wren looks over at the males talking. "This is the first time I've seen him smile since the tenth game."

I sigh. "Sorry it had to happen under this situation. You know Damek and Iella will be happy to see you too."

I let what Wren said settle into my skin. Kutar in pain, suffering as his body tries to accept its new status as mortal, something it wasn't designed for. It makes me think of what Death told us about where humans really came from.

When Inspiration has his idea for creating these lands and some of the gods disagreed, how did the nineteen of them do what they did, stripping their godliness from them to make them the base of the people who would be subjugated under them? How much did it hurt them? How much agony did they suffer to become us, against their will?

Kutar had Wren to help him while his body fought and he suffered. Who did they have? Who was there to teach them their new body's needs? Everyone around them was suffering in the same way, as newly made mortals. How many of them died because they had no idea how to be mortal and no one to hold their hand and guide them through it?

Anarus called the punishment the gods get for failing one of the games torture, and he was right. It is torture. Kutar was tortured. But so were those original humans and they had no Wren to help them through it.

Kutar did everything right in the games. Being denied his very identity, in pain and abandoned, scorned with no idea how to even live? They lost everything, everything, all at once. Friends, family, a sense of who they are in the world, a sense of the future. They were lucky Wren's father was willing to help them. That she figured out how to contact him to ask for that help.

I shake my head. None of this, from the creation of the world to the creation of the games and Kutar's pain, none of this is right. Evil doesn't even begin to cover it.

We stay only a few more minutes, letting them both know that, for us, nothing has changed. Kutar may not have powers anymore, but that means nothing to friends. Ydum promises him that, once this is all over, he'll help Kutar find a way to belong, a new way forward. He fails to say the if we win part. All of us know that without the words needing to be said out loud.

Back at our tent, I contact Kinshra. It's late, and she would normally be hunting at this time, or at least getting ready to, but I think this counts as an emergency. We really haven't talked since Anarus reconnected the bond. A quick conversation of what the crap was that and where the fuck did you go for a month, but nothing more. Winter is as hard for wolves as it is for people and life has not been easy for me either.

The tent we were assigned, the one that was supposed to be for Death has a large camp cot in it and not much else. Not that Death would have been able to use that cot. It's big but not eight-foot-tall hulking god big. I sit on the floor instead, leaning back on Anarus. Byder and Ydum sit on the cot, nearby in case we need anything.

She's quick to respond when I call for her. *Jinx! I'm on a hunt. What do you need?*

I give her a quick rundown of the current situation, explaining Byder's thoughts that their pack might be able to help us.

These people you are going against, are they the ones that hurt Anarus? Interestingly, that question does not come from Kinshra and I'm startled by that.

Who is that, Kinshra, and how are they talking to me?

Alpha, she tells me. *I'm touching him as you and I are connected. He didn't know if it would work, but wanted to try. He doesn't know a lot about a god-guided familiar bond, since he's never seen one before us, and is going off instinct to direct us about it.* I feel what would amount to a wolf version of a shrug. *It worked. We won't question it if you don't.*

I chuckle. I think I'm past questioning anything with you and me, Kinshra. But to answer his question, yes. They're the ones who made us do the games and the ones who said Anarus couldn't touch me to take his mantle, then made us wait so long to revive him.

I feel a low growl form in Kinshra's throat that is echoed in her alpha's. *Wait,* Kinshra tells me. For a few minutes, I feel both the alpha and her disappear, as if they are talking to others in reality. They quickly return.

We will come, the alpha tells me. *The whole pack will come. We will see if other packs will come too. Familiar bonds are sacred. They killed the god of your bond. Hunting them would be an honor.*

I give them a sense of where we are and they let me know that, if we can promise a feed for them when they get here, they will abandon their hunt and can be here in a few hours.

I can promise something to eat. Not sure what or how much, there are a lot of humans to feed too, but they will be respected and fed something. Let me know when you are close so I can let Esnir prepare the people not to freak out over the wolves strolling through our camp.

Ayja comes into our tent just as I finish up with Kinshra. I tell her what the wolves said and she informs us that, having heard our plan to interrogate the original gods, she thought it would be best if Death stays in the tent to monitor them, and she will bring them, one at a time to us. She will release them after to Esnir, who will keep them separated so they can't talk to the ones who haven't met with us yet.

We agree to this plan and shift things around in our small tent to make it appear less like where we are staying and more like a place for conversations. We initially plan to snag two chairs and a small table from the strategy tent, as well as a small oil lantern, but Esnir stops us with a smile.

"Are you or are you not a witch, Jinx?" He raises an eyebrow at me. "Make your own and stop trying to steal Isis's work."

I laugh but know he's right. Damn him. Ydum gets me a small block of wood and I make us a, I'll admit, crude table and chairs. It is much harder to direct the wood to expand into not just more wood, but wood in a specific shape. It takes me a minute with the table legs as I add too much to one to even them out, then another when I do too much again. Eventually, Byder has to manually cut them back because the table is so tall, we would have to stand at it.

I flatly refuse to try again with the oil lantern, afraid of messing something up and having it work, starting a fire. Esnir relents at that, understanding and definitely not wanting that mess, and gives us one.

Instead of hanging the lantern from the hook on the ceiling in the middle of the tent, we set it on the table that's in one corner. The flickering of the low lamplight creates shadows in the opposite corner and Anarus slips into them, allowing it to appear the shadows might be his. Ydum and Byder stand just inside the tent flap, carrying an air of bodyguards. I sit in one of the two chairs, facing the tent flap. When the gods come into the tent, they will have to sit with their back to Byder and Ydum while Anarus will only be a dark outline in the corner of their eye.

Ayja starts with Hunt. Hunt slips into the seat and hums appreciatively as she looks around. "Good set up."

I need truth, I think as I take a deep breath, tapping into my magic. Hunt must tell me the truth. She needs to fear lies and half-truths. "Why are you here, Hunt?"

She turns to glance at Byder, wrapping her thin fingers around the top of the chair as she twists in it to see him. "Do you know how long it has been since there was a true full hunt god? I watched your progress through the games and knew I would have to give up my seat to you. I was ready for the break. Honestly, when we created these lands, I didn't realize I would spend the next thousand years on politics. I want to hunt. I want to be in the woods. I don't want to be in a damned stone building, bickering about how much annual salary some half power god of fluffy clouds that just gained their mantle deserves. I was ready for the break, damn it! Then, Winter has to go and fuck it all up because she's a stingy bitch who doesn't want to share powers unless she doesn't care about them."

"You didn't know who Anarus was, or what he could do? What Winter did to him when he was born?" I ask, keeping my tone flat, empty.

Hunt gives a derisive laugh, turning back to face me. "No. I guessed that Anarus was something to her when she always managed to be there when the council met about him, even in the wrong seasons. But fuck all if I guessed he was her son. And the thing with the wilde hunt?"

She snorts, turning her gaze to Anarus lurking in the shadows for only a moment before sitting straight in her seat to look at me again. "We don't do the death penalty, just making gods mortal, but for that, I would make an exception. The torture he must have been under his whole life. And part of that torture was our doing. My doing. Had I known, I would have fought for him. I didn't know, but that doesn't negate my guilt. The others just want to say it was her right as his mother, as a council god with him under her pantheon. Which, one, is wrong because no mother should have the right to do that to their child, no matter who they or their child are. Two, because his real power has nothing to do with winter at all. Anarus's actual powers were inherited from Death and Death alone.

"And, three, if anything tells me that we original gods have taken too much power for too long, the fact that we fought about what to do about him at all is proof we have failed to be what we set out to be. Even without the whole extra mantle and the oddities that gave him, the things we've learned that were happening to him as a child should never have been allowed, never been possible for any god to feel like they could get away with doing to a child. Any child. We failed him in so many ways. We kept failing him by refusing to admit we failed him."

"What was your role in the subjugation of the gods before creation that disagreed with Inspiration's plan?" I'm making up these questions as I go along. I have no idea what I'm doing. "Did you help strip them of their power and lie to the beings left behind that we are less than you are?"

Hunt ducks her head shamefully. "Unfortunately, yes. I did participate in making the humans. A thousand years, or more, gives you a lot of time to think.

Like I've already said, none of this is what I thought it would be. Given the same choice today, I would never go along with Inspiration."

I tap my fingertips on the table. The female seems to be telling me the truth, but she still hasn't given me much about what the council knows about us out here in the woods and what they plan to do about it. I try to think of a way to get her to say it without asking outright. "That's all well and good, but you did do it. So, again I ask, what are you doing here, Hunt?"

She huffs and gives me a knowing look. "You want to know what the council is doing. Fine. As soon as Peace told the council that Anarus's bonds had come back to life, they all knew exactly what had happened. You three and Death had left the hall, and Anarus's bonds were back? Doesn't take a genius to figure it out."

"When the arguments about what to do with you three and what punishment Winter should get shifted to debates about if Death should be made mortal or just outright killed for his transgression, the transgression of using his power exactly how he can use his power and for his own son, no less, with everyone knowing without even debating it that you would be executed, along with Anarus, again, I knew I was done."

Her voice turns bitter. "They're going to let Winter get away with what she did because you four are too much of a threat for them to care. They want you dead. The Fates that made your destinies want you dead for what you are. What they made you. I'm over it. Done with this bullshit lie that we are anything better. Why should we get to make someone a specific way then get mad at them for being exactly what we made them? I sought Death out at his home and he just told me, if I really thought it was time for a change, go to the woods. I did and here I am, still clueless what you and a bunch of humans are planning or think you can accomplish."

"So, you know nothing of what the council is doing now? What they plan to do?"

"Except kill you," Hunt shrugs with only one shoulder. "No."

I nod and look at Ydum and Byder. Ydum sticks his head out of the tent flap for a moment and, when he leans back in, Ayja is entering the tent.

"Done here?" Ayja asks.

"Sadness next, please," is the only response I give her.

Once Ayja is gone with Hunt, I roll my shoulders and stretch. We say nothing while we wait and Ayja quickly returns with Sadness in tow.

Before her butt even hits the chair and Ayja can fully leave the tent, Sadness is spitting. "I know what you think and what you want. They killed my son. Modes should have won the games. Nothing against you four, but you know it's true. He was the most powerful god in that whole group. They want to tell me he didn't even find his mate in that cave."

She laughs bitterly. "A child of Fate didn't find his destined mate in the cave? The only way that happens is if his mate wasn't ever in the cave. I want to claim that I'm mad because, if it happened to him, how many others died for the same reason, but I won't lie. I don't give a damn about any of the others. He was my son! Mine! And he's dead now, so fuck all of them."

Well, Sadness is angry. Didn't know that was possible. "Are you here looking for change in the system or just to burn out your anger?"

"Neither." She says, her voice stronger than I've ever heard it before. "My anger will never burn out. And changing the system won't work either. What needs to happen is that we burn all of this to the ground. The whole damn thing, to the ground. Every single one of the original gods and our children who are full gods needs to die. And I say that knowing that I'm including myself in that statement. There is no way the power in Nazus can ever be fairly and judiciously shared if any of us live. We have been in power for too long. It's time for the next generation to give it a try and see if they can do better."

I open my mouth to speak but Sadness doesn't give me the chance. "And before you ask, no, I don't know what the council is up to now. I lasted only five minutes in the hall after Death left. I think it shocked the other Fates when I walked out without even conferring with them. But, like I said, fuck this, fuck them, and fuck Veirveil."

Anarus comes out of the shadows and puts his hands on the table, leaning against it to hover over her. He thunders. "Where is my mother?"

Sadness turns her head slowly towards him. "Contained to her home, last I knew. She has been left enough of her powers to keep the season properly, but other than that, we, the Fates, bound her powers. My binding is still active, but if the others have removed theirs, I cannot tell. I'm not exactly open to sharing with my brothers and sister right now to find out."

"It would help if you did enough for us to know what is going on with Winter." I tell her. She's not a spy. Not a chance. Can we trust Hunt? I don't know. But we can trust Sadness, I'm absolutely sure.

Sadness shakes her head, her loose tarnished gold hair falling into her cloudy blue eyes as she does. "If I do that, they will know what I know as much as I know what they do. I may not have seen much of this camp, the army you are amassing here, but I saw enough that they would be able to figure everything else out. You should be blindfolding us before moving us out of the tent. Hunt, Nature, and Fire you can trust, I think, but do not trust Fertility."

I let Ayja take Sadness back, saying she's trustworthy, and have her bring me Nature, then Fire in turn. We take Sadness's advice and have them blindfolded, and I add hands bound, when brought over. Nature's responses mimic much of Hunt's.

Fire professes an affinity to both Byder as a follower of the four disciplines and Ydum's control of volcanoes. She also feels that the power the council in Nazus has outlived its appropriateness, and that maybe some new blood would be good. I'm still not sure if we can trust those three, so we release them back to Death to keep an eye on.

When Ayja brings the Fertility goddess to us, we treat her with more hostility than we did the others, following Sadness's directions with this too. We leave her blindfolded and bound and let her stew for a few minutes after being placed in the chair on the other side of the table from me.

I work to lay a magical working of truthfulness, as I did with the others. With them, it felt like a cloak settled over them and they just accepted its warmth. With Fertility, it feels as if the cloak chafes and she wishes she could figure out where it's coming from and move it away.

"Why are you here?" I ask, startling her. None of us had moved since she sat down. I think she thought she was alone.

Fertility turns to the sound of my voice. "I disagree with the decisions of the council as of late."

That's true, technically. She voted Nay against having the council members that were active at the time of the ending of the games have their terms of service extended. The vote went against her.

But that's too simple an answer. Too rehearsed sounding. I silently move to another part of the tent. "Where is the Fertility god?"

"We disagreed." She shrugs as if this is enough of an explanation.

Byder, who moves to stand over her right shoulder, speaks loudly, startling her again. "Bullshit. I don't think anyone knew you could go anywhere without each other. You want us to believe you suddenly decided not to get along and share one brain?"

I move again, keeping her guessing at where we are in the tent, confused and disoriented. "What does the council know of our plans?" The plans we just cemented hours ago with Esnir. "What are their plans?"

She sighs. "They understand your anger and that you think you were justified in attempting to bring Anarus back. They are willing to negotiate with you to get his body back where it belongs and may even un-banish Death. But they believe your overreaction to losing the games cannot go unanswered. They are willing to discuss the possibility of changing the nature of the games so that humans are not so susceptible in them and resources are made more widely available to the human communities, but only if you meet with them in Veirveil, at the council hall in two days."

Wrong answer. I move again around the tent. But before I can say anything, Ydum silently sits in the chair I was in. When he speaks from that spot it only makes her more confused. She can't tell where anyone is or even how many people are in the room.

"So, you admit you are a spy?" Ydum says casually. "That sounded less like you are giving us information we can use against them and more like a well-rehearsed list of demands. Not sure what makes the council think they have a right issuing demands at this point, but…"

"I'm not a spy!" Fertility's voice is high and shrill, fighting under the truth I demand from her. "That's just the last discussion I heard before I left. I disagreed with those decisions."

"Which ones?" Anarus's growl makes her jump and squeal. She obviously didn't know we were successful at bringing him back. "The ones where they say they might un-banish my father for defending their creations when they failed to? Or the one where they want my body back, the body I am currently using?"

He strides up to her in quick, loud steps and takes her throat loosely in his hand. Anarus is not putting any pressure on her neck, but she pales anyway. "If that's the best you can give us, what use are you to us?"

"You can't. You wouldn't threaten me. I'm a council god. When the council hears of this, they'll…" Fertility is panicking.

Anarus twitches his fingers. "When this is all said and done, more than likely either the council will be dead or we will, so what the fuck do we care what the council thinks when they hear we threatened our prisoner of war when she became worthless to us?"

Even without being able to see her eyes, I can tell Fertility is searching for something, anything, she can give us to make us think she's worth keeping alive. Not that we would kill her right now, I think. Anarus might have different ideas.

"Your bonds! The bond between you and Jinx." She shrieks when Anarus wiggles his fingers again. "Did you even look at them, Anarus? Did you even notice—"

If it wasn't for how quietly he speaks, I would say that Anarus roared. "You don't get to talk about my bonds! You don't get to speak at all anymore. Ayja!" Ayja pokes her head back in the tent. "Take her away. And leave her bound and blindfolded. Gagged too. Treat her as a hostile threat."

Ayja's eyes go wide, but she does as Anarus says and takes Fertility away.

As soon as they are gone, Ydum stands, hands in his pockets, an air of casualness that is obviously hiding very not casual feelings. "Do you want to tell us what the fuck that was about, Anarus? What was she talking about? You and Jinx's bonds?"

Anarus's eyes flick to me for only a fraction of a second. "I don't know."

Byder caught the look between us. "Why did you just look at Jinx? What's going on?"

Ydum and Byder both look from me to Anarus and back as the silence stretches tight between us.

I try with everything I am to fight the slight panic, hoping that none of them feel it. We don't have the time right now to deal with this shit. "Could she be just trying to cause issues? Spewing nonsense?"

"Doubt it. Might have thought so, if Ani hadn't immediately done everything he could to shut her up quickly then his eyes hadn't shifted to you like that and made me think he at least thinks she isn't." Ydum answers, his voice tight. "What do you think you know, Anarus?"

I'm not sure if Anarus knows what Fertility is talking about. The possibility scares me. Anarus's shoulders slump and he seems about ready to say something, but he's interrupted before he can.

"Um, Jinx?" Kutar's voice outside the tent sounds nervous. "There's a whole bunch of wolves just to the east of camp and Esnir said to ask you if you knew anything about that. One of them is currently trotting through the camp and people are kinda freaking out."

Fuck. I forgot about Kinshra. I check quickly that the wolf in the camp is in fact her and then let Kutar know to let her come to me unhindered. I also tell him to prepare leftovers from whatever meat people had for dinner to leave on the eastern edge of camp for the wolves, and a small bit brought here for Kinshra. He leaves to do as instructed just as an enormous gray and black wolf strolls right through the tent flap and butts against me.

You smell upset. Kinshra says. *Were you and your mates fighting?*

Not really, Kinshra. Don't worry about it.

After getting a small scratch hello from me, Kinshra moves on to Anarus. I can tell by his face that she is talking to him through the touch of his hand in her fur, but I can't hear what they are saying.

Well, that's new. And annoying. I could hear their conversation when we did this in the games.

"That is a fucking big wolf." Ydum says under his breath, his earlier frustration forgotten. He and Byder have never seen Kinshra before. Not even in my mind. Anarus and I were the only ones in the fifth game to see her and her alpha in person.

Standing on her four legs, Kinshra's head comes up to my shoulder. On Ydum, she comes up to the bottom of his ribs. After a moment, Anarus lets go of her fur and Kinshra talks to me again.

I assume the tall one and the broad one are your other mates?

I speak out loud for everyone else's benefit. Anarus can only hear her if they are touching and I don't think Ydum or Byder could hear her at all. But then again, I didn't think her and Anarus could block me out either.

I try not to laugh. "Yes. The tall one is Ydum and the broad one is Byder. You knew their names before, Kinshra, but yeah." Byder snorts back a laugh.

Would they let me touch them? Alpha is curious if the crossed bonds between all four of you will let me talk to them too.

"Can she touch you?" I ask them.

Ydum, ever inquisitive, immediately reaches out a hand. "Absolutely."

Kinshra walks up to him, placing her head under his hand. Ydum instinctively moves his hand to scratch between her ears.

The tall one has nice hands. Tell him a little left, it itches there.

Ydum smiles, and moves his hand. "I'm glad you... Fuck. That's interesting. I heard her, but don't share the bond. I wonder." I know his mind is reeling over everything he thought he knew to assimilate this new concept.

While Ydum thinks, Byder talks. "Hey, the broad one wants a turn."

Kinshra whuffs a laugh and moves to him.

As soon as her head is under his hand, he digs his fingers gently into her fur. "She is really soft, Jinx."

You smell like a good hunt, broad one.

"Hunt god." Byder's eyes go wide. "Wow, that's weird. That's how it is when she talks to you all the time?"

I nod. "Yeah, you get used to it."

Tell Anarus and the tall one to touch me too.

I tell them and once they do, Kinshra talks.

The pack will stay outside the camp until you tell them what to do. As long as meat is given to keep us fed, we will stay as long as we are needed. If meat is an issue, feeding this many people, let us know and we can hunt in shifts. I will stay here with you four, though.

"Sounds fair enough, Kinshra." Ydum says. "We appreciate you and the pack coming. We're not sure what's going to happen here but having your support makes it just that little bit better."

Make sure if the wilde hunt does come, they stay away from the pack. Too many of their numbers hunted us when they were alive.

"Will do." Anarus tells her. "Well, will try. Not sure how much control I will have yet."

You will do your best, guide. I trust you.

Kinshra shakes her fur, making the three gods let go. She moves over to a corner of the tent and lies down on the ground, curling up in a ball with her tail over her nose and appears to doze.

"Well, that was fun." Ydum puts his hands in his pockets again. "But I believe we were in the middle of a conversation." He looks at Anarus and me.

So much for them forgetting all about that. Anarus doesn't look at me, but answers.

"When Jinx put the bonds back," Anarus says carefully, "there was something different about it."

"Do you know what?" Byder asks. I can tell he feels concerned.

Anarus shakes his head. "Not exactly. I know something is different and I have a feeling I know what. A suspicion, but nothing concrete yet."

Ydum turns to me. "Do you know something about the bonds being different?"

I do, at least I think I do. But I do not want to tell them. Not yet. But I won't lie either. "I didn't know there was an issue with the bonds per say." I look at no one, even though I very, very much want to look at Anarus. What does he think he knows?

"Per say?" Byder grumbles. "Do you know of an issue or not, Jinx?"

Fuck. "This is not the time or place for this. We have bigger issues right now. If Anarus and I both noticed the same thing, then is it not a right now issue. It can wait..." I feel just a little panic and don't hide it in time. It isn't the same type of panic they usually feel from me and it makes all three males look at me with concern and frustration.

"Fuck"!" Ydum yells. Ydum never gets mad, not easily. But now he's yelling. "Could you be more obtuse about it? Just say it. If it's not a right now issue, we can all know and set it aside. But right now, this feels like you and Anarus are keeping secrets."

Anarus grunts. "It's not me keeping secrets. I've been dead for a month."

They're watching me. Byder and Ydum are watching me. I start to pace, nervous energy making me need to move. They're all watching me. I rip my hand through my hair and groan. They won't let it go, I know. I haven't wanted to think about this. Talk about this. But I have to now. They won't let it go.

I stop, dropping my hand with long exhale. "Fuck." I say under my breath, having no idea how to say this, when even I'm not sure. Even just trying to shape my mouth around the words makes me panic just a little more.

There is so much. There is so many ways that this won't be good. That they'll be unhappy. I can't know how they will all feel, and that makes me worry. I open my mouth to say it and the words just get stuck in my throat.

"Jinx." Ydum's tone is much kinder. They are feeling my emotions through the bond and know I'm struggling. "We love you. All three of us. You know that. You can tell us anything."

Groaning, because I know that, but this seems just too big for words, I decide to just say what I can and hope they understand. "Red clover."

I wait while the three of them try to process what my words mean, looking at each other to see if someone else understands what they don't. I will not cry. I will not worry.

Ydum gets there first, of course. His long legs make it across the tiny tent in two steps. He grazes his knuckles down my cheek. "Are you sure, beautiful?"

I shake my head, tears still threatening even though he isn't mad anymore.

"No. No, I'm not. But I—" I shudder from trying to contain all the fear and worry and every fucking thing else I have hidden feeling.

Ydum's hands move to the top of my hips, his fingers splayed as they rest on either side of me. He closes his eyes and places his lips on my forehead. It's not a kiss, I know he is looking at me with his power, the interconnectivity of nature, and our bond.

He pulls back and actually kisses my lips. "I am."

From the bond, I know the moment Byder understands. He feels something that is quickly overshadowed by panic. "Fuck. This just became a more important fight. If we don't end the games..."

There is the sound of all three of them sucking in a breath between their teeth. If we survive but don't win, and the games continue, our child will have to go to them. If the original gods were willing to use the games to try to just get rid of the four of us for being problematic, what will the original gods do to the child of traitors?

Ydum steps away from me, Anarus immediately taking his place, holding me tightly. He is conflicted, concerned, worried. "You don't have to do this. There are ways. Your choice, Jinx. It's your choice."

The suddenness of the rush of protective feelings in me surprises even me. On instinct, my arms wrap around me, hugging my middle. As terrified as I feel, have felt for a while now, I can't fathom doing anything to change this. My feelings are echoed back to me in all three of them.

Ydum chuckles. "Well, I think that answers that question."

"Good. Mine." Anarus growls then kisses me passionately. Every line of his body is suddenly taut with the need to protect me, keep me safe. Keep us safe.

"Shit." Byder swears under his breath and moves quickly to stand behind me, his lips grazing the back of my neck. "And we thought the pull of the bond was strong before. This is intense."

Anarus looks over my shoulder at Byder, then to the side to look at Ydum. "You two, too?"

Byder is behind me so I don't know how he reacts, but Ydum answers. "It appears that it doesn't matter who the biological father is, all three of us will feel the urge to protect Jinx and the child as soon as we accept it as our own."

Anarus eyes glaze over for a moment then he looks back at me, as if he doesn't ever want to take his eyes off me again. "The extra bond was just a tiny, hesitant extra thread between you and me. I thought at first it was just a loose thread, a frayed edge or something. It's not tiny now. It's strong, and branches to all of us. Ydum and Byder just as strongly as between you and me."

I step out of the dual embrace of Anarus and Byder. "You three can't go crazy now. Especially right now. You can't try to treat me as defenseless or push me to the side to protect me. Not now, not with all this." I gesture around to the tent, but they know I mean the whole war we just started.

Ydum puts his hands in his pockets with a quirky smile. "Oh ho ho. Yeah. No. I don't think you would let that happen. I'm quite sure vicious Jinx will be ten times worse right now. I'm very happy to sit back and watch as you shred the world to protect your family. You were already powerful, beautiful. Now you'll be unstoppable."

I turn my attention to Byder and Anarus and see that Byder has a dark smile. Anarus is struggling to control his feelings, but I expect that from him right now. This means family for him. Not just the chosen family of the three of us, or the unknown family of a father who was kept from him and a mother who would rather he die than deal with him. But a real family, ties that bind permanently. His child. Him as a father. A role in life he was never taught, has no examples to follow. And that family is already being threatened.

"We tell this to no one else." I say firmly. "Not yet. Except, just so you know, I think Death knows. Right before we left to bring Anarus back, he said something, asked me if I should be doing this with how I am right now. I told myself he meant the mourning, the pain from the broken bond, but I think he knows."

"And the Fertility goddess knew, so they both probably do." Ydum adds.

"Which means the council probably knows too." Byder grumbles. "So, I think not telling others, at least Esnir, is out of the question. He'll have to know what they'll want to use against us."

"Well, I guess we tell him everything." I sigh. "And soon. It's late and tomorrow may be kind of a big day. If we figure out how to draw the council to us instead of us going to them."

We head back to the strategy tent. In that short walk, I realize how late it actually is. The sun is already set completely and the night sky clear and bright with stars. People are still moving around the camp, but not as many as there was before.

As soon as we filled in Esnir, and Ayja, on everything, the interrogations, our assumptions about the Fertility goddess, and me, he had the gall to laugh. Full outright laugh. "Of course. It would be you, Jinx, that manages to use the magic in the strongest ways possible. I mean, with you capable of making the plants in a burn salve able to protect you from the fire of a volcano in Ydum's eyes, did you really think a little red clover in your coffee every morning would be harmless?"

"Well, when you put it like that." I grumble, making all four males laugh.

Esnir gets serious again, leaning back on the strategy table, his arms crossed over his chest. "Ok, so, tomorrow. How soon will you know about the wilde hunt, Anarus?"

"Not sure." He twists his mouth. "I can feel them close. Like an ache in my chest. But I don't know what that means. Close to me physically? Close to the bridge? Just close to needing to return in a time sense? No idea. The actual solstice is not until the twentieth, so tomorrow is the last day they should be free. But does that mean I won't see them until the day after tomorrow? I don't know. And what does see them mean? Again, I just don't know."

Esnir nods and looks towards his mother, who's standing on the other side of the table, hands braced against it as her face scowls over the maps in front of her.

She looks up and there's a strain in her eyes. "We currently have about a thousand humans. I have gotten them reorganized mostly in the formations Byder suggested, and new groups coming in will be added to their proper magic platoons, each one being led by a god or gods with a power akin to their magics.

Kutar, Wren, Damek, and Iella are watching out for stragglers while Isis has been back and forth, keeping us updated in numbers and setting up tents we are magicking up for the incoming groups."

Esnir interrupts her. "I think, if the council is assuming you have two days to respond to their demands, we should use that time to our advantage. We have planned everything based on having the wilde hunt, but that was before we realized the extent of humans we would have. Since we don't know if we'll actually be able to use the wilde hunt, I say we plan that we won't. We use the time we have been given to plan and train the humans and gods better. If the wilde hunt is available, then we will find a place for them. If not, then it won't mess anything up for us."

"With that in mind then," Ayja says, "tomorrow, we should have each platoon god work with the witches in their groups to help them craft for war. I've already been formulating battle plans for waves of magic and weaponry attacks based on if we are here in the woods or in the city. I'm also strategizing a plan in case the only people we are actually fighting is the council themselves, which would be a different type of battle. Right now, I'm not sure what help the wolves can be beyond in open conflict. The wilde hunt, if directable, will be their own division but I won't bank on them, like you suggested."

She nods at her son. "The biggest questions we still have are who does the council have on their side beyond themselves and how does engagement go down? I want to work on this more, but if we stay up all night, we'll be too exhausted to be rational and plan well tomorrow."

"They won't leave the city." I say, pacing. "Fertility made it clear they expect the four of us and Death to come to them. They won't leave their stronghold without provocation." An idea forms and I share it. "What if the wolves aren't necessarily a fighting force but a distraction?"

Ayja stands taller, her eyebrows raised in curiosity. "Go on?"

"You just said that we need to sleep or risk not being in a good place tomorrow, not rational to plan, right?"

Ayja nods, so I continue. "Veirveil isn't used to so many wolves close by. Or really any. It's too big a city, too many people normally. So, what do you think would happen if half the city was kept up all night by howling wolves that seem like they are right outside the council members' windows? Yips and growls all over the city all night long and they can't even get any rest? Wolves running through the city, especially at the council homes, destroying things, spooking the horses, but not hurting them obviously, letting the animals free to run wild, havoc and mayhem all night long."

Esnir's eyes light up and Ayja smiles. They look at each other for only a second then both say, "Do it," at the same time.

I step a pace or two away as the others continue talking. Kinshra?

Have a job for us?

If you can. While I give her the rough idea of a map of the city and the northern wedge that is the homes of the council members, she heads back to her pack to be near enough to tell them the plan, if they agree to it. Terrorize them? Leave the innocents in the rest of the city alone unless actively provoked, obviously defend yourself if you can't flee, but focus on driving the council of the gods mad with lack of sleep, causing damage without actually hurting any innocent animals?

I wait while Kinshra confers with her alpha. I can feel her excitement with the plan. *On it,* she tells me. *Better than hunting.*

As soon as I feel her leave me, I hear the woods to the east come alive with wolf calls, howls and barking yips. The sounds are moving away from the camp, towards the city.

"I take it they liked the plan?" Esnir says, looking up as if he could see the noise through the tent roof.

"Destruction and mayhem, all night long." I smile.

"With that, I think we should all call it a night." Esnir sighs. "We have all done the best we can and have to wait to see what tomorrow brings."

Back at our tent, I surmise Isis has been by because, instead of the sole cot that had been in the tent before we used it for interrogations, a large pile of furs is tucked into one corner. She must have just decided that we could work out whatever sleeping arrangements are best for us with that instead of cots. I appreciate it and we do end up just spreading everything out to make one large nest of furs for the four of us together.

Once we are settled, me between Anarus and Byder, with Ydum on the other side of Byder, I finally feel the exhaustion hit. We had been going almost nonstop since before dawn the day before and it's probably close to midnight.

I want to sleep but I can't. There is trepidation running down the bond. It's all of theirs, but Anarus is feeling it the most. I turn to face him, and snuggle close.

"I love you, Anarus." I tell him, burying my head onto his chest under his chin. His arms sneak around my waist to pull me closer.

"Are you sure—" Anarus tries to say but I interrupt him.

"I love you, Anarus." I say again, pulling my head back so I can look at him as my body presses tighter against his. "I love you. I'm sure that I want to give you everything. Every part of me. Even this one. We're yours, me and it."

"Her." Byder mumbles into my back. He's nuzzling my back.

I twist to look at him as Anarus raises himself up on one elbow.

"You know something, Byder?" Ydum asks from Byder's other side.

"Not really." Byder sighs and flips onto his back, his arm under his head. "Well, maybe. I don't know. Call it an educated guess."

"Her." I can feel Ydum's smile as he talks. "Why does that make me insanely happy?"

Anarus pulls me back to him, to bury myself into him again. "I don't know but me too, Ydum. Me too."

Chapter Seven

I'M WOKEN UP RIGHT at sunrise as Anarus gasps and clutches at his chest, sitting straight up. He's pale and shaking.

"Anarus?" My worry wakes up Byder and Ydum. "What's wrong?"

"The wilde hunt." He pants out. "They're coming back."

"Where?" Ydum asks, sitting up as well now.

Anarus's face is getting paler and he's struggling to take a full breath. He points to his chest. "Here. Me."

Shit. Oh, shit. Anarus is taking on the full mantle of the god of the wilde hunt. I know it without even question. I can feel it. The wilde hunt isn't going to the bridge between life and death to cross it, but are confused and going to him because Anarus is the bridge. They are going back to where they knew for the last twenty-two years.

"Take my hand, Anarus." I shove my hand into his, but he pulls it free before I can completely grasp it.

Shaking his head, he groans. "Salve." He curls himself up, bringing his knees to his chest and his head to his knees as he moans again.

"Fuck the salve!" I grab at his hand again. "Take my hand!"

Anarus roars wordlessly and shakes his hand out of mine again. His words come out between gritted teeth. "Not. Without. Salve."

The salve is back in the city, somewhere in Death's bedroom. There's no way he can do this alone and there's no way I can get the salve. My brain scrambles for anything to do instead.

Ydum slips behind me, trapping Byder between the two of us with Byder's chest pressed hard to my back and Byder's back to Ydum's chest, both of their legs sprawled out to either side of me. Ydum reaches his hand over Byder's shoulder to grab mine, his palm to the back of my hand. As I look at him, to question what he's doing, he furrows his brow and his hand turns icy cold.

Byder, between me and Ydum, quickly yanks off the shirt he's wearing, and grabs my free hand, clasping it to the tattoo of the earth, wind, fire, and air symbols. Covering my hand with his, he places my fingertips on his chest between the blue water and the yellow air symbols. Then, he reaches out and wraps his other hand around the wrist of the hand Ydum is covering. I feel a damp, cooling breeze move from my wrist to coat the hand that was already chilled by Ydum.

"Ice, water, and wind to cool your hand." Ydum says. He pushes my hand to Anarus's chest, right over his heart, right as Anarus lets out another loud roar of pain.

I cringe at his pain but force my mind to calm. I need to see Anarus's power. The well, let me see the well. I open my eyes and see that our already dark tent has gotten even darker. Shadows are moving everywhere, agitated and confused.

"Go to the well. Go into the well." I tell them. "Not into him, but the well."

I look at Anarus's chest right above his heart where the well of the wilde hunt always was. All I can see is a pure shimmer of the gold bonds he anchors within his heart as the ender of bonds.

There's no well there anymore. Shadows are trying to go back where they knew to go, but it's gone. Every time a shadow dips into him, looking for the well, Anarus screams and writhes again. But they find no place within him and leave to circle the tent, more agitated, only to try again.

"There's no well for them to go into!" I yell. I need help. I don't know what to do.

There are noises of people outside. I can hear them. I think they see the shadows and hear Anarus's screams and don't know what's happening. Fuck, please work. I need help.

"Death! Death!" I scream as loud as I can. "I need Death now!"

I hear Esnir outside the tent yelling for someone to get Death.

Good. Help. "Hold on, Anarus. Help's coming."

Anarus twists his face in pain. His eyes are roving everywhere and finally land on me. "Help me. Please."

The words are so quiet. No. No. Not again. Don't do this again.

I keep my eyes on Anarus, but hear the tent flap open. "What? Why?" Death's voice sounds next to me.

"The well's gone." I tell him. "What do I do? The well's gone. There's nowhere for them to go."

He stops, thinking, before he starts coming across the tent to us again. "The well was Winter's. She made it to contain the mantle and put it in Anarus. It wasn't part of the mantle, just the place to put it when she forced it into him instead of passing it on the right way."

Death slings himself around to sit on the other side of Anarus and pulls him back to lean on his chest. "If they've accepted him having their mantle, now that he can take on mantles, they should listen to him. They shouldn't be going to him but to the bridge to cross it, under his command to."

Anarus pants through the pain. "They can't tell... difference. I am the bridge. They know me... They... no difference to them."

Death grumbles under his breath. "They should be able to tell the difference. Damn Winter ignoring them too long. They're too confused. It's the mantle confusing them. They feel the mantle settling on Anarus and are confusing his physical body with his essence as the bridge."

"That's wonderful to know." I scowl over Anarus's shoulder. "You try telling them that!"

"If they are choosing him as the bridge, he'll have to make a place for them, then." Death says, as if that's the easiest thing in the world.

"Great idea." I growl. "How?"

I keep my focus moving between Death and Anarus, who is howling more than ever, eyes unfocused and roving again. The entire time Death was talking, Anarus was writhing in pain, barely able to focus on what we were saying. The last time I saw him this pale… No. I'm not thinking about that.

Death rolls his jaw. "Anarus."

Anarus doesn't seem to hear him, so Death tries again. He places his hand on top of Anarus's head. His voice is deeper, resounding through my bones. "Anarus, calm. You need to let Jinx help you."

Anarus is taking short, sharp breaths, but his gaze finds mine again.

"Good." Death nods his head even though Anarus can't see it. "Now, where do you want them? Where will you make their home, Anarus?"

"I don't know!" Anarus screams.

"You have to choose, son! You need to control them and tell them where to go. Choose!"

Anarus starts crying. "Jinx, where? I can't. Where?"

"They were over his heart." I start to say.

"No." Death forcefully bites out. "Not over his heart again. You'll strain the tether of his mantle as the ender of bonds again."

I reach blindly through my mind. Where? Where should Anarus keep the wilde hunt?

I think of Byder's tattoo under my fingers and Ydum's tattoo on his arm and shoulder. They are both tattoos of power. If Anarus's human-made tattoo of a wolf can cement my bond with Kinshra, maybe his other tattoos can be put to magical use too. "His arm. His left arm. Bound by the barbed wire tattoo to stay there unless he lets them go."

Death grabs my hand on Anarus's chest, with Ydum's and Byder's hands still on mine, and moves it to Anarus's barbed wire tattoos. "Tell them, Anarus. Command them. You are the commander of the wilde hunt. Tell them where to go."

Anarus groans and the shadows start moving. They flood through my hand into his arm, searing cold making my bones creak.

"Too cold!" I gasp out and immediately I feel Ydum's hand over mine change to warm. Byder shifts my hand on his chest and his hand at my wrist warms too. The pain in my hand relents as Ydum's volcano and Byder's connection to fire warm me.

"Jinx." Death says. "Make the tattoo a bind. Don't let them come back out."

I look at the tattoo as a guide of what words to use. "I need the tattoo to bind the wilde hunt to Anarus's arm. I need the barbed wire to be a fence and a gate made at his wrist that can open and close to let them in or out, but the rest of the tattoo holds them there and nowhere else in him. I need the black lines to bind the arm tattoo to contain the wilde hunt. Let the symbols there infuse the fence with power to keep them there, safely in the tattoo, but not in Anarus. His to control and command, but not in him just with him. Bind it with the salt tattoo. Bind it with the gold tattoo. Bind it with the iron tattoo. And bind it with stone tattoo."

Anarus grits his teeth, grinding them as he groans. The tattoos on his arm, thick black bandings and barbed wire, move and shift making a fence that weaves between the symbols for salt, gold, iron, and stone. A new design appears on his wrist, a barbed wire topped gate. I move my hand to the gate and press my thumb to it. The gate opens and the shadows flow in faster and faster. Smoky swirls move along his skin behind the tattoo.

When the room brightens, all the shadows of the wilde hunt inside Anarus's arm, I let go of his wrist. The tattoo of the gate closes and all the shadows stay in the arm. The shadows look like smoke against his skin, but are not going inside him, but just inside the tattoo binding.

I look back at Anarus's face and see he's covered in sweat and still pale but breathing easier. Death slides back, away from him, and I pull Anarus into me to hold him tightly. Ydum behind me moves his hand from mine to rest it on top of Anarus's head while Byder lets go of my wrist to touch Anarus's non wilde hunt arm.

"Man, you gotta stop it with taking on these crazy power mantles. You keep trying to die on us." Ydum teases. "You can't do that anymore. You gotta be here for your girls."

Anarus chuckles weakly. "That's the last one. I hope."

He reaches his arm up to cup my face. His left arm. I see the dark swirls still moving on it. The actual tattoos are still now, but the shadows that look like tattoos of smoke still move, swirling there. His hand, when he touches my face, is that familiar cool then warm, making me smile.

"Do you control them?" I ask. "Will they listen to you?"

Anarus shakes his head. "Yes and no. They seem like they will do what I say but you made the gate. I think you might control the gate, little human."

I sputter. "I didn't mean to make it that way."

"Gotta be careful with those magic words, baby girl." Byder chuckles.

I hear a noise and turn in time to see Death hunch his shoulders and dip out the tent flap. I extricate myself from between my gods, leaving Anarus with Ydum and Byder to take care of him for the moment.

I follow Death out of the tent. "Death, wait."

He turns back to me. I can see he's worn and tired. He was helping Anarus with his power too and it drained him as much as it did me.

"Thank you. For helping." I say.

Death only shrugs. "He's my son."

As I watch Death just walk away, Esnir stands next to me, concerned. "What the fuck was that?"

I sigh. "Anarus now has the full mantle of the god of the wilde hunt. They are with him and under his command."

"Shit." Esnir swears softly. "I think that makes him the only twice mantled god. At least the only one I've ever heard of."

"Thrice." When I correct Esnir, he furrows his brow until I explain. "The bridge, the bonds, the hunt. All three are separate mantles that he now fully carries."

"So, let me get this straight. Between the four of you, who are entangled in a four-way bond, there is a full hunt god, a full nature god, a thrice mantled god of death, and a witch that uses words to manipulate emotional magic with a bonded familiar wolf?" Esnir whistles, tucking his hands into his pants pockets and walking back to the strategy tent. "Who needs an army with you four around?"

I shake my head at him as I go back into the tent. Inside, I see Ydum and Byder talking at the small table in the corner while Anarus is lying down on the furs. He looks more relaxed and his color has returned.

I lie down on the furs next to him and pull his arm to me so I can look at it. The swirly smoke is still moving around in his skin, staying inside the fence his tattoos now make around his arm.

"It feels the same as it did before." Anarus says softly. "Just, only in the arm. It's not so heavy or angry anymore."

"Could you move them like before, do you think? Hiding people with them or making a room dark?" I watch the smoke move. It's almost hypnotizing.

Anarus's voice is a low rumble as he moves himself over me. "I don't know. Why don't we give it a try?"

He brings his mouth down onto mine as he curls his hand into a fist. As he kisses me, his soft lips moving over mine, a slow trail of shadows envelope us. He opens the hand and the shadows stop coming out of the tattoo. He moves the hand under my shirt, using the cool and heat to tease my breast, making me gasp.

He should be resting. He just took on a full mantle and who knows what we'll have to do today. I try to stop him. "Anarus, you just."

"I just gained a fuck ton of power." Anarus breathes out, his mouth trailing down my throat. "And I want you."

I relent, arching into his hand with a sigh.

"Is this a closed party, or can anyone join?" Ydum is staying just outside the shadows.

Anarus looks at me, one eyebrow arched. I nod and he pulls the shadows back into his arm with a twist of his hand. "Guess I can control the gate after all."

Ydum looks at Anarus's arm for one moment, muttering, "Interesting." But then he turns his attention back to me. He spreads his long body out on the furs next to me, on his side, his head propped up on his arm.

Byder sits at my head, close enough to touch but not touching me yet.

Anarus is still hovering over me, his hand in my shirt. He moves, lying on my other side.

I'm surrounded, Anarus on one side, Ydum on the other, and Byder at my head. Three months ago, I would have been in an absolute panic about this. But now, I feel safe and protected.

Ydum pushes on my shoulder, making me roll onto my side facing Anarus.

"I'm gonna ask you something, beautiful and I need you to be honest with me." Ydum rubs a hand on my ass cheek. "You ever been taken here before?"

Now I know why he rolled me towards Anarus instead of him. He knows that when it comes to talking about history, Anarus and I have a different type of bond that lets us feel safe talking about these things.

I look only at Anarus's eyes as I answer. "Yes."

Anarus's eyes move from mine to look at Ydum only for a second. From the slight growl I feel more through the bond than actually hear, I assume that Ydum was looking at Byder and Anarus for confirmation it was one of them and all three of them got angry when they both denied it. They know from that alone when it happened. But they let go of that anger quickly, replaced with a resolve from all of them to erase that memory and replace it with a better one.

"If I said I wanted to do it now, would that make you excited or panicked?" Ydum asks softly, his hand gently stoking up and down my bottom.

I trust them with every fiber of my being. "Excited."

Ydum's hand stills, and I amend my answer. "And nervous."

"Yes or no?" I know that question from Ydum is not for me but Anarus.

Anarus looks at me as he answers. "Yes, but hands stay on her."

"Noted. Byder?" Ydum's hand starts to move again.

I tilt my head up so I can look at Byder as he talks to me. His eyes are dark. "Hand or mouth, baby girl?"

Gods, I love these three. They're establishing everyone's boundaries first. No assumptions, but everything with consent from everyone.

When I don't answer right away, Byder amends his question, thinking it's discomfort making me not answer. "No is an acceptable answer too, baby girl."

I bite my lip. Desire to be bold floods me, but I know what I feel now may change. "Mouth, but."

"Two taps or butterfly. You remember that, right?" Byder says quickly, that deep commanding tone starting to fill the edges of his voice. "Everything stops with two taps or saying butterfly. From any of us."

He looks over at Anarus, who nods, before he looks back at me.

"Two taps. Butterfly." I repeat, knowing Byder will insist on hearing it out loud.

"Are we done with the consent discussion yet?" Anarus rumbles. "Jinx has far too many fucking clothes on."

"We all do." Byder amends before taking his own shirt off.

In a flurry of hands and lips, all four of us strip down until we are all naked. I know I take off my own shirt and Ydum's pants, and Anarus discards my underwear furiously with a growl. "Still hate these things."

Anarus kisses my lips and palms one of my breasts, rolling my nipple between his fingers while letting the cold heat from his wilde hunt hand spark my desire. Byder and Ydum kiss while Ydum's fingers brush their way down my spine, causing me to shiver in excitement, until his hand reaches my thigh. His hand wraps around to the front, pulling on me until I'm pressed back against him, my top leg is draped over his knees and his hard length is pressed against my backside.

His hand goes between my thighs to cup me. "I need you dripping, beautiful." His fingers taunt and tease at me, running up and down my opening, putting slight pressure on my clit before moving away to run his fingers back down me again.

He keeps edging me towards the desire he wants me filled with, bringing his fingers close to where my body is longing to feel pressure, friction, but then moving away before I ever feel like it's enough. He chuckles at me when I let out a frustrated groan, tilting my hips to try to force him where I want him.

When he uses one finger to circle my entrance over and over, my thighs clench together.

"Soon, beautiful." He tells me, moving his fingers completely away from me, frustrating me even more. I know he goes back to kissing Byder, and stroking his cock while Byder strokes his.

Anarus takes Ydum's place, his fingers trailing down my stomach to follow the same pattern Ydum did, only giving me the briefest moments of pressure at my core before moving his hand away to trace designs on my thighs, then returning to my clit, then higher to my nipple and back down again. The two of them keep changing places, while Byder spends his time divided between toying with my neglected breast and teasing Ydum.

When Ydum finally slides a finger inside me, I gasp against Anarus's mouth and he uses the opening to dip his tongue into my mouth. Byder brushes my other breast with his hand, using his thumb to rub my nipple as it pebbles against his touch.

My body warms as the fire burning low in me becomes a raging burning need coursing through my limbs. Ydum's finger doesn't move and I feel frustrated. Friction everywhere but where I want it the most.

When I arch myself against Ydum's hand, wanting more, he tears his lips from Byder's. His voice is rough, his breath rasping. "Fuck, Jinx. You feel so fucking good."

He uses the heel of his hand to grind against my clit as he moves his finger in and out of me. I feel pleasure moving over me, in me, and I moan as he curls his fingers. My body tightens and I feel that spiral of heat get close to the edge.

"Sit her up." Byder's voice is deep, commanding, and Anarus and Ydum do as he says.

Anarus sits up first and, after Ydum moves his hand, he pulls me up. Still facing him, I wrap my legs around Anarus's waist. Anarus moves me onto his lap, lining me up so that he slowly enters me as I sit down on him. I moan as he fills me and he dips his head to kiss along my collarbone.

Byder moves away from us for a moment, and from the sounds, it seems as if he is grabbing something from our bags. He comes back and Ydum moves away from my back for a moment.

When Ydum is at my back again, there's a slickness to him, all over him, that feels different than I've ever felt. His hand spreads my ass cheeks, rubbing between them, spreading more of the slickness while he also uses my own wetness to lubricate me and himself. My half-working brain realizes the slickness is lubrication. I have felt it before, on Byder when he's been with Ydum.

Once Ydum is satisfied with his work, his fingers circle my back hole and push gently into it. Anarus still holds still, while Ydum works his fingers in and out of me a few times. He goes slow and keeps his lips on my hair.

When he adds a second finger, he asks me, "Still good, beautiful?"

I nod, feeling nothing but the frustration that Anarus isn't moving and Ydum seems to be going so slow.

Ydum scissors his fingers inside at me, making me gasp at the stretch. He does it a few more times, then removes his fingers.

Byder uses a finger under my chin to turn my face towards him. "Deep slow breaths, baby girl. Relax."

I do as he says, taking slow breaths. Ydum replaces his fingers with his cock and pushes himself inside me slowly. The stretch of it burns slightly, but Ydum goes slow, allowing me to adjust before moving a bit more. Anarus's hands hold my waist while Ydum's hands are holding my hips and I try not to, but I squirm against the overfull sensation.

I squeeze my eyes shut and shake my head. "It's too much."

Byder grips my chin tighter. "Look at me, Jinx." I open my eyes and look at him. "Do you want to stop?"

All three of them still, waiting for my answer. "No."

Byder nods and, as Anarus goes back to trailing kisses along my shoulder and neck, Ydum moves again, pushing further inside me. Byder keeps telling me to breathe slowly and I listen, my eyes on him as my hands grip Anarus's forearms tightly.

When I am sure there is no way I could feel more full, Ydum lets out a sigh against my ear. "You did that so well, beautiful."

He kisses the spot behind my ear. "Anarus, you still okay?"

I look at Anarus as he contemplates his answer, his gaze on me instead of on Ydum, who asked the question. "Yeah. Honestly didn't expect to be, but yeah."

Ydum starts to move, slow gentle thrusts, and I moan, my head falling back against Ydum's shoulder. I can feel both of them and it is unexpectedly delicious, so much, so overwhelming.

"Fuck, I can feel." Anarus shakes his head. "I didn't think I would feel you, Ydum."

Ydum stops moving again. "Do you want to stop, Ani?"

Anarus looks at me, his brow furrowed. I can feel his confused and tangled feelings, but he asks me. "Do you want to stop?"

I run a hand down his cheek, caressing him gently. There are so many feeling in me, so much desire, I know I don't want to stop. But I need him to know it's okay if he does. "We're asking you right now, Anarus. What do you need? It's your choice too."

Anarus blinks a few times, as if the idea that he can say no is novel for him. "I trust you." His eyes move to Ydum. "And you. I'm okay."

He moves my hand from his cheek back to his arm, whispering. "Don't let go of me, please?"

"I won't let go. I'm right here." I grip his arms tightly for a moment and he nods before returning his lips to my collarbone and nipping gently at my skin. He starts to move inside me, moaning against my skin.

Ydum starts moving as well, timing his thrusts against Anarus's so that the feeling of fullness swings between them, never leaving me empty but alternating from Anarus to Ydum and back. Everything is overwhelming quickly, my breath coming in shallow pants as the tightness in my core grows rapidly.

Byder turns my face back to him again. "You still want mouth, baby girl?"

I nod, unable to drudge up words.

Byder moves his hand from my chin to the back of my head as he rises to his knees, bringing his cock level with my mouth. He doesn't push me, but waits, his hand on my head relaxed, as I kiss along his cock before licking his tip, tentatively.

"Fuck." He groans out slowly and his free hand instinctively reaches out. When he finds himself gripping Anarus's shoulder, he pulls back quickly and changes which hand is behind my head so he can grip Ydum's shoulder instead. "Shit, sorry."

Anarus doesn't respond, but does bite down just a tad too hard on my skin for only a fraction of a second. I squeeze his forearms once and he relaxes, moaning into my shoulder again. Ydum and Anarus increase their paces and I forget what I was doing with Byder, moaning as they both manage to find that perfect spot in me at the same time.

"Fuck, I. Oh fuck." I moan again, feeling my muscles tighten and a pulsing pleasure making my mind empty of all thoughts but how my body feels. The heat of the two of them surrounding me, the feeling of the two of them filling me, overwhelms everything and my body explodes, lightning racing throughout me as my body tenses. Both Anarus and Ydum keep moving, riding out my orgasm until all I can do is quiver between them.

When he senses I have come down some from the euphoria, Byder brings me back to him, pushing his cock against my mouth with the gentlest of pressure.

I open my mouth and let him enter me. As I close my lips around him, allowing him to control the pace, fucking my mouth as I use my tongue to run along his soft skin, he groans.

He uses his hand to keep my head still as he moves in and out of my mouth, sliding a little deeper each time until he is filling me up completely without hitting the back of my throat. He knows from before that I'm not ready for that. Someday, but not today.

The sensation of all three of them, moving inside my body, completely overpowers my senses and I moan against Byder.

The vibrations of my voice makes him growl. "Fuck. Oh, do that again, baby girl."

I do, moaning deeply as Byder's fingers twist into my hair. I dig my nails into Anarus's arms as my body spins pleasure through my veins. I close my eyes against the need to explode making dark flashes spot my vision.

A voice comes from the front of the tent. I think it's Isis, but my brain doesn't have enough power to register it completely. "Hey, guys. Esnir wants…"

Byder, Ydum, and Anarus all yell at the same time. "Fuck off!"

"Oh shit, sorry!" There's a giggle that is definitely Isis, but I don't care.

Anarus moves one of his hands from my waist to press his thumb to my clit and it is the last piece that throws me over the edge again. My entire body tenses and I scream around Byder, my lips clamping against him hard as he drags himself in and out of my mouth furiously.

His voice is ragged as he says, "I'm fucking gonna come, Jinx. Fuck. In or out? One, in. Two, out. Fuck."

I tap Anarus's arm twice and he tells Byder with a harsh, "Out."

Byder immediately pulls out of my mouth and lets go of my head with a long groan. He turns away from me as he comes, groaning my name over and over.

My head, not gripped by Byder anymore, falls back onto Ydum's shoulder as I pant and feel my body tightening again. I quickly crest again, right as Anarus's breath starts to hitch against me.

I feel Anarus's muscles in his arms tense. "I don't. Ydum. I want to." He presses his lips hard against my shoulder as he stills his thrusts. There's a confused feeling through the bond as his pleasure overtakes him. He shudders through his release, but doesn't move away from me.

Ydum follows close behind and we all stay still as our breathing come down to a more normal rate.

Anarus is the first to move away, sliding out of me quickly and out from under me to back away from us.

"Shit." Ydum mutters under his breath as we all feel the confusion coming from Anarus. "Hold on, beautiful." He tells me as he slides slowly out.

I groan slightly as the feeling of emptiness takes over and a slight soreness replaces the pleasure I had felt. Ydum doesn't let go of his hold on my hips right away.

"You okay?" He whispers into my ear.

I nod. "I don't think Anarus is though."

I feel Ydum sigh. "No. Me neither."

Ydum backs up from me, letting Byder help me up, before the two of them move away to the table, leaving space for me to talk to Anarus, who didn't go far, just a few paces back from us. I throw on someone's shirt, not mine I know since it reaches my thighs, and walk softly over to him.

Anarus has pulled on his pants and is standing with his back to me in the corner of the tent, his back muscles tense.

I touch his shoulder gently. "Hey. What's going on?"

He doesn't turn around. "Nothing."

"Nope." I say firmly. "Not doing that. Talk to me."

He turns to face me and there is a tortured look in his eyes that conflicts with the confused but satiated feeling from him in the bond. He mouth is drawn tight, like he has words he doesn't want to say, but also does.

I take his hand in mine. "You're safe, Anarus."

He groans, running his free hand over his hair. "I had. Um, I had a similar experience to you when I was younger." He clears his throat and I know he is talking about Jacob and his friends. "Except I was much younger and it was a male who was supposed to be my guardian."

Fuck. I try not to feel angry. I had guessed some things based on stuff Anarus had said during the games, but an adult? When he was a child?

"How much younger?" I ask, keeping my voice as neutral as possible.

"Ten." His voice is so low I doubt I heard what he said right until his eyes can't settle on where to look anymore.

Fuck. Fuck, fuck. He was a child! I cannot tamp down the anger growing in me. I know he'll feel it so I struggle to find peace.

With my voice as calm as possible, I ask. "Would this be the same male that suggested the originals put you down like a rabid dog?"

He only nods at me. Without meaning to, I squeeze his hand tightly while I grit my teeth.

"You said Ydum's name as you came, Anarus." I try to help him say the words he's looking for. "Were you trying to ask him to stop?"

Anarus's eyes settle on staring at a spot on the floor. "No. I liked it. I shouldn't have, but I did and." He groans again. "I said I would never let a male near me again like that. I told myself I would kill any male that tried, but then I liked it and I wanted... It made me think maybe I, when I was younger, I actually did too and maybe it was." His voice trails off, but the feeling of shame down the bond finishes the thought for him.

I grab his chin and yank his gaze to me. "That was not your fault, Anarus. Not yours. You did not deserve it, you did not cause it, you in no way instigated it. And just because you enjoyed sharing me with another male now, does not mean you in any way deserved or instigated what happened back then. That was an adult and you were a child. You were innocent, and they are the rabid dog that should be put down. And if they are still alive when all this is said and done, I will make sure they aren't anymore. Not. Your. Fault."

Anarus's eyes flick up to me for only a moment, and from that alone, I know there's more to his confusion and feelings of guilt and shame.

"Anarus, what is it?" I wait, letting him come to it in his own time.

"You love me no matter what?" He repeats the line he used during the games before he was willing to tell everyone about his power being death and the extra mantle of the wilde hunt, making me know he is feeling more than just exposed and raw. "I know it, I just need to hear it. You love me no matter what?"

I pull him close, hugging him. He wraps his arms around my shoulders. "I love you no matter what, Anarus."

Anarus buries his face in the crook of my neck and shudders against me. "I wanted." He pauses, then starts again, barely whispering this time. "I wanted Ydum as much as you. In that moment, I wanted Ydum as much as you. I wondered what it would be like to kiss him instead of you. Or maybe even Byder."

I try not to laugh. I know he's feeling so much, his pain from his childhood making this hard and confusing for him, but he had just been sitting with the three of us, all of us sharing love with each other. Byder and Ydum kissing each other just as much, if not more, than he and I had. For him to feel a desire to expand that physicalness to them isn't as shocking as I think he feels it is.

"Oh sweetie, I think Byder would definitely understand that feeling. He was just as upset at first to suddenly have such feeling as I think you are now. And I'll tell you the same thing as I told him. This bond? It's the four of us, together. What you loving one of us means can and will change over time and doesn't have to be the same as how you love someone else. If you feel that, there's no shame in exploring it."

I pull back to look him in the eyes, and speak firmly. "None, Anarus. Just be honest about how you feel, your insecurities with it, with them and I'm sure they will understand. Like you told me, we do this at your pace. Yours, mine,

Byder's and Ydum's. Together."

He grips me tight, hugging me again. I can tell he isn't crying, but only by a sheer force of will. I wrap my arms around him and hold him until the shudders pass. He pulls back from me enough to whisper in my ear. "I love you, little human."

"And I love you, my beautiful, beautiful man."

He pulls out of my arms completely, wiping a hand down his face, before schooling it to his normal grumpy demeanor. In a more normal voice, he says. "Alright. We gonna go see why Isis so rudely interrupted us?"

Oh yeah. Forgot about that. I find some clean clothes and actually dress for the day. Out of the corner of my eye, I see Ydum ask Anarus if they're good and Anarus nods curtly, saying he's talked out about it right now, but that the two of them can talk more later.

While I'm happy that Anarus feels safe enough to leave the door open for the two of them to explore what his new feeling might mean, I will have to find out that god's fucking name. I will kill the male who harmed my god as a child. Or hold him down while Anarus does. Whichever makes Anarus happy.

"Hey, vicious Jinx," Byder says with a small chuckle, "can we go or are you not done planning murders in your head yet?"

I quickly finish dressing and rebraid my hair as we walk to the strategy tent. Inside, we find we are the last to arrive. Esnir, Ayja, and Death are standing at the table, looking at the maps there. Damek, Iella, Kutar, Wren, and Isis are all standing in a group away from the table chatting. When Isis sees us come into the tent, she smiles and winks at me, making my face heat from a blush.

Esnir looks up at us. "Glad you all could finally come." He says with a knowing smile. Damn Isis. She told them why we were delayed.

We go to stand at the table, and the others join us there. Esnir leads the discussion. "Alright, so first, status updates. Where are we with the humans and gods not from the games or their families?"

Damek answers. "There are about twelve hundred humans. Another fifty gods, from many pantheons. We have several groups made up from a lot of them."

He points to a spot on the map of the camp on the table in the middle of the tent. "Any able-bodied humans that can hunt have been put in one group here and the hunt and war related gods are working with them to turn their abilities towards combat. This group is the best one we have, and our best bet as soldiers."

He moves his finger to another section of the map. "Any witch with the knowledge of how to work with plants is with the nature gods, learning to craft plants in combat ways here. There are fewer humans in this group and they are going to be shakier with their magic. One day, or less, is not long enough for that type of training. Any humans that were village healers have been turned to medics. The able-bodied ones are making packs so they can go into combat, if need be, while the less abled are setting up medic stations here in camp."

He points to where the healer's tent was set up, then points to a fourth spot. "Any human with a weather-related skill is being turned to that with weather gods and their camp is here. Everyone else is divided between the able-bodied general skills working with whatever other gods are available to do basic, non-magic skills of defense or offense. The not so able-bodied have been put on food duty, clean up duty, or other basic housekeeping chores with the same said for gods not suited for other positions."

Esnir nods at this information. "I think that's a good setup."

"It is, mostly." Damek sighs and rubs his forehead. "There are still a few problems with some of the humans. Like Jinx and I said before, the power of the High Priest or Priestess being generational unless someone else in the village showed more promise than they do has led to a lot of witches being improperly trained. Many of them have no idea what their magic can really do, and therefore have no idea which group they should be in."

Damek looks around the table. "Someone needs to help these people, guide them to the right place. For the healers, that was pretty easy and most of those people knew their skills. But for hunt versus weather or nature? Many of them didn't even know those could be magical skills at all, much less if they possess them. We have put them with groups based on their physical experiences, if they have ever hunted before or not, but they may be with the wrong group."

Ayja turns to Ydum. "You have a full mantle for nature. While hunting may be more Byder's thing than yours, do you have the interconnectedness that comes with full nature?"

Ydum nods at her. "I do. I can feel the animals even if I can't work with them, and weather is obviously as much a part of my full mantle as plants and such are."

"Could you guide the unknown witches to their proper group with that power?" Ayja asks him.

"I could." Ydum tells her. "And Byder could determine if someone who is with the hunter group doesn't actually belong there and send them to the weather or nature groups to give that a try." He looks over at Byder, who gives him a quick nod. "We'll work together, and with any other partial nature, hunt, war, or weather gods already working with those groups to sort out anyone who is unsure where to go to make sure they are best utilized."

Esnir places a hand on Ydum's shoulder. "Always good to have your amazing brain on a problem, man. I know I can leave it to you to figure out."

He looks back at the whole group. "How are people getting along? Any group dynamic problems between gods and humans or between one village and another?"

"For the most part, the humans and gods have all accepted the setup well." Iella explains. "We haven't even really had any issues as far as people struggling to get along. Humans from different villages, gods of different types working together, or really any clashes between gods and human, even. Everyone seems to just see each other as equals and on the same side."

Esnir moves us on. "What about the original god defectors?"

Esnir looks at Death for this information. "Sadness is definitely on our side. She has asked if Jinx would like to work with her, seeing as emotions are part of her specialty. Hunt, Fire, and Nature are most likely good too. I think we could release them to help the human divisions they're best suited for, under careful watch of the other gods already there. Maybe extract a blood oath from them that they will submit to whichever god has been put in command over those humans. Fertility is raging against her bonds and definitely not here to help. She needs to be talked to again, maybe with a little more pressure."

Ayja furrows her brow. "You think a blood oath for Hunt, Fire, and Nature? Really? Those haven't been done in a while. I don't know who could."

"I can." Death says. "I could do an if, then oath. If you break these rules we give you, then you die. Sadness, as a Fate could do it better, though. An actual destiny bound oath. Or Anarus could learn it as a Fate. I would have taught him a long time ago, if I knew... He should learn how eventually, but it doesn't have to be now." Death looks down at the table, tapping a finger against it.

Anarus slides his hand into mine, squeezing tightly. I look at him from the side of my eye. His jaw is tight, but his head held high. "I'll go with you to learn."

Death looks up at Anarus, surprised. He only nods curtly.

"And I'll talk to Sadness." I say.

"Okay, next." Esnir continues. He looks down at the table and I realize he has a list of things in front of him he's referring to. This is his first time really using his power as a god of war. I would have missed that he felt nervous or unsure if I hadn't caught him fingering the edge of that list anxiously. "The wilde hunt. Anarus, you took your mantle as the god of the wilde hunt this morning. Where are we with using them? How long do we have and under what stipulations?"

Anarus rolls up his sleeve to show everyone his arm swimming with shadow smoke. "I have them. It's fairly what I had before with my shadows, just only in my arm and under more control. I don't think Death's rules for them, limiting them to being out to only between October thirty-first and the winter solstice, applies if I allow them special access. But I can't be totally sure yet. I can let some of them out and recall them now, under better control than I could before, but the solstice isn't actually until tomorrow, so I can't be sure until then."

"Sounds like that's a maybe still." Esnir confirms. "We know that Fertility said the council has given the four of you and Death two days to report, meaning by the end of tomorrow. Obviously, we have no intention of giving a damn about their demands, but knowing what they're thinking helps us figure out a timeline. Whatever we are going to do, that first interaction, I think we need to do it before their deadline expires. Or at least have a solid plan before then of what we want to do."

Esnir looks to his mother now. She is the battle goddess, so she was the one planning the first interaction. Ayja clears her throat. "My first thought is we need to control where the battle, or first interaction as Esnir called it, happens. I think between the issue of bad sightlines in the woods and too much potential innocent collateral damage in the city, we would be best containing the issues to the government wedge of Veirveil. If the nature gods and human witches could work in secret to surround that wedge with plants and whatnot, trapping everyone in that wedge from getting out, and anyone else from getting in, except through the opening we allow in the north woods, we could create a safe zone for discussions, combat, whatever this comes down to. The wolves would make a nice scouting party since they have already established their presence there and can communicate to Jinx, who can communicate to Ydum, any issues as the nature team works."

Esnir looks to me. "Would the wolves be willing?"

"Let me ask." I say and step from the table. As I reach out to Kinshra, I hear Esnir ask Ydum if he is willing to go to the nature group, and Ydum agree.

It only takes me a moment to confer with Kinshra. The pack is willing as long as they can rest as they scout, since this is normally their down time.

I give them the idea to assign one wolf to one original god, and leave the rest on boundary duty, preventing innocents from accidentally getting stuck in the wedge. Since most of the original gods would be in the council hall by now, the wolves assigned to the gods would be able to just rest outside the building for now.

They agree and I let Esnir know what we worked out.

"That's actually perfect, Jinx. Thanks." Esnir says, relieved. "Mom?"

Ayja continues laying out her plan. "With that settled, I say we shoot for a small party going to the government wedge to begin talks with the remaining council tomorrow afternoon when we know we will still have the backup of the wilde hunt. We will have an advanced infantry, probably the hunters Damek said were best suited, just outside the wedge in the northern woods, and a signal in place if combat occurs to bring them in and relief platoons of the nature that don't craft today and the weather behind them, infiltrating the wedge as needed. I would leave the general humans back here at camp for defense and to hold the other wedges of the city. We'll want a different area, close to but not in the camp, set up for refugees fleeing any violence but not necessarily on our side as soldiers. Families with children and so forth."

Esnir shares with the whole group the main concepts of the plan and what our true goals for this are. Everyone agrees that the best first step is to tell the original gods still with the council that they need to step down, have their powers bound, and submit to an inquiry about their actions.

If they agree, Sadness can bind their powers through their destinies, and we can restrict them to their homes like was done with Winter. If they don't, or some subset doesn't, we do it by force, with whatever level of force is necessary to make them submit, including open warfare as a last resort.

Once they are contained, we can run through the systems of gods individually, calling on all the gods in each pantheon one at a time for them to either agree to the new, democratic system of government and be included in the trial for their original god, or not and join them bound.

Kutar makes a good point during this discussion. "We need to separate the government from the pantheons as well. Someone, a full god, will have to be the leader of each pantheon. A full hunt god will need to lead Hunt's pantheon, for instance. We'll still need some system in place assigning which god does what for their pantheon, since we can't just have a hundred full nature gods running around, each trying to control all of nature. But that god, that pantheon leader, needs to not be allowed to be on the council. Or any council. We need to separate those levels of control. A separation of the godly aspects from the government, same as we are doing with the humans with the High Priest being separate from the government."

We all agree to this adaptation of our plans. But before we get much further, I think of an issue we haven't covered. "We are assuming that we can bind the original gods, cut them off permanently. Or, if need be, strip them to mortal or even kill them. What happens when an original god is stripped or killed? What happens to what they made? If they built these lands, will severing them from it permanently destroy what they have created? Will the sky be unmade if the goddess of Sky is unmade?"

"It hasn't happened yet, so we can't know." Ayja answers. "But there are existing full gods for each pantheon. There is a full sky god, Tomnio. If we do one pantheon at a time, we can start with something simple, like fire, see what happens with that first one and be ready for the next, after assuring we have a full god in that pantheon on our side to take over first. Tomnio can make sure the sky stays the sky, even if he has to do it by remaking the sky when Sky is no longer in power."

Chapter Eight

WITH ALL THE PLANS in place, and a timeline set, Esnir assigns everyone to tasks. Death and Anarus will go to the original gods to extract blood oaths of loyalty to the plan and submission under whoever will be the new pantheon leader and the new government. Ydum and Byder will go to their respective human platoons to assist in getting them ready, with Ydum taking his humans to build the trap around the government wedge of Veirveil. Iella and Damek will go to the general human group to lend their support, make sure all the tasks like feeding the wolves and humans is taken care of. Kutar will head up clearing the space on the other side of the river as a refugee camp of some sort. Wren is sent to work with the healers since she still has her magic and has some experience with that. I am sent to work with Sadness and monitor incoming information from the wolves that Ydum will need. Esnir and Ayja continue to maintain the strategy tent, running interference on any major issues and keeping an eye on Fertility.

We all leave the tent and my gods and I move to the side for a moment, finding a hidden spot to talk alone. Death waits for Anarus a short distance away, giving us some privacy. We are all supposed to meet back up this evening, but, especially with Ydum going into the city, we want to talk first.

Ydum gathers me into a tight hug as soon as Anarus pulls a few shadows to seclude us more. He kisses me quickly. "Be careful with Sadness. She's on our side, but she's also angry, which is weird to say. Sadness is angry. Her power may not be stable because of that, and her separation from the other Fates."

I kiss him again and hold him tightly. "You be careful taking the humans into the city. You come back, understand? The wolves so much as twitch, I'll send a panic down the bond and you get the fuck out of there."

Ydum smiles as me. "I'll be back in your arms tonight, beautiful. Don't you worry."

He lets me go and Byder only gives me a swift kiss. He's staying in the camp, so we're not as worried. Byder and Ydum move a pace away to say goodbye to each other while I talk to Anarus.

"You okay going with Death?" I ask him, wrapping my arms over his shoulders.

He leans his head into the crook of my neck, inhaling deeply before responding. "Yeah. Actually, I'm kind of nervous. But an excited nervous. It's the first time we will get to spend time together where I'm not dying or already dead." He looks up and snort softly. "Maybe. Maybe this will be good."

I kiss him gently. "It will be. I think you two have a lot of time to make up and maybe this will be a good start."

Byder and Ydum step back over to us. Anarus steps out of my arms and, before Ydum can even react, Anarus clasps his hand around the back of Ydum's neck, placing a swift kiss on his lips. While Ydum's eyes widen and Byder looks over the both of them with his jaw hanging open, I only chuckle.

Anarus lets go of Ydum quickly, backing away and grunts at him. "Fucking come back, okay?"

Ydum collects himself quickly, gives Anarus a smile and pats his shoulder. "Same thing you said before game six. And I'll follow it the same as I did then."

"You better, or I'll split your lip again." Anarus grumbles before pulling away the shadows and walking off to go with Death.

I hide a grin while Ydum outright laughs. Anarus threatening to split Ydum's lip has become his way of telling the other god he loves him. I'm glad some things haven't changed with Anarus's death.

Ydum and Byder also take off, headed together to go to the part of the camp where their humans are, while I go the opposite way to the small tent given to Sadness. I feel nervous about interacting with the original goddess by myself, and to some extent working on the emotional manipulation everyone seems to believe is my specialty as a witch.

Everyone has said it so many times, including the council during the tenth game, that it's just become assumed that it's true. But I worry about it being wrong. I walk slowly between the tents as I think.

Sure, I am really good at making peace for myself and sometimes others. But that was a mastered skill out of necessity. It was the only way I survived the last six years of nightmares and panic attacks before I felt safe because of Byder, Ydum, and Anarus. Before they taught me how strong I am and that I can keep myself safe.

At different moments, I feel as if I have manipulated emotions of other people for things other than with peace, like forcing truth with when we interrogated the original gods. But how much of that was just how my magic works and something anyone could really do, and how much was something unique to me?

Sadness would be able to tell easily. And I'm scared she will tell me everyone is wrong and I am nothing special. A word witch, something never heard of but, other than my unique way of performing magic, nothing spectacular or unique.

Not that I want to be special or unique. Just, everyone else has assumed I am and have now rallied around that, as if it matters somehow. As if they wouldn't be doing what they are doing if it wasn't for the 'Jinx is different and the gods screwed her over because of that difference' factor.

I arrive at Sadness's tent faster than I want to, despite my slow pace. The camp on the north side isn't that big. Just a smattering of hastily constructed tents between trees that are bare of their leaves and all their low-hanging branches stripped for warming fires. I take a deep breath, blowing it out slowly to calm myself.

When I finally knock against the post situated just behind the tent flap that works as a door, Sadness answers quickly, telling me to come in. I walk in the tent, that's half the size as the one we have, and look around.

Just as ours did before we adjusted it, there's only one small camp cot in the tent with a few furs to keep warm with on it. Sadness doesn't even seem to have brought any clothes or personal items with her to litter the floor or corners of the rest of the tent like there is all over ours. But then again, there are four of us and I'm not sure how much an original goddess can do magically. She may be just calling up clean clothes to her, or staying clean magically too. Or just too pissed about her son's death to care.

"Death said you wished to speak to me?" I say, standing just inside the tent.

Sadness looks up from her spot sitting on the cot. Her cloudy blue eyes are no longer snapping with the anger she held when I interrogated her, but rather look like I interrupted her thoughts just before she could start crying. Her tarnished gold hair is still limp and hanging flatly down her back. She's not wearing the nice, neatly pressed fine silk and velvet clothes she was in the council hall, but the same basic blue shirt and a soft flowy black skirt she was wearing yesterday.

I realize now that I have no idea what Sadness looked like before. She may not have looked so limp and curved in on herself on September fourth, the day before her son Mode's death. She may have been what I expected from a goddess, especially a Fate. Powerful, dominating, and self-assured. Who knows what toll her loss has taken on her beyond the anger I saw yesterday.

"Jinx." She gestures for me to join her sitting on the cot. It really is the only place to sit, so I take her up on the offer, sitting on the opposite end. We both look at the same wall of the tent as we talk. "I felt your power when you interrogated me and, well, it was a nice attempt but clumsily done. If we are going to fight against the powers that be, everyone needs to be at their best, don't they? Which means someone should help you learn to do what your power can do, and the only available one to do that now is me."

Sadness sounds, well, sad. But as she speaks, she seems to find something other than what was plaguing her to think about and her demeanor hardens with determination.

I speak carefully. "I would appreciate whatever help you could give me. Honestly, I went into the games not knowing that what I did was magical in any way. I thought it was just good meditation. But through working with my gods and the other humans, I realized not only is it magic but I do it in a rather unique way. I really haven't had a chance to explore that much since the games ended."

"Your power." Sadness says. "You said magic. I don't know if you remember that the council said for us four Fates to examine your destiny to see if we could figure out why your blood test was off. But we did and the results were interesting, to say the least. It's not your magic, it's your power."

I furrow my brow. "Powers are what the gods have. Unless you mean that, as a witch turned immortal, they are called powers now. But I've not heard anyone else speak of it that way, and I haven't been made immortal either anyway."

"I don't mean that at all." Sadness shakes her head, giving me a soft smile. "This is why I knew I needed to talk to you. I know from hearing the testimonies about the games what you and your gods think about your magic. You were so close to the truth, it's actually a testament to how incredibly smart all four of you are. You figured out that you are not a beginning magic witch nor an end magic witch, but both and neither."

She cocks her head to one side. "Although, Drila let that one slip too, so I can't give you complete credit for that. But you also figured out that needing something, not just wanting it, but having a real purpose for it, intensifies your abilities. You know that you don't need supplies but an already constructed start and can build from it without gathering more base parts. You also discovered that your power comes from the words you say, or think, rather than images or feelings. You were so very close, if you had only had the truth about humans back then, I think you would have truly pieced it all together."

"The truth about humans?" I think about what Death told us, the story that humans were actually fashioned from the gods who disagreed with Inspiration's plan to create these lands. "You mean, that we are all descendants of gods, just not the ones who created Nazus?"

Sadness nods and shifts in her seat to look at me more fully. "Yes, the gods the rest of us vanquished in that first war. Think that through, Jinx. If those vanquished gods were made into the first humans, both the magical and the non-magical ones, and the witches aren't descendants of humans that were gifted magic by us, but are actually humans who managed to retain some of the powers of those vanquished gods, what does that mean about how your so-called magic works?"

I look at my lap, twisting my fingers around themselves as I consider this. The original gods all have a pantheon, and their descendants gain their powers from within that pantheon. Or at least, that's what I was taught.

I ask Sadness to clarify this. "Can a god be born from one pantheon and have a power from a different one? Say a hunt god have a nature child?"

"Yes, but no." Sadness tells me, confusing me more. "That nature child would have to have a nature god in their ancestry. Which isn't all that unlikely. Gods and goddesses intermingled a lot in the early days. It quickly developed into a sort of caste system where the pantheons became more insular. Now, with children only ever born from one god and one witch, the pantheons are fairly straightforward. Every once in a great while, one of those old connections will pop up in a child making the child belong to a different pantheon than its god parent. It just means they had an ancestor from a different pantheon very far back in their bloodline."

Sadness waits while I assimilate this information to what she wants me to think about. Gods can be born, rarely, to a pantheon other than their parent's, but only if they have an ancestor from that different pantheon.

It would make sense, then, that the same could be true of humans. Occasionally, there are humans born to two witch parents who have no magic whatsoever. Maybe it could also be true that a child could have a very different magic type than their parents too.

But for all the humans I know, and according to Damek and the other witches at the games, magic all works the same, with feelings and images, not words. And my gods told me that humans don't actually have specialties in magic. Things they may be better at, of course, but magic is magic to the humans. There're no pantheons in the witches' magic, just better abilities. At least, until they are bonded to a god and their magic develops in alignment with their god's power. Other than me, magic is feelings and images and what you are most comfortable with.

Feelings and images. I groan inwardly. I focused so much on the images rather than words part, I didn't even think about the feelings part. I don't use feelings, I create them with words. Just like Sadness and the other Fates do. Could it be that my magic is akin to Byder's and Ydum's, a full mantle type thing?

"Is my magic just closer to one specific god's power? One of the vanquished gods made mortal to create the humans?" I ask.

Sadness actually chuckles. "Oh, so close. You really are smart. Not closer to but actually is one specific god's power. The use of words is how the gods did everything back then. The world and everything in it was created with words. The world is words made flesh and bone. Back then, we were nothing but thoughts. We didn't have bodies until we made them before we made the rest of the world. That's why so many of us look like our powers. We created our bodies from them. Now, most gods don't have that because of the witch contributions to their makeup. Some pantheons' looks are stronger, so they retain it. Nature the most, but sometimes sky or fire too."

She shakes her head, as if to clear away the distraction of what doesn't matter. "But we were all thought and word before we made ourselves physical beings as well. Your use of words as your form of power is the rawest, and oldest, form of all power and magic. It is how all gods used to use their power, the vanquished and us, the victors. But most new gods feel their powers as part of themselves, similar to an arm or a leg."

I know that from working with my gods to help them take their mantles. The tides and phases of the moon are on Ydum's spine and the volcanoes in his eyes. Byder's hands know the weapons for hunting, while his heart knows the thrill of the kill.

Sadness keeps talking. "Your power comes from an earlier version before changes happened throughout the generations. More beginning than a beginning witch, or even a new god. Fully mantled gods can make a full thing they want or need from nothing. New, unmantled gods can make the base part from nothing quickly, then build something they either want or need faster than normal. Beginning magic witches can call the base parts that exist somewhere in the world to make only what they need. End magic witches can only make the thing that they need with all the parts already there. Because you are an end magic witch carrying a power like a god, you need the base parts, and the need, to start, but then can magically make more base parts after that like an unmantled god."

I shake my head, looking back up at Sadness. "I need more than the base parts. I need the whole thing. I would need a whole carnivorous plant in front of me to make more, wouldn't I? I have to draw from what is right around me. I needed water first before I could make rain. Even when I got better at it, I needed a cup of water to make more water to make rain."

Sadness raises an eyebrow at me. "You did then but do you now? Do you need as much of a start as you think you do? For the plant, sure. But would you need an actual water source anymore? You have a god that has the power to work with and make water. Would you need the actual water if Ydum is right next to you? Or could he just make the water particles in the air and you could use them to make more until you have actual, substantial water? And what about the wind? The clouds? All the other parts of a storm beyond the water? Did you ever need those to make the storm, or just the base parts, water and air?"

"I…" I stop. Would I? We never tried it again after they had their mantles. We just assumed because that's what worked and was our running theory throughout the games. Just as much as Byder and Ydum never really did much to work with their mantles after Anarus died, I didn't do much with my magic—or power, I guess it actually is—either. And none of us ever even thought about the fact that we never had wind or clouds before I made them with my magic just from the air and water. That's sky power, not the same as water.

"As you saw when you worked with Ydum and the rosebud, you need to have a start for what you want to do. But what counts as a start? How much of a start? You were told you were both a beginning magic witch and end magic witch and made assumptions about how that works. Assumptions that make sense for a witch. Making rain, making it warm, making potions, salves and protection circles, they would all still work for you like an end magic witch's would, with the notable exception of not needing supplies past that starting point. But the moment you understood that your magic worked differently than all other witches, words instead of images, creating more of something by just duplicating what you already have, why did you keep assuming you are just a witch?" Sadness looks at me from the side of her eye, watching how I take that question, I think.

"What would I be besides a witch?" I ask, trying not to panic. Is this more of that my dad may not really be my dad stuff from the start of the games? "My parents are both witches. My mom swore my dad is my dad. I'm not anything else. I can't be. The council even tested me again. I'm not part god."

Sadness chuckles slightly. "I am in no way questioning your mother's faithfulness to your father. Or suggesting your parents are not witches. But just like a god can be a nature god born to a hunt god because somewhere way back in their family history there was a nature god, so could a human be born something else. Even if no one else in their family has that trait now. A blonde child in a family of brunettes doesn't mean their mother was unfaithful. Nor does someone being born more than just a witch born to a family of witches.

"Before we fought with the vanquished gods, there were five Fates, not four. Myself, Happiness, Peace, Anger, and Fear. We are not actually separate pantheons, but one pantheon with multiple gods leading it and Happiness, Peace, Anger, and I have just agreed to stay in our own chosen domains.

"Fear was the last god to back out of Inspiration's plan. He was the last god to be vanquished and made mortal, or mostly mortal, and stripped of his power. But cutting his power as a god is not the same as taking his power as a Fate away. Even as a vanquished god, now mortal, he still had the power to create destinies. So, Fear made himself a new destiny. I would guess he made a revenge that would come when we least expected it. A destined descendant to bring back his power and seek revenge for him.

"You, my dear, are that descendant. Fear's descendant. Fear's destiny. While many witches can use Fear's power in their magical ability, use feelings in their magical working, you have Fear's destiny completely. I heard a rumor you even reattached mate bonds, remade them, to Anarus when you brought him back to life. Something a simple witch could not do, even one as powerful as everyone believes you are. Which you are, powerful that is. Just not only a powerful witch. You are also a powerful Fate. The result of very recessive power coming out into the open again. An end magic witch with the power of a Fate."

"That's why my blood test was wrong." I whisper. "Because I'm not a god, and have no ancestors that are from the original gods. But I'm not a witch either."

"You are a witch, Jinx. You are the child of two witches." Sadness corrects me. "You are also a Fate. Just like Anarus is both god and Fate, so are you both, a witch and a Fate. You are a witch with the power of a god, but no original gods as your ancestor. Instead, your ancestor is a vanquished god who was also a Fate. Fear's last stand against the rest of us. He agreed with the creation of Nazus, but not the type of control we wanted over other sentient people. Seems you have a lot in common with your ancestor. And this time, I'm going to do the right thing and agree with the Fate Fear made to be his new destiny."

I go back to looking at my twisting fingers. "Could there be others out there? Other descendants of the vanquished gods carrying their full powers?"

"No." Sadness sounds confident. "When a life is made, whether it is a god or a human, there are many strands braided together for them. Their life line is one. Gods have potentially infinitely long life lines, but humans have a finite one. This line is what Anarus examines as the bridge to determine if someone should cross into the land of the dead.

"There is another line weaved into the life line and the two are connected. Gods have their mantles, that power line that determines the pantheon they are in. Witches have a small, ghostly remnant line left over from their ancestors, the vanquished gods. Magic-less humans have the life line but no line for power at all. Part of the blood test humans take is examining that line to see if it is a descendent of a power line, a god, or a ghostly remnant, a witch. The last part of the braid is the mated bonds. You have four such lines, your three gods and your familiar. Byder has three. Some people have none as they have no mated bonds."

I nod, understanding this. I've seen the lines Anarus has anchored in his heart. They are all braided strands of gold.

Sadness stands for a moment, adjusting her skirt, then sits and continues explaining. "Anarus has his own infinite life line as a god, weaved in with his power line as a god, the one for his mantle as the bridge between life and death." She tilts her head to the side, thinking. "Actually, he would have two power lines now. The second as the commander of the wilde hunt. Hm, interesting. He would be the first one ever with two power lines."

Sadness shakes her head with a smile. "Thoughts for later. Then Anarus has his four mated bond lines. The bond to the three of you and his fourth bond to your wolf, as the god guide. But Anarus has yet another line. His Fate line, as a god who works with destinies, the ender of bonds. Only a very select few people have that line. I have my life line, weaved with my god power line, no mated bond lines, but I do have the Fate line as a creator of destinies. For me, my god power line and my destiny line as a Fate is the same thing. The same is true for Anger, Peace, and Happiness. Anarus would have his god power line and his Fate line as two distinctly separate lines.

"Fear also had those same lines, life and the combined power and Fate line. We cut his power when we made him mortal, or attempted to. The creation of witches shows we were less successful cutting it than we thought. And we put a finite end on his life line, actually attached it to death in a way god life lines aren't. But we had no way to cut his destiny as a Fate. There was no Anarus to end destinies back then. We could end lives, we could stop power, but we could not end destinies, either bonds with mates or the destiny of a Fate. So, when Fear was mortal, he still had his destiny line as a Fate, the line that gave him his ability to create destinies. He was the only Fate we made mortal, so was the only mortal with such a power."

My mind turns all this information over. I speak hesitantly, giving Sadness room to say I'm still wrong, still misunderstanding. "So, I have a mortal life line, since I haven't been made immortal yet. I also have a ghostly remnant of a power line as a witch. Then, my four mated bonds to Anarus, Ydum, Byder, and Kinshra. But I also have that extra destiny line of being a Fate. Fear made his destiny include having a descendant who was human, a witch, but also a Fate and that descendant is me. That's the whole reason my blood test was both, because Fates should be gods, but I'm not. I'm a witch, a human, but also a Fate."

"Exactly." Sadness tells me. "So you know, when you take them down, you will have to have Anarus end Anger, Peace, and Happiness's destinies as well as strip their power if you want it to work. Not even killing them will be enough unless you end their destiny lines. We didn't end Fear's destiny, so even from the land of the dead, he still has some control over destiny. Enough to make you, a witch and a Fate."

Sadness stands up, pacing in the tent. "You are not a creator of destiny, like the four of us, nor the ender of them like Anarus. Your Fate power, that Fear gave you, is to manipulate destinies. This is how you can use emotional manipulations so well. They are intertwined, destiny and feelings. Your control of peace, and Peace's power, comes from the ability to make people accept what they are destined for. Anger makes people buck against that destiny, want to change it. Happiness is more than just acceptance, but actually liking the destiny in front of them. And sadness, it is acceptance while not wanting it. The same as anger without fighting back. Fear would be a lack of knowing what that destiny is at all, an inability to accept or not accept their destiny because they are not sure what it is. This is what you manipulate when you manipulate emotions, Jinx."

She stops directly in front of me. "You know peace. You know how to control it. But you think it is just meditation or the need for it. Try manipulating it now, knowing what it is. You know what destinies look like from helping

Anarus. Look for my life line, Jinx. Find my destiny within it and give me peace about it."

I look up at Sadness. "I hurt myself when I touch the lines. It burns my hand."

Sadness shrugs. "Before, when helping your gods take their mantles, you were trying to manipulate their power lines. When you brought back Anarus, you were manipulating the mate bonds. Your power is not supposed to be used on those two lines. You were brute forcing your power to do something it shouldn't have. The life line should not burn a Fate to touch. Try it. Manipulate how I see, and react to, my destiny on that life line."

She has a point. The lines are different. I burned because I was using my power on the wrong line. I am supposed to work my power on the life line, not the power line or the mated bonds. For a moment, I wonder what the other witches in the games were actually doing when they were examining their god's mantle, if I was actually manipulating their power lines as a Fate, albeit badly apparently. Even though we watched each other practice, we never really talked about what exactly we were doing. Once again, I was doing the magic differently.

I shake my head slightly. Thoughts for another time and potentially Ydum. Deep breath. I need to see Sadness's life line. I open my eyes again and see a soft gold shimmer in Sadness's heart. There's a lot of gold shimmers all over Sadness, but they are the wrong gold, just like with Anarus when I realized the bridge and ender of bonds were different mantles. The gold line in her heart is the destiny over her life. Give her peace over her destiny, I think to myself.

Sadness speaks softly, trying to not break my concentration. "You are not using your magic, but your power as a Fate. You are not giving me peace. You are not creating an emotion, Jinx. You are manipulating how I see my destiny. If you try to give someone an emotion they do not currently feel, you are changing their destiny. The emotion has to already be there somewhere, even if they have rejected it, so you can just build on what is there. Peace is an emotion I could have about my destiny. I have either accepted my destiny, and you only need to encourage me to accept it more, or it is a destiny I've rejected and you have to reject my rejections of it. Intentions matter. Why would this emotion about my destiny matter? Why do I feel what I do now? What do you have to change in my destiny to make the new emotion one I would have? You have to have a need for your magic to work. For you to manipulate a destiny takes a need for their feelings about it to change."

Another deep breath and I examine Sadness's life line. I know why she is not settled or peaceful. She's mourning her son. But I want to see it, the braided rope that is her destiny, then figure out how to see the different emotions about that life's destiny. It comes to me in bits and pieces, each feeling its own strand in the braided gold rope. Heartache, love, mourning, loss, anger at the original gods.

Focus on the love, I think. She loves her son. In my mind, I pluck at that part of the bond and give it a new way to grow. I change how she feels about his destiny. She needs to think differently about his death. He's in the land of the dead, a place of beauty, from what I saw. Death held his hand and took him where he needed to go. He wasn't alone in his journey. The one person I saw cross the bridge before Anarus took his mantle was not stressed or worried when Death met him in the land of the dead. He was peaceful. Modes would have felt that same peace meeting with Death.

I hear Sadness sigh and look at her face. One lone tear is tracking down her cheek. She brushes it away roughly and turns away from me, breaking my concentration and hold on her bonds. "Good. But you took too long. What will you do when you have fourteen original gods, all feeling different things at the same time? Make me angry now."

That shouldn't be too hard. Sadness is already angry. She keeps her back to me as I look for those lines again. I find the anger and pluck on it with my thoughts. My words. This one. Focus on this one. I don't give her a story for it like I did with peace. I'm not manipulating the strand, making her feel something she doesn't want to, but using how she already feels.

As Sadness's face hardens with a low growl in her throat, I lose my concentration as a thought occurs to me. I say it out loud. "This is why Anarus was always the most affected by my attempts to manipulate emotions. I was actually drawing the feelings I manipulated from the bonds he was holding. They're not his bonds, not all of them, but I drew from them, making the emotion go through him first before anyone else felt it."

"Exactly. But can you let go of my anger now?" Sadness says this through gritted teeth. I realize that, while I broke my concentration about what I was doing, I never stopped making her feel the anger.

"Oops, sorry." I think about letting her destiny of anger go and she relaxes, twisting her neck to stretch it before turning back to face me again.

"That was better. Quicker. But now you need to do it with more than one person at a time." Sadness walks across the tent and opens the tent flap. "Are you coming?"

I jump up and follow her. She leads me to the strategy tent. When we go inside, Esnir and his mother are both at the table and Isis is sitting on a chair in a corner of the room, looking at something in her hands that's too small for me to see.

When Esnir looks up, quizzically, Sadness waves a hand at him.

"Ignore us." She says blandly. "Just keep doing what you are doing." She speaks softer, only to me. "Jinx, make them sad. All of them at once."

How? I can't examine their emotions on their life lines that quickly and pluck at the sadness they may or may not have about their destinies. I need to do something else, but what?

"Do you not know what sadness is?" Sadness whispers, standing very close next to me. "Even if you yourself are not feeling it right now, do you know what sadness feels like? You know what their lives are right now, which is part of their destiny. You are seeing their destiny playing out right in front of your eyes. Their destiny to be in a war rather than comfortable at home. You know why that might make them sad, rather than whatever they may be feeling. Give them the directions of where to focus their feelings about that destiny and let it go to build in them itself."

Right. Sadness. Heartache. Despondency about your destiny. Make Ayja, Esnir, and Isis choose that feeling about their destiny. I watch them, looking at each one in turn. Your destiny is not what you want. You won't fight it, but it won't be what you hoped.

Isis lets out a small sniffle. But Esnir and Ayja don't seem to react, having gone back to looking at the papers on the table, conversing softly, and Esnir writing something down.

I step further into the tent, and see Isis is looking at a necklace with a locket on it in her hand. Inside the open locket is a small tuft of hair. Blond like hers, but with gray traces through it. Whatever that necklace is, it has some sadness already attached to it, so she was easily accepting of something she was already feeling, rather than a change. Esnir and Ayja are determined to make this campaign of ours work and are using each other to deflect anything not attached to that determination.

I focus on the sadness more. You can be determined and sad at the same time. This is not what you thought you would be doing after the games ended. This is not what your destiny should have been, either of you. Esnir and Isis should be staying in Ayja's home, teaching Isis all about Veirveil and growing closer together, preparing to make a home and family of their own. Not this. Not fighting for freedom from tyranny. That peace is just another thing the original gods stole from them when they fucked with Anarus, and the loss of that life hurts.

Esnir's mouth twitches. "What are you doing, Jinx?"

"Practice." Sadness answers for me.

Ayja turns her face toward me, her eyes shining from unspilled tears. "Well, can you stop? We're busy."

"Yes." Sadness says, then turns to leave. "Come along, Jinx."

Before I follow her out of the tent, I make sure to let go of the sadness I created. "Sorry."

Esnir only waves a hand at me, dismissively. "You gotta learn somehow."

I follow Sadness again and she leads me to a mess tent in the southern portion of the camp. When we go inside, there are a few dozen humans sitting at tables eating what looks like oatmeal. There are four humans standing at a table, serving the oatmeal from large metal pots. I spot Byder at a table, talking to a few of the humans. He looks deep in conversation, but after a moment, he looks up, spotting me with a confused smile.

"Now," Sadness says, standing close to me again so that she can whisper, "make them happy. Make them feel happy about their destiny, everyone in this room but the cooks and Byder. Do not give it to the cooks and Byder."

Happiness. Joy at what their destinies hold. I look around the room, making myself see each face, but purposely skipping over the cooks at the serving table and Byder. You are absolutely happy about your destiny and what it will bring. Thrilled. Ecstatic about it.

It's much harder trying to spread it through this many people and I start to sweat with the effort. Especially because most of these people are actually afraid of what's to come and making them accept happiness about it is instead of fear is not a normal shift in emotions in this situation.

Byder looks at me curiously. I feel his question of what I'm doing down the bond, but I push it away. Later, Byder. I keep my focus on the rest of the people in the room. My hands tremble from the effort. Happiness, you want to feel happiness.

"It isn't working." I grumble under my breath as I keep pushing.

Sadness sets her hand on my shoulder. "Isn't it?"

Her question makes me take a second look around the room. The people at the tables eating had been either having quiet conversations or just sitting quietly when we walked in. The quiet ones are talking to others at their table now, the volume in the room having gone up a bit with the added conversations. The previously chatting ones seems to be more animated. Is that happiness from them? Or a start of it?

"What reaction were you anticipating, Jinx?" Sadness breaks my concentration completely. "You are in a room full of humans set to potentially go to war with the gods they always thought were invincible, unstoppable. They are preparing to become soldiers tomorrow when yesterday they were lowly villagers who had never killed anything but animals they planned to eat. They are scared, trying to find their strength and determination to see this through. And you made them relax and talk to one another. You got them out of their own heads enough to share their fears and find the hope in their new destinies. That is a major change in their emotions."

She's right. I never thought about that. I don't know what difference I was expecting. Laughter? Smiles? Why would they have that right now, even if they did feel it?

Sadness turns and leaves the tent and I follow her again. We walk slowly back to her tent. "You will be strongest with the five main emotions that people have about their destinies. Happiness, sadness, anger, peace, and fear. Eventually, with enough practice, you may be able to combine some of them. Happiness and peace. Sadness and fear, or anger and fear. Sadness and anger. With even more practice, you may be able to confuse their emotions by giving them conflicting ones. Happiness and fear, like you just attempted and honestly did better than I expected. The more you practice, the larger your influence can be. I could, if I wanted, bring this entire camp to its knees in tears of anguish. But that all will take you time to master. Time we do not have now."

"What about other emotions? Desire? Frustration? Things like that?" I ask.

As we are walking through the camp, I look around at all the people. They're moving through the camp, walking around tents and in and out of open areas between the tents. Some of them seem bent to one activity or another. Others are chatting. I see a god giving several younger males a lesson with bows and arrows. He appears to be showing them how to arch the arrows, sending it up to the sky before it arcs back down to the target. How to shoot over the people in front of them to hit the enemy past the allies, I realize.

Sadness doesn't answer me at first, but stops walking to watch the archers work. "What is desire? What is frustration? Really, what are they?"

I think about that as we watch the archers practice shooting over a tent. There are more people on the other side of the tent, standing out of the way of the falling arrows, guarding the spot so no one accidentally walks through the target zone. Several arrows hit the tent instead of the ground beyond it, and the god goes to those archers to assist them at trying again.

"Desire is just wanting your destiny to be something. For your destiny to include something you want." I suggest.

"Yes." Sadness says. "But think about the five emotions. Which emotions would create that?"

I furrow my brow. "Depends on the destiny, I think. If the thing they want is part of their destiny, it would be happiness and peace. If not, anger, maybe sadness?"

Sadness looks at me. "And fear. Both would include fear. The fear you won't get the thing you want. Even something that could be a part of your current destiny might not be part of your future. You are happy with your destiny, Jinx, the mated bonds with Anarus, Byder, and Ydum. You desire to keep those bonds for a long time. That desire is the happiness you have with it now, the peace that they want the same thing, and the fear something will change and take it away. There is still fear in the desire. All the other emotions are a complex weaving of those five. Just like the colors you taught Ydum are all a complex weave of red, yellow, and blue."

I sputter. "You know about Ydum?"

"Of course, I do. You four talked about it often during the games." Sadness shrugs, smiling. "But I also knew it before then. Fate, remember? We create all the destinies of both gods and humans. We knew that he would be colorblind before he was even born. I do find it rather interesting how you manipulated that destiny with your magic to give him the colors anyway. Twisting his destiny so that, instead of not having the ability to know colors, he only did not have the ability to see them, and making him able to feel them with your magic? It is really amazing what you were able to accomplish using your witch magic and Fate power together when you didn't even understand what you are, much less what you were doing."

"Do you control it, then? Things like that? Did you choose to make him that way?" I twist my mouth, ignoring for the moment that she said I actually manipulated Ydum's destiny. Not just gave him a new way of thinking about it, but changed an established destiny. "Is everything already decided by our destinies? Do you know how this conflict will end before it even starts?"

"We don't know everything. That's not how destiny works." Sadness sighs heavily. She gestures to the archers. "I can no more predict which archer will successfully shoot the arrow over the tent than you or anyone else can. That is determined by how much they pay attention to the lesson they are given, how confident they are in themselves, and a myriad of other factors that are in their own control or other's control. What I can tell you is which ones have a natural ability to be capable of such a shot and which ones don't. The one that don't will have to work harder, but that hard work will give them just as much of a chance of success as the ones that are destined with the natural ability to shoot. And the ones destined to do it well have just as much of a chance of failure if they are cocky about their skill or fail to try hard enough."

Sadness turns away from the archers, continuing to walk. I follow as she continues. "Your relationship with your gods was destined from before your birth. We, as the Fates, knew that you would go to the games if you survived until then. We knew you had the potential for matches there and to develop an intensely strong bond with those matches, if they found you, if you accepted them, if you managed to survive the games.

"In the same way, we knew that Anarus had a destined bond with a witch in the games, but his destiny with it was more tenuous than yours. Knowing what I know now, that was because Winter had to make choices about her son's life in the way that made him go early. Other gods had a hand in that too, including the council. Your choices that affected finding your bonds were minimal, while his were astronomical and mostly out of his hands. But until those bonds between you and Anarus connected to each other, we did not know the other person in the bond for either of you, just that there would be one.

"We made Ydum's destiny, the destiny to be a part of a bonded group, and that much of that bonding would happen because every member of the group is different in some way that is important. We made that part. We did not make the part where that group was his mate bond or that his difference would be his colorblindness. We make the basics when making a life line, and we do not make the mate bonds at all. Those details are filled in by life itself, by destiny itself. Ydum's father needed to be someone who had the propensity to make a colorblind child. Ydum could have just as easily been left-handed, or deaf, or some other something that came from his witch father's blood that set him apart as different to fulfill the destiny we gave him. And his and other's life choices could have made that bonded group a group of friends from school rather than his mate bonds. We make the basics and life fills in the details."

Sadness says nothing more until she stops just outside the tent flap and turns to face me once more. Her face tells me she is considering whether or not to say something. When she nods, I know she made her choice.

"The destiny of your child is already made. We did not make the choices of what that destiny was, just spun that she has one." She shocks me by saying this. "It was almost nothing when it was first created, when she was first created. Now, with all three of them accepting her as their own child, and you as well, her life line's connection to her destiny, and yours, is stronger. I could tell you what she will look like, what her attitude will be like, what her potential power as the child of a Fate witch and a Fate death god will be if and when she is born. But other than those set in stone beginnings, the rest of it is still hazy, with many loose threads in the rope because there are too many moving pieces, too many choices to be made by too many people to determine what will happen for her. Will we win here and she will grow up safe and loved? Will you lose one of your gods and she grows up with only two fathers instead of all three? Will we lose and she has to go to the games, a female god with almost no hope of finding her bonded mate? Will we lose and she never gets the chance to be born at all because you die? We cannot know because too many people have too many choices that will influence which threads will strengthen and connect and which ones will burn away."

My mind is running away with thoughts. Destiny isn't set in stone the way we thought. Sadness called my child "she," like Byder called her "she." I can influence what people feel about their destiny. That's how my magic, or power, really works. Sadness knows what my child will look like if she is born. There's an if to her being born. I made an entire mess tent of people feel a little slice of happiness in a situation where they have no reason to feel happy. Even the Fates don't know the outcome of this whole thing. I am the destined descendant of the Fate Fear. A Fate no one but the original gods knew existed.

Sadness chuckles. "Jinx, I can see that your own destiny is making you confused and your thoughts are too much for you to do more now. Go. Settle your thoughts. We've done what we can for now. The rest is up to you." She leaves me standing there and goes into her tent alone.

Chapter Nine

MY FEET MOVE WITHOUT me asking them to. My thoughts swirl in my mind and I don't even know where I'm going until I enter the strategy tent and crash into Anarus, my arms wrapping around his shoulders to cling to him, pressing my face to his chest. I'm not even crying, more stunned.

Anarus brings his arms around me to hold me, dipping his head to speak into my ear, confused by my behavior. "Little human? What's wrong?"

I don't know the words to say. There's too many of them. I just let the first thing that clearly makes sense pop out of my mouth, muffled by his shirt. "Sadness said she. Just like Byder, she said she. I'm the Fate Fear's descendant with his power and Sadness said she."

None of this helps Anarus understand. He lifts me up into his arms and, on instinct, I wrap my legs around his waist. "I'll be back." He tells the others in the tent.

I know he is carrying me somewhere, probably our tent. But I don't lift my head from his chest to see. There're too many thoughts. My test was red and blue because I'm not a god, and not just a witch, but a Fate too. The child of witches, the descendant of a Fate, bonded with gods. I'm both and neither.

When Anarus sits down, me still in his arms, he leans back from me, his hand lifting my face to look at him. We're in our tent, sitting in one of the interrogation chairs. "Do you want to clarify all that? What did Sadness tell you?"

Anarus's eyes on me, confused and concerned, unlocks everything. I take a deep breath and start talking. I don't stop until I've told him everything that happened with Sadness, everything she said, everything I did. At some point, Byder must have come into the tent as well, because occasionally he or Anarus ask me to explain a detail or make a grunting noise of surprise or comprehension as the pieces of what we thought about my magic during the games make more sense.

"Well, fuck." Anarus. says when I finish. "And here I thought my time with Death was eye-opening. But Jinx has to go and learn she's a fucking Fate-god-witch combo thing. You really made a whole room feel happiness?"

Byder answers for me. "It was the strangest damn thing. That's why I came here. She and Sadness were just standing there, Sadness with a weird smile on her face, and Jinx concentrating so hard she started sweating. Then, suddenly, everyone in the room was all relaxed and talking and the humans who had been talking to me with all this anxiety just weren't anxious anymore. Then, the two of them left and it was like the spell broke. Which, I guess it kinda did. No one else really even thought anything was strange about it, but I knew it had to be Jinx's doing."

I'm still sitting on Anarus's lap, sideways to him, with his hands wrapped around my waist. "Anarus, she said she."

"I know, little human." Anarus places his lips on my temple, a soft kiss.

Byder lets out a short laugh. "I think you gotta change your nickname, Anarus. Wouldn't you calling Jinx little human be the same as when she kept swearing by saying oh my gods?"

I feel Anarus jerk slightly as he suppresses a laugh too. Which just makes me want to laugh too. Which sets Byder off again, and we all just end up laughing.

"Fuck." I sigh, feeling less overwhelmed. "Esnir already thought the four of us are our own fucking army, what's he going to think now?"

"Baby girl, we are our own army." Byder tells me. "But unfortunately, I have to get back to the actual army we're making. I just wanted to make sure you were okay."

I nod. "I'm okay. Just wow." He kisses my hair and leaves, leaving Anarus and I alone. "How was it, with Death?"

Anarus groans for a moment. "Awkward as fuck. But good too. I know how to extract blood oaths now, which might come in handy. And I get it, at least some, why he never tried to come back before he felt me die. We talked. Well, he talked, I mostly listened. Winter made all sorts of promises to him about me. He was banished. He didn't want me to suffer because he's my father. He didn't want me banished or something because of something I couldn't control. I'm not sure I forgive him for never checking in, at least, but," he shrugs with one shoulder, "maybe someday."

I wrap my arms around him again. "At your own pace. When all of this is done with, you two can work on things at your own pace."

We sit quietly together, just absorbing everything that has happened, everything we both have learned about ourselves.

Eventually, Anarus speaks again. "We should probably tell Esnir he has two Fates instead of one to work with."

"Three." I remind him, with a chuckle. "Sadness, me, and you too, Anarus. Two Fate gods and one Fate witch."

Anarus shakes his head. "I think it's going to take both of us a while to accept what we are. The reality of everything we are. But at least now we understand why you and I are so connected. I'm glad it's nothing more, nothing like I feared. For a while there, at the end of the games, I worried it was that you and I had a deeper bond than we had with Byder and Ydum and it would make more of Saffron's accusations true. I'm glad it's not that."

I agree and we go back to the strategy tent. When we enter it, Ydum and Kinshra are both inside, along with everyone but Byder. I'm startled to see my wolf familiar there, standing next to Ydum, her tongue lolling as he absentmindedly scratches between her ears like it is the most natural thing in the world.

Ydum's talking, pointing to a map of Veirveil as he does. "There's a barrier of vines that is woven around the entire border of the wedge, minus a small opening here to north that is blocked by wolves and a few human guards. Woven into the vines is wild and cow parsnip plants. Inside the wedge, there are poison oak, sumac, and ivy plants spaced every two feet apart, built up to wind around the parsnips to make a tight netting, meaning no one can go through them to the vine border without touching them. Between the poisons, is oleander that, as it sits, is not an issue but could be burned or otherwise used as weapons later. Outside the vine border is rows of rose bushes, magically enhanced to have extra thorns of substantial lengths."

I smile slightly at Ydum's description of how they used plants to hem in the government wedge of the city. It's close to the plan we used against the yetis in the copse in the first game. My plan that I had him do.

Ydum turns the map slightly. "Within the wedge, we have made caches of plants here, near the council homes, here near the council hall, and here near the sole entrance and exit. These plants are primed with power from various nature gods and have a trigger that any mature god or witch can trip to make them explode with rapid growth to be used offensively or defensively. Thorn-laden vine whips, poisons of various types and sap that can be used as a fuel for fire or as their own toxic substance in each plant. We also made a cache in each of the other wedges, just in case, and have them guarded by a sole wolf."

Ydum stops talking and looks down at Kinshra. I realize he's listening to her and that's why his hand was on her head. After a moment, he continues. "Kinshra reports that the council members are all accounted for, all fourteen remaining as well as the human seat. They have not moved since they arrived there this morning. A person did come into the wedge before we sealed it, they believe to deliver food, but they led him, nicely, out the north exit when he left. There are no other humans or gods inside the wedge besides the fifteen of them and one more god inside the building. I assume the god they don't know is the door guard in the council hall, Drew or whatever the fuck his name is."

"That's perfect, Ydum." Esnir claps him on the back. "Love the cache idea. Can Kinshra understand me if I speak to her?"

Ydum looks down at the wolf then back at Esnir. "Yes. For the most part."

"Thank you, and your wolves, for your assistance. Will you continue guarding the council gods and the northern exit? Will you make sure Drew is allowed to leave the government wedge as an innocent at the end of the day, when he leaves the council building?" I love that Esnir looks at the wolf as he speaks even though he knows Ydum will be the one to speak for her.

Ydum waits only a second then answers. "Yes, to all of that. She requests food be provided near sunset if possible. She can move the food to the wolves if it is given to her in a way she can distribute easily."

Esnir nods at her. "We'll see it done." He notices me and Anarus have returned. "I'm going to assume the time with Sadness was enlightening, Jinx?"

I square my shoulders as Anarus and I move to stand at the table with everyone else. Ydum gives me a look like maybe I want to take over with Kinshra, but I give him a quick headshake. He's got that under control, no need to change what's working.

"Very. She believes I am a Fate as well as a witch. Specifically, the destined descendant of the Fate Fear that was stripped of power, but not his destiny, and made mortal to become one of the ancestors of the humans. As such, I have the power to manipulate the emotions of fear, anger, sadness, peace and happiness in relation to one's destiny, a very, very beginning power, on top of being an end magic witch who just happens to not need more supplies because, as a Fate, I can create them like a god would. I am not totally an end witch, and not totally a Fate with god powers. I am neither and both. I made an entire mess hall of humans, minus Byder and the cooks, happy. And made the three of you in this tent at the time sad as practice."

"That's what the fuck that was." Ayja breathes out. "I was wondering."

Ydum's eyebrows are in his hairline and I feel his curiosity through the bond. Later, I send him with a small smile. That male is going to want all the details and to try experiments, I know. Ever the academic.

But at that moment, Ydum's fingers must hit a good spot on Kinshra, because her back foot starts to twitch and she lets out a small whine. I have to hold back the laugh, as does almost everyone else.

Ayja shakes her head, smiling, and goes back to the plans. "We have decided that tomorrow the first wave will be Anarus, Byder, Ydum, Jinx, Esnir, Isis, Damek, Iella, Death, Hunt, Fire, Nature, and Sadness. You thirteen will breach the council hall and state our objectives of them stepping down and submitting to being bound. Second wave, the hunter group Byder is working with will enter the wedge but hold the exterior of the building with the wolves currently there. Third wave, will be the nature group who did not go with Ydum today. We had said they would remain at the northern exit, but with the addition of Ydum's caches, we will add a team of one nature and two hunters acting as guards for the nature witch to be stationed at each of them. Fourth wave, weather group will stay in the woods surrounding Veirveil covering advances and retreats to the northern exit. Everyone else stays back here, Kutar and myself manning the camp and Wren manning a refugee station to the south of this camp, past the river."

Esnir looks at Kinshra again. "We will need a signal system. Something to tell each wave to either advance into the council wedge, or building as the case may be, or retreat back toward camp. Would the wolves be able to help with that?"

Everyone looks to Ydum and Kinshra. Ydum only looks at Kinshra. "If Jinx can relay to her which direction is needed, she suggests one long howl means advance, three broken howls means retreat. This is their traditional signal system, all the wolves are comfortable with it. If all the groups move both forward and back as a unit, hunters advance in the building as nature moves to surround it, and vice versa, that makes it a clear signal for everyone. Sustained howl without let up means everyone descend on the council building, all the groups. Sustained broken howls means get the fuck gone, everyone, even the people at camp. Alpha will assign one wolf to each group to spread the signal along."

"I never want to plan another war without wolves. So fucking helpful." Ayja says, then cocks her head, amending her statement. "Scratch that. Let's just never have to plan another war. I like not doing much with my power."

"Where do you want the wilde hunt?" Anarus asks.

"With you." Esnir cross his arms over his chest, stepping back from the table some. "Since their use is iffy, I want them as the first defense for everyone in the building with us. The powers of two hunts, two natures, two deaths, fire, war, chance, two witches, and now not one but two emotion wielders? The council is going to be hard pressed to refuse us. But if they try anything and you can still get the wilde hunt to do what you want, add to that making them blind and deaf to each other? We may not even need anyone else."

"Don't forget all the power they have in there." I say. "We sound great in theory. But compare that to their inspiration, sky, water, wind, knowledge, curiosity, half fertility, at least three seasons, and three emotion wielders of their own? Are we really? Plus, that Drew fucker and whatever he can do."

Death, who was silent and standing away from the table the whole time, paces back towards the group. "Inspiration, Knowledge, and Curiosity are great for coming up with ideas, but useless in a fight. The hunts and war can take them down easily. The seasons are outmatched by the two natures who pantheons technically encompass the seasons, as are Sky and Wind. The witches can balance their numbers to our side, and take care of Fertility who has almost nothing to add to their power of offense or defense. Water and Fire cancel each other out. And they don't know you are a Fate, Jinx. The other Fates will fight Sadness, thinking it is all her. And that Drew fucker, as you put it, will probably run, pissing himself. And Anarus and I have not even lifted a finger yet. Much less the wilde hunt."

"The only question left," Death adds, "is who is our spokesperson? If we are going in with the initial idea of this being a peaceful surrender, someone is going to have to do the talking."

Slowly, every head in the room turns to look at me.

"Oh, fuck no." I breathe out slowly.

"You were the one to start this party back in the games." Isis says. "You should have the honor of ending it."

I blanch. "I didn't start it. Aretha overheard me and she did it all. It was never me."

"Who united all the humans?" Esnir asks.

"Aretha." I retort.

"She may have been the outspoken one, but it was you we rallied around, Jinx." Damek says with a wry smile. "Who got the gods teaching us all to fight?"

"Anarus." The fuck if I'm being the spokesperson.

Anarus chuckles behind me. "For you. To protect you. Who always tried to make Drila acknowledge the lives lost?"

"Okay, that one was me, but damn. No."

"Who was always vicious Jinx demanding this shit change from the first moment her bare feet hit the sandy floor of the cave?" Ydum asks.

"It's not a fair question if you use my name, Ydum." I run a hand through my hair. I'm not winning here, I can tell. "Fuck. You all want it to be me?"

Every single one of them nods, even Death.

"It was always going to be you, Jinx." Esnir tells me. "All of this comes back to you. Starting with your shitty birthday and ending with an army made in your name. This was all planned by destiny, literally by a Fate, your ancestor, for you, because of you."

"Do I get a vote in this?" I ask sarcastically, knowing the answer is no. I groan and deflate. "Fine. Somebody better give me a clue what the fuck to say, then, because if not, I'm going to be a bumbling idiot and make us all look bad."

For the rest of the afternoon, I sit with Ayja and Esnir, working on what exactly I am to say when we negotiate with the council of the gods. I keep throwing up oppositions they may say and the two of them help me strategize answers and when to say fuck it all and start with force.

Ydum heads back to his nature group, to assign roles of who will be where tomorrow. Anarus runs messages to Byder, letting him know to coordinate with Ydum on the groups defending the caches and inform everyone else of their positions and the signals to be on the listen for. Anarus also informs the weather group of the same things, since no one from their group was in the meeting. Everyone else goes to their groups to prepare as well. Wren snags Isis to help prep the land on the other side of the river for potential refugees.

Interestingly, Death stays behind in the strategy tent. He doesn't participate with Ayja and Esnir talking to me, but doesn't leave to do something else either. I don't know what he is staying for. I wonder who is guarding Fertility but don't ask.

Eventually, Anarus comes back to the strategy tent, bringing food for everyone including Death. He also carries packages wrapped up in bloody looking paper. At first, I'm nervous about them. But then Anarus kneels next to Kinshra, placing a hand on her head, and I realize it's dinner for the wolves. He devises a system for her to carry the packages where she can trot while carrying them, but still only drop one at each spot. Kinshra takes off and Anarus joins us at the table.

He leans into me, placing a kiss in my hair. "Eat food, Jinx."

"Okay, Byder." I tease him, but grab a bowl of the soup and a piece of crusty bread anyway.

As we all continue discussing what to actually say when we confront the council of the gods, everyone eats. I pick out the soft innards of the crusty bread to use as a scoop to sop up the last remnants of the soup at the bottom of my bowl, leaving the crust in a perfect unbroken shell. Anarus, as soon as I have the last bit of soft bread picked out, swipes my hard crust and eats it.

Ever since he did that at the beginning of the games, it has been our tradition. I don't like the hard crust and he does. During that month he was dead, I wasn't able to eat crusty bread at all because the leftover ring sitting untouched made me beyond sad. It's weird the little things that become so important.

When we decide that we have covered every contingency we can think of, and I have almost accepted my role as the voice for the group, almost but not totally, we call the game.

I realize that, since we arrived, I have not checked on my father or sisters. Anarus and I decide to wander the camp and figure out where they are. Dad and Finnegan are probably with the hunter group, so we start there.

When we get to the area that has been assigned to the hunters, we find that they have rearranged their tents to make a circle around a small clearing in the trees. There are several circles and clearings, as the hunter group is the largest, but one circle has the largest clearing and the most tents. In the smaller clearings, there are handfuls of people wandering, talking, or practicing.

In the largest clearing, people are working with the different weapons they brought. Byder, Xolios, and a few other partial hunter gods are moving around the group of about fifty humans to correct angles and grips. These hunters are used to their prey being animals, rabbits or deer, not people. Just like the group Sadness and I saw in the morning with the archers, they need to adjust to the two-legged, upright targets and the fact that there may be allies between them and their target to avoid.

I scan the crowd and quickly see my dad and Finnegan working with a hunter god I don't know. They seem to be learning dual-wielding knives. What surprises me is when I see Dahlia and Catarina with a large group of other females. They're watching as a female hunt god overpowers a male hunt god, their gazes intent on the female's every move.

When the gods stop and slowly recreate a move, I realize the gods are teaching the human females how to overpower a larger attacker. It's the same instructions my gods gave me in the games. As I watch, the male god calls Catarina forward and she practices breaking out of a hold, successfully. Dahlia takes a turn and she struggles more, but gets there after a few tries.

"Looks like you aren't the only tough as nails Bloodmorrow girl." Anarus snickers behind me. I nod in agreement.

We leave them to their work and wander to the nature section of the camp. They set up their tents in a similar fashion as the hunt section, but instead of many small clearings, there are only two, one large one and one small one. In the large clearing, everyone is gathered together in two different groups. One group is obviously watching the instructions while resting, sitting on logs just outside the tents.

The second group is closer together, standing in the clearing center, something small on the ground in front of them as they listen to Ydum, Nature, Otuna, and Zimuna talk. Nature bends down as Ydum talks and does something to the little bundle on the ground in front of him. The bundle explodes into a tangle of thick vines with sharp looking thorns. They're teaching the witches to trigger the caches.

In the training group, I spot Samantha and Myrna. They're giving Ydum rapt attention before bending down themselves to attempt triggering their own practice cache. Myrna's blooms immediately. Samantha's takes a couple of tries before exploding. I look through the resting humans and see Shearah. She's chatting with a few other witches sitting on logs in front of a tent together. I walk over to her and she waves me closer as soon as she notices me.

"Jinx. Meet Mina, Sirene, and Sybil. They're my tent mates. Guys, this is my youngest sister, Jinx and lurking behind her is her god, Anarus."

I suppress a smile at Shearah's introduction of Anarus. He really does tend to lurk sometimes. I give them all a slight wave.

"I thought you said she had three gods." The one I think Shearah said was Sybil says.

Before I can answer, Shearah does for me. "She does. That blonde hottie that took us out this morning to the city, the one who had the wolf with him the whole time, that's her god Ydum. Byder, her other god, is with the hunters." She yanks a thumb toward Ydum, prompting a fake moan from Mina.

"Aw, so he's spoken for? Damn." I try not to bristle at the way Mina is eyeing Ydum, or blush at the fact that Shearah called him a blonde hottie. Instead, I focus on what Shearah said.

"You went to the city with Ydum this morning, Shearah?"

She nods vehemently. "All four of us did. It was amazing, using my magic completely unrestricted like that. I mean, we couldn't do what your nature gods could, but once they got stuff growing, being able to make it weave around like that? I've never felt anything like it. It was such a rush! I didn't realize how limited we were by High Priest Breedlove and all his rules about how we could use our magic."

Huh. Guess we all were taught wrong by him. We'd always been told that my sisters and I didn't have much magic at all. My dad is more potent than most male witches, but that was always said in a comparison way. Like, that if he was female, he would have been considered average, but since he is male what he can do is impressive. But only a little impressive. I wonder if he really is more powerful than I thought too. More like Damek than I thought.

How many people in our village thought they really had nothing much magically, but in reality were just never taught well, all because High Priest Breedlove was afraid of losing his family's position of power?

"Do you know where Ganna and Ophelia are?" I ask my sister.

"Ganna is over working with the healers. She actually started apprenticing with Granny Helen while you were at the games." Shearah tells me. "Ophelia is with the weather people."

Both of those statements shock me. No one told me that Ganna is working with our village healer to learn the trade when we were in Greenbriar. That's not a small thing. Granny Helen is very selective in who she will teach. And Ganna isn't just learning from her but actually apprenticing? Is Granny Helen thinking of handing over the reins to Ganna once she is fully trained? That would mean Ganna really is extremely talented at the healing crafts.

And Ophelia with the weather magic group? When did that happen? How? My whole life we had only ever been taught about protection magic, basic healing magic, and about stones, crystals and other helpful objects. We were never taught anything about weather magic. But then again, I did make it rain in a washroom with only a few days instruction. Maybe the idea of my sister being talented in weather magic shouldn't surprise me so much.

I let Shearah get back to talking with her new friends. Anarus and I take off to the healers tent, which is a hive of activity. There are people bustling around everywhere. Some are making bandage rolls, while others seem to be coming and going as they deliver plants to a table where I see Ganna and some other witches working furiously.

As I meander over, I see that Ganna is using magic to quickly dry and grind up parts of the plants. She is putting each ground up plant part in a labelled jar. There are a good twenty jars in front of her already full.

When I look at the jars with my magic, I see a green glow around them. Ganna has infused them with her magic, a really potent magic, to make their natural properties so much stronger. They are prepping plants for making salves for all manner of injuries. Ganna's forehead is furrowed and her back bent to her work, her complete focus on what she's doing. I'm loathe to interrupt her, knowing you never interrupt a casting witch, so we leave the tent and find the weather group.

The weather group is the smallest in the camp. There's only one small circle of tents around one small clearing. About fifty people are gathered in the clearing, and I think that's everyone for this group. Fire is there, as are a few partial weather gods, working with the witches, but the group seems to be struggling. There are several groups of people sitting in circles together, about four or five in each, all staring up as Fire and the other weather gods move between the groups talking to each of them individually.

I see Ophelia and another four witches, three females and a male, sitting on the ground, facing each other with their heads tilted up. They are all slouching as if feeling defeated, but their faces still show intense concentration. Fire seems to smile and nod nicely when talking to each group, but as soon as she stands up to move to a different group, her face shows a level of defeatism too.

"They seem to be struggling." I say quietly to Anarus.

Anarus nods. "Maybe we should help. Weather is not really Fire's forte. And I don't know how much the other weather gods would know about trying to teach this to witches."

"Us?" I turn to see his face. "How could we help?"

"You made it rain in a washroom. You know how a witch would do this."

He's right. My magic, or power, whatever, isn't weather based, but I do have experience with it. Even if I use words instead of images. I walk actually into the clearing and Fire notices me.

"Please tell me you are here to help." She pleads with me as soon as I am close enough.

"I can try." I tell her. "It's not really my thing, but I've done it before."

Fire relaxes visibly. "It's not mine either, but fuck if these humans aren't determined. Tell them they can do a magic and they will fight tooth and nail to figure it out."

"I know that feeling." Anarus quips behind me.

I scowl at him playfully. "What have you tried, Fire?"

"Rain. Figure with the cold what it is, they get rain, other weather stuff won't matter. The rain will freeze all on its own."

Sounds familiar, I think to myself.

"But how?" I push her. "How are they supposed to make the rain?"

Fire's lack of an answer and blank stare tells me everything I need to know. She isn't giving them a good how. I nod and move over to the group Ophelia is sitting with.

"Struggling?" I say as they all shift to give me space in their circle.

They all nod. "This is my sister, Jinx." Ophelia introduces me. "She won the games, so if anyone can help us, it would be her."

Thanks, Ophelia. No pressure or anything, right?

"You're trying to make rain, right?" I say but don't wait for the answer. "What are your intentions? What is the need you are trying to fulfill?"

When the five of them just stare at me, I try again. "Okay, back to basics, then." I think of how my gods taught me to make the rain, and what Damek told me about how other witches' magic works. "Let's start easy. Meditate. Find your peace, find your magic."

I watch. All five of them close their eyes and I can tell by the change in their breathing and the straightening of their spines that they are all grounded in their meditation.

"Now, think of all the possible reasons this spot right here in front of you needs rain. Don't think of the rain itself yet, just reasons why you need it."

The male speaks without opening his eyes. "It doesn't need it, though. We want it because we want to use it as a weapon."

"That's true, but does the water you want to use know that?" I explain. "What are the reasons this piece of land might need rain that the water would understand? Say them out loud to each other."

Ophelia catches on first. "It's too dry for the grass to grow."

"Good." I say. "What else?"

A female with blonde hair pipes up. "To put out our fire?"

"To give us something to drink?" A black-haired female adds.

"Nice." I shift in my seat a little and glance up at Anarus standing a few feet away. He's watching me but not saying anything, his face impassive. I can tell he is thinking something because of the bond, but he is actively trying not to, I think, so he doesn't distract me. "Now, hold onto those reasons, those intentions and feel the air with your magic. There is water there. Imagine it coalescing together to make the rain cloud you need to fulfil those intentions." I would just tell it to do it with words, but I adjust for what Damek said most witches do.

Small wisps start trailing through the air in the center of our circle. I don't know if it's all of them doing it or only one. I need to figure out if any of them need more help. "When I touch you, open your eyes and look at the center of the circle, your intentions clear in your mind, and add to what is there."

One by one, I touch the knee of everyone in the circle. I go with Ophelia first. She opens her eyes and stares at the small tendrils of clouds. As she furrows her brow, the tendrils start swirling together.

I nod at her and touch the knee of the male next to her. He opens his eyes and the small swirls Ophelia had shifted closer together get thicker, having more substance. I give him a smile when he looks at me for approval.

Next is the female with black hair. She opens her eyes and gasps when she sees the others' work. Her concentration falters for a moment but she recovers quickly. As I watch, I see she is cycling through using her thumb to crack the bottom knuckles on her fingers on each hand over and over, a nervous tic that helps her focus better. I ignore it as she adds more dimension to the swirly tendrils and they begin to look more like a cloud than just puffs of white air.

Next is a female with red hair that hadn't spoken to me yet. When she opens her eyes and looks at the almost clouds, she straightens her back as if seeing that others have done it emboldens her. Quickly, the almost cloud takes definitive shape and grays slightly.

Finally, it's the female with blonde hair's turn. When she opens her eyes, she stares at the cloud apprehensively. Her mouth moves with no sound coming out. Nothing happens with the cloud, though.

"What are you thinking and saying?" I ask her quietly.

Her cheeks blush. "Please work."

I bite my lip, understanding the frustration and worry she's probably feeling. "Know you can do it. You have to insist on it. This is what water should want to do. It should want to gather in clouds to make rain. You just need it to do it faster than it normally would, and in this one specific spot. So, tell it to. Be bold and know that you can tell it what to do."

She shakes her head, tears gathering in her eyes. "My magic is weak. High Priestess Pauline always said it. I'm not that good. I don't know why they even put me in this group."

"Who put you in this group, do you know?" I ask kindly.

She bites her lip. "Some male god. He was really tall with blonde hair, super green eyes and greenish skin. He was nice but when I said I couldn't do much magically, he shook his head and told me to come over here. I don't know how he decided."

"Ydum. I think that was Ydum." I look at Ophelia, who nods, telling me I'm right. "He's one of my gods from the games. If Ydum said you can do this, you can. So, fuck what your High Priestess said. That's bullshit. Even I made it rain in the games and I have no weather skill at all. So, recenter yourself and show your High Priestess who you really are, who a god of nature believes you can be."

The female closes her eyes and takes a deep breath. I encourage her with a little tug of peace. When she opens her eyes to focus on the burgeoning cloud, she is more determined as her lips start moving soundlessly again.

"Say it out loud if you need to." I tell her. "State your intentions clearly."

"The flowers need a drink. The grass is too dry. Make mud for building a house. The refreshing smell after the rain. Peaceful background sounds for sleeping." As the female lists her reasons for needing rain, which are far more creative than I ever was, the small cloud darkens and drops of rain start to fall in the center of the group.

The female squeals in delight. "I did it! I actually did it!"

"You all did." I beam at all of them. "Now, keep going. Make it cold and ice, or snow. Should be easy right now. Then, change it back to rain. That'll be harder because it's winter and the water wants to freeze, but try."

I stand up and realize that Fire and Anarus, as well as all the other groups had been watching this little group. The other groups move away to sit back in their circles and try what I had told this little group to do.

Fire shakes her head with a smile. "That was impressive. Thank you."

"Glad I could help." I say, then Anarus and I leave to let them get back to work. As soon as we are out of sight of the group, Anarus grabs me by my waist and turns me into him, kissing me deeply, his hands running through my hair.

By the time he lets my lips go, I'm panting slightly. "Not that I'm complaining but what was that for?"

Anarus gives me a half shrug, looking down. "Seeing you that powerful and teaching others to be too was kinda hot."

"Mm. Then, I guess I'll have to do it more often." I tighten my arms around him and kiss him again.

Anarus moans into my mouth and steps forward, walking me backwards until my back runs into a tree. His hands are roving everywhere as he kisses down my neck. One of his hands finds the back of my right knee and hikes it up to rest on his hip as his body presses tighter against mine. I can feel his hardening length through our clothes and know exactly how hot he found it.

I gasp, pushing my hips against him in return. Then, I hear a few snickers and instantly blush. "Anarus, people." When I look, several people are walking between the trees and looking at us with mischievous grins.

He drops my leg, swearing under his breath. "Fuck. I miss the games where we had so much privacy all the time."

I chuckle at him as he disentangles himself from me with a distinct snarling frown. "Missing the games? Who would've ever thought that would happen?"

Chapter Ten

WE GO BACK TO our tent and wait for a while, sitting at the table. Anarus is looking over copies of the maps of Veirveil Esnir had given him. I, on the other hand, am just looking over and over the paper where we had written down things I should say to the council. Before too long, Byder and Ydum both come back as well. They walk into the tent together, discussing which plant witch to put with what two hunters at the caches tomorrow.

Ydum drops ungracefully on the furs as soon as he enters the tent, letting out a long groan. "Fuck, that was a lot today."

He looks exhausted. Of course, he would be. He spent the morning building the defenses around the government wedge then the afternoon teaching witches to trip his caches and what to do with them after they trip them. This was probably the biggest use of his power ever, including in the games, and his first time really using it at all in such a big way since taking his mantle. According to everything I heard, he was pretty much everywhere, a finger in every pot.

I walk over and sit on the furs, pushing a curl of hair off his forehead. "Did you eat at all today? Or rest?"

Ydum captures my hand in his, kissing my fingers. "Okay, Byder. No, I haven't but I'm fine, beautiful."

I laugh internally at Ydum making the same joke about Byder being all about everyone eating as I did with Anarus, but I also turn to give Byder a questioning look. He answers by immediately standing and leaving the tent again.

"I heard you had a little fun with the weather group." Ydum continues talking to me. "Fire said you were incredibly helpful, teaching them to use intentions to make rain. Wonder where such an enterprising witch learned that?"

This time I laugh out loud, playfully pushing on his shoulder. "No clue.

Guess it was all just raw talent. It's not like I had three smart gods to teach me it or anything."

Ydum toys with a loose hair that escaped my braid, looking very much like he is going to kiss me, but then a thought crosses his mind and he changes course, becoming the pure academic I knew he would eventually. "What was that in the meeting about you being a Fate? Being Fear's, which by the way who the fuck is Fear, Fated descendant?"

"Damn, knew you'd remember eventually." I mutter. "Fear, one of the vanquished gods turned human by the original gods when they created us. He was one of the five Fates. Until he disagreed with Inspiration's plans for humans, that is, and was made one of us. They made him mortal but couldn't stop his control of destiny since no Anarus at the time to end a Fate's destiny." I explain.

When he raises an eyebrow, I take that as my cue to keep talking. "According to Sadness, Fear basically got revenge by fating a descendant that would inherit his entire power as a Fate, and, well, here I am, messed up blood test because I have the power of a god but am not one, but not completely just a witch either. A human that uses words to create, just like the gods did when they created everything, can manipulate destinies as a Fate, and do all the other magic stuff like an end magic witch can."

Ydum gets a faraway look, staring into nothing. I can tell he is making connections in his brain with everything we had thought and done during the games. His brow furrows. "What about the whole needing the thing to make the thing? Sure, you can create from there, but you always needed that starting jump off."

I give a wry smile. "That's the both and neither part. I'm a witch, the child of two witches, and my blood test should have been red because I'm an end magic witch. But, since I'm also a Fate with the power of an original god, I also got blue because I can also make the supplies from nothing like a god can. I need the base start like a bound god who hasn't completed the games yet, when it's magic stuff, but don't need more supplies because my Fate power takes over and creates them for me."

He sits upright, quickly, draping his elbows over his knees. "Both and neither! Shit, that makes so much sense now. And words because it is the old type of god power, not what we are now as all descendants of a god and a witch. But you wouldn't need that start for the emotions because as a Fate, you'd just make a new destiny, or build on what's already there."

I nod, smiling at how smart Ydum is. "Yeah. Damn, you figured that out a lot faster than I did. Only one thing wrong. I don't create destinies, that's the four gods of Fate. I don't end destinies either, that's only Anarus. I manipulate already created destinies, like changing a colorblind god's destiny to never know colors to just being never seeing them, but able to know them through touch. And I can manipulate the way someone feels about that destiny, make them feel peace about it when they don't want to. At least for a little while. We didn't cover making it stick. That'll be something for me to work on. But for now, while I'm pushing it, someone will feel what I want them to about their current or future destiny."

"Damn." Ydum shakes his head and looks at me with a smile. Then, his eyes glaze over and he stares off into the distance. From what I saw in the games, I would guess he's about to slip into a thought bender. But then Byder returns with food and pulls him out of it.

The four of us sit together while Ydum eats, each working on our own thing. Ydum and Byder return to their discussion of who to put at the caches. I try to focus on being confident in what I will say to the council, but Anarus keeps distracted me, antsy and grumbling while staring at a map of Veirveil.

"What's wrong?" I finally ask him.

Anarus shakes his head. "I don't know. I feel like there's something we are forgetting, or not taking into account. Something's missing."

"Well, I know we all want to get good rest tonight," Byder interrupts us, "but there is something I think we need to do." He digs through his bags in the corner of the tent and comes back over to us with several daggers. "It's been a minute since the sixth games and I want to review weaponry with Jinx. If shit goes sideways tomorrow, you'll need to be armed, baby girl, and I'll need to be assured you remember what the fuck to do with them."

Ydum pushes back from the table and grabs two of the daggers from Byder. "Good idea." He hands one of the daggers to me.

I take it but shake my head at him. "Uh uh, not you. You're exhausted. You rest. I'll work with Byder."

"You expect me to rest in here while you and Byder are reviewing the information you may need to stay alive tomorrow? Not happening, beautiful."

Anarus plucks the dagger out of my hand. "And we aren't using these either. Not yet. Too much of a risk for accidents with Jinx."

I glare at him, but know he's right. I spent a good majority of the games, including game six, injured because I lost a fight with the floor.

Byder shrugs and takes the daggers back and all three of them step out of the tent flap. I follow them grudgingly. If Ydum thinks it's important enough for him to not rest when he obviously needs it, I should be willing too.

Outside of the tent, Byder picks up, then discards, several sticks until he finds a few he likes.

He hands one of the sticks to each of us, but keeps a sheathed dagger in his hand. "Show me your grip, Jinx."

I look at the stick in my hand and try to determine what parts of it Byder was probably intending to be the pretend blade, hilt, and pommel. Thinking back to their training three months ago, I wrap my four fingers around the hilt and lock my thumb over the first and second finger, squeezing my third and fourth fingers tightly.

Byder examines my grip closely. "Good. Where are you imaging the sharp part of the blade?"

"Both sides." I tell him. "Your daggers are double-edged."

"She's got you there." Ydum chortles.

Byder raises his eyebrows and bounces his head from side to side as if to admit I did, in fact, beat him with that point. "Fine. How are you standing?"

I shift immediately, moving my body so that my knees are more relaxed and I have my weight evenly distributed, hands up to protect my sides and core.

Anarus shakes his head. "Wrong. You're not going to stand in the council hall like that. That's hostile. In game six, you wanted hostile. In the council hall, you want ease of movement but to appear non-threatening until you are threatened. But by then, it's too late to shift stances. You're going to have to be able to move from talking to fighting in one fluid motion without even thinking about it."

Ydum comes behind me, resting his hands on my elbows to move them down to my sides. "You want the loose stance, but the weapon not visible and not the protectiveness that makes it look like you anticipate an attack. You're ready for an attack but don't look like you're ready for an attack. Eyes open, seeing everything, changing in a second to a threat."

He takes the stick out of my hand and puts it in the pocket of my pants. He sweeps my braid over my shoulder and kisses the back of my neck. It feels nice and would be distracting, but I know this tactic. I inhale sharply at the sensations he is making in me, but keep my eyes on Byder and Anarus.

When Byder steps forward with his stick moving up, I grab for mine, pulling it into my power grip and going on the defensive quickly.

"Damn, thought I'd get her with that one." Ydum steps back as I move to show Byder what I remember about fielding off a knife attack. After a few parries back and forth, Ydum crosses his arms over his chest, frowning. "Jinx, in the games we didn't actually want to hurt anyone unless we had to. This time, you have to be ready to hurt them, kill them even. This isn't strike to get away, but strike to keep striking until they are stopped or run away."

Fuck, he's right. I'm still fighting the way they taught me in the games. Move however you can to get the fuck out of there and away from the danger. But we would not be trying to get away from the danger tomorrow. We will be the danger.

I roll my shoulders. "So, show me what to do differently."

"Why am I not surprised to find you four training instead of resting?" Esnir says with a laugh from behind me. I turn to see him and Isis looking like they are just coming back from the mess tent, food in hand. Esnir glances at Isis, with an eyebrow raised. "If you can't beat 'em, join 'em?"

She nods and Byder gives her the stick in his hand. "Unless you plan for her to have something other than a dagger, Esnir?" Byder asks.

Esnir plops on the ground, leaning against a tree and digging into the food. "Rondel. One edged."

Byder nods. "Alright." He spends a few minutes making sure Isis remembers her grip, and how to move the knife differently than I would because it only has one sharp edge while Esnir eats.

"Like we were explaining to Jinx," Ydum tells her, "this is different than the games because we aren't training to hit and run from the threat. You want to be the threat. If shit goes down, you take them down, no stopping to run. You want them to run from you."

"Or never run again." Anarus adds.

Isis's eyes go wide at that. She didn't kill, or really even hurt anyone, in game six. The memory of killing Aretha still haunts me, and I settle it in my mind that I might have more deaths to remember happening at my hands after tomorrow.

As soon as Esnir is done eating, the four gods step away from us to talk in a circle alone. Isis stands next to me, relaxed and twiddling the stick she is pretending is her knife.

"What do you think they're talking about?" She asks me.

I shake my head. "Nothing important. They're waiting until we forget to be vigilant. Then, they'll attack. They want to see if they can catch us off guard."

"Well, fuck." Ydum laughs. "If you're not going to fall for any of our tricks anymore, Jinx, why wait?"

He steps out of the circle of gods, quickly on the offensive. I know as he comes at me that his movements are much slower than he could be. Ydum is a blur when he fights. But he wants to give me time to remember how to defend. And figure out how to attack.

I expect this from him, so am ready. Isis, I barely notice out of the corner of my eye, was not and Esnir knocks her off her feet quickly. I pay attention to blocking Ydum. He picks up his pace, thrusting attacks at me and defending when I try to attack, as he sees the muscle memory coming back to me. I know I'll never land a blow to Ydum, but if I can get close with him, I can actually land it with someone else.

What I don't expect is when Anarus steps up to attack at the same time I'm still fighting Ydum. I step back a few paces, trying to put distance between me and them to think. We hadn't done this before, dual attackers, so it's new and I'm not sure what to do. I think through everything they ever taught me quickly, while still dodging and focusing on evade for the moment. I know I need to get it back one on one. But how?

Without turning my back on either of them, I dart between two trees and circle around one to come up behind them. As I do that, I scoop up a handful of the detritus on the ground in my free hand. When Ydum and Anarus both turn to face me again, I lob the dirt and leaves at Anarus. He's shorter, so my aim towards his eyes would be better.

"Fuck!" He yells as my handful lands true.

I hide my smile at the fact that my idea worked, and focus on Ydum, still moving backwards to draw him away from Anarus, who stopped to wipe his face.

"Fucking perfect, beautiful." Ydum tells me as he lunges at me again. "But stop being on the defensive. Take me down."

We circle each other for a few more steps before Anarus catches up to us. Out of the corner of my eye, while still trying to figure out how to defend against the two of them, because that detritus trick will not work again, I know, I spot Death leaning on a tree watching all six of us. He has a large stick in his hand he must have picked up absentmindedly while watching. I bite my lip, stopping the smile at the idea that forms.

I take several large steps backwards towards him quickly. "Hey, Death, swap my knife for your sword."

He looks startled for a moment, then looks at the long stick in his hand. He lets out a loud laugh and tosses me the larger stick as I toss him the small one in my hand. Catching the longer stick, I now have the reach to tap Ydum on the shoulder without him being able to hit me back. I do it, then run to hide behind Death's hulking frame.

"Hey, foul!" Ydum calls out. "Death wasn't part of this training and where the fuck did you magic a sword from?"

Unable to hold back my laughter, I peek back out at them. "I didn't magic it from anywhere. I got it from an ally. And you've told me before to use all of my surroundings. My surroundings just so happened to include an eight-foot-tall god with a really big stick."

Death glances down at me, still half hiding behind him. "She's got a point. In a real fight, if she has two attackers, her best defense is to find an ally to help her. The question is, in this situation, do you know I'm actually an ally, Jinx?"

"You gave me the big stick." I shrug. "Figured that was good enough to claim you for my side."

Anarus huffs. "Fine, whatever. You claim Death on your side. Are we doing this, or what? You won't learn to be more offensive if you just hide behind that mountain the whole time, little human."

I look up at Death, who shrugs at me, handing me back my stick dagger. I give him back the stick sword, which he immediately breaks into a more appropriate dagger size, well, appropriate sized for his massive hands size, and we square off against Ydum and Anarus.

Quickly, the whole things dissolves into two teams. Me, Isis, and Death against Byder, Ydum, Anarus, and Esnir. The males all keep throwing out suggestions and reminders to Isis and me, no matter which side they're on.

"Remember your hand-to-hand training too." Esnir says, as he comes closer to Isis. "If you can reach them, you can hit them with a fist as much as the knife."

"And so can they." Death adds as he proves his point by lobbing a soft, open-handed hit at Ydum's unprotected side. "Watch their blade, but also watch everything else."

"Protect your back." Ydum tells us. "The worst part of a large melee like this is how chaotic it can get. Is that person behind you foe or friend? Try to keep someone at your back, and you at theirs, to know you are defended there."

He and Byder demonstrate as they fight Death and me, moving close enough to each other to know their backs are to each other but far enough apart for free range of movement.

Anarus slips between two trees. "Think of choke points. You want an easy out for you, but a hard out for a group coming against you. Inside the building, doorways, narrow halls, find any way you can go that makes them funnel down to one versus one, but leaves you an exit strategy works. Don't get pressed against a wall or somewhere you can get surrounded or cut off from your allies, though."

"Use stuff around you, like Jinx said. Chairs make a great range weapon when thrown, or a shield in a pinch. Throw books. Slam doors closed behind you if you know there's another way out of the room. If someone comes in close quarters and you kill them, or incapacitate them, don't be afraid to use their body as a shield until you can reestablish your bearings." Esnir tells us.

He snags the bowl he had been eating from and tosses it toward Isis, who ducks it while Byder feigns a hit to her chest with his stick dagger. She groans, knowing that she would be too hurt to still fight if this was real.

We keep moving, fighting, and listening to the advice from our gods for long enough to become sticky with sweat. Eventually, I wave a hand at them to indicate I need a break, leaning against a tree to catch my breath. Byder is by my side quickly.

"You good, baby girl?" He asks me as I lean over, bracing my hands on my knees, fighting a wave a dizzy nausea I know means I didn't drink enough water today. Or overdid it between the magic with Sadness and the fighting practice. Either way, the sun is setting and we should probably call it a day.

"Yeah." I lie. "Just, long day."

"Liar." He holds out a canteen of water with a smug smile.

I take the canteen and drain it as I roll my eyes. Of course, Byder would notice. He was the one who noticed that I had stopped drinking coffee after Anarus died and made me start again. He was also the one who would notice every time I didn't eat enough food or drink enough water then too.

Even though they had been hurting from the bond breaking too, Ydum had made me get up and do things, like start running again, and Byder had made sure I ate. And I made sure the both of them talked instead of shutting completely down.

I look over at Anarus, who is across the small area in front of our tent, talking with Death. I'm glad he's talking with Death. I'm glad for that for him. But this small interaction, Byder knowing I neglected myself again, reminds me of how fucking hard that month was. Something that in the last week or so, we had almost seemed to forget. How easy it was to forget now that he was back and okay.

But it really has been only about a week and a half since the three of us had been shrouded in so much pain, we could barely make it through each day. And tomorrow we are going to face the council and more than likely have to fight them, meaning any one of them could be taken from me again. And this time, we can almost be certain there will be no undoing that loss. The fear hits me so hard I vomit up all the water I just drank.

Byder's arms are around me so fast, holding me up as my stomach continues to heave, even though it is empty. "I've got you, baby girl. I've got you. It's okay. It's going to be okay."

I shake my head, tears threatening to overwhelm me. As soon as I am sure my stomach won't recoil anymore, I turn in his arms to bury myself there. "I can't do this anymore. I can't. I can't do it again. What if I lose one of you again tomorrow? What if I lose all of you? I'm so tired, Byder. I don't want to have to keep fighting, scared I will die, scared I will lose someone I love. I cannot do that thirty-two days again. Not when I know it will be forever this time. I can't."

Byder sits down with me, leaning his back against the tree while cradling me in his arms. I feel Ydum's hand on my back, rubbing it in small circles.

"We are all going to be fine tomorrow." Ydum says.

I huff derisively. "You can't say that. You don't know. We thought we'd all be fine when you took your mantles and it ended up ripping my heart apart. Anarus died and we almost died from the grief of it. Thirty-two days. We only dealt with that for thirty-two days. I couldn't do it forever. I can't. And there is nothing stopping it from being all of you and me left completely alone tomorrow. I would drown under the weight of it."

"No, you wouldn't." Anarus says. "Because you have something to fight for this time. We all do, which is why we will all survive, no matter what tomorrow brings."

I look up at Anarus. He's standing with his arm braced against the tree above Byder's head. For the first time in what feels like so long, he is swimming in shadows as he looks down at me. I don't even think he realizes he lost control of the wilde hunt in his arm. But he looks so much like he did that first day I met him, the anger simmering just under the surface and the shadows simmering just above it, I say nothing. His usually neatly groomed facial hair has gotten longer and wilder. His braid down his back, that's almost as long as mine, is messy too when he never let it get even slightly tangled before.

I look over at Ydum. His blonde curls are a mop on his head, in desperate need of a haircut. His facial hair is so pale, it's hardly visible against his skin and the few-day old scruff looks like fluff on his cheeks.

Byder's just past shoulder length hair is pulled into a messy bun at the crown of his head and there is patchy brown facial hair smattered across his cheeks. Ydum had been right during the games. His beard does grow in patchy and uneven. I run my fingernails through it and almost smile.

I'm sure I look just as much a mess as they are. All of us with dark circles just barely receding from a month of too little sleep, or being dead in Anarus's case. All that pain is still there, we just stuffed it down with the four of us back together and so much else to distract us. We are truly in no shape to be taking on anything, much less fourteen original gods.

But for some reason, people have rallied around us as a cause to finally fight back. The tipping point in their ability to deal with the shit they've made us live with our whole lives. We can't not be strong and lead the charge. There are twelve hundred humans camped out in these woods, looking to us to help them free themselves and so many more waiting back in their homes, hoping they didn't sacrifice their loved ones to this cause for nothing.

I look across the space we just trampled while we practiced fighting. Esnir and Isis are walking hand in hand back to their tent. If we give in, if we give up, they go down with us. They do, their families and a bunch of other gods. Damek and Iella are somewhere in this camp, praying they don't have to ever worry like Iella's parent did, like Ydum's parents did for his sister, with too few male witches for too many female gods. Like we will have to if we don't at least try to stop this.

I take a deep breath and look at my three gods again, who are watching me with worry. I don't want to fight. I don't want to have to. But we weren't given that choice. That choice was made the day my test turned red, then blue, ten times.

Before that even. I know Sadness said it doesn't work like that, but our choice was made for us that day, however many hundreds or thousands of years ago when the twenty original gods stripped Fear of his power but not his destiny and made him a human just so that they could have some rational beings to subjugate.

If we are going to have to fight, and we are going to have to, we aren't doing it like this, I decide. I refuse to go in front of the council looking as broken as they tried to make us ever again. If we are a threat, if they think we are a threat, then we are going to be a damn threat that strikes fear into their hearts as deep as they have made it live in mine my whole life.

"There you go. That's my vicious little human." Anarus holds a hand out to help me up. I take it and the four of us go into our tent.

Without any real discussion, I take a seat in one of the chairs and Anarus sits on the floor in front of me. I pull his hair out of the tangled braid, combing it out. Then, I add the braids of totality, three braids from his temple to just behind his ear on the left side of his head closest to his heart, filled with all the strength, safety, and power I can into each one that represents his body, mind, and heart.

After I finish righting the rest of his braid, he moves away to clean up his moustache and goatee. Byder sits where Anarus just was, rubbing his cleanly shaven cheeks as I give him his three braids of totality.

When I'm done making sure his hair will stay neat through the night with his hair creams, Ydum sits in his place. With shorter hair, the braids of totality are harder to do for him, but I weave them through his hair anyway, making sure to give him just as much strength, safety, and power as the other two in his short locks.

Still in silence, Anarus picks me up out of the chair only to settle me down on his lap to braid my braids of totality. Ydum and Byder stay close and I know by feel alone that all three of them are adding their power to my braids the way I did with theirs. Their powers are so much stronger than the last time we did this, just before the tenth game. It makes me feel better to feel that strength in all of them, those full mantles that will help keep them safe.

When my three braids are done, Ydum holds a red shirt from his bag out to me. "Red enough? It feels it, but I want to check first."

I know what he's asking me. He can still feel colors from the magic I gave him in the games, but he wants to know if it's the right red for new protective bracelets. When I nod, Ydum sets to work with the fine tip of a knife to pick at the threads of the shirt until he has enough for all of us. While he does that, I take the bracelets we have left, mine, Byder's and Ydum's and burn them. Anarus didn't have one anymore, having lost his when he died, the same time I lost the one he made me.

Once Ydum has enough string pulled from the shirt's fabric, we all sit on the furs together. This time, I don't have to teach them what to do. They know.

The only change I make is each of our bracelets are one string. No more doubled or tripled up strings in any of the bracelets. We are all one group, one family, with no one being second or third. Each of us makes three this time too. We all will make the same bracelet for everyone else, with love and safety. The bond isn't just between me and each of them individually, but all four of us with all four of us, and we all give our strengths to protect each other.

We each take turns tying our strings on Ydum first, only speaking for this part, feeling that the ritualness of it deserves it.

"Red for protection." I say as I tie it around his wrist, then I kiss his wrist where I tied the string.

"Red for the fire that burns in our hearts." Byder adds as he adds his bracelet to Ydum and kisses that same spot.

"Red for the blood that we are willing to spill to make this world safe." Anarus murmurs as he ties his around Ydum's wrist. After a moment's hesitation, where we all say nothing, Anarus kisses Ydum's wrist too.

"Red for our love, the four of us." Ydum says, tying his bracelets first around Byder's wrist, sealing it with a kiss, then Anarus's, waiting until Anarus nods before he kisses his wrist, then finally mine, and he corrects himself. "The five of us."

Then Byder gives me and Anarus his bracelet, repeating the kissing of the wrist with the both of us in silence. Then, I give mine to the two of them in silence. Anarus gives his to Byder, then me. The only change in the way any of us do the whole process is that, instead of Anarus only kissing my wrist, he also kisses my lips.

When he steps away, Byder moves in front of me to wrap his arms around my waist. "I love you, Jinx."

I wrap my arms around his shoulders. "I love you, Byder." He kisses me gently, with none of the assertiveness he usually laces through his desire, but only a tenderness that warms me.

An odd hesitancy in the bond makes both Byder and me look up for a moment, distractedly watching Ydum and Anarus.

Anarus scratches the back of his head as he seems torn between moving away from Ydum and moving closer. "I, um, I don't know how to..."

Ydum's eyebrows hitch up a slight bit and he glances over to me briefly before looking back at Anarus. He speaks quietly. "I love you, Anarus. Just like Byder and Jinx. We don't have to do anything you don't want to."

"But would you want to?" Anarus interrupts him. "I hit you. A lot."

Ydum chuckles and, slowly, allowing time for him to move away or say stop, he wraps his arms around Anarus. "We'll just pretend that was foreplay." He leans down to kiss Anarus, who turns his head to meet him.

Byder pulls my attention back to him, smoothing my hair back and tracing the shell of my ear. "That's good, I think."

"Taking a piece of himself back." I agree then kiss him.

The four of us find our way over to furs in the middle of the tent. Byder and I are kissing while Ydum and Anarus talk softly with each other. At one point, Anarus catches my attention.

"Jinx, can you..." Anarus stammers, his hands tightly fisted in his lap. I wait, letting him figure out how to say what he wants on his own. "I know I should say it. I should be the one to say it, but I can't. You said to tell Ydum, but I can't. I can't say the words. Can you tell him? Tell him why..." Anarus groans, shaking out his hands.

I figure out what he means. He can't find the words to tell Ydum what he struggles with and why so Ydum will know how to make him feel safe. I nod. "Anarus was hurt in much the same way I was, but he was much younger and it was another male. He's struggling to know he's not to blame for what happened then, especially with his new desires so closely related to that act that hurt him."

"That explains the war of emotions I've been feeling from you." Byder says.

Ydum moves slightly away from Anarus, so they aren't touching any more than Anarus instigates purposefully. "Anarus, can I ask you a question about what happened?"

Anarus nods and Ydum speaks softly. "When males are together, there's sometimes a power dynamic with that. Do you understand what I mean?"

"Do you mean who is," Anarus clears his throat, "who is giving and who is receiving?"

Ydum nods. "Yeah. Can you tell me how that power dynamic played out for you?"

Anarus takes in a deep breath and looks at me rather than at Ydum. Ydum doesn't react, knowing that, yet again, our bond that has nothing to do with destiny helps both of us feel safer. "He was always in control."

Byder catches on to where Ydum is taking this conversation. "You know that my first time with a male was with Ydum. I was very unsure about what I would like and not like, even with no trauma behind the relationship confusing things. Ydum understood that and was very accepting that a lot of it was trial and error. It's okay to say yes but then change your mind, figure out you are not comfortable with something and change that yes to a no. Ydum is very good about that. Very patient."

Byder laughs for a moment. "Everyone, even the most experienced person has those moments. Jinx likes some of my more dominating tendencies, but Ydum called that off very quickly. He made it very clear he was not at all a fan."

Ydum laughs too, probably remembering the same thing Byder is. "Yeah, the first time you put your hand around my throat, I ended that quickly. You are not the only one that gave any of us a split lip during the games, Ani."

I tilt my head to the side, wondering when that was. I never noticed Byder with a split lip.

Anarus seems to relax at that comment some and snorts softly. "Must have been a weak punch if we never saw the evidence. I thought you were our best fighter, Ydum."

"The point is," Ydum drawls, rolling his eyes, "if you are interested in exploring where a relationship between me and you may go, and where your boundaries with that are, there are a lot of things we can experiment with long before we get to anything quite as intense as sex. And the dynamic of that, if and when we do get to that, can be many things. If you never want to be the one you called receiving, because of your history, I understand and accept that. I accept that with Byder because it's his preference, so can definitely accept that with you. You lead. I will let you always lead, so that you always know this is not that, not what happened in your past, but now. Two people who love each other enjoying loving each other and no power dynamic at all. You can control how and where we touch, kiss, what clothes stay on or come off, how far anything goes. All you, always you, and I will be more than happy with everything you are willing to do and will want nothing you don't also want."

"Clothes stay on. All of them." Anarus says sharply. But then, he softens and looks at Ydum. "For, for now."

"Done." Ydum nods, then looks at Anarus, his eyes taking on a hooded look I know very well. "Can I kiss you, Anarus?"

"Do you want to?" Anarus asks, his tone hesitantly teasing.

"Badly." Ydum rumbles, then leans over, moving close but leaving enough space that Anarus has to bridge the gap to kiss Ydum. As he bridges that gap, Anarus fists Ydum's shirt to haul him closer.

Byder turns back to me, seeing that Anarus is now trusting Ydum to guide him and doesn't need me as a buffer anymore. "Speaking of. I do not want

161

clothes to stay on, Jinx." He smiles, a little mischievously. "But I would like to not have any power dynamics either."

"I think I'm okay with that." I pull Byder to me, kissing him as I shift us so that he's under me. We slowly undress each other, exploring each other's bodies with our fingers and mouths.

Byder takes his time, finding each spot on me that makes me squirm and a damp need build in between my thighs. I do the same, discovering exactly how much Byder likes it when I nip at his nipples, playing with them until they become tiny, hard buds and his cock presses hard into my stomach.

A sharp note of pleasure courses through the bond and both of us are drawn to watch Ydum and Anarus for only a moment. All their clothes are still on, as Anarus requested, but Anarus's hand is inside Ydum's pants, Ydum panting hard with his eyes closed.

As Byder and I return to our quiet explorations, I hear Ydum swear. "Fuck, hotness. That feels, shit."

"Not that nickname either." Anarus grumbles, making me almost snort. Ydum must have already tried several nicknames Anarus didn't like. "I'm not sure how to..."

"Just like you are. What you do when you're alone but on me. Do you want me to reciprocate?"

Byder moves to undo my braid, but I stop him. My braids of totality need to stay tight.

I hear Anarus answer, "Yes." After only a moment, I feel panic through the bond and he yells. "No! I changed my mind. No."

"Okay, sugar." Ydum says softly.

"Not that either." Anarus growls as Ydum laughs.

Byder pulls me back on top of him. Maintaining our focus on each other with Anarus cycling through so many intense emotions so close by is hard. Byder slides his hand between us and lines himself up with me. He waits, letting me sink down on his length at my own pace. I go slow, teasing him and watch as his eyes darken with desire and enjoyment as I take in his tip only to retreat again over and over.

"Jinx." He groans and his hip flex as he chases me. My teasing tortures me just as much as it does Byder and I give in, wanting to feel him inside me. That fullness I know makes me gasp. I lean down and kiss him, then sit up and sink all the way down on him.

I moan as I glide on him, moving my hips in a slow pace, relishing the feeling of pleasurable heat every time he hits that perfect spot inside me. Byder grips my thigh with one hand and moves his hips to meet mine, keeping my slow pace. He brings his other hand up to graze my stomach and I think he is going to trail it down to my clit, but he doesn't.

Instead, he spreads out his fingers, almost cradling my lower belly. There's nothing there, nothing to indicate what is going on inside me, but he holds his hand there anyway. We stare at each other, speaking only through our eyes our devotion and love. A slow building need burns through me and I brace my hands on Byder's chest, running my fingers through his sparse hair. I close my eyes and groan. "Byder."

"Yes." He grabs my hips and tilts them. The slow burn peaks as he drives even deeper and I tense around him.

"Fuck, baby girl." Byder and I both moan as my body explodes. His hands tighten and pushes me down as he drives up. He groans as he comes.

Byder's hands move from my hips to my back as he pulls me down to lay on his chest. We spend several minutes just lying there, enjoying the warmth of the afterglow together.

Eventually, as I finally slide off Byder's chest to lie next to him, still in his embrace, Anarus and Ydum both find their way to curl into a pile with us. As we all fall asleep in each other's arms, I know that the two of them never went further than kissing and touching, Anarus giving that pleasure to Ydum but not being able to receive it back. But for someone who has lived a life as devoid of affection and love as Anarus has, and with as much pain given in ways that should have only ever been pleasure, accepting as much as he did from another male is a huge step.

Even though we are all four terrified of what tomorrow will bring, none of us are terrified of the love we can give each other today.

Chapter Eleven

WAKE UP, JINX. THERE'S a problem.

Kinshra's worried voice in my head has me wrenching my eyes open and sitting up without disentangling the arms and legs surrounding me, which wakes up everyone else. I speak out loud for their benefit. "What's wrong, Kinshra?"

People. A lot of them.

"Not the council people?" I place a hand on Anarus's chest tattoo, thinking about him being able to hear Kinshra at the least.

Not the council people. Other people. Through the north opening. Five wolves are dead.

"Fuck." Anarus bites out and fills in Byder and Ydum. I guess my quickie magic worked.

"Where are they now, Kinshra? Where are the people? How many?" Ydum throws clothes at me and I slip then on one handed, while Anarus keeps telling them what she is saying for me.

Here. One hundred and two, all but one are gods, all but two armed. At the building that the gods were in all day yesterday. One hundred staying outside. We hid. They are circling the building. Council gods and the other two are inside the building.

"Fuck." I am the one to swear this time. "Stay hidden. We're going to Esnir now. Let me know if the situation changes."

"All but one gods and all but two armed?" Anarus asks.

I can only shrug as I strap the daggers Byder is thrusting in my hands to my legs and, for old time's sake, shoving one down my breast band. I know the three of them are doing the same, minus the breast band part.

Anarus, Ydum, and I run to the strategy tent while Byder runs to the mess tent. He's hoping to grab a ton of food to make sure everyone eats, ever the hunt god with a special affinity to feeding people.

Our plans are just shot to shit and now there is no waiting until the afternoon. Something is niggling in the back of my mind as we walk. One hundred and two. That's a really specific number. Especially when only the two are unarmed.

Inside the strategy tent, Esnir is sitting down at a table in the corner with Isis, eating breakfast. As soon as he sees us, he jumps up. "What happened?"

"One hundred and two people, all but one gods, all but two armed, broke through the north exit, killing five wolves and are surrounding the council hall. The wolves are in hiding but still watching. The council gods and the two are inside the hall." I tell him quickly.

"Fuck." Esnir downs the coffee in his mug in one gulp. "Isis, get everyone."

"Set up the waves ready to deploy." Ydum adds.

"We need to talk to Fertility." I tell Esnir. "Who are the hundred armed? Who are the two? That two is itching my brain."

Esnir nods. "I agree. Tell Death to bring Fertility, Isis."

Isis takes off at a run.

"Can we get more details from Kinshra?" Esnir asks me. "Position of each person? That type of thing."

"I'll ask." I touch Anarus's chest again. He grabbed a shirt to bring but didn't put it on. We guessed I might need to keep talking to my wolf with him listening in as the guide so he can relay the conversation to the others. "Kinshra? Is there any way to get more details about the people around the building?"

I'm scouting it now. I can't get too close, so it's taking a moment.

"Be safe, Kinshra. Do what you can, but do it without getting spotted." They already killed five wolves, I don't want to lose my familiar too.

I'm going to do something, Jinx. I think it might work. Are you somewhere safe where you don't need to be able to see what you are doing?

"You need me to be able to be blind for a bit?" I glance at Esnir and Anarus, who both nod that they will cover me. "Do it, Kinshra."

I close my eyes, keeping my hand on Anarus's chest. He wraps his arm around my waist to guide me closer to the strategy table. In my mind, I see the road around the council building appear. It's an odd angle, and even odder colors, and it takes me a minute to realize I am seeing through Kinshra's eyes.

Don't let go of Anarus, she tells me. I'm not sure how this is working, but it is.

"Don't care about the magic of it, either, right now." I say with a chuckle. As Kinshra moves closer to the building, crouched and belly crawling to stay hidden, I ask Anarus if he can see what I'm seeing.

"Not really, I'm getting a sense that you are doing something through your bond with her, and using me as a go between for the added power, but I don't see the vision." He tells me.

I nod and start detailing what I see. "South side of the building, the side with the back entrance. Twenty gods, five have bows and arrows, three axes, ten daggers, two with some sort of hammer looking thing. Ten directly in front of the door, the other ten ranged along the walls of the building. East side, fifteen gods, ranged along the wall, all daggers. North side, fifteen ranged along the walls, all daggers. West side, front entrance, ten with hammers, ranged along the front, about twenty paces from the building. Ten more behind them with bows and arrows. Directly in front of the front doors, under the awning of the building, are ten with daggers, ten with axes. All one hundred looking outward, not inward. They are guarding the building. We'll have to fight our way in if we want in."

"Any specifics you can see about the gods guarding the building?" Esnir asks. "Green skin tint of a nature god? Reddish tint of a fire god? Blue of a weather god? Anyone you recognize?"

I shake my head. "Wolves are red-green colorblind. Can't make out colors. No one I distinctly recognize either."

"Anyone moving around, look like they are in charge?" Ydum asks me.

Again, I shake my head. "Not that I can tell. No one is moving, it looks like they are waiting, just guarding."

Anarus speaks next. "Your math gave us one hundred, but Kinshra said one hundred and two. Where are the last two?"

Kinshra, are you sure about that number? Where are the last two?

They are inside the building. Wait. One of the two are not a god, but they don't smell like humans normally do.

"The one that smells wrong for a human, does it smell anything like Isis?" I ask.

I hear Anarus talking and know he is relaying what Kinshra is saying to everyone else. I feel that there are more people in the tent now, but don't open my eyes to look who.

Yes. She is different like Isis is different.

"Immortal witch. She's a witch who survived the games. Probably the god's mate." I explain. "How many of the council gods are in the building? Anyone else besides the fourteen gods, the door guard guy, the human council member, and the two new people in there?"

No. Just them. No door guard today. He did not come back. There is a lot of fear in the air, though. Either everyone is scared or someone is terrified out of their minds. I'm going back to hide with Alpha.

"Thanks, Kinshra. Stay safe, all of you." I say and open my eyes.

The strategy tent is full to bursting. Besides all of us that are in the first wave Ayja set up yesterday, minus Death, there is also Kutar, Wren, Ayja, Xolios, Zimuna, Otuna, and a god I saw yesterday working with Fire and the weather group.

Byder is shoving a bowl of oatmeal and a coffee in my hands. "Eat, baby girl."

I take the food and coffee and set it in front of me, scarfing it as Ayja talks. I see remnants of food in front of everyone else.

Ayja rubs her hands together. "Alright, change of plans. Fasnas, your weather group will surround the city first, securing the woods around the city on both the east and west sides up to the northern break. Make sure your people know that, if anyone is trying to escape the city from anywhere not the government wedge, they are to let them through and direct them to the refugee camp on the other side of the river. Especially if they have children with them. You may want to make the groups bigger, or join them with some of the hunter group people, so that someone can leave and escort the ones with children to safety." Fasnas nods at this idea, pulling a piece of paper in front of him, and starts a quick conversation with Byder.

Ayja continues giving directions. "Once weather is in place, Zimuna, your nature group will follow behind to secure the northern break. While the northern break is secured, Otuna you will send in your nature and hunter teams to secure the caches, both inside and outside the government wedge. Once that's done, Xolios, your hunter group and the games group will go to the council hall, secure our access to the building and the games group will get inside to the council. Otuna, keep the wolves on each cache with your groups. Xolios, the wolves outside the building, keep Kinshra plus one with you and send the rest to range out to the northern break with Zimuna and east and west around the city with the weather groups, as a warning system and extra defense."

Ayja takes a small breath. She seems to be steadying herself. This is her first real war just as much as it is Esnir's. Battle is her power, so everyone is looking to her for this as much as we had been looking to Esnir for the overall war planning.

"Now, for the plan." She says with a long sigh. "Once everyone is in place, which will be communicated through a bark rather than a howl from the wolves, weather will create a distraction, give us a first advantage, wind, rain, whatever you think is best. Then, the hunt group will attack to take control of the exterior of the building. Once the building is secured, the games group will breach the building. From there, advance or retreat as told to by wolf howls. They sound the alarm to full retreat, feel free to rip down the plant barriers to exit that way if need be. Just remember some of those plants are dangerous."

Ayja looks around the room, giving space for questions. When no one has any, she continues. "Any groups not physically armed at this point, find your way to the armorer next to the main mess tent. We don't have much in the way of extra weapons, so arm your humans and gods judiciously. Hunter group first, then weather. Nature can use the caches and anything they find, so arm them last. I put the mess tent on filling canteens and making trail packs last night. Make sure every human collects a canteen and food ration. We don't need to lose humans to dehydration or hunger. Wait for the signal, one long howl from the wolves, to move out."

Xolios, Zimuna, Otuna, and Fasnas, done with his conversation with Byder to reassign some of the hunters, curtly nod and leave.

Esnir, who had been looking outside the tent, turns back to everyone still inside. "Alright, from this point on, we need silence in the tent. I'm going to have Death bring Fertility in. Sadness and Jinx, you'll question her. We need to know who the hundred are and who the other two are. If any of the rest of you think of a question, write it down on a paper and hold it up. I will give it to them. We do not want Fertility knowing how many of us are in here listening. If you don't think you can handle staying completely silent, step out now." He starts handing scraps of paper and writing tools to everyone.

"What do I do if Kinshra tells me new information while we are talking to Fertility?" I ask him as he moves around the tent.

"Talk internally with her," Esnir says, "and let Anarus hear. He can relay it to me or whoever needs the information, in writing."

He pauses, then comes to stand directly in front of me, placing a hand lightly on my shoulder. "Jinx, be ready to use force to get Fertility to talk. I know you said no to torture, but we need to know who the hundred are and who the two are. Can you do it? Could you hurt her to make her talk if you need to?"

I take a deep breath. "Honestly? I don't know. I want to say yes, but I don't know if I will be able to convince myself to actually do it in the moment."

"Go as far as you feel comfortable, then." Esnir says kindly. "If you can't bring yourself to actually harm, and we feel it is warranted, one of us will do it instead. But prepare yourself for that potentiality."

I nod at him, taking deep, steadying breaths. This is war. People's lives are on the line. Innocent people's lives. They already killed some of my familiar's wolf pack. Over sixteen thousand people dead in three hundred and seventy-five years. They started this, we're here to end it.

With that, the tent becomes a flurry of quiet activity. Everyone finds a perch to sit or stand, out of the way of the front part of the tent where a chair is set away from everything else. Anarus stays close to the front of the tent with me, but back along the tent wall to be out of the way.

"Truth?" I ask Sadness. "What emotions create truth?"

"They don't. Truth is a choice, not a destiny." Sadness tells me. "But you did a pretty damn good job of trying it when you talked to me."

I mutter under my breath. "What I wouldn't give for a bit of Eecret. Truth leaf would be so helpful right now."

Isis pops up from her seat and rummages in a bag by her feet. "I don't have Eecret, but I do have some daisy. It's not as strong, better for divination than truth telling, but it's not nothing."

Isis hands me a small jar of dried flower petals. "Thanks." I tell her, then turn back to Sadness. "How are we playing this?"

"You talk, I'll focus on emotional control." Sadness says. "You interrogated her before, she'll expect you. I can jump in when we need to throw her off from getting too comfortable."

Sounds like a plan. Esnir gestures out the tent flap and Death brings in a squirming Fertility goddess and plunks her down hard on the chair. She's blindfolded, hands and feet bound, and gagged.

Without speaking, I hand Death the jar from Isis, and touch my mouth. He nods, then takes one leaf out of the jar before ripping down Fertility's gag and shoving the leaf in her mouth. He holds her jaw shut, but looks at me with his eyebrows furrowed.

When Death runs his free hand down his throat, I know he is asking if she needs to swallow the leaf. I look at Isis, who shakes her head. She holds up a hand, as if to say stop, bouncing her head from side to side as if she is counting in her head.

After about sixty seconds, she waves her hand, telling us to go ahead, and Death drops the hand on Fertility's mouth but doesn't move away from her. She spits out the leaf quickly, complaining of the bitter taste of it. I wait for her to go silent again, and for Sadness to do what she wants with Fertility's emotions.

"Fertility." My voice echoes in the silent tent. I've never heard fifteen people be so quiet before. Fertility jumps slightly at the noise and turns her head to track my voice. "What is the council planning?"

"How would I know?" She whines. "I've been stuck in a tent, bound and gagged. I smell. Couldn't you at least allow Death to let me bathe?"

I move as I talk, just like I did last time. "You seriously want me to believe you and Fertility god don't have some sort of hive mind brain? What is the council planning?"

She keeps her voice overly high pitched, making her whine seem more forced than real. "We don't, I swear. I don't know anything."

I step carefully to the strategy table and pick up the bowl from my breakfast and drop it on the table with a loud thud that makes Fertility jump. "Wrong answer."

"I. Don't. Know." Fertility drops the fake whine. "I can't connect with my mate that way. Not without physical touch."

"Well, then you must know the plans the council would have if they fear an attack." I say calmly. "Tell me."

Fertility shakes her head. "There are no plans. It's not possible to attack the council."

I kneel in front of Fertility, so close she can feel my breath as I speak and it startles her again. "Wrong answer." I whisper. I reach out one finger and touch her cheek gently. "What would the council do if they were worried about an attack?"

Fertility fails to repress a shiver at my touch. "There are no plans."

I look up silently at Death, then Esnir, my finger still on Fertility's cheek. Death shrugs and Esnir nods. I remove my finger from her cheek, wait one second, then slap her as hard as I can, cringing at my own actions. Nope, did not like doing that. But I ignore my distaste at hurting her.

While her cheek turns pink, I repeat myself. "Wrong answer."

"Sadness? Is that you trying to make me afraid?" Fertility laughs, all trace of fear gone, replaced with anger. "I'm not afraid. You can't make me afraid. You're all dead. You just don't know it yet."

I glance at Sadness who nods. She wants me to help her push the fear. Give Fertility fear. An uber fuck ton of it. Let her fear her next breath. Her ability to have a next breath if she lies again. I weave the fear of Fertility's destiny into her choice to either lie or tell the truth. Which one she chooses decides that destiny, I try to make her believe.

"What is the council planning?" I say again.

A small trail of sweat glistens in Fertility's hairline at her forehead. Her breaths start coming in short bursts. I go back to the table and slam the bowl again. I wait a beat, then do it again.

"Tell me, Fertility." I guess I am good at interrogations. I don't like being good at this, though. It feels wrong. But we have no choice.

"A secret force." The words come out of Fertility as if she's fighting saying them. "Pure children of the original gods. More than you could ever fight. If there is ever a threat of the council being attacked, the council is to sequester in the council hall and the force will surround it."

"How many?" I crouch in front of her again.

Fertility grits her teeth, turning her head away from where she knows I am. I stand and walk around her slowly. She needs more motivation, but I don't want to be the one to do it again. I can't make myself.

Looking at Death, I trail a finger over her shoulder, telling him silently that I want him to do it instead. Death nods, and as I circle the rest of the way around

Fertility, Death lays one meaty hand on the shoulder I touched.

Again, I hate it. I hate doing this. But she made it them or us. Just like Aretha in game six made it her or me. We have to know what we are up against to survive it, and it's us, the humans and gods who want to be fair and safe, or them, the original gods wanting to maintain power that they never deserved. It's us or them and Fertility chose them. I have to choose us.

When I am back in front of her, I ask again. "How many gods in that force?"

I can tell Death is exerting just enough pressure on Fertility's shoulder to make her fear what he would do. Gods heal, and quickly, but a dislocated shoulder would still hurt and need to be reset before healing. I know from personal experience.

"A hundred!" She shrieks out quickly. "There are a hundred of them."

Death removes his hand from her shoulder.

I nod even though she can't see me. "Good. Now, who are the other two?"

"What?" Fertility actually sounds confused.

"A hundred and two people came to the council hall this morning." I tell her. "A hundred outside, guarding. And two went inside. Who are the two?"

"How do you?" Fertility sputters.

I chuckle, letting venom spill with it. "You think you know what we have going on here, but you have no idea. A force of one hundred guards is nothing to us. A minor inconvenience. Who are the two?"

Fertility clacks her mouth shut so hard, I swear I hear her teeth crack. Death puts his hand back on her shoulder. From the face she is making, he's putting a lot more pressure on it than he was before. Enough to actually hurt.

I look up at him, my eyes glancing over to Esnir and everyone else, a nervousness coming over me. I was fine with the threat of physical force, even the slap, but actual harm? Suddenly, I'm not so sure.

Silently, Anarus walks over to me. He picks up my hand and places it on his wolf tattoo, while looking me in the eyes. I can tell what he's saying. Wolves are already dead. People may be soon too. They would have no compunction against hurting or killing us. This is war. A dislocated shoulder is nothing to a god. Painful but nothing in the long term. I swallow back bile and nod at Death.

He squeezes Fertility's shoulder and there is an audible pop as her clavicle breaks. I thought he would dislocate her shoulder, but he didn't. He broke her clavicle. I don't know if that's better or worse. Without moving his hand, Death sets the clavicle bone properly while Fertility is still screaming from the pain of the break. It will heal perfectly fine in a few hours, but until then, it will hurt like a bitch.

"I won't tell you!" Fertility screams. "I won't! You already know. You should!" She pants in pain, trying to control her shaking. "What good friends you are if you don't know who the two are."

Fuck.

"Fuck." Esnir whispers.

I turn my head to him. The eyes of everyone from the games widen at the same time as we pale. We know who the two are.

"What did you do to them?" I growl, anger surging. The people in the room who weren't in the games with us look to each other, confused, while everyone from the games instinctively steps closer. "What did you do to them, Fertility!"

Fertility only lets out a caustic laugh. Out of the corner of my eye, I see Ydum and Byder grabbing Anarus as his fists ball up. They aren't speaking but making far too much noise. Enough for Fertility to realize they're in the tent. Ayja is holding Esnir back, but struggling to and she's unsure why she has to at all. No one is holding me back though, so when I ball up my own fist, I expect no one will stop me.

I expect no one will stop me until Damek shoves in front of me, that is. His fist lands in Fertility's nose with a resounding thud and blood pours down her face.

"What the fuck did you do to Raven and Uesis?" He yells, his voice deeper and angrier than I've ever heard it. Even when he attacked me in the sixth game. Iella is pulling him back before he can hit Fertility again, or she is trying to. She is significantly smaller than him, but he relents anyway.

"Answer the question, Fertility." I seethe. "Raven and Uesis wouldn't have joined the council willingly. What did you do to them?"

Fertility bares her teeth in a grotesque, bloody version of a smile. "Guess you'll have to go through that minor inconvenience of a guard force to find out."

I lunge but Sadness steps between me and my target, shoving Fertility up roughly into Death's hands. "Get her out of here. She's no more use to us now."

Death wrangles the manically laughing Fertility out of the tent.

Sadness looks over all of us. "Calm the fuck down, now!" I feel the press of her power behind her words and my anger yields to her words, but only by a small margin.

"They have Raven and Uesis as hostages." Isis spits. I have never heard that girl speak with so much contempt. Or any contempt. Her sweet voice twisted in anger and fear. "They've had them for a month and a half. What have they done to them?"

Ayja uses a soothing tone that helps nothing. "We can't know until we rescue them. Which we will. Today. Now." She turns her son to face her. "Forget Fertility and help me figure out how to adjust the plans to include a rescue party for them."

Esnir's jaw is tight, a muscle twitching there, but he nods and turns to the strategy table to look over the troop assignments.

The rest of us from the games try to contain our anger. I whirl on Sadness, Fire, Nature, and Hunt. "You knew! You knew they have Raven and Uesis as hostages and you said nothing this entire time." I stalk to stand in front of Sadness, waiting for her to give us any explanation.

"I didn't know." She claims. "I know what happened at the tenth game, but not what was done after that. Inspiration said he would deal with them."

"What happened at the tenth game?" Anarus is swirling with shadows, his hold on the wilde hunt very tenuous.

Sadness sighs, knowing she lost our trust. "Music isn't a pantheon of its own. It's under Inspiration. Normally, that power only enhances other powers. Sing a creation song while another god creates, and the creation goes smoother. Fire god is trying to burn something? Music gods can sing a song to enhance the range, but not one to set the thing on fire themselves. And most music gods have only one type of song. But Uesis took on a full music mantle like we've never seen before. He can create all types of music as a power. He could burn down the world with a song if he wanted.

"Inspiration said that was too much power in one god. Every pantheon's power in one music god. He had Uesis restrained. Uesis, Raven and their families were put under Inspiration's control. I thought he would be made mortal to strip him from his overly enormous power, but Inspiration must have had different plans."

Sadness stops talking and I turn to Fire, Nature, and Hunt. They nod at Sadness's story.

Fire shrugs. "Music is in the Inspiration pantheon. It was Inspiration's job to hobble a god from his pantheon with a mantle they couldn't control. He should have made Uesis mortal, like we've done for other gods with the same issue."

"Why didn't you tell us?" I ask all four of them.

"You never asked." Hunt says, her voice impassive. "We thought they were made mortal and were just living in Raven's village. We thought you would find them there, like you did Wren and Kutar."

This changes everything.

Or does it, really? The four of them may be claiming that the council is hobbling gods because their mantles are uncontrollable, but what if it wasn't about that god being able to control their mantle? What if that only meant they couldn't be controlled by the council?

I look around the tent at the gods that were with us in the games. They tried to stop Anarus because of his power. They tried to stop Ydum and Byder because of their powers. Esnir came through unscathed, but war gods are a newer creation of the original gods. Maybe they thought he would be controllable. And he isn't a full mantle for his pantheon. I really haven't asked too much about Iella's mantle. Is she a full chance goddess? Is there such a thing as a full chance god, since it's the combination of two original god powers?

Modes never made it out of the cave, as a destiny god. A destiny god while I'm a Fate witch? That would have been bad for them if we had teamed up. Tholdir was flames, or at least that's what we thought. How much power would he have gained had he lived? What about Wilros as a messenger god? What about Kara as a victory goddess? Victory would just be an extreme version of chance. Iella's power magnified infinitely.

We said it when we figured out Anarus is the child of Death and Winter. The purpose of the games is to make a mating pair, using the cave to match a god and witch. We thought it was to stop gods from being born with twisted powers because they are too pure as the child of two gods. But it wasn't. The games were never about saving the gods, but about controlling them.

How many gods were just bumped off because their powers were greater than the council would have been able to control? We can't know. How many times have the original gods done this before? How many times have the original gods claimed a new god failed to take their mantle and just made them mortal because they were too strong to be controlled.

This time, though, Inspiration knew what the four of us in the games were thinking. He knew what we were planning and he planned ahead for it. He took them hostage rather than making Uesis mortal to hold them as bait. Or leverage. Yeah, this changes nothing. It's just more of the same bullshit.

"We'll get them out." Esnir says, throwing the paper he had been looking at back onto the table. "It'll have to be us going in there. If they brought Raven and Uesis into the council hall, then surrounded it, they know we're coming today. So, the plan doesn't change. Everyone does what they know to do, we just get Raven and Uesis out first."

All of us from the games give Esnir a terse nod. "What about these fuckers?" Anarus gestures at the four original gods.

"They gave blood oaths." Ayja says. "Blood oaths you extracted, Anarus. They may have withheld crucial information, but they couldn't defy us now if they wanted to. Not really. They can choose to not offer information, but they couldn't refuse us or lie if we asked them outright. Not if they want their blood to stay on the inside of their bodies. Nothing changes."

"Are we doing this or what, then?" Damek growls.

Esnir looks at me. "Give the signal."

I relay the command. Kinshra, long howl.

At once, the air around us reverberates with the howls of wolves, a wave of howls that spreads from one wolf to another. The twelve of us set to breach the council hall leave the strategy tent together, meeting up with Death on the way out.

I take Anarus's hand in mine as we walk and give it a squeeze. We don't speak, but he pulls his shadows into his arm, forcing them back under his control for now.

At the northern edge of the camp, we meet up with the hunter group. Following Xolios's hand signals, the group splits in two, half of the hundreds of people move to circle the city to the east, staying within the woods, and the other half move to the west. We go with the group to the east. We are not quiet about, nor do we attempt to stay hidden.

As we walk, we pass witches in teams of two or three with a wolf. Each group is close enough to see the previous and the next group by line of sight. The weather group is encircling the city.

At the first group or two, I see a few gods with children rushing past them, out of the city. The weather witches stop them, and the families recoil at first in fear. But the witches speak calmly and kindly to them, weapons lowered, hands too, so they aren't threatening as warriors, gesturing towards the south, before letting them continue on. They are guiding the families to the refugee camp Wren set up past the river. Good. The children will be safe. The innocents. No matter what happens, we won't become like them by threatening the innocents.

As we walk, I see teams of three break off from the group and head deeper into the city. The hunter and nature witches manning the caches heading to their assigned post.

Jinx, weather and cache protection is in place. Kinshra tells me. *Wolves headed to them to be guards and messengers now.*

I relay this to Esnir. The city of Veirveil is now completely surrounded. My heart upticks. There's no going back now. Not that there was any chance of going back for a long time now, but this feels more like the first act. It feels odd to be walking this calmly to go to war. My hand trembles and I ball it in a fist to stop it.

About the time our route around the city starts to shift from northeast to northwest, Kinshra speaks again. *Nature is in place, Jinx. They have taken back control of the northern break. No losses on our side.*

Thanks, Kinshra. Again, I tell Esnir who only nods. We didn't know the council had left anyone at the northern break, so the fact that we took no losses from taking it back startles me. The fighting has already started and we are still just casually walking.

After what my nerves make me feel like is a long time, but is probably closer to thirty more minutes, we reach the northern break. The hunters that went west meet us there at almost the same time.

From what the gods taught Isis and me last night, this is the most dangerous moment for us as an army. We created the choke point to slow down the council's ability to leave, but it also slows down our approach. We need to get several hundred people through the choke point without the guards around the council hall noticing us and using it against us, taking us out before we can even breach the government wedge. Not an easy feat, but a necessary one.

Xolios uses hand signals to direct the hunters through the choke point and to the west. The council building is to the east, but we want to stage inside the wedge before we go there. So far, there have been no unexpected obstacles, besides the few guards at the northern break that the nature group dispatched without an issue.

It seems to me like the council is going to try the same tactics as they did with the non-magical humans. Shelter in place to create a stalemate where we can't enter the building and they won't leave. I wonder how shitty their intelligence is if they think that will work. They can't know about the sheer volume of humans with magic and gods coming at them. Either that, or they grossly overestimate the power of their god guards. Or we grossly underestimated them.

Once everyone is past the choke point of the northern break, Esnir takes over the directions. Archers first, now we creep through the government wedge, using multiple streets and open areas to move as a somewhat fluid group until the council building is in sight. The thirteen of us meant to go into the council building stay together, just behind the archers.

Slowly, under the direction of Esnir and Xolios, the hunters circle the building, using the city terrain to hide their movements. We wait at the front, hidden in the shadows of a building that I have no idea what it is used for, ready to enter the council building once a path is cleared. As we wait, Kinshra finds me.

Esnir gives a slight nod to Kinshra, who lets out a small bark. The guards around the building hear it, but with so much interference by wolves already, they don't react. They still don't react when the small bark is passed from one wolf to another, spreading the message that everyone is in place until it reaches the weather group surrounding the city.

The weather changes swiftly. Too swiftly to be natural. The day goes from cool, with a small brisk wind, to downright freezing in moments. The wind starts swirling around the building, whipping our hair around us. From our hiding spot, I can see the guards in front of the council building glance around nervously. Clouds gather just above the council building and a freezing rain that changes to sleet in the natural cold of winter starts to fall.

A few steps behind me, I hear Damek snort softly. "Of course, they get sleet on the first try."

I hold in a laugh that's completely inappropriate at this moment. Damek fought hard to make sleet in the second game, only succeeding because I let him after I made rain against him to win the game. Ydum next to me catches my eye, a smile on his face he's trying to suppress. We really, really should not be laughing at this right now, but I think we have all been broken just a little too far by all this shit.

Turning my attention back to the guards in front of the council building, I see two gods drop their bows. They must be weather gods and working to stop our weather group. I'm not sure why they bother. It's not like it wasn't already winter and they're gods. They won't freeze very easily. Our humans can, though, so trying to stop the extra cold actually works against them.

Then, it dawns on me. They aren't trying to stop the cold but the wind that is blowing straight around them. Their archers are going to have a harder time shooting in the tailwind swooping down over the roof of the building and out in front of them.

The wind holds in our favor. Esnir gives a signal and our archers let loose a volley of arrows. This is the first sign beyond the unnatural weather that the guards get to prove they are actually under attack.

In response, they close ranks, closer to the building. Or attempt to. Our archers in front of the building took out five of their ten archers and eight of the hammer wielders before they could get out of the way. In their place, ten dagger wielders come from both sides of the building to replace the ten that had been ranged along the walls. The stone awning over the front doors of the building makes their archers fairly useless. But it also makes our archers useless against the forty-seven gods crowding in front of the door.

What isn't useless for us, though, is our over four-to-one odds. Esnir gives the signal and with a yell, the hunter group charges the doors. I try to watch the clash and keep track of who belongs to us and who belongs to the council, but the mayhem that ensues makes it impossible.

I know people fall. I see them get hurt and some of our hurt people are dragged back to the woods, towards us, but I can't tell in the mess who they are. My father, two of my sisters, and my brother-in-law are out there somewhere, but I don't know where. For all I know, they are on the other side of the building and I would never be able to see them. Knowing this doesn't stop me from looking and worrying anyway.

In a shorter time than I thought it would take, there's a whoop from the hunter group as we take control of the front door. I see most of the guards from the front of the building kneeling, their hands raised in surrender and their weapons on the ground. We didn't kill unless we needed to kill.

Several people with backpacks rather than weapons, are still moving around, moving between our still armed people, and some of their unarmed, kneeling people. I realize they're the medics, treating the wounds of our people and the enemy equally.

An echoing whoop from the other side of the building tells us the building is now surrounded by us and under our control. A few of the medics, now recognizable to me with their backpacks, run around the sides of the building to offer their services where they are needed for the backside forces.

It feels too easy, though, and my brain itches, chafing against the thought that we are missing something.

"That was too easy." Anarus echoes my thoughts from behind me.

If we were following the plan, Esnir should be signaling for the thirteen of us to enter the council building now. But one look at his face says he's struggling like Anarus and I are.

Something is wrong. Something is missing. Something big. There's something we don't know and that something means the council isn't showing their true hand with the guards outside the building.

Esnir looks at Damek, Ydum, Byder, Death, and Anarus. They are saying something only with their eyes. With only the slightest of nods, Esnir, Damek, Ydum, and Byder all instantly grab Fire, Nature, Hunt, and Sadness, pinning their arms as they force them against the wall of the building next to us with daggers at their throats. Iella, Isis, and I scurry out of their way while Death and Anarus pace in front of the four original gods. Anarus has his own dagger pressed against his right wrist, the wrist that isn't the wilde hunt gate, which confuses me.

"What would the council do if the building is breached?" Death asks the four original gods in a whisper-growl.

None of the original gods answer or even move, but a feeling of calm washes over me.

"Jinx." Death says. "Stop Sadness."

Shit. Sadness is making us calm. She's using peace to try to distract us from the fact that we know we missed something. Clear thoughts. We need clear thoughts. I push everything I can against Sadness's peace.

"Who took Sadness's blood oath?" I ask, realizing that while Death and Anarus were getting blood oaths of loyalty from Hunt, Fire, and Nature, Sadness was with me. And no one came to her to get an oath while I was there.

"Fuck." Anarus glances at Death. No one. The answer is no one.

Fear. Make Sadness fucking afraid because she is about to die if she doesn't tell us what we missed right now. Byder presses the tip of his dagger harder into Sadness's throat. The other three don't let Hunt, Nature and Fire go, but they give a little more space to Byder and Sadness.

"What would the council do if the building was breached, Sadness?" I ask again. We don't have time for this. Whatever the answer is, they are doing it right now. I look Sadness in the eyes. I trusted her. I shouldn't have trusted her. I'm completely foolish for trusting her.

Sadness smiles, a sad smile. "I didn't lie to you, Jinx. About Fear. I didn't lie about that. And I didn't lie when I said I believe that all the original gods should die. Even me."

Before any of us can think, Sadness presses herself forward, dipping her head and turning it to the side as she pushes herself against Byder's knife, slitting her own throat. Byder yells and tries to pull back but it's too late. Blood rushes out of the original goddess, flowing over Byder's hands as Sadness's body goes limp.

"Shit!" Byder pales.

"Anarus, cut her Fate line." I say as I pull Byder to me, away from the body of the original goddess. Byder is panicking, but trying not to. I wrap my arms around him. For all we've done in the games, the only ones of us in the group from the games to actually kill anyone before is me, Ydum, and Damek. And Byder wasn't even trying to kill her. I'm not sure if it is my heart or Byder's that is pounding against my chest so hard. Probably both of us.

Death turns to the three remaining, blood oathed original gods. "Answer the question."

Esnir, Ydum, and Damek shift, returning their focus to the gods under their knives. Fire squirms under Damek's knife and, instinctually, Damek pulls the blade back a bit so it's not actually touching Fire. Fuck, how many spies did we miss?

Anarus had been looking into nothing for a moment while he cut Sadness's Fate line, but now he turns to Fire, pressing his own blade to his own wrist harder.

Fire turns red around the edges of her face. She squirms again and Damek, regaining his composure, pushes the knife back where it was.

"Safe room." Fire pants out. "Behind the council hall. Fire proof, with the controls for explosive fire traps throughout the building inside the room."

"How many traps?" Anarus asks.

Fire's redness spreads to her cheeks. "Four in the hall, two in the lobby. Triggers are individual. Can be exploded from in the safe room or set to explode from movement near them. The four in the council hall will bring down the roof if they are all detonated."

Anarus takes a step closer to Fire. "Anything else?" He presses his dagger harder against his wrist, causing the tiniest drop of blood to well up. The way Fire whines at this drop of blood, and the flush now covering her entire face, makes me realize that Anarus's wrist must be the trigger for the blood oath. If he makes the blood oath on his wrist actively bleed, Fire's blood will boil inside her.

"No, not unless they changed anything without me here to help." Fire's eyes are darting from Damek to Anarus, not sure who is the greater threat against her right now.

"You lied." Anarus swipes the blade at his wrist, leaving a fine scratch that wells up with blood. As Fire collapses, screaming, the scratch on Anarus's wrist heals instantly and the scar that was there disappears. Within seconds, Fire's body is as lifeless as Sadness's is, only red and blistered instead of pale and bloodless.

Anarus looks at Hunt and Nature. "Anything to add?"

Both gods shake their heads slightly.

"No." Nature says quickly. "Fire knew the traps since she made them. I know of no others." He swallows hard, his Adam's apple bobbing against Ydum's blade.

"Why didn't you tell us about them?" Death asks.

"Forgot." Hunt says, then she whimpers and cringes. "Honestly. Fire and Inspiration made them in the war against the non-magical humans. The safe room too. We never even thought about them after that. It's been a long time, more than hundreds of years. It just never occurred to me. I wouldn't have kept it secret purposefully."

"How do we prevent them triggering?" I ask. "How do we stop it?"

"You can't, as far as I know." Nature tells me. "The controls are in the safe room and the traps high up on the walls, higher than anyone could reach, even Death. Even if you could reach them, the only option would be to trigger them, not disarm."

"Fuck." Three of us say it at the same time, but I'm not sure who the other two are. I'm the one who continues talking though. "What's the trigger? Inside them, what's the trigger?"

Nature answers. "If I remember correctly, the box contains an explosive powder, Fire's creation. A flint and steel fire starter mechanism is kept apart, flint on a turning mechanism is kept from turning to scrape against the steel by a glass piece. Shatter the control in the safe room, the glass in the box breaks instantly, allowing the flint to turn, rubbing against the steel until enough sparks set the powder ablaze and it explodes from the box, knocking down the support column for the roof. Trip the control the other way, the glass will shatter when there is enough vibration from movement through the room to trip its breaking rather than shattering the glass instantly. Not sure how much of a vibration will trip it. I wasn't part of the design for it."

"So, the box can be disarmed if you can remove either the flint or steel without the glass shattering first." Esnir says, thinking. "But the council could have already set them to trip under vibrations that could be as little as just one person walking."

"Hey, Anarus?" Damek paces a few steps, not guarding anyone anymore. "How much actual physical manipulation can your wilde hunt do?"

Anarus twists his mouth. "Not sure anymore. They could before." He looks down at his hands. To test it, he would have to let a shadow free, but that means taking the dagger away from the blood oath marks on his other wrist. Knowing what he's thinking, I move to his side.

"Keep your eyes on them." I jut my chin at the two original gods left, besides Death, and reach my hand to his wrist that is the gate. I press on his wrist, letting just one shadow out. Then, I hold out my own dagger, asking it, "Can you pick this up?"

The shadow tilts its head, or what I think is its head, at Anarus, who nods for it to do as it was told. I feel a shiver of cold against my skin as the shadow picks up my dagger then sets it back down in my hand nicely.

"That'll do." Esnir says. "Let's move. We've wasted too much time as it is."

Before Esnir and Ydum let go of Nature and Hunt, Anarus gets very close to their faces. Close enough for his breath to ruffle their hair. "If you so much as sneeze wrong, I cut this and you boil like Fire. Got me?"

Both Nature and Hunt nod and Ydum and Esnir let them go. The eleven of us left finally move to the council building. At the door, the fifty or so witch hunters stand to the side to let us through. One moves as if he will open the door for us, but Anarus stops him.

"Where are the boxes in the foyer?" He asks the original gods.

"I don't know." Nature says.

"They'll be visible, though. Near the ceiling, large, black rectangular box." Hunt adds.

Anarus nods at Ydum and me. Ydum opens the door to the council building very slowly and only a crack. I press on Anarus's wrist again, letting a few shadows into the building. Ydum keeps the door open, peering through the crack. Anarus closes his eyes to focus and Death takes over holding his dagger to Anarus's wrist while his son focuses on directing the shadows. After a few minutes, the shadows come back through the door and drop two pieces of flint into my hand.

"Open the door the rest of the way but do not go in." Byder says behind me. When I look, he has a bow and arrow he snagged from one of the archers in his hands, and a quiver full of more arrows slung across his back.

Ydum does as he says and he steps into the doorway, glancing up and down the hall for the black boxes the shadows disarmed. He spots one, its cover hanging loose but not fully off, and fires an arrow into the box, shattering it. A black dust puffs out of the box and slowly falls onto the carpet below. He spots the second box and shoots it as well, with the same results.

Byder nods, nocking another arrow. "Just to be sure."

"Go slow." Esnir tells us. "We don't know who is where in the building or how much vibrations will set off the ones in the hall."

Carefully, we all move one by one down the hallway to the spot the god Drew usually sat. Kinshra moves to follow me into the building but I shake my head.

Stay out here, Kinshra. You need to be able to send messages to the rest of the wolves to sound alarms.

Kinshra shakes out her fur, showing her displeasure at this, but does as I say.

Again, Ydum opens the door to the council room only a crack and I let a few shadows loose from Anarus's arm to go through the door.

After a moment, Anarus's eyes go wide. "Room is empty except Raven and Uesis tied up on the dais. Raven appears unconscious and Uesis is gagged."

Esnir swears. "Fuck, do this carefully."

Anarus nods and I know he's communicating with the shadows. It takes longer this time, but the shadows come back, dropping four pieces of flint into my waiting hand before going back into Anarus's arm. Ydum pulls the door wider and Byder finds the four broken boxes along the four long columns I always thought were just decoration. He shoots each one with an arrow and we watch as the dark powder from them falls to the floor.

"Go slow. There could be more that Fire didn't know they added." Byder says, stepping back to let everyone else in first.

As soon as I enter the almost empty room, my eyes go to Raven and Uesis. Raven is tied up, her hands bound to her feet behind her back and she is lying on her side, her eyes closed as if she is asleep. Uesis is right behind her, tied in a similar fashion, but upright on his knees. His eyes are wild and roving over all of us. Raven's black hair is matted and dirty, and her umber skin is pale. Uesis has a beard, shaggy around his lips, his greasy and sweat-soaked hair long enough to flop in his eyes.

Both of them are dirty, bruised and far too thin, wearing the same clothes they wore the day of the tenth game. I can see from the other side of the room there is a black something in Uesis's mouth, held in by a strap around his head. Uesis is shaking his head at us and I'm not sure if he is trying to say something or just desperately wants the gag out.

Damek doesn't wait but charges up the dais. "Hang on, man. We'll get you."

Uesis is shaking his head harder. I look at the black in his mouth again and realize it looks just the same as the black boxes on the wall, just smaller.

I scream. "Fuck! Damek, stop!"

He doesn't listen to me. I scream again. "Damek! It's a-"

I'm too late. Damek undoes the strap around Uesis's head and I see Uesis try to grit his mouth together tighter around the box, but Damek pulls. I only have enough time to scream and turn away, falling to the floor behind a chair before the blast ripples through the air. My ears ring and I'm not sure if that's from the explosion or from the racing of my own heart.

I don't have to look to know what happened. Iella's screams piercing the air tell me everything. I've heard that type of scream before. I've made that type of scream before. That scream is the scream of a mate bond ripping apart.

I'm pushed down further, I'm not sure by whom, but when I try to stand, Ydum and Anarus are both still over me, dust that floated down from the ceiling coating them. Slowly, Anarus stands. Ydum moves to a crouch next to me. As he stands, he pulls me up with him.

"Don't look." Ydum's voice cracks as he shields my vision with his body, lifting me up and wrapping his arms around me to plaster my face in his chest. "Don't look, beautiful."

"Isis. Take Iella back outside." Esnir says quietly, his voice shaking. I turn my head that is held tightly by Ydum's trembling arms to look at Esnir. The dark tan skin of his face nearly white as he stares in the direction of the dais Ydum won't let me look at.

Iella's still screaming and it's hard for me to catch my breath. I know the pain she's feeling right now. Nothing in the world hurts the way a snapped bond hurts. Iella goes with Isis without a fight, but she doesn't stop screaming the whole way.

Once she's outside, the room is too silent and all I can hear is the rush of blood as my heart beats too hard and too loud. Ydum's arms are squeezing me tighter than I think he means to. He knows that pain too. I turn my head to look at Byder. I can see the arrow nocked in the bow he is still holding shaking. Even the memory of the pain is too much to think around.

"Is Raven?" I can't get the rest of the words out. I know Damek is gone. I know Uesis is too, but maybe the blast was small enough. Maybe.

"No, baby girl. She's gone." Byder tells me, his voice just as cracked and raw as Ydum's was. There is a puddle of vomit at his feet.

I try to swallow the sob. We should have looked for them harder. We should have looked for Raven and Uesis harder. Gods, Raven. She was only ever there for the gossip. She gave me rosemary, basil, and black pepper. She knew Saffron from home before the games and was afraid to tell her family she survived when Saffron didn't.

Uesis sang for the wilde hunt. He played his violin for us. He couldn't fight well, but easily accepted Raven teaching everyone else when the petunias split our group in two.

Damek. Damek who was the only human male in the games. He taught me how my magic was different without judgement. Who thought that my magic was "fucking cool." Who should have been on the council if I wasn't.

I'm not able to stop the sob this time. But I try anyway. We aren't done here. I can't mourn yet. The original gods need to pay for what they did. This was a trap. They used our friends as a trap. They will answer for it.

Anarus moves faster than a blink, pinning Nature against the wall, his dagger digging into the god's neck. "Safe room. Where is the fucking safe room?" His growl doesn't stop when his words do and shadows are moving around him without him asking them to.

"Through the back door to the hall." Nature squeaks out.

Byder raises his trembling hands, finally looking away from the dais to look at Hunt. He points his arrow at point blank range to her head. "Any other way out of it?"

Hunt shakes her head. "Only the one door in or out, reinforced walls around it. But it's magically locked. Blood of each person that goes into the room unlocks it. If you don't add blood to the lock, you can't get in. Once the door is opened from this side, then closed, all the same blood used to unlock it from the outside have to be used again to unlock it from the inside or it won't open."

"What's the door made of?" Death asks.

Nature answers. "Solid metal covered to look wood."

Death nods and walks away, calling back over his shoulder. "Give me five minutes."

Unsure what Death is planning, the seven of us wait right where we are. Anarus doesn't let Nature go and Byder does not take his aim from Hunt. Ydum doesn't let me go either. His arms are still strong bands around me, only the slight tremors in them, and his pounding heart, giving away that he's still holding me because of his own feelings rather than to protect me.

The smell of the explosive powder settles and a coppery scent mixes with it. I tell myself not to think about the smell or what it's from. I shiver because I can't lie to myself. I know that smell from Aretha. In a way, not seeing is worse because my mind has a chance to make up its own ideas about what the dais looks like.

Death returns with a group of hunters struggling to help him carry something. I can't tell what it is with half my face still pressed into Ydum's chest but Death gestures down. "Found the key."

Ydum lets out a small, strangled laugh. "That might work."

He finally loosens his grip on me and I can turn to see that between Death and the ten hunters, they are carrying a full fucking tree as thick around as me with the top, leafy crown broken off and a lot of somebody's belts used as handles, wrapped around the trunk.

Anarus lets Nature off the wall. "Lead the way."

Nature takes the lead, Byder pushing Hunt to the front with him. He and Anarus follow right behind them, weapons still trained on them. We aren't trusting anyone anymore.

I'm moved through the room squished between Esnir and Ydum, both of them trying to stop me from seeing the dais. Not that I'm trying to see it very hard. I can tell that neither of them want to look at it either, but they both seem to have their eyes drawn to it over and over. Like a carriage crash, they can't look, but can't look away, shuddering and paling as they do. Death, the hunters, and the tree follow behind us.

The two original gods lead us through the door to the left side of the dais. As we walk past the dais, I can see enough to know I really don't want to see any more. The red pools there are far too large. I avert my eyes, training them on Byder's back, and walk through the door to the back hallway of the council building.

Halfway down the empty and only dimly lit hallway is a door on the right side that looks just like any other wood door. Death taps the door with his fist and it thuds in a way that confirms what Hunt and Nature said. The door may look wood but is actually solid metal.

"Anarus," Death turns to his son. "Tell a few shadows to go into the room. I want to see where the weak spots in the seal of the door are."

Anarus nods and I press his wrist to let a few shadows loose. The shadows circle around the door for several minutes, not finding a way in. They slink back to Anarus and I open the gate to let them back in his arm.

"Nothing." Anarus says with a head shake. "They found no gaps."

"Alright then. We'll make some." Death and the ten hunters position themselves so that the tree they are holding onto by belts wrapped around the trunk is angled towards the spot where the door handle meets the doorframe. The rest of us move down the hallway to be clear of them.

The eleven of them do a few test swings, with the back end of the tree breaking through the wall behind them easily. But that wall is just regular wall, not reinforced like the safe room walls. The broken wall behind them allows the males to swing the tree more fully, allowing them to use the energy at the top of the swing to hit the door harder at the bottom of the swing.

After a few initial test swings, under Death's instructions, they all take one step forward and start swinging the tree in earnest. The first few hits are weaker until they build up more momentum. They hit with a dull thudding that probably just sound like someone knocking on the door inside the room. The force of the hits gets stronger, reverberating in the air, the steel rattling with the impact. Tiny chunks of wood fly off the tree at each hit.

After a few attempts, Nature pushes out from under Anarus's guard, whipping off his belt. He adds it to the belts there to add his power to the swinging tree. Hunt, Ydum, Esnir, and Byder do the same, adding their strength to the swings. Anarus stays back with me, moving back down the hallway towards the council hall to stay out of the way, knowing that he has to man the wilde hunt. I know that there is no more space along the long tree for me to add my, probably less than helpful, strength right now.

From my position at the end of the hallway, back by the door to the council hall, I can't tell if they are making any headway on the door, but the sounds of the tree hits are louder now. A few more hits and something cracks. On the next swing back, I see the crack was from the tree. A large chunk of the end of the tree has fallen off, but I don't see it in the hallway. It either fell through the door, meaning there is a hole now, or is wedged in the door, meaning there will be a hole soon.

They swing the tree a few more times, then Death holds up a hand and they all stop adding to the motion. The tree slowly stops its swings and they all set it down with a grunt. Death nods at the hunters and they leave back out the way we came.

Death crosses his arms over his chest, not even winded. Ydum, Esnir and even Byder are all at least a little sweaty and short of breath. Nature and Hunt are gasping. They're a lot more out of shape than they thought. The hunters are all trembling from the effort.

"Now, shadows, Anarus." Death says.

We come back over to the door. There is the tiniest of slivers between the door and the doorframe right next to the door handle. All that work and there is only a crack formed from the door bending a slight bit in the doorframe. The broken part of the tree is lodged in the crack. Anarus pulls the wood out and flexes his wrist. Shadows, all of the shadows, pour out of Anarus's arm and into the room. Even through that tiny crack, we can hear the shouts from inside.

"Jinx." Death nods toward the door and I know what he wants. Fear. Give all the council in that room indiscriminate fear. You are afraid of your destiny after this. They are blind in the dark. Be afraid. Be terrified. Your safe room is safe no longer.

Someone on the other side of the door presses up close to the door. "Sadness, why? Why are you doing this to us?" They call out, their voice shaking.

Death laughs. "Sadness is dead, Inspiration. That's not her. Open the door."

"Death." Inspiration gasps. "You're lying. The other Fates are all in here. Only Sadness could be creating this fear."

I snort. "Did you forget about Fear the minute you made him mortal, or did you at least give your fellow god the courtesy to wait until he was actually dead to forget him?"

Inspiration's gasp is audible through the crack in the doorframe. He sputters, still under my fear. "Jinx. Fear couldn't. He's dead. Been dead. Your emotional control." I wait as he tries to connect the dots in his mind. I know when he comes up short.

"You made Fear mortal, but did you cut his destiny?" I know the answer is no. I know Inspiration and the rest of the gods have no idea what or how I am. So, I fill in the gaps for Inspiration, telling him everything Sadness told me. Then I spit, "So, are you going to open the door, or should we leave you in your blind fear to stew a little while longer?"

Inspiration doesn't respond to me, so I turn to Anarus. I can hear talking through that tiny gap in the door, but can't make out what's being said. Anarus looks at the floor, his hands moving slightly at his side.

"They're deliberating. They can't see each other, but are talking. There are… fifteen people in the room. Inspiration, Sky, Water, Spring, Summer, Fall, Winter, yes actually Winter, male Fertility, Anger, Happiness, Peace, Knowledge, Curiosity, Wind, and the human immortal. They seem to be debating opening the door for us. The seasons, minus Winter, the male Fertility and three Fates say yes. Everyone else but the human says no. The human has not voted, and now they are arguing if the human tie-breaker should be used or if they should listen to each other's reasons for their opinion."

Hunt rolls her eyes. "They are literally debating about if they should debate about this. They have been attacked while hiding in their safe room, as much of a declaration of war as we could give them, and they are politically analyzing the situation as if their lives are not in any danger. How the fuck did I put up with their bullshit that long?"

"Make them deaf, Anarus." Esnir says.

Anarus nods and shift his stance slightly. Creating silence under his shadows takes a more concerted effort. I put my hand on his shoulder to lend him strength. Not magically, just more moral support. The pitch of the murmuring sounds coming from the crack in the door swings up significantly as panic takes over.

Death moves back to the tree. "A few more swings? Blind, deaf, and feeling reverberations as we attempt to breach their door could push them over the edge."

I agree but look around. The hunters that had been helping are long gone now. Thinking we were done, and physically spent, they had left as soon as they set down the tree. There's only the eight of us, and Anarus has to concentrate on the wilde hunt. I think Death picks up on my thoughts, and everyone else's.

"They don't have to be effective hits, just scary." He shrugs. Byder, Esnir, Ydum, Hunt, and Nature all take up positions around the tree to grab the straps.

When I move to stand next to one, it's Death that moves to stop me. "Not you."

"What?" I look up at him, my arms crossed over my chest in anger. "Why not me? Because I'm human, or because I'm—"

"Neither of those." Death says quickly, with a chuckle. "You might be human, Jinx, but I am under no illusion that you aren't extremely powerful. Your gods taught you well. But someone needs to mind Anarus, and you can control the gate for the wilde hunt. Concentrate on making them pants-pissing scared instead."

Well, fine. If he's going to be rational about it. I step back again and stand with Anarus. As the others hoist the tree up with grunts and swears, I look at Anarus and see that he is sweating a little. Controlling the wilde hunt is taking a lot out of him.

I feed my hand into his, not planning to give him any magical help, just let him know I am here as he stares down at a random spot on the floor. I stare with him, focusing my mind on every person in the safe room and trying to determine what they would fear the most in their minds.

Chapter Twelve

KNOWING EXACTLY WHO IS in the room, I start with the human tie-breaker. She was last year's Gods Games winner, which means she is a strong witch and now immortal, but I don't know who her god is to know where her power is leaning now.

I saw her so many times, sitting on the dais in the council hall, but never paid her much attention. With an odd number on the council, she was basically just a token human so the original gods could say humans did have a place in the government. She shouldn't still be there, on the council. By all rights, that position should be mine, or if Anarus's death counted, Damek.

I stop my line of thought. I don't want to think of Damek right now. Focus on the human. She needs to be terrified of her destiny when we breach the room.

I stop, having a better thought. Rather than afraid of us, I want her afraid of them, the council in the room with her. We are nothing to fear because she's a victim in all this too. She needs to be afraid of her destiny if we don't make it in the room, if the council wins.

I can't send actual thoughts to her like I can Kinshra, but use my thoughts in my own mind to direct the flow of my magic—my power if I can still believe Sadness—to make the intense feelings I want to create. Sadness said it would take time for me to learn to weave the different emotions together, but I don't have time. I need to do it now. So, brute force and hope, like in the games when I didn't know what I was doing, will have to work for now. I meditate, weaving the story in my mind and letting my magic do the rest.

I focus on all the ways the council could mistreat this single human token representative. Have mistreated humans like her before. They'll make you mortal again. They'll take you from your god, break your bond, the most painful thing you've ever felt in your life. If you don't get out of that room now, they'll sacrifice you if they think it will keep them alive and in power for even just a minute longer. You need to get out of that room, and you need to get out now.

Right when I feel the fear latch onto her, I hear the tree collide with the door with a resounding thud. They aren't swinging it as hard, or hitting the door with as much force as before, but they are hitting it. I feel the human flinch at the feeling of those reverberations. She's blind, deaf, and only feels them, knowing exactly what it is. The terror she was feeling before I even started stacks on top of itself from those reverberations. She is literally clawing at the walls to find the door and give her drop of blood to unlock it. My work with her is done.

I turn my attention to Knowledge and Curiosity. They are a mated pair, I know. I feel them holding hands in the darkness enshrouding them. They can't hear each other, or see each other, but are grounded in that touch. Knowledge jumps at every reverberation of the tree hitting the door. He knows exactly the tensile strength of the door and how many more hits it will take before we breach it. Curiosity leans into Knowledge, knowing he knows, but unsure of that amount herself.

I do the same thing for them that I did for the human. Make them both afraid of the people in the room and what their destiny is with them, rather than fearful of us. Are you sure that is your mate's hand you are holding, I feed both of them the fear. Are you completely sure? What if it is actually Inspiration? You know he wants you both gone. Your powers are worthless without him and his worthless without yours. Inspiration wants to be in control. He wants all the control. Without you, he could have it. He could be the only god of the lands of Nazus if you two were just out of the damn way. So, are you sure? Are you totally confident that is your mate's hand?

I feel the moment Curiosity crumbles under my fears and yanks her hand out of Knowledge's. He roars, seeking her hand again, fighting my fears, but blind and deaf, they cannot find each other again. The only way you will see your mate again alive is to get the fuck out of that room, I tell them both. Find the door and unlock it. Get out and maybe you can survive. Survive together.

Does it hurt gods who are bonded as much for that bond to snap as it does witches and gods who are bonded? Anarus doesn't have to wait until you are dead to snap your bond. What if he does it now? Are you willing to risk that the pain isn't the same?

Another reverberation of the tree hitting the door rolls through both Knowledge and Curiosity and they fight towards the door. My fear is latched into them and I can move on.

I try for the three nature type gods, Wind, Sky, and Water. All of your powers are low tier pantheons, I tease them. Should you really have your own pantheons at all? Are you sure? The seasons have a hand in what you make. Nature has a hand in what you make. Death is the only thing that makes what you do have any strength or reason for people to be afraid of you, and Death is against you too. Fuck, Ydum can do what you do and he's not even an original god at all. Should you really be going against the gods that control everything you do? If you win, if you stay in power, what are the chances anyone will listen to you anymore?

The tree hits the door again. Feel that? Can you really feel that? We are coming. The door will give eventually. Do you really think you can stand against Death, Nature, and Ydum? Did you ever really believe you could? You three are all useless gods, unnecessary. Get to the door and let us in and maybe we will at least keep you around to make our lives easier.

The gods that voted for opening the door are all joined together, scrambling in their blindness and deafness to find the door and give their blood to unlock it.

One more hammer of the tree against the door and all the gods break, scrambling to the door in their fear of becoming obsolete. I'm not even having to try hard to make them fear their new destinies if we breach the door. Most of them are halfway there already. But I still bring them the rest of the way.

Most but not all. Two are not. They'll be harder to convince. I focus my energy on the two hard ones. Inspiration or Winter first? I debate this while the tree hits again. A twitch of Anarus's hand in mine makes my mind up for me. Inspiration first. I want to save Winter for last. I want to save Winter for him.

My thoughts turn to Inspiration. The one in charge, the one in control. This is your council, isn't it? That's what you've told yourself over and over. From the first moment of creation, you knew it was all really yours. No one acts without your consent. No one dares to defy you. They couldn't. Without your inspiration, they wouldn't be able to have the ideas to act on.

But if that's true, how the fuck are there so many people on our side? Over a thousand humans defied you with only a slight push. The inspiration for this fight was already burning in their hearts. Your creations were ready to revolt, they just needed someone to say they could. You lost your control on them a long time ago.

The thud from the tree hitting the door changes its tone. I think the door cracked more. What do you think about that, Inspiration? Your idea, this safe room. And now it's a sarcophagus, you and all the gods that followed you into it will die in there. Because a handful of gods and humans decided they were done following you and made their own inspiring thoughts. You are worthless, powerless, done. Just give in and open the door before we knock it down.

Maybe you can save some of the gods you claim to care about. Maybe you can plead your case and we'll let you live. Or at least make your death quick. Not turn you mortal and watch as you shrivel away in the agony you have caused so many other gods. Maybe we'll be merciful, something you never were. That's the only destiny you don't fear, our mercy. Because your destiny is sealed, Inspiration, and it's putty in my hands. The only decision left to be made about that destiny is whether it will contain mercy. So, open the damn door and pray to yourself that I choose mercy.

The tree hits the door again, that change in the tone stronger. Inspiration knows. The door is almost breached and his chances at gaining mercy almost taken from him. He rushes to the door, bumping into other gods, all clamoring to be let at the door, ignoring the risk that we will breach it while they are pressed against it.

Winter is now standing alone in the room, but she doesn't know that. All of her fellow gods are by the door, and she is the last stand against us. I look up to see where we actually are with the door. I'm not sure if the idea that we have almost breached the door is just part of the fear I have created or really true.

When I check, the crack at the door has widened. The gods swinging the tree have had to shift their holds on it as more of the tip of the tree has splintered away.

I feel a stickiness that is more than sweat along my skin and look down at myself. Splinters from the slowly breaking tree must have hit me. There are tears in my shirt and pants. A few are oozing blood, nothing too significant, but enough to be annoying. Now that I noticed them, the splinter wounds sting.

Especially one on my left arm. I run my hand along that arm and find it, just above my elbow, a small chunk of the wood embedded in my arm. Oof, that is a little more than a splinter. As I touch it, the flare of pain tells me to leave it be. I can't pull it out now without risking heavier bleeding or leaving tiny pieces behind that will fester. Better to ignore it for now.

Screaming behind the door tells me that the gods are warring within themselves on whether to do what my fear says and unlock the door or back the fuck out of the way as the gods swinging the tree make it finally break. Getting out of the way must win, because they all scramble out of the way as, with a booming clang, the final bits of the metal lock on the door shatter at the same time that the tree splits down the middle, chunks of wood flying everywhere.

I turn around, blocking Anarus from the projectiles with my back since he is so bent on his work that he doesn't notice them. I feel more burning scratches as some of the flying splinters hit me, but I ignore the pain.

The door is open. The six of them swinging the tree drop the shattered remnants and pull their weapons out into their hands. Death looks at me. Anarus needs to drop the shadows so we can see and hear in the room.

"Anarus." I say softly in his ear as I push on his wrist. He lifts his head to look at me. His dark eyes are bright, his face pale, and sweat is cascading down his face in fat drops. He's trembling as the shadows slide back into his arm and Anarus heaves a shuddering sigh.

"The sun has set. They won't come back out now." He tells me.

That explains why he had to fight so hard to make them do what he wanted. They should have been back in his arm already. Our ability to use the wilde hunt is as done as the shortest day is. The wilde hunt will rest now until Anarus opens the bridge again next October thirty-first.

With the shadows gone, the original gods in the safe room can finally see and hear each other again, but my fear still resides in all of them but Winter. I watch as Knowledge and Curiosity slam into each other, grabbing each other in a desperate hug they won't let go of for a long time.

The rest of them, besides Winter and Inspiration, cower back from the door, putting as much space between us and them as they can. Inspiration is trembling, but tries to stand tall, letting the others cower behind him as if he will protect them. I notice that the human is in a corner of the room, squatted towards the ground, her panicked face looking everywhere as her fingers drip blood on the floor from clawing at the walls so hard she tore off all her nails.

Winter is looking around the room, perplexed by everyone else's behavior. I haven't given her any fear. Yet.

I step into the room and glance around. It isn't as big as I suspected. Just four basic, plain white walls, the same red carpet as in the hallway, and one large table with twenty-one chairs around it.

There doesn't even seem to be any provisions in here. Gods don't starve easily, or dehydrate, but the human would have. A bitterness runs through me as I realize the gods here would have let her if we had decided to wait them out instead of attack. And the gods would have starved too eventually. We could have just blocked the door and let them die in there slowly, never even bothering to do anything but ignore them the way they ignored all the humans in the villages while they starved.

But the human in this room didn't deserve that destiny. Nor does she deserve the one we are planning for the gods. She is as much a pawn as any of us. I walk over to her and crouch down in front of her. I know the others are rounding up the original gods and controlling them as my fear still works on them.

I let my fear drop from the human female, but it doesn't change anything for her right now. I make a concerted effort to give her peace and know we will not threaten her.

"Go out of the building and across the street. Do not look at the dais as you go past. You don't want to see that. Ask anyone for Isis, tell them Jinx said to take you to her. Tell her I said to protect you, that you're innocent. She'll keep you safe. She's human too." I add a little more peace to my words, hoping to undo some of the torment I gave her, knowing Isis will help too.

The female nods at me and, as soon as I back away, she flees the room.

I turn back to the rest of the room. The original gods are all sitting in chairs at the table, one of our gods holding weapons to them, except Winter. Someone must have rearmed Hunt and Nature. Someone decided they were trustworthy now.

Nature is holding two knives against Sky, Wind, and Water, who are all three shirking away from him, my fears seeming to come true for them. Hunt has the male Fertility and Inspiration under her knives. Ydum has the three seasons held together, two of Byder's daggers loosely aimed towards them. Esnir has the three Fates, arms crossed over his chest and no real weapons in his hands, but they are cowering from him all the same. Byder holds Knowledge and Curiosity in one chair, Curiosity sitting in her mate's lap as Byder aims an arrow at their touching chests. Anarus is the only one from our side not guarding or standing. He is slumped into a chair, trying to hide just how tired he is.

Death does not have Winter sitting in a chair either but pinned against a wall by her throat. The low, constant growl coming from his throat belies the serene look on his face. So does the flashes in his eyes. Everyone looks at me for direction.

"Tell me I can snap her neck." Death growls.

"Not yet." I say, surprised by how calm I feel. I don't think the Fates are making me calm, just that I actually am calm.

I thought this would be the worst part of this whole day, the moment everyone looked to me to be the spokesperson for the group. Instead, I only feel disappointed I didn't get to make Winter afraid before we breached the door. I'm angry, I'm sad, I'm hurting, my feelings a mess on the inside, but when I look at the council of the original gods, held hostage by my gods and friends, I feel nothing towards them except contempt.

I thought I would be scared of their combined, overwhelming power. But now I know they don't have some overwhelming power that makes them stronger than everyone else. They just use cruel torture and fear to make themselves appear to. And fear isn't theirs to use anymore. I'm Fear's descendent, his destiny, his revenge. It's mine.

Everything we planned for me to say, I abandon, a new plan forming in my mind that is right for the situation we are in now. Those words were planned for a negotiation, and this is not that. The time for negotiations ended the moment we saw Raven and Uesis on the dais in the council room.

I slowly, very slowly, walk up to the head of the table to stand next to Anarus. "Modes, Dorlios, Kara, Bokysus, Leander."

"What are you doing?" Inspiration asks. "If you think you'll scare us by listing off your dead friends, it won't work." Hunt digs her knife into Inspiration's neck a little more and he stops talking.

I look at him, that calmness I feel making my face stay neutral and impassive, even though my feelings inside are nothing neutral or impassive. "You made me lose track. Guess I'll have to start over. Modes, Dorlios, Kara, Bokysus, Leander, Amanda, Tholdir, Aretha, Zodum, Saffron, Velmos, Asteria, Wilros, Anarus, Raven, Uesis, Damek." My voice breaks on those last three names, but I don't stop. "At least thirty-four others in the cave whose names I don't know. That's only this year. This one year of the Gods Games. You killed them. You murdered them in cold blood for your fun. Tell me why we would let any of you live."

"We didn't kill anyone." Winter cackles. "I distinctly remember the report saying you killed Aretha. Your blade, your hands, Jinx. You killed her not us."

Death squeezes her neck tighter, cutting off her words.

"That's true." I say. "I did. But if I didn't, my name would just have replaced hers on that list. I had no choice. Aretha had no choice. But you did. All of you did. So, tell me why!" I slam my hand on the table to emphasize the last word.

"We didn't kill Anarus. He's sitting right there." Inspiration holds out a limp hand towards Anarus, but drops it when I stare at him again.

This time I'm the one who laughs. "Really? If you didn't kill him, tell me why I had to go into the land of the dead to bring him back!"

Winter's voice is rougher under Death's grip. "You should have left him there. He was the worst mistake of my life."

Anarus looks up at her, his nostrils flaring. He looks like he's going to stand, but I push on his shoulder to make him stay put. The low growl from Death gets louder and I know he's squeezing her neck harder. I grit my teeth as the fury threatens to overwhelm me. I need to deal with the council. I know I do, but the desire to rip Winter's mind apart is too overwhelming.

I bury her in fear. Not the fear of her destiny, that's sealed. But the fear she made in others. The fear Anarus had of his destiny. Everything Anarus has told me about his time growing up. Every secret story, every sharp pain he carries, every fear of his I make hers. Abuse from males who treated him as a plaything then told him he was a rabid dog that needed to be put down. Hits and punches instead of hugs and bedtime stories. Never hearing the words 'I love you' for twenty-two years. Thinking he never would, that he was unlovable.

Never knowing where he would sleep tomorrow and how much the new people would fear him. Being thrown into the games too early and expecting to die. Powers he couldn't control. Putting himself last so that those he loves will live even if he didn't, afraid he will never be loved back by them. Fear of his future with a family because he didn't know how to be a family. I give her it all.

Then, I give her Death's fears. Or at least the fears I think he would have. Never knowing his son. Thinking his son is loved and cared for, but too afraid to check in case he's hurt because of who his father is. The moment he sees his son in the land of the dead, the fear of what happened to cause his son to die. Finding out what had been done to Anarus and the anguish of knowing he could have stopped it if only he hadn't been so afraid. Fear of that son never forgiving him now.

I make her afraid of me, Ydum, and Byder, who love Anarus and will not let her take that away from him. Ever. We will kill her to stop her from ever even looking at him again. I push on her every torment, every heartbreak, every moment of pure pain we felt when the bond was severed.

The more fears I pile on Winter, the larger her winter storm gray eyes get until they are almost bulging out of their sockets. Her pale skin pales more and becomes covered with a sheen of sweat. She trembles under Death's hand, still holding her up against the wall, her feet dangling just a few inches from the floor.

Fear your next breath, Winter. Fear the world that will exist if you stay in it. Your only hope is pain. Pain and anguish and loneliness. No one fears you anymore. No one cares for you at all and they never did. Death is preferable to what awaits you if you breathe again.

"Jinx." Anarus's voice brings me back to myself. I look down at him. "She's bonded to Death. If you kill her, the bond will snap. I don't want to hurt my fath—" He stops himself, cutting off the word he isn't ready to say. "Not that pain. Not for him. Let her live. For him."

I nod, not even realizing I had gone that far with the fear I gave her. Not realizing I could. I take a deep, centering breath and let go of the fear I was giving Winter. Death lets her go slightly, at least allowing her feet to touch the ground.

I turn my attention back to the council. Our initial thoughts of what I should say to them aren't right anymore. The plan of getting them to accept blame for the things they have done and understand why they are being bound and their powers gagged isn't the right way anymore, and now, I don't know what to say. I left them trapped in the fears of losing their power, their mates, the whole world as they know it. I don't know what more I can do to them.

I'm relieved then, when Esnir speaks for me. "The fourteen of you will be held, accused of conspiring to murder gods who should have been under your protection and humans that you should not have controlled at all. If you would like to accept your guilt, say so now, and you will be freed, stripped of your power, and made mortal."

We look around the room. None of the original gods speak up. Esnir shrugs. "Alright then. Death? How do we bind them?"

Death peels his eyes off Winter to turn to look at Esnir. "Blood oath on their life line. That'd be the best way to do all of them quickly. More than the blood oath Nature and Hunt gave Anarus, but one that binds their power line away from their life line, made on the life line itself."

I look down at Anarus. "That's not happening right now unless you do them." Anarus is still pale and weak. He couldn't do it. I won't let him.

"I can help, but I can't do it myself." Death tells me. "I can do a regular blood oath, but not a life line one that binds their power. I can't do anything with a life line except end it. It has to be a Fate, to tie their destinies. So it has to be him, unless you want to trust one of the other Fates to do it."

Fuck no. "If I'm a Fate, can you use me?"

"Fuck no." Byder, Ydum, and Anarus say at the same time. They all look at each other, surprised at the others' reactions.

When I glare at each of them in turn, they all state their reasons. "You're a Fate but you're human, Jinx." Byder says. "You haven't even been made immortal yet."

"You're as exhausted as Ani is. You used a lot more energy than you think making everyone afraid, and you're injured." Ydum has a tightness around his eyes that tells me he's trying to suppress his worry over me.

Anarus stands up, bracing a hand on the table to support himself. "I'm not gonna lie. You know exactly why I said no. I won't risk you both carrying this many blood oaths."

"Then we find another way." I growl, frustrated. "Because there's no way you're doing it either, Anarus. Not how you are right now."

Death shakes his head. "There is no other way. Not that I know of. Not to bind their powers as gods against them, so they can't use them. We could do a lot without a Fate, but not stop their destinies as gods."

Anarus grits his teeth, a muscle in his jaw tensing. "Then, I'll do it."

"We." I say, refusing to let him carry all this by himself. "We will do it. The both of us. You already have two blood oaths to carry and there are fourteen more to carry. I'll take eight and you take six of them. That way we can share the load, each of us with eight. I'll even relent enough and say you can take female Fertility when we get back to camp, so you have more."

"No." Anarus tries to argue but his knees give way a little before he catches himself.

I raise an eyebrow at him. "You want to say I'm too weak, but only one of us is standing under our own power and it isn't you, Anarus. Trust me to know my own limits. If it's too much, I'll say so."

He scrubs a hand down his face. "Fine."

Death grabs Winter's arm and lets go of her throat before roughly shoving her into a chair next to Knowledge and Curiosity. Byder shifts his aim immediately to be point blank on Winter, leaving Curiosity and Knowledge effectively unguarded.

"Let go of the fear you are creating, Jinx." Death tells me as I move over to Curiosity and Knowledge. We'll do them first so that their lack of guards isn't a problem. I roll my shoulders and actively think about letting go of the fear I was still holding over thirteen of them. I had already let go of the fear for Winter.

Once I'm next to Curiosity and Knowledge, I look up at Death. "What do I do?"

"Know the words you will say first." He explains. "That should be easy for you as a word witch. We need them to have no access at all to their powers. Their destiny is yours to control. Put in the limits. For how long, what ends the oath, both successfully or unsuccessfully, and a punishment if they violate the oath to not use their powers. The details are important and need to be airtight."

I bite my lip. According to Sadness, and my own practice, the details are where I struggle. And if I mess this up, any of them could slip through our grasp. I need to know exactly what to say and not miss one word of it. I snag a piece of paper off the table and a writing tool. I need to make sure I cover everything and the best way is to write it down and read it.

I scribble furiously, then show it to Death, who nods. "That'll about do it. But they must agree. Blood oaths cannot be forced."

"Well, that defeats this whole thing, don't you think?" I flap my arms in frustration. "Why would they submit willingly?"

I realize that we are having this argument right in front of the gods we are threatening.

"Because it's that or we slit their throats now." Esnir says dispassionately. "Just because they need to agree doesn't mean they can't agree under duress, right?"

Death nods at him. "They get to make that choice. Agree and submit or die now."

I adjust the words I have written down and, after approving my changes, Death directs me on what to do next. "Since you have no power to create life or death, only manipulate it, I will assist. Pick where you will carry the oath. A wrist is usually used, but any place on your body that you can access and draw blood from yourself will work. It will scar."

I roll up my sleeve on my right arm. Not my wrist, but higher up, I decide. Just below my elbow on the inside of my arm.

Death approves my choice and I follow his directions. "Now, make a slit in your skin, one straight line just deep enough to bleed but no deeper." I press my dagger to the spot I chose and bite the inside of my cheek against the sting as I open up my skin. It's only a scratch but it is enough.

"Good, now, Curiosity, will you submit?" Death asks.

The small female, large brown eyes wary in her soft, heart-shaped face darting between me, Death, and Knowledge, doesn't answer until Knowledge gives her a small nod. She holds out her arm and Death makes the same slit at her wrist with his dagger, then makes one on his own wrist as well. Death pushes our arms together, mine and Curiosity's, so that the slit in her wrist matches up with the one on my arm, then lays his wrist over the spot where our skin meets, allowing drops of his blood to mix between ours. Then, he nods at me.

"Find her life line with your essence and hold your conjoined hands over it. Then, read the words you wrote." Death tells me.

I look at Curiosity closely. Taking a deep breath, I close my eyes for a moment, then open them. I see two lines of gold coming from her heart. One line runs to Knowledge, then through him to Anarus. Her mate bond with Knowledge. Another line, her life line with its magic of her godhood, runs straight to Anarus. Seeing her mate bond to Knowledge separate from her life line makes me think about the talk I had with Sadness about the different lines destiny weaves.

I know, from looking at Anarus's power so much, that our mate bonds are not separate from our life lines. Those are intertwined for us four. I thought that was how everyone's lines were, all the lines twisted together into one rope, even with what Sadness said about some people have more or less strands than others. Maybe that's why everyone assumed our bonds would get less painful over time after Anarus's death. Because the bonds between my gods and me should not be entangled like they are. Maybe our mate bonds being intertwined with our life lines is unique to us four and not the norm for mated bonds.

I shake my head slightly to stop my thoughts. I need to focus. I use my essence to hold onto the life line that runs straight to Anarus, the one that contains her magic as a god alone in her own right. Once our arms are over it, I read the words I wrote.

"Do you agree to bind your access to your powers, magic, and rights as an original god, as the creator of curiosity in the lands of Nazus; to it being bound completely, totally, unusable in any way by you until such time as a trial to determine your destiny is conducted and completed? Do you agree that any and all control of anything in Nazus that should be yours will be relinquished to a god of our choosing from your pantheon until the decision of your innocence or guilt is made after that trial? Do you agree to remain our prisoner, with no freedoms of any kind, physical, mental, emotional, magical, destined or undestined, only able to leave the prison of our choosing as needed to attend your own trial? Do you agree that, should that trial end in a guilty verdict for you, that you will relinquish your powers, and your right to live, to us in perpetuity? That a guilty verdict means your destiny will be either to die or be made mortal with no magic or power as either god or witch, as is decided by that trial? Do you agree that failure of you to honor this oath will result in your immediate death by the stopping of your heart, the snapping of all your mate bonds and life lines, and the boiling of your blood within your own skin?"

"I agree." Curiosity says, her voice only wavering slightly. "Do you agree that the trial will be fair and impartial, my deeds and my deeds alone used to judge my guilt or innocence, no one else's?"

I didn't expect her to add a condition, but it's a fair one, I think. I look up at Death, who nods in agreement. "Only if you agree to be completely honest during that trial. Not a word of a lie, not one half-truth, and lies by omission are also lies resulting in the oath being violated."

"I will agree to that as well." Curiosity says.

"Then, I agree as well." I say.

"Then let it be so." Death concludes. As I watch through my essence, a drop of our mixed blood falls on Curiosity's life line. The rope seems to fray slightly, the strand that is her god power pulling back from the life strand slightly. Not enough to unravel the rope totally, but enough they aren't touching anymore.

Death lets go of our hands and, as I watch, the small scratch on my arm heals instantly, leaving a small pink scar that tingles faintly in its place.

After a breath to collect myself, and adjusting the words of the blood oath to include what Curiosity and I added at the end, Death and I move to Knowledge. I make a scratch just below the one I made for Curiosity, find his life line as a god, and read the same words to him.

Knowledge agrees quickly, making no changes.

I move on, skipping over Winter. I'll leave her to her son. She deserves that. The male Fertility asks for his blood oath to be for both him and the female Fertility. I vehemently disagree to that condition. The female Fertility will stand or fall on her own, forced to speak to her own actions, the same as him. We have a moment of a standoff as he decides if he'll agree or not without that condition, but he relents and submits.

As I move to Sky, to extract her blood oath, I notice how tired I'm getting. But this is only the fourth of the eight I need to do. I will not allow Anarus to take it all on himself while still recovering from keeping the wilde hunt out too long. I can do this. I will do this.

Sky, Water, and Wind easily submit to the blood oaths. When I move to Spring, Ydum stops me, pulling me away for a moment to a corner of the room where no one else will hear us.

"You need to stop, beautiful." Ydum's eyes are searching mine. "You're exhausted, aren't you?"

"And so is Anarus." I retort, trying to not let him see how much my hands are trembling.

"Anarus is a god." Ydum holds me by my shoulders, keeping me facing him. "Everyone here is a god but you. Tell me. When did you last eat? Drink something? Do you even have the canteen or rations the humans were all supposed to get or did you leave yourself exempt from that?"

I turn my eyes away. "I'm fine."

"You didn't answer me." Ydum whispers furiously. "It was that oatmeal and coffee hours ago, wasn't it? The last time you fed yourself was before sunrise and it's now after sunset. Damn it, Jinx. You're performing powerful magic with nothing, no fuel at all! You're bleeding, in pain, starving, and dehydrated and still won't stop. You are not immortal."

Ydum turns away from me and stalks back to the table before I can stop him. "Ani, you need to do the rest. Or we need to find another way. Jinx hasn't even eaten since sunrise and she's bleeding. She can't do any more."

I spit out a "Fuck you!" at Ydum, but before I can counter his decision on my behalf any further, everyone in the room, even most of the gods we are actively working against, mutter or exclaim in shock.

"Fuck, Jinx. Are you trying to kill yourself?" I hear Esnir say as Byder's face goes hard. "Find her some fucking water, someone."

"Shut up!" I yell above all of them. "All of you shut the fuck up!"

Twenty-one sets of eyes turn to me, mouths open in surprise. Yeah, I may have put a touch of fear in my yell by accident. Oops, not sorry.

"When the fuck did this become coddle the fucking human who is too stupid to make her own choices? When did I give any of you," I give a venomous stare to Byder, Ydum, and Anarus especially, "any of you the right to make choices for me? I thought that was the whole point of this fucking thing, that gods and humans deserve to make their own choices about their lives. And you want to start it all by telling me what I need? What I can and can't do? Well, fuck all of you! You want to scurry off and find me some food and water? Fine, I won't deny you, but fuck off if you think you know what I can and can't do."

I walk up to Spring, use my dagger to make a new scratch on my arm and hold it out to him. "I said eight, I'm doing eight. We doing this thing or am I bleeding for no reason?"

No one moves for a tense minute. Spring takes the dagger from my hand and creates his own blood oath line, then looks at Death.

Death comes back over to add his blood to the oath, muttering. "Your gods are gonna kill me for this." But he squeezes his arm to add his blood anyway. Since he isn't making the actual oath, he doesn't need to make a new cut every time, just add some more blood.

I close my eyes and take several deep breaths. I need to calm myself down before I can look at Spring's life lines, but I won't use my magic to do it. I might be mad at him now, but Ydum is right. I have overdone it and am too tired. He's probably even right I shouldn't do these last two oaths, but damn it if I don't feel too stubborn to back down now.

Once I get my mind to quiet down, I open my eyes and look for Spring's life lines. He isn't mate bonded so he has only one gold rope coming from him to Anarus. I walk us through the blood oath and, before I talk myself out of it, I turn and do Fall's too. It takes me longer to work the magic to see his life line because my concentration is slipping, but I muddle through, if only to make the point that I can.

As soon as Fall's blood oath heals on my arm, I walk to the wall by the ruined door and slump to the floor. Anarus can do the rest now. I did what I said I would and they can all leave me alone. Sure, I feel like I'm going to pass out and the room looks like it is tilting in a way I know it can't possibly be actually tilting, but I did it. Maybe Kinshra can bring me a canteen and food or something so I'll be able to walk out of here under my own power, because otherwise, my little temper tantrum is going to get even more embarrassing.

I don't watch as Anarus takes over, doing the blood oaths for Summer, Happiness, Anger, and Peace. I just sit against the wall, my eyes closed, and rest.

About the time Anarus gets to Anger, though, a wet snout pushes at my hands. Huh, I must have actually asked Kinshra for the food and water because she's here, inside the council hall, with a canteen hanging from her neck and a bag held gingerly between her teeth. I take both from her.

Thanks, Kinshra.

Eat, foolish human. Isis says she is going to punch you for forgetting to get food. She also said not really, so I have no idea what that means. But I'm tempted to bite you myself.

I take a long drink from the canteen and that actually helps enormously. I didn't realize how dry my mouth was. I open the bag and find a mix of nuts, dehydrated berries, and jerky. I eat a few handfuls then lean back against the wall.

There. I ate and drank. Happy now?

No. Eat it all and drink it all. Alpha would bite the heels of any wolf in the pack that forgot to take care of themselves like that. I'm still not sure I won't do that to you.

You're not my alpha, Kinshra.

Then, who is? Because you obviously need one to keep you in line.

I roll my eyes at her.

At first, I think Kinshra's growl is at me for rolling my eyes at her, but then

I realize she isn't looking at me anymore. While we had talked, Anarus had completed all the blood oaths besides Inspiration. Even Winter submitted without too much fuss, which surprises me.

But now, Anarus and Inspiration are standing in front of me, right by where I am leaning on the wall by the door. Anarus is standing in front of Inspiration, a small scratch on his wrist welling with drops of blood, but his dagger is in Inspiration's hand and Inspiration doesn't look like he has any intention of using it on himself.

"Inspiration." Death says slowly. "Give the dagger back to Anarus."

One glance around the room as I stand up shows that Esnir, Byder, Ydum, Nature, and Hunt all have their weapons trained on Inspiration. All of them except Byder are carefully stepping closer to Anarus.

My heart is in my throat. What did I miss? Why is Inspiration threatening Anarus? Doesn't he know it's over? He doesn't make it out of this room alive without the blood oath. I pull my dagger out as I drop the canteen and food on the floor.

That was a mistake. The canteen clatters as it hits the floor and everyone's eyes turn toward the sound for a fraction of a second. Everyone's but Inspiration, who uses the minor distraction to thrust the dagger at Anarus.

Time is really a weird thing. There's no god pantheon over time, so it must not be a creation of the gods but exists all on its own. Why does it slow down like that at certain crucial moments? Why does it let you see in absolute clarity exactly what's about to happen when you least want to have that power of divination?

I know, with every ounce of my being, that the dagger Inspiration is moving towards Anarus will kill him. I know it. I also know that no one else in the room is close enough to stop it. And I also know I fucking cannot go through that again.

It's not really a choice. I don't choose to move. I don't choose to throw myself between Anarus and the blade. I just do. I'm shorter than Anarus, so the blade aimed for his heart hits me higher. I push back on Inspiration at the same time as I move between the two gods, so the cut is shallower than it would have been too. But shallow is not exactly a word that make a wound from a dagger better. I feel the blade skitter along my collar bone and leave a trail of heat on it before getting stuck in my shoulder.

Apparently, this is the moment time decides I no longer need the power of divination and kicks back to its normal speed. I hear the twang of an arrow being fired just before one erupts in Inspiration's temple and he collapses to the floor. While also being yanked sideways? Or maybe I'm falling sideways. I'm not sure. I know there's a lot of yelling and I end up on the floor with lots of hands all over me.

Ydum is sitting on my chest choking me and I try to tell him I can't breathe but he isn't listening. I try to push on him but my right arm feels like lead and my left screams when I try to move it.

Oh right, there's a knife in my shoulder. That would hurt to move. And Ydum isn't choking me. He's putting pressure on my wound. I'm really tired. Maybe I should just rest while they all argue or whatever they are yelling for.

"Do not close your eyes, little human." Anarus tells me. Ydum shakes me a little as Anarus keeps talking. "Keep your eyes open and on me."

Okay, okay, jeez. You don't have to yell. I look at Anarus and his eyes are full of panic. Wow, is it really that bad? I only feel a little bit of burning on my collarbone and the pain at my shoulder. That should be superficial at most. I pushed Inspiration back. His blade couldn't have dug that deeply. For some reason, nothing happens when I try to talk.

"Make her immortal!" I hear Byder yell. "Make her immortal right fucking now so she can heal."

"She might not survive it if I do it now." Fertility says, far more calmly.

Out of the corner of my eye, I see Byder slam Fertility against the wall roughly. "She might not survive anyway. Do it now!"

Hey, guys. I think you're being a little overdramatic here. Sure, my shoulder's fucked but other than that, I just feel a little tired. But I was already tired so that's not surprising. Just get one of the medics and I'll be fine in a bit.

"Without my mate, it could kill the child." Fertility pants out. Byder still hasn't let go of him. "Without my mate, I'm not even sure how well it will work."

No! Fuck no! I try to move, to squirm, to yell, anything. Ydum is holding me too tightly, sitting on top of me. I'm fine. No. Don't do that. I must move enough to get Anarus's attention because he looks back down at me.

His eyes are so pained. "It's that or both of you, little human. I can't lose you."

I want to fight. I want to struggle. I want to get up and tell them they are all worried for nothing. But then I blink and it's really hard to open my eyes again. They are just so heavy and I'm just so tired.

Anarus screams. "Do it! Do it now! She's slipping away. Jinx, open your eyes. Open your eyes."

Everyone is screaming now. I can't make out a lot of their words, but only catch bits and pieces. Ydum is screaming at me. Byder is screaming at Fertility.

Death is screaming at Anarus. I hear that one. "Do not touch her, Anarus! She's too close to the bridge. Don't touch her."

Anarus groans, his voice full of pain. "I know. I can't come for her. I can't help her. I promised her I always would. Jinx, please. Open your eyes. Please."

Just a minute and I will, Anarus. It's okay. I'll be fine. Just give me one minute. I need one minute to breathe. I take a deep breath in and the sounds of screaming get muffled then fade away completely. My body relaxes and my eyes don't feel quite so heavy anymore.

Where did the snow come from? There's snow under me. I can feel it but the cold isn't bothering me. That's interesting. I open my eyes back up and see open sky. Huh. I'm outside. When did that happen?

I try to move and find I can easily. No one is sitting on top of me anymore. And nothing hurts. Not even the shoulder with the knife in it. I feel my left shoulder with my right hand. Someone must have taken the knife out because it's not there anymore.

I feel very confused, but also, peaceful. I'm not even worried about the fact that I'm confused. I wonder which Fate is controlling my emotions right now because I should be worried about how I am outside in the snow when I was just inside, hurt.

I roll over and push myself to standing. I'm not tired anymore either. And nothing hurts. Literally nothing. Not even my right hip, the dull pain in it that I've learned to just live with since the sixth game is gone too. I'm not thirsty or hungry either.

I look around and see trees bare of their leaves all around me. To my left, I see a streak of gold. No, not a streak. It's a rope of it, stretched out to hover above the ground about five feet in the air.

I know this place. Why do I know this place? I should follow the gold rope. Somehow, I know it will take me where I need to go.

I follow the gold rope to a tiny creek. The creek is frozen over from the cold I can't feel. The gold rope runs to a bridge. The stone bridge is pretty. Just a small bridge over a tiny creek, but it feels so important.

Such a nice bridge. I should cross it and see where it leads.

At the bridge, a male stands in the way of me crossing the bridge, one hand resting on either stone railings and one foot on each side of the bridge, on the ground on both sides. It looks like an uncomfortable position to stand in, but he looks so graceful doing it. He's beautiful. A beautiful, beautiful male.

His dark brown skin is visible to his waist because he's not wearing a shirt. That's nice because he has some really nice tattoos. Symbols, barbed wire, and shifting smoke on one arm. Symbols and colorful flowers on the other. A wolf howling at the moon on his chest. Phases of the moon and stars on his back. I love those tattoos and feel a strange urge to touch them. Especially the wolf.

My hand hurts. I look down at it. It actually feels strange for my hand to hurt when all the aches and pains I usually have had disappeared.

I ignore it and look at the male again. Do I know him? His face is just as beautiful as the rest of him. Or would be if he didn't look like he was in pain. Dark amber eyes that have streaks of black in them. His lips, surrounded by a trim moustache and goatee, are soft looking, like they might be nice to kiss.

I shake my head at that thought. Totally inappropriate, I tell myself. His black hair is down his back, in a long braid. Someone put three tiny braids just above his left ear too. Probably someone who really loves him. They look cute there.

My hand really starts hurting now, a pulsing pain that arcs and makes my hand curl up on itself over and over as the pain comes in waves. I look down at it, expecting to see some reason for the pain. But there's nothing there.

"Go back, Jinx." The male cries out, his voice rough like he's been crying for a long time. "Don't cross the bridge, please. Please, go back."

He's pleading with me not to cross the bridge. Why? I should cross it. Somehow, I know I should. I need to meet... someone? I think I need to meet someone across the bridge. But the male is in the way and he seems to not want to let me cross it.

"Excuse me, but I need to get across the bridge." I say politely. Maybe he doesn't realize he's in my way.

"No, Jinx. Go back. Don't cross it." The male says it more insistently this time. He knows my name. How does he know my name?

My whole arm hurts now. The pain is spreading. The pain I can't see what's causing is spreading. It keeps hitting me in waves, over and over. Streaks of hot needles, sharp knives running from my fingers up to my shoulder with no origin

I can see. I have the feeling if I go across the bridge and meet whoever I am supposed to meet there, the pain will stop. But the male still won't move.

I step forward towards the bridge and the male jerks, like my step forward hurt him. I step again, and again he jerks.

"No. No, Jinx. Please. I can't stop you, but please don't go across the bridge. Please don't die. Please." The male is actually crying now. There are tears running down his face unchecked, turning his dark umber skin shiny in their wake. He doesn't lift a hand from the sides of the bridge to wipe them away, but just lets them fall.

There's a part of me that wants to wipe his tears away, stop his pain, hold him until he stops crying and realizes there's no reason to be sad right now. But his words stop me.

Die. He said don't die. Is that what this is? Am I dying? It would make the no pain make sense. Except the pain in my arm that is rapidly spreading.

Oh gods, that pain. It burns. It burns so bad. It's spreading through my shoulder. It's not pulsing pain, not waves anymore, but sheer, unrelenting pain.

Across the bridge. I need to get across the bridge to make it stop. Whoever I am supposed to meet over there, they'll make it stop. I know they will. Death will make it stop.

Death. If I'm dying then it's Death I need to meet on the other side of the bridge. But that doesn't make sense because if I'm supposed to meet Death on the other side of that bridge, then that means it's the bridge between life and death. Anarus controls the bridge between life and death, though.

I look at the male again. Anarus. The male is Anarus. Oh fuck. Oh no. I'm dying and that's Anarus.

"Anarus." I can barely whisper his name. As soon as I do, that burning pain in my arm hits my chest. My heart. Oh gods, it hurts. My heart is trying to squeeze but it can't. Not squeeze. Beat. My heart is trying to beat because it hadn't been before.

"Oh gods. Anarus, it hurts." I gasp, clutching at my chest. I bend over at the waist, curling in on myself as the pain becomes overwhelming. "Help me."

"Go back, little human. Please." Anarus doesn't move. Why won't he move? Why won't he help me? "I can't leave the bridge! If I touch you, I'll move you over it. Go. Back. Jinx."

"It hurts. Make it stop hurting." I fall to my knees. The pain is everywhere now. In my legs, in my arms, my heart, my head. My stomach clenches painfully. I can't breathe.

No. That's wrong. I can't not breathe. My lungs are screaming for me to breathe, but I haven't since I woke up in the snow. My heart wants to beat, my lungs want to breathe. But if I do it will hurt. If I let them, I can't go over the bridge to where it won't hurt anymore.

"Breathe, Jinx!" That's Byder. How do I hear Byder? He's not here.

"Do it, little human. Please, breathe." Anarus's tears are rolling down his cheeks faster in fat streaks.

"It'll hurt." I can barely speak anymore.

"I know." Anarus sobs. "I'm sorry. I'm so sorry. Please. You're running out of time."

A shadowy figure appears on the other side of the bridge. He's huge. He looks just like Anarus but huge. Death. That's Death and he's here for me.

"I don't want to do this." Death whispers to Anarus. Death is crying too. Everyone is crying. All these strong, tough males are crying. "I have no choice. Her essence called me here to collect it. I don't want to do it, son, but if she crosses the bridge, I have no choice."

I'm struggling to my feet. I don't want to go towards Death but also want to so desperately. Every step I take towards the bridge make Anarus jolt as if he feels it in his soul.

"Please breathe, Jinx." He pleads again. "One breath. I know it hurts, just do me this one favor before you cross the bridge. One breath. Take just one more breath."

One breath? He only wants one more breath? For him. Okay. I can do that for him. Because I love him. Just one more breath.

I breathe in and fire is everywhere. It hurts. It hurts so bad. I fall and feel like I keep falling. Everything burns and I scream. Everything is black and burning and I'm screaming and I can't stop.

Anarus, please make it stop. Please make it stop. "Please make it stop!"

"I've got you. Fuck, beautiful. I've got you." Ydum's arms are so strong around me, holding me tightly, but it hurts so much. "Open your eyes and look at me."

I try to open my eyes only to squeeze them closed again. The light is too bright. "It hurts." My voice is weak and jagged.

"I know it hurts. I know. Open them anyway." He tells me.

I open my eyes to the too bright light as the raging fire burning through me subsides only the smallest bit. I'm immediately dizzy and Ydum turns me just in time for me to vomit. Gods, I hate vomiting, but it feels like I have done it so many times lately.

I try to look around but Byder is crowding in too close and I can't see Anarus. By the red carpet on the floor, I guess we are still in the council's safe room. I let myself sink into Ydum's arms. I am so fucking tired. So very, very tired.

"You can sleep now, Jinx." Ydum says. "It's okay now. You can sleep now."

Oh good. The last edges of the burning pain recede and I fall asleep.

Chapter Thirteen

I HAVE FLASHES OF awareness. Being carried by Ydum out of the building. Ydum handing me to Byder while surrounded by bare trees. Byder laying me down on the piles of furs in our tent and carefully removing my clothes while swearing quietly. Gentle hands washing me with a warm cloth. Ydum propping me up while Byder spoons small sips of broth into me. I groan at that because it hurts to swallow.

When consciousness really finds me, Ydum is lying on the furs next to me, his fingers brushing small wisps of hair off my forehead as he watches me. His face is pale and tired, small dark circles under his eyes. He breaks into a smile as soon as he sees my eyes are open.

"Hello, beautiful."

I open my mouth to speak but all that comes out is a croak. My throat is so dry and it hurts. I try to swallow but there is nothing there to swallow but a sandy, gritty feeling.

"Byder? Water." Ydum looks away from me. I follow where he is looking and see that Anarus and Byder are both sitting at the table. Anarus is nursing a mug of something I assume is coffee by the smell. Byder jumps up at Ydum's words and grabs a canteen that's hanging off the back of his chair.

When he brings it over, I expect he will lie down on the other side of me, or sit there, but he doesn't. Instead, he sits on the other side of Ydum, handing the canteen to him. Ydum helps me take a sip and I realize how utterly weak I feel. My voice is still jagged feeling but at least the sand is gone.

"What happened?" I look from the two of them to Anarus, who is still nursing his mug, looking into it as if it will tell him the future.

"What do you remember?" Byder asks. He's as tired looking as Ydum is.

I furrow my brow, trying to put all the flashes together. "Inspiration. He took Anarus's dagger. He was going to kill Anarus. I pushed him away but the blade hit my collarbone and got stuck in my shoulder."

"Not just your collarbone, beautiful." Ydum says tightly. "Your throat. He slit your throat. The cut along the collarbone and the dagger getting stuck in your shoulder were the least of your injuries. He slit your throat."

"Oh." Well, that makes everything make a lot more sense. "Is that why swallowing hurts?"

Byder lets out a tense chuckle. "Yeah. That should get better quickly now. What do you remember after that?"

"Anarus." I say as I try to filter through the memories. "At the bridge. But I think I didn't know who he was. Or was confused. I didn't hurt, but then I did." I shake my head, trying to make the random images in my head make sense. "A lot of pain. I remember a lot of pain, burning and I just wanted it to stop."

"You died." Anarus tells his mug. "You died and we argued at the bridge between life and death because you wanted to cross it."

"The male Fertility made you immortal to save you." Ydum brings my attention back to him. "That was the burning feeling. Death told us you were so close to dying that he was actually called to the bridge to collect you, but Anarus wasn't letting you cross it. Fertility made you immortal and he, Byder, and Esnir, along with the other three Fates worked to heal you before you were too far gone. But it was a near thing. You've been in and out of consciousness for two days."

Two days? I struggle to sit up, but there's something very warm and heavy pinning my side down. The other side than where Byder and Ydum are sitting. I turn my head and see Kinshra dozing at my side, her head lying on my abdomen.

Following my gaze, Byder snorts. "Yeah, she wouldn't leave you alone. When we tried to make her move so we could do something, like sit you up to feed you, she would growl at us. We eventually just gave up trying to get her out of the way and worked around her."

Sliding my hand out from underneath her, I scratch the top of her head to wake her up. "Hey, Kinshra."

She opens her yellow eyes and peers at me, lifting her head and tilting it to the side. *You really awake or is this just more screaming?*

"Screaming?" I ask, puzzled.

You were screaming. A lot. You kept tearing the wound in your neck back open doing it.

"Yeah, um, you screamed a lot." Ydum said, scratching the back of his neck, not realizing Kinshra was saying the same thing.

The burning. As I thought about it, I could feel a ghostly trace of that burning pain in my veins. "Is that the immortality? That burning pain?"

"Isis came by and said that being made immortal hurt her too." Byder explains. "Not quite as much as it seemed to hurt you, but then again, she wasn't actively dying as she did it and she had both Fertilities."

So many things. I rub my face trying to keep them all straight. Two days. I was out for two days, except when I woke up to scream in pain. Fuck, no wonder they all look so haggard.

"What happened with the council? The original gods? We're still in the tent." I look around and thoughts assault me. "My sisters! My dad and Finnegan. Are they okay? What about everyone else? Esnir? Iella. Oh fuck, Iella. Is she..."

Ydum cups my cheek in his hand. "Slow down, beautiful. Everyone is okay. Well, everyone who was okay when you got hurt is still okay. We checked on your family. They are all fine. All the other gods, including Winter, had already given their blood oaths and are now being held in one of the council homes, each in a room alone and guarded by people from the hunter group. Esnir and Ayja are going through the city and talking to the different gods and immortal witches. Seems like not many are too upset that the council has been disbanded."

"Iella is managing." Byder's voice catches slightly. "You know how that is. She, well, she's doing as well as can be expected."

It doesn't escape my notice that Anarus has said almost nothing this entire time. When I look at him, he's still eyeing his mug as if it owes him money and he's trying to determine what part of it to break first.

I force my body to stand to go over to him. As I move, I realize I am only wearing one of Ydum's shirts. I know it's his because it goes to my knees and I spent so much of the games in nothing but his shirts.

At the table, I take one of Anarus's hands into mine, moving his arm out of the way so I can stand between his arms, facing him as I move between him and his line of sight of the mug. He flinches at my touch and doesn't look up, but keeps staring at the same spot, like he can see through me to the mug.

"What's going on in your head, Anarus?" My voice breaks his concentration.

"You threw yourself between me and Inspiration." Anarus's voice is rough, like he hasn't used it in days. "You were screaming in pain and begging me to help you. To let you cross the bridge. And I couldn't do anything. If I touched you, you would have been dead. For two days, you screamed for me to help you and I couldn't do a damn thing. Not here, not at the bridge, nothing. Immortality doesn't fix those types of wounds, Jinx. It makes it easier to heal, but doesn't solve them."

Anarus finally looks up at me. "You were dying for two fucking days and I couldn't even hold your hand because if I did, you would go right back to the bridge and cross it. You were screaming for me, tearing your throat apart screaming for me, and I couldn't come for you. I promised I would always come for you, and I couldn't."

I take one of his hands in mine, noticing how he flinches at the touch but understanding it now. I bring his hand up to my face and kiss his knuckles. "You came for me in a different way. You kept me off the bridge. It's only flashes now, but I know I didn't recognize you at first and you wouldn't let me cross the bridge. You begged me to breathe. I didn't want to and you made me. I only breathed for you, because you begged me to. I'm not dying now, Anarus. You came for me how I needed you to and I'm not dying now."

With a pained groan, Anarus stands so fast that the chair he was sitting in falls over. He wraps his arms around me, pulling me into a hard kiss, like just touching me will heal all my wounds, his, the whole world.

When he finally lets me go, or at least lets my lips go, one of his hands ghosts over my throat, tracing a scar I feel under his gentle touch. I have a feeling that scar will never go away, even with immortal healing abilities. Just like Ydum's dead pinky, it will stay as a reminder of how dangerous these games and the original gods really are.

"It was so close." Anarus whispers. "If you hadn't pushed him back enough, or hadn't turned your head. Any tiny difference and he would have hit the main vein in your neck and there would have been no time to save you."

His eyes and his hand flit down my body, stopping just below my belly button. His fingers twitch as he rests his hand just above my pelvis. "We don't know. Fertility couldn't know. We had to choose, and I chose you. She could be gone, but I had to choose and chose you."

I close my eyes against the pang in my heart at that, but open them quickly, knowing Anarus is just as gutted over having to make the choice. "You did what you had to do, Anarus. You saved me. You came for me and saved me. Everything else. Everything else will be what it will be."

"We all gotta stop dying. Every single one of us has tried to die now." Byder jokes.

I turn to him with a wry smile. "Not you. Ydum died in the games. Anarus died taking his mantle. And I died, or tried to, now too. But you haven't died yet, Byder. Just a little mauled by a bear and one attempt at being a succubus's dinner."

"And we're keeping it that way." Anarus mutters.

Ydum laughs. "Agreed. No trying to go and die now, Byder, just so you can say you did too."

"Aw, man. Why do I have to miss out on all the fun?" Byder makes me laugh, which makes Anarus laugh and we all end up laughing. Laughing about how many times we all keep dying. What a crazy thing to laugh about. But there is too much pain if we don't laugh about it. So, we laugh. And we push down the pain, refusing to allow it to engulf us. At least for a little while longer.

Chapter Fourteen

IT TAKES ME ABOUT two weeks to realize staging a coup, dismantling a long-standing government system, and trying to rebuild it is really not very fun. In those first few days after I wake up, most of the humans leave and go back to their villages. Some stay, especially ones from the hunter group that are working as guards at Winter's home, which is being utilized as the prison for the original gods. Some of them send for their families to come join them in Veirveil and they are all given lodgings in the city so that the camp can be fully dismantled.

My mother is one that refuses to come even though my father is staying until we get the rotation of the guards settled. All of my sisters and Finnegan, except Catarina who stays with Dad, go home. As we rewrite the laws of Nazus, we try to pull at least one representative of each human village to assist us, not the High Priest or Priestess though. We also call for a representative of each god pantheon, including war this time. It's a temporary council until we can have a vote to make a permanent one.

At the same time, we are acutely aware of the fact that it's still winter and many of the villages are struggling, especially because of their abandonment of their homes to come here for the coup. There wasn't much in the way of loss of life, fortunately. Besides Damek and Raven, only three humans died in the whole thing, and about seven severely injured but they heal fine. It's awful but that's much less than we expected.

For the gods, besides Uesis, Winter, Fire, and Inspiration, about fifty of the hundred guards around the building died on their side, since the rest of them surrendered once they realized they were truly outmanned. And the five wolves.

All of this means that, on top of trying to figure out how to rework the government, and provide basic rations to the starving villages, we are a land in mourning. It's not as bad as it could have been. Really, really not as bad as it could have been. But there still is death and pain.

A week after the coup, we hold funerals for everyone from both sides. We treat both sides no differently with this. Many of the guards that surrounded the council building had families. They were only doing what they were told to keep their families safe. The guards still alive are questioned and it becomes apparent quickly that, given the choice, many of them would not have fought us or the changes we want to make. They didn't know, they were only told there was a threat to the council, come do your job and protect the council building. They were never told what that threat was or why. So, the guards get honorable funeral pyres alongside everyone else.

There's just so fucking much to do. Gods to assuage that we are not just going to kill everyone who isn't completely on board with what we want to do. We make sure that they all understand we are willing to listen to suggestions. We want something more democratic, humans and gods on more of an equal footing. But killing humans or gods for breeding purposes in the games is an absolute no go. We want everyone to be happy in this new world we are creating, as happy and safe as we can make them.

There are a few tense moments when some of the children of the original gods try to establish their dominance. Phylidria is one of them and ends up joining her mother, Winter, at her home under guard and a blood oath when she refuses the idea of a voted-on council outright. She's very much like her mother, power hungry and oblivious to the rights of anyone else. It's seriously odd to think about the fact that she is technically Anarus's half-sister. They are so different.

It takes until almost the end of January before we have the pantheons set back up enough to hold the trials. Fortunately, the things created by the original gods continue to exist just fine after their death and we don't have to try to remake fire or anything. Just assign a new full god to take over the maintenance of it. We celebrate Byder's twenty-fifth birthday by interviewing gods to find ones that agree to the condition they cannot be on any government councils since they will be pantheon leaders.

Those are two different councils now, too. Veirveil is now a village, like any other human village, just the biggest village and the capitol of Nazus. It's not special except that it also houses the Nazus government as well as its own, or will when we finish getting all that set up.

The pantheon leaders for the gods, now considered basically faith leaders with a separation between faith and government, all get an office in the council building, so that they can work with the council easily, but they are not the council and can never be. The pantheon leaders are the ones who decide that the jury for the trials gets to be everyone still alive from the Three Hundred and Seventy-Fifth Gods Games and one human from every village that sends us a representative. We will have the villages and pantheons hold a vote for the actual council in a year.

We have given ourselves one year or less to finish the trials of the original gods, determine their destinies, create the full new constitution and establish voted for councils in each human village that will determine who their representatives and High Priests are, two separate people, and install them.

Then, there will be a vote for who is on the Nazus council and we will be dismissed, gladly, from our positions. Just like the gods' pantheon leaders are now a faith leader rather than a government leader, so too are the High Priests. They will not be part of each village's local government, but just an advisor and the one in control of faith things.

Even the schools will no longer be in the High Priest's control. And the position isn't familial anymore either, but elected by the community, after certain requirements in education are met. Requirements that are still being worked out between the temporary pantheon leaders and the current High Priests, and education systems, such as a college for those wanting to go into the faith careers, that is also still in process of being created.

In the meantime, no humans are being tested. There will be no more Gods Games. None. Never again. The pantheon leaders have been tasked with devising a new, safer way for twenty-four-year-old gods within their own pantheon to take on their mantles. And the council, once a real one is established, will figure out what to do about finding the witch and god mate bonds. But for now, we are functioning in survival and rebuild mode and everything not essential like that can wait.

What can't wait is the trials those involved in creation and the games. By a very much not unanimous vote, the decision is made that Drila will not be put on trial for her part in the Gods Games. The others, the humans and the new pantheon leaders argue she was acting under orders from the original gods and had no control over her own actions really. Those of us in this last games round disagree, all of us remembering Saffron bleeding out right in front of us while Drila picked at her nails and ignored us. She could have done something, at least looked like she cared, been sympathetic about the deaths. Something. But we lose that vote so she is pardoned without a trial.

The only ones on trial at all is the nineteen original gods that ran the council all this time. This means that, every day, we go to the council building and listen to the pantheon leader question their original god about their actions during creation and the set-up of the games. It's tiring and mostly boring. But necessary.

The four of us have been staying with Death to make it easier to get to the council building every day. Anarus and Death kill the barrier plants and caches Ydum and the nature witches made, so the wedges of the city are back open and fully operational, but still. That walk every day from Ydum's or Byder's home would be a bit much. Especially for me.

Plus, I think Anarus likes staying with Death. I think he's enjoying learning about his father. I know Death is happy about it, glad to not be banished and getting a chance to make up for lost time with Anarus. He's the only original god who won't be put on trial and has been given a full pardon for whatever role he played in creation. He was already gone when the games were made, so he's innocent of all that.

We are surprised shortly after the start of the trials when Iella stops us after one long day at the council hall, asking if she could talk to Anarus and me privately. We meet with her back at Death's house, and the four of us sit to talk with her.

"I don't mind Byder and Ydum being here, but only really needs Jinx and

Anarus." She tells us as we get comfortable in Death's sitting room. She heaves a sigh, looking down at the floor, her fingers twisting in her lap. "Anarus, can you double check my mate bond with Damek? Make sure it was completely cut?"

Anarus tries to be kind. "The bond wasn't cut, Iella, but broke when he died. It would have to be completely severed after a death like that."

"I know that. Rationally, I know that, but," she sobs slightly, "this? What I'm feeling? It's too much. Far too much for it to be severed right."

I hold back my own sob of sympathy. "Snapped mate bonds are brutally painful, especially when they snap from a sudden, violent death like that, rather than cut by Anarus at the end of a life well lived." I remind her. I should know. I lived with the pain of one for thirty-two days.

"Just... please?" Iella gives Anarus a desperate look.

Anarus humors her and checks the bond just in case, his eyes glazing over as he accesses that part of his mantle. When he looks at Iella again, his emotions are so mixed, I'm scared what he'll say.

"Your bond to Damek is severed completely, Iella," he says so softly we have to strain to hear him, "but your bond to Damek's child is not."

It takes all four of us, Byder, Ydum, Iella, and me, several minutes before we get what he means.

I hold her for a long time as she sheds bittersweet tears, and I go with her to tell Damek's father, Beck, that he will be a grandfather. Beck becomes one of the first humans to move full time to Veirveil, moving in with Iella and her parents to help support her through her mourning and pregnancy.

Some of the trials are easy. Winter's was pretty much open and shut. When questioned about her role in Anarus's life, she of course was honest about all of it. She had to be with the blood oath on Anarus's arm.

We spend a week hearing the truth from her about how she gave birth to him in secret, loaded him with the full mantle of the wilde hunt when he was only hours old, then abandoned him outside the council building, pretending to be just as shocked by his appearance there as the rest of the original gods, and it takes its toll on Anarus. Most of our evenings are spent finding things for him to break to vent out his rage after he spent the day listening to Winter detail how she knew exactly what happened to him in one instance or another and didn't care to do anything to protect him or keep him safe.

When she talks about his placement when he was ten, and how she knew exactly what was happening in that home, it's me who is throwing things Death just bought to decorate his mostly empty home. Death stops trying to fill the house with furniture and other stuff until Winter's trial was over after that. It takes everything in me not to just go off on my own and kill her when the seasons pantheon decided to only make her mortal as her punishment.

Fortunately, or maybe unfortunately, the god who had been Anarus's guardian when he was ten was one of the ones who died when we took control of the council building, so his destiny was already sealed. It makes me angry that he got an honorable funeral pyre, but how were we to know at the time that he didn't deserve one?

Apparently, making a human Fate immortal makes their power over emotions stronger but at the same time makes it harder for them to control their own emotions. It's going to take some time for me to learn to tame my fear and anger, the two emotions most closely tied to the Fate Fear and thus my own power.

Hunt's and Nature's trials are also easy, but for the opposite reason. They had meant what they said when they came to the camp to turn against the council. They gladly submit to no longer being the leaders of their pantheons, and, while not pardoned like Death, they are given lighter punishments than the rest of the original gods. They will never have access to their power again, their mantles stripped from them, but are not made mortal. They will be almost no different than human witches made immortal for the rest of their lives, a ghost of power lingering but no ability to do much about it.

Byder and Ydum are their respective pantheons' first choice for leaders but they both decline. When the year ends and everything is settled with an elected council, none of the four of us want to ever see the council building again if we can help it.

As a pantheon of two, Anarus and Death decide that they don't need a pantheon leader and Death will be the only original god allowed on both the Nazus and Veirveil councils. He's also the only person allowed to serve on two councils at all, but with only two of them available, and Anarus staunchly refusing all of it, needs must and all. We made sure the new constitution includes the death pantheon in its every five year votes for new pantheon leaders, who can stay the same if the pantheon votes that way, and new council members, who can't stay the same even if people want them to, so that when their pantheon does grow larger, it won't be a gap in the balance of power in Nazus.

By the end of April, the trials for most of the original gods are almost done. All the seasons are done, and the Fates, the Fertilities, Sky, Water, and Wind. Now, we are on to Knowledge and Curiosity. They have both been found guilty of crimes against the people of Nazus, and sentenced to mortality. The main discussion at this time is do we allow them to keep their mate bond or cut that as we make them mortal.

For all the other gods except Winter and Death and the Fertilities, this wasn't a choice that was needed. None of the others had mates. Death specifically said he wanted that damned bond between him and Winter cut. He absolutely did not want to be bonded to her anymore and, somehow, I don't think the bond being cut really hurt him. Maybe because he had already rejected it. For the Fertilities, the choice to sever the bond was made easily. They could not be trusted with that bond in place.

Anarus had to spend time for all the gods teasing out their destinies to only cut their god power and end the destiny power of the Fates, since none of the pantheons chose a death penalty for their original god, only making them mortal. He did shorten the life lines, adding death to them, but didn't add mortality the way the original gods did it. Their bodies won't burn and chafe with the ability to age and get sick, but will only have a finite end, an end determined by destiny not us.

But now, with both Curiosity and Knowledge found guilty and sentenced to being made mortal, we have to decide if their mate bond should be cut as well or just their power. Which means debating. And I hate political debating.

After a particularly long day of negotiations, I groan as I basically toss myself onto the couch in the sitting room of Death's house, our house now too, I guess. Death has done a really good job decorating the sitting room now that Anarus and I have stopped trashing it. It actually looks a lot like the sitting room from the games and I'm not sure if he did that on purpose or if it was completely accidental.

Two large leather couches, larger than the ones in the games of course because an eight-foot-tall god needs really big furniture, form an L around a fireplace with a mantle made from the tree he used as a battering ram in the council building. Hanging above the mantle is the painting of our carnivorous plant. The shiny wood floors are only partially covered by a white rug with small pink rosebuds on trailing green vines all over it. Dark wood side tables sit beside each of the couches. The room is comfortably lit by a chandelier of gold and black that works with magic, and the three windows opposite the fireplace are separated by bookcases that Death and Ydum are slowly filling up with all sorts of reading material.

The two of them have found a lot of common ground over books and talking about obscure information. Last week, I laughed myself almost sick when I woke up in the morning to find neither Death nor Ydum had ever gone to bed after starting a debate over how the cave magic worked. Ydum said the mate bonds already existed prior to the cave and were just recognized by the meeting of a witch and a god there, while Death argued that a possibility of a bond existed, but not that bond specifically, and the witch and god made the bond by choosing each other.

Anarus finally had to step in and tell them that they were both right. The bond existed, and was set to be between that specific god or gods and witch, but that they also had to choose it and each other. I think he just said that to shut them both up about it.

Anarus sits down at my feet, pulling them into his lap and stripping my boots off to rub my feet. Byder and Ydum land on the other couch, and the whole thing feels so reminiscent of the games, I half expect dinner to pop onto the table in the corner any minute.

"Can we as the council just overrule the jury and say that the bond can stay so we can be done with this already?" I grumble.

"Already wanting to abuse that small slice of power you have, beautiful?" Ydum laughs.

"No." I retort. "I just don't want to listen to people yammer for hours on end tomorrow. I will gladly give up all the power others seem so desperate to give us if it means I can finally sleep in."

"You didn't seem to mind waking up early this morning." Byder's voice is deep and I flush a little remembering exactly what woke me up early this morning. Or really, who. Byder.

I wiggle to the edge of the couch and turn my head to look around the couch arm at him and my belly heats from the look in his eyes. I know that not all the desire burning through me is mine. A lot of it is, but not all of it. Byder and I just stare at each other for a long, burning moment as the intensity of need in the room grows for all four of us. Lately, it feels like all three of them are tinder boxes and I am constantly just the match, ready to combust with one touch.

Anarus breaks first, sprawling along the couch until he is hovering above me. He won't lie down all the way on top of me like I wish he could. My flat belly isn't so flat anymore.

"Fuck. Byder, kiss her." Anarus's hand is pushing my shirt up and his mouth is on my breast before I can even gasp. He sucks my extremely sensitive nipple into his mouth, dragging on it hard as his teeth graze the skin in the gentlest of bites that I feel all the way down between my thighs.

"Oh shit." My words are muffled as Byder obliges Anarus and kneels on the floor in front of me to kiss my mouth. His tongue slides into my mouth to meet mine and any chance I had at more words is gone. Not that I'm complaining. I curl my hand around the back of Byder's head, tangling my fingers in his hair to press him closer.

Ydum slaps Anarus on the butt playfully. "Budge up, move down or get sandwiched. Your choice, Ani."

Anarus lets go of my breast only long enough to glare at Ydum, whose eyes are twinkling deviously. Anarus has come a long way in telling us about his past traumas, especially after they were all so openly talked about in front of all the gods during Winter's trial. Talking about his experiences has helped him heal some and become more comfortable with a lot of things surrounding the relationship between the four of us. But not totally comfortable. And Ydum loves pushing his buttons, by doing small things like that, slapping him playfully on the butt, to help him heal just a little more each day.

Anarus huffs, but slides his legs down to the floor to kneel next to Byder so that he still has access to me how he wants. Ydum, still smiling, moves first to kiss Anarus, then interrupts Byder to kiss me, then him. Anarus moves his attention to my other breast, extracting another moan from me.

With Anarus out of the way, mostly, Ydum lifts my legs and sits down. He places my legs down across his lap and starts teasing the edge of my pants with his fingers. He takes his time, slowly working his hand into my pants, but avoiding the spot I really want him to touch. Between the ministrations of the three of them, the slow burn in me builds rapidly and Byder catches my moans with his kisses and Ydum stills my squirming hips, my desperation for friction growing.

A noise in the room barely distracts us and I try not to laugh as I hear Death grumble. "They have a perfectly good bed upstairs. A nice one. A big one. But, no. The couch in the sitting room." It's not the first time Death has walked in on us and it probably won't be the last. At least he's good humored about it.

"You know, he's right." I say. "This would probably be much more fun in a bed. I'm not as small as I used to be and definitely not as flexible."

Anarus groans as he pulls my shirt back down. "But if we go to the bed, how will we make up for all the lost time of embarrassing my dad?"

I manage to sit up, and pat Anarus on the cheek. "I'm sure we'll find other ways."

Epilogue

I WILL NOT SCREAM. I will not scream. I bury my face in Anarus's shoulder and will myself not to scream. This pain is overwhelming and I'm only partially successful at not screaming.

Distraction. I tell myself. I need a distraction.

I lift my head and look over at Ydum. He's sitting in a chair in the corner of the bedroom we took over in Death's house and have lived in for the last eight years. His attention is completely focused on the small bundle in his arms, an overwhelming awe making him almost glow. Good. That's where his focus should be right now.

Byder is sitting on the floor behind me. I want to look at him, but I can't right now. So, I look at Anarus instead. He's holding me up as I kneel on the floor and lean against him every time the pain hurts too much. I pull back some to look at his face.

"Raven?" I ask. It's as much as I can get out.

Anarus chuckles at me. "Raven is downstairs with Grandpa Death, doing her spelling homework. And before you ask, Damek is with Grandpa Xolios and Kinshra outside."

Fuck that. No. "I told him not until Damek's fifth birthday. No dagger throwing until after his fifth birthday. He's four for two more months. If they're..." I can't finish, because fuck it hurts.

"If his power is hunts with small weapons like I think it is, even you can't stop that interest level, Jinx." Byder tells me as he rubs the small of my back and I groan into Anarus again.

"She was the same way with Raven when we realized she could open the gate in Anarus's wrist, Byder." Ydum says from the corner. "Tried to say she couldn't do it again until she was five, and that lasted, what? Two weeks? Vicious Jinx is now overprotective mommy Jinx."

"I'm still vicious, just for very specific reasons now." I say between gritted teeth. "And you don't get to talk right now. This is your fault."

I'm not really angry at Ydum. He knows that. I yelled at Anarus when I was giving birth to Raven too. And Byder with Damek. I've actually been kind to Ydum in comparison. Considering all it took to get here.

Raven was totally on accident when the red clover from the games worked too well. When she was two and we decided it was Byder's turn, we barely even thought about it and I was pregnant. So, when we made the same choice when Damek was two for it to be Ydum's turn to become a father, and it didn't happen for over a year, we worried it would never happen.

But, of course, the ass had to take forever then double whammy me with twins. "Shit. I am never doing this again."

All three of them laugh and, while I would love to yell at them more, I can't. I need to concentrate now. My focus narrows down to just this. One single focus that takes all of my attention.

In what feels like forever, but also only moments, Anarus is helping me to sit, leaning back against him as Byder hands me our fourth child, and third daughter. I love that his hunt power also included so much for healings and other work with animals, including birthing. It means that he has been able to basically be the midwife for me each time. It's just the four of us in the room and I like it like that. Of course, there is an actual midwife downstairs within shouting distance because all three of my gods are worriers.

I'm exhausted but happy as Ydum switches places with Anarus and we hold both of his blood daughters together. The blood part will only matter for the next few minutes. Starting with Raven, we all agreed that for those first few minutes, the blood father gets first attention with their new child, but after that, there is no difference between any of them as far as who is the father of our children. They are all the father of all of them.

And that has worked out well. If it weren't for looks, no one would be able to tell whose child was whose based solely on behavior. While Raven is the spitting image of Anarus, and by extension Death, just as Damek is the spitting image of Byder, the three of them have always treated both of the children as if they are their own. So do all the grandparents, all seven of them.

When we thought it would never happen for Ydum, he was sad but claimed only mildly. He had two children he loves to death already and if that was all there was, he would live his life happily being Papa to them, while Anarus is their Daddy, and Byder is their Baba. And, after these first few minutes, it will be the same for these two, I know.

"Tell me I'm wrong, beautiful," Ydum says softly in my ear, his finger stroking down one twin's cheek then the other's, "but the younger one doesn't have the green tinge of a nature goddess, does she?"

I look at that tiny face, the tiny pink mouth yawning, and know he's right. She has no tell-tale greenish tint to her skin like her sister. They are identical in all ways, as far as I can tell from first looks, both with blond hair that looks like it might end up curly, bright eyes that have a rather greenish glitter, and long fingers.

Both completely identical except for the shade of their skin. The first born has a definitive green tinge to her cheeks like Ydum while the second one's cheeks are pink like mine. "No, she doesn't. What could she be if not nature like her father and twin?"

Byder looks over Ydum's shoulder, smiling, as the younger one grasps his finger tightly in her tiny hand. "My guess? Fear's destiny is still throwing curveballs at us. This one decided to take after Mom as a Fate."

"Fuucckkk." Anarus moans from where he moved to sit on the bed. "Death goddess, hunt with small weapons god, some sort of nature goddess and a Fate? Fuck. No more kids, okay? We are screwed trying to raise this crew as it is."

"Names?" Ydum asks me. "We need two of them now."

"You still like Leander for one?" I ask him.

He nods, whispering. "Something for her. The forgotten first loss in the games. The one none of us even really paid attention to but you." He runs his finger along the cheek of our daughter that obviously will belong somewhere in the nature pantheon again. "You choose the other."

I look at my youngest daughter. My destiny from the Gods Games. From my shitty birthday to this, a Fate as my own child, my world and family complete. From when my gods played games to when my gods learned about all the lies, from when my gods waged war to now, when me and my gods finally get to live in peace. "To remember the one who really set all this in motion. Aretha."

Acknowledgements

Whew! We made it. Three books, a million rounds of editing and it's finally done, out there, in the world.

Brent. My love, my muse, thank you for everything you've done and keep doing. For always supporting me. For standing back and watching while I chase my dreams, ready to catch me if I fall but confident I won't. I don't need a mate bond to know you are my fated love from the gods.

To everyone who helped me edit, process, fix ugly plot holes, I love all of you. It's mostly the same lineup of culprits. Shoshana Kronfeld, still the most awesome biggest sister ever. Heather Douglas, your editing skill 100% count as end magic! Everyone else, you know who you are and what you did. Since you didn't answer the email asking for permission to reveal your names, you're just gonna have to know you belong here too with my undying gratitude. (Check your email more often.)

Mom, you said you'd read the first book. Holy crap, you actually said you'd read it. That is a lot of motherly love there. I know what I said in the Author Note, but, um, if I can't look you quite in the eye next time I visit, don't hold it against me? It's Dad's fault I'm weird.

Finally, to all the readers who stuck this out with me. Thank you to the ones who didn't get mad at the pregnancy trope. To the ones who did, sorry, not sorry. I will be back with more books, some spicy like this, some not so much. An artist's craft is only as good, and important, as the art aficionados who show up to appreciate it. Writing is an art I am so lucky to get to do. And I'm even luckier that people appreciate it. So, thank you all. I'll keep writing. You keep reading.

About the Author

Kefira Zink is an author from a little town in Michigan. She has a bachelor's degree in Sociology from Arizona State University and a master's degree in Sociology, with a specialty in Religion and Deviance from American Public University. She loves buying books, especially rescuing old books and giving them a loving home as well as reading books (which any reader will tell you, buying books and reading them are two very different hobbies). She is married to her wonderful husband/muse and together they have six grown children, one cat, a dog that thinks it is a cat, and a lizard that thinks it is a dinosaur.

Connect With The Author

Website: https://sites.google.com/view/kefira-zink-author
Email: kefirazinkauthor@gmail.com
Facebook: Kefira Zink Author
TikTok: kefira_zink_author